The
Camel
of Soloma

D C Bourne

Trevennick Books

Published by Trevennick Books
2009

Copyright © D C Bourne 2009

ISBN 978-0-9559577-1-0

Printed by
TBC Print Services Ltd, Blandford, Dorset DT11 8ST
Typeset by the author
Cover and artwork by the author
Cover photographs, rocks near Trebetherick

To those who have hoped, when hope seemed
impossible

Time is but a moment, escaped eternity

Preamble

In part this novel is set in the Cornwall of recent memory and in part in an older landscape – not so far distant in time, nor so far below the surface – when a great ice-sheet lay perhaps 30 miles off the coast and sea-levels were 100 metres lower. Into that marginal environment the first stirrings of settlement began.

The Camel of Soloma

Chapter 1   Living History

As in a dream, Nathan turned the vehicle. They drove in silence past the blacked out windows of the town and onto the top road. Wind was scattering the fog, and by the old, stone bridge they saw the screech marks of their tyres. There were no road markings nor signposts at the junctions. Near Trewosa two horses were pulling an empty farm wagon into a field. The moon was setting dull orange in the far west as the sun rose in the east, and they pulled to a halt outside the farmhouse at Little Vennick.

Side by side they stood as Nathan lifted the heavy lion-head on the door, waiting as the echo from the bronze knocker faded, and pushing at the unlocked door. The house was dark and quiet. Drawing the thick, velvet curtains in the kitchen, dawn light showed the table. A fresh newspaper lay folded beside a plate of hard-boiled eggs and bread and a note that read, 'Help yourself, Love M'.

"What's the date?" asked Nathan, pointing to the paper.

Zadie picked it up and put it down again. For a long while she stood, staring unseeingly into his eyes before hearing her own distant voice.

"It says, September the tenth … nineteen forty-one."

Long he remained silent. Finally he asked hesitantly, "In the cave at Polgodoc … what were you thinking?"

With equal reticence Zadie replied, "I was thinking that we were in a war … a war with the Mortan. The explosion of the flare … the noise … the incessant, deafening noise – it was as I imagine being bombed."

"Yes," answered Nathan in a tone that sounded tinny and remote as he fought to push down emotions that were a churning, bubbling crater of molten lava, kept in place from some pyroclastic outburst only by the shallowest skin of logic and exhausted will. "Yes, I was thinking it was like a war."

Again they stared. Her eyes looked older than their twenty-something years, he thought, and they were flecked with green and white again – an Atlantic surface lashed and tormented by the elements, although the turmoil, he knew, was rising from within: fear, doubt, hope dashed, exhaustion. Gold-blond hair fell, dirtied, against a dirt-streaked skin, and he wondered what his own face looked like – the early furrows of a few more years and the crinkles where part shut eyes had fought the glare of sun on ice felt taut with embedded grime.

A droning of propeller blades rattled the windows and a single, distinctive shape lurched landward, smoke trailing from its fuselage, circles of red, white and blue punctured by canon-fire, as if some careless marksman had sprayed an archery target. Hunched over the controls, a figure fought to keep the damaged craft aloft.

"This is a dream. This is a horrid, horrid dream!" exclaimed Zadie. "I'm going to wake up from it in a minute and find myself in my own bed … or at least in my own time."

"There was nothing imaginary about that steam engine at Padstow, nor about those soldiers … nor their guns," countered Nathan softly. "That aircraft was no more imaginary than the eggs and bread on that table."

Suddenly, mention of food brought an intense realisation of hunger. Days, weeks, months it seemed since they had eaten proper food. Eggs – big eggs – were staring at them; slices of home-baked bread were beckoning, and a note that said, 'Help yourself'. Thus began an unfair contest: pangs of guilt against pangs of hunger; thoughts that this was someone else's food, their precious food in a time of rationing, against thoughts that they were desperate; the certainty of something that was tangible, edible, normal, against the uncertainties, the fears, the doubts of what might lay ahead.

"We need food," stated Nathan's voice more strongly. "There

is nothing left in the rucksack. I think she will understand ..." and he touched the bread, lifting a piece towards his mouth.

Barely had his hand moved before Zadie grasped the other piece, chewing alternately upon it and the large egg – its slight blue tinge betraying its origin was duck, not hen. All too soon, even moistened fingertips could find no more crumbs to gather from tablecloth or plate.

"I'm still very hungry," announced Zadie, "and what did you mean by someone understanding?"

"Maybe there is more food ... outside," Nathan responded cautiously.

"Why outside? And what did you mean by someone understanding?" interrogated Zadie.

"If this is wartime Britain, it's not like our time – not like 2007. Every available plot of land was dug up to give food – gardens, golf courses, common land – anything that could be eked out to supplement the rationing. There will be no sugar or jam in this house; no fruit unless it is in season or pickled; only a little butter – unless someone made it locally and was not caught for hoarding or trading. It was the worst time for the convoys ... only the barest essentials came through – fuel, armaments, basic foodstuffs. They expected invasion ... the beaches were strung with barbed wire; the dunes near Rock were mined; the cliffs fortified and patrolled."

"How do you know all this?"

"My grandfather ... sometimes he spoke about it ... and once an old man came to visit the bungalow in Trevennick. They reminisced for hours and I listened. I was interested. He had been a young flier in the First War ... based at Crugmeer ... there was a camp there – maybe before the Royal Air Force was properly formed. They flew sorties in aircraft that looked like something out of the Wright brothers to protect shipping hugging the coast from attack by the early U-boats. He showed me some old, faded photographs of the planes ... apparently, he only crashed three of them. After the war he settled in a village near here, at St. Eval. In the Second War he lost his home, along with most of the villagers ... it was demolished to make way for an airfield built with stone from the quarry at Stepper Point. I expect St. Eval was where the plane we saw was trying to land."

"There was a place like that near where I went to school in Dorset," Zadie observed poignantly. "They had a week's notice to leave; those who were in rented accommodation received compensation only for the value of the vegetables in their gardens. The villagers wrote a message on the wall of their little church asking the army to take care of it until they could come back. It must have been a pretty village ... but it was never given back ... the army still has it; people lost their homes for ever."

"That must be Tyneham?"

"Yes."

"Good geology down there – Houn's Tout, Warbarrow, Lulworth, Stair Hole –"

"Nathan! Don't start! I don't want a geology lecture." More gently, she added, "You said something about food outside."

Morning sun streamed beyond the opened back door onto what had once been a pleasant garden, and a robin perched on the wooden handle of a fork, inviting them to dig. Bare earth reflected darkly in places; in others, rows of beans and peas clung to improvised supports, their leaves withering with the passing of the season. Three rose bushes flowered defiantly in their midst; half-dug rows of potatoes and carrots led to a wire cage from which an expectant hissing issued, magnified by the dry-stone wall behind. Geese fixed Nathan with a beady stare. Spectres of another existence bit into his mind and he reached instinctively to touch his calves. Only with an act of will did he join Zadie unearthing a potato plant, seeking for each tuber, brushing it clean of earth. Soon he retreated to the safety of the peas, searching for remnant pods amongst the drifting fragrance of faded rose.

"How about some eggs?" enquired a satisfied Zadie, balancing a pyramid of potatoes in her open hands. "I can hear ducks as well as geese."

"No."

"What do you mean, 'No'?"

"I mean, No. I'm not going near those geese."

"Why?"

"It's a long story –"

Urgent hissing turned to a screaming whine as five aircraft roared over the wall, barely a hundred feet above, and banked, climbing into the eastern sun. In the distance, beneath them, another aircraft pottered slowly across the landscape on its bi-plane wings. Somehow the spell of placid harvest-gathering was broken and, by unspoken consent, they retreated to the kitchen. Enamelled pans, the outsides of which might once have been yellow and the handles brown, lay near an electric cooker, its narrow top boasting but three rings. Washed potatoes and de-podded peas sat stubbornly in pans of cold water, whilst a whistling kettle on the other ring refused to sing. It had been with great pleasure that they had found a tea-caddy half-filled with leaves, and a brown, earthenware teapot. Frustration was mounting as neither the large red switch marked 'Cooker' on the wall nor any of the other switches produced a comforting red glow in the coiled rings of the cooker's top, and Zadie walked over to the door, flicking the ugly brown switch to the ceiling light.

"No electricity," they said in unison.

"Why do we have to have a power cut now?" demanded Zadie. "Cold peas I can manage; uncooked potatoes, I can't. I had been looking forward to a cup of hot tea too, even if there is no sugar and no milk."

"Try the meter."

"What?"

"Find the electricity meter," continued Nathan. "It will be grey and on a wall – like the ones you and I know in the holiday lets. See if it has run out of money."

For an object that was fairly essential, it proved remarkably elusive. A quick search of walls failed to reveal anything: it was not in the cupboard by the back door; it certainly was not outside; there were cupboards with plates and utensils, but no meter. At last, it emerged from behind a pair of dark-stained cupboard doors near the kitchen sink. A fuse box with bare wires sat alongside and the main cold water pipe ran nearby.

"Health and Safety would have a nightmare," commented Nathan.

Zadie was more practical, pointing to the little lever that sat on zero credit.

"Look for coins," prompted Nathan.

"Any suggestions as to where?"

"Yes ... nearby in the kitchen ... probably in a small container on the –"

" – mantelpiece," ended Zadie for him. "Got them! They're old coins ..."

Separated into small piles, the contents of the pot lay on the kitchen table. Two coins had been deposited in the meter and the big, metal butterfly-lever turned until it clicked. Rings on the cooker glowed red. Zadie was examining the remaining coins one by one whilst Nathan had uncapped a fountain pen and was writing with its gold nib on the pad of blue paper, water-marked 'Basildon Bond', that lay under the 'Help Yourself' note. Occasionally, Zadie looked out of the window at the buzzing bi-plane ploughing its lonely furrow up and down the landscape, but most of the time she was engrossed in the coins. Large, round pennies, bigger and heavier than a fifty pence piece, were embossed with figureheads of monarchs past: Georges and Edwards, and three different images of Victoria. There was a halfpence with a sailing ship on its obverse side, a farthing with an engraving of a wren, a smart bronze one with straight sides and a picture of a portcullis. A heavy, silver one bore the legend 'half-crown', but the largest pile – the ones that had fitted the meter – said 'one shilling'. In the past her strange grandmother had let her play with coins like these and she knew something of their value – the shilling, for instance, was worth 5p – but it was peculiar to think that they were once real currency.

Whistling from the cooker broke into both their trains of thought. The kettle shrieked notice of its boiling contents and, within a few minutes, under-done potatoes and over-done peas joined the hot, black tea in a meal that by all other standards would have been unsatisfactory. It was a hurried meal, and a hurried clearing up: gnawing at each was the thought that they must move; the food and message had been left in expectation of someone's return. Fetching the rucksacks from the old landrover, Nathan stood in the doorway, hesitating over the note he was holding. The bi-plane was buzzing noisily nearer – a dragonfly patrolling. Suddenly its wings glinted and, abandoning its linear exactitude, it circled twice – low, slow, peering to penetrate the farmhouse walls.

"Let's go!" called Nathan urgently, rushing into the kitchen, as the insect beat its path to some waiting point with increased acceleration. "That was a spotter plane," he continued in answer to the unspoken question, whilst urging Zadie through the back door. "Someone must have been suspicious about seeing the vehicle in Padstow this morning … not surprising really … all the private vehicles were registered … less than a hundred in this area in total. I should have thought of this; we shouldn't have delayed," he ended, grabbing roughly at a handful of carrot tops as they stepped over the row and slipped through an opening in a dry-stone wall. His fingers touched the stones of slate and granite – casually stacked to an unobservant eye but carefully fitted in reality, the outcome of a craft passed down the generations – and his mind cried out, 'Just let the walls be the same as I know; just let the places be the same.'

"Where are we going?"

"An old barn … a mile and a half away … maybe two miles. It is six fields from here … I remember it as a ruin."

Not for the first time, he blessed the builders of these old, dry-stone walls. They were lower here on the moor but still high enough to screen them from the road as they hugged their eastern side. Sunlight blazed in late morning perfection upon moss and ferns covering the stones or clinging improbably to niches between them. Fading explosions of pink dog-rose, separated from their cousins by eight feet of earth and stone and blooming a full month later, vied with golden outbursts of gorse, while two meadow browns flirted along the wall, and stonechats called from the highest sprigs, their colour reflecting the budded flower of prickly growth upon which they perched. Tall cow-parsley hid brambles that delayed progress momentarily with their September bounty, and blooms of convolvulus waved in the gentle air amid the last fragrance of honeysuckle. Sheep moved with minor bleating at the intrusion into their stone pen, reluctantly leaving the shade and water trough to shamble onto rough pasture in the field beyond. High enough for sheep to stand, the exit through the wall was low enough for Zadie and Nathan to crawl, hands resting on recent droppings, until they unbent their bodies to walk upright again. To the east and south the view was opening now: the scarred remnant of St. Eval village; St. Breock Down; hills near St. Columb. Above, the first faint fingers of cirrus caressed the sun, clawing their slow advance eastward into a ceiling of pastel blue.

The sound of aircraft engines spluttered and grew, carrying intermittently with the breeze until it became more constant. Almost too late, they threw their packs into the brambled parsley and ran, diving into the sheep-pen's narrow opening, huddling together beneath its granite cap, heads bowed, hands hidden, as three planes lumbered and yawed, touching the wall as it seemed, dislodging fragments with their draught, scattering sheep, pursuing their landing at St. Eval. Plaintive bleats from sheep so scared that they sought the return of their own hiding place forced Zadie and Nathan back into the open. Silently they walked, sensitised to sound, aware of their visibility, craving darkness at this zenith noon, desiring a sanctuary and time to think.

Two fields later, it happened. This time there was no escape – nowhere to run to, nor to hide. The field ends were distant; even the stone-wall sprouted only a meagre crop of brambles at its base. The plane had taken off towards the west and banked north; in twenty seconds it would be directly over them; they could not be missed.

"Throw your pack in the brambles," screamed Zadie, "and kiss me! Do it! Now, Nathan!"

Suddenly, he understood. Bodies embraced, and limbs entwined. Lips kissed lips, breath held. Hearts raced as the plane roared overhead, unbalancing them with the nearness of its noise. For a lingering moment longer than was necessary, the embrace lasted, until they rolled slowly apart.

"After all that we have been through," chided Zadie

mischievously, " you seemed a bit reticent to kiss me."

A multiplicity of emotions turmoiled to find expression in Nathan, as they walked on up the field. Not least, logic demanded admiration for the quickness of Zadie's thinking in turning complete exposure into a moment of near-normality. It would be no more than an amusing story for the pilot when he returned to St. Eval. Nathan spluttered incoherently and Zadie laughed at him, putting a grubby finger to her lips.

"No. Don't say anything. You'll only put your foot in it. Just take us to that barn, then we can talk in safety."

Its old slate roof was in sight now, peering over the wall two fields away, and he felt strangely buoyed, confident that shelter lay within their grasp. Individual slates began to dissemble from the mass – heavy, thick slates, feet square, lichen covered, local quarried, weighing on timbers of ancient oak. Part-hewn blocks identified themselves in each thick wall – a random collection of what had lain within dragging distance from the surrounding surface – and narrow slits opened like cats' pupils into an interior little more than one storey high. Less of a ruin than he remembered it, the six inch thick door was bolted and barred with a shaft of double that diameter. Perhaps four feet high by two feet wide, a smaller door was recessed between quoins of dressed granite into one of which a single hole had been drilled at great labour and a bolt inserted. A wider hole, sufficient for an arm to reach through, lay above the bolt, and muffled noises emanated from within.

Nathan knelt, peering through the hole. Neither door was part of his memory. This barn had been a half-ruin to him. Eventually he straightened, turning to face Zadie.

"I think I will first go and check the ladder, if you don't mind. There's a tap that feeds a trough round the back … the water is OK, although I wouldn't touch the trough," he added, unearthing a handful of muddied carrots from his rucksack. "They're not much but they will be something to chew on while we wait."

There was the suspicion in Zadie's mind that he was being overly polite. Nevertheless, she took the carrots and found the tap. She could see why he had said not to use the trough – green algae crusted its surface and slime extended from the sides to such an extent that only one small patch of water was visible. Nathan slid the bolt as noiselessly as possible and half-knelt to put his shoulder to the door. Reluctantly it gave, and he slipped inside. Shortly he reappeared, fastening the bolt again.

"I thought I heard noises," observed Zadie as he sat beside her on an old mounting stone next to the trough. Carrots glistened orange and wet between them.

"Just an animal," said Nathan reassuringly. A while later the now-dry carrots were back in Nathan's rucksack and he ventured, " Listen, I feel too exposed out here."

"You want to go into the barn?"

"Yes."

She nodded and rose, taking a few steps before he added unexpectedly, "What are you like with cows?"

"Fine. Why?"

"What about large cows?"

"Fine," came the answer again, more impatiently, as they rounded the corner of the barn.

"What about other animals?"

"Nathan, what are you talking about? I've told you I am fine with animals!"

"OK, OK," he answered, his hand resting on the bolt. "There is an iron ladder just inside the door, fixed to the wall. Go straight up. Be careful of the first plank in the hay-loft – it has a hole in it. I'll be right behind you. And try not to show any fear or aggression. Animals sense that kind of thing ..." he ended, loosening the bolt and shoving the small door half- open.

Zadie pushed by him. Darkness struck her after the brightness of the light outside; stench hit; a buzzing swarm of flies rose, their sound drowned by laboured, heavy breathing from an immense shape. A head, half the size of a car bonnet, swivelled slowly in her direction, and Zadie's mouth opened in a soundless cry. She felt her hand being placed on a rusted rung and Nathan pushing her upwards. Now he must turn his own back to the beast. The screech of old hinges as he applied his shoulder to close the door was buried by the scrabbling of hooves as a lumbering body raised its forequarters. Sweat dripped as Nathan stuck his arm through the hole, forcing the outside bolt back into place. He could sense the animal was fully on its feet. It could sense his rising panic. His elbow jammed in the door, and a single, prolonged bellow crushed his senses, reverberating around the enclosed space, flattening him against the wall with its power. The great head loomed, gathering pace.

Nathan wrenched his elbow free and leapt, scrabbling up the rungs as three feet of solid stone shuddered from the animal's lunge against this unwanted invader of its privacy. Once more it bellowed, lifting its head and snorting through nostrils that brushed the rafters of the loft. Slow in its immensity, it circled until the effort of movement led it to lie down as laboriously as it had risen. Shivering in the warm hay-loft above, Nathan lay, a tirade of ire and pent emotion pouring over him from the figure alongside.

"You didn't tell me it was a bull ... a big bull ... a huge bull! You didn't tell me!"

Sentences were peppered with adjectives garnered from boarding school – a rich vein of anglo-saxon derivatives – and Nathan wondered at the breadth of Zadie's education as his mind clawed its way back into some semblance of control. Finally the storm of invective passed and a still, small sobbing plunged more deeply into Nathan's heart.

Chapter 2   The Creature Within

Soft crunching awakened Nathan. Something was stabbing into the nape of his neck, and his eyes were troubling to focus. He seemed imprisoned in a world of trees and branches that made no sense; amongst them, giant creatures moved. One was moving his way. He stirred. A voice cut through the horror, vision snapping into place. Ants shrank into tiny forms moving along a piece of hay.

"Welcome back," said the voice. "You've slept a good hour longer than me."

Mid-afternoon light shafted into the hay-loft from an aperture, catching the gold in Zadie's hair and reddening the half-eaten carrot in her hand as he rolled awake. Her other hand held the binoculars from Nathan's opened pack, and she was examining a segment of landscape studiously.

"There's been movement down by Little Vennick –" (munch) "– a bicycle with someone who looked like a policeman … only he had a different kind of cap … walked round the farmhouse …" (swallow) "…was inside a long time –" (munch) "– stood around outside a while … haven't seen him go."

Zadie discarded the stubby end of the carrot and picked up another, offering him the binoculars before sitting cross-legged, eating with both hands together in fair imitation of an over-large rabbit. Fortunately, the binoculars were the greater matter of Nathan's attention, and he avoided any comment as a figure moved into view and he began his own (carrotless) commentary. Zadie abandoned the rabbit pose.

"I think it is a special constable. They were an extra set of ears and eyes … worked with the local police force … maybe did mundane work for intelligence. He seems to be waiting for somebody. Ah! There is a car moving on the road … black … old Wolseley … flag on the bonnet … must be a staff car … just about to encounter that farm wagon drawn by the two big horses.

The land-girls are not managing them very well … that will be interesting … there is a narrow section of road with deep banks and no gates … no room to squeeze by … somebody is going to have to back up."

Zadie could see with her own eye the ignominy of the shiny staff car reversing a quarter of a mile as the carthorses lumbered forward at unchanging pace, plodding towards their feed, dragging the wagon laden with main-crop potatoes that would become rations for some distant city.

"What are our options?" asked Zadie, taking over the binoculars again as the staff car ground through its forward gears.

"Not a lot. On the negative side of zero, to be honest," began Nathan slowly.

"It's turned up the track to Little Vennick …"

"We have no papers, no ration cards, no travel passes, no identity …"

"There is a man getting out of the passenger door … flat cap … peaked … army uniform …"

"Our clothes are not of this time; even our packs are made of material that didn't exist in 1941 …"

"The constable and the officer are going into the house … the driver is standing by the car having a smoke …"

"We could give ourselves up but five minutes of questioning would give us away. We don't know the detail of this time … worse, we do know some of the outcomes that they do not know yet. We would be regarded with great suspicion … probably as spies. We cannot even answer a simple question like how we arrived here."

"They have come out again. That's strange – the constable has climbed in the back. The car is leaving …"

"Maybe I could join up … false name … 'John Smith, Edward Street, London'. There is bound to be a recruiting office at Bodmin, if I could walk that far … sent to some distant front … 'lost in action' … more difficult for you, though."

"It's turned the other way on the main road, towards St. Eval. Nathan, did you leave anything in the house? What about that note you wrote? Why were you writing it anyway?"

"I wrote it because I recognised the writing on the table ... much younger, of course ... but the 'e' was quite distinctive – similar to Soloma's. However, I didn't leave it. Here: it's in my pocket; you can read it if you want," he finished, offering her the piece of folded, blue paper and picking up the binoculars.

He scanned the distant west as she read. Gulland stood clear, white waves lapping its island crown, untroubled by human wars. Beyond, the veil of cirrus merged imperceptibly into thicker altostratus; and above, the great orb sank, two thirds descended towards the destiny of that day's end. Long the glasses lingered on Gulland's broken silhouette.

"That was a generous note," a soft voice intruded into his thoughts. "She would have understood; she would have liked the greetings from Polgodoc's further shore." Sadly, he tore the note and let it fall beside the gnawed carrot tops as the gentle tone continued, "You were a long time looking at that island. You're thinking of her, aren't you?"

"Yes. I was wondering what she was doing ... and I was thinking about Polgodoc. It is our only option. Maybe we can return to our own time. If not, maybe our future would be better with Soloma ..."

Silence lay long between them. Fears churned in Zadie's heart. She had known it would come to this; he had feared it would come to this; she had dreaded the moment when he would vocalise the thoughts she was suppressing.

"So," she said eventually, "you want to take me back to a place where I have nearly fallen to my death, nearly been crushed to death, nearly lost my mind, and nearly been driven to insanity." It was a statement; its tone was flat; and, if it had possessed a colour, it would have been the greyest of greys.

"Do you want to stay here?" he questioned in words tinged with the faintest hint of lighter grey threaded through with darkest black.

The sun's weak shadow moved three inches across the hay before three words more ancient than she had cause to know were uttered with a single nod: "So be it."

Distantly, noise splintered the moment of acceptance. Both pairs of hands reached for the binoculars but hers were faster. Raising and focusing in one action, she confirmed what his eyes suspected.

"Larger vehicle at Little Vennick … six soldiers … no, seven … the constable, too … he's pointing. They've gone through the vegetable patch and are fanning out across the first field. The constable has gone inside the house."

"How are they holding their guns – slung over their shoulders, or in front?"

"In front, but across their chests – not pointing. They are in the second field now, coming straight up the slope. Can we get out of here? There are still four fields to go …"

As if in answer, a second noise penetrated the four narrow openings into the hay-loft. Coming from the east, it roared low overhead, clipping the sun's shadow to the west, circling so impossibly close to strands of gorse on top of the old, dry-stone walls that fragments of golden flower followed in its wake. Circle by circle it inscribed its pattern, ascending the slope field by field, circumferencing the old barn tightly twice, wing dipped, face peering, moving on, widening its search. Above the retreating roar, a third sound drowned reasoned speech. Clattering, skidding, sparking on ancient stone, old life levered itself alert and lifted its head, bellowing as it had never bellowed before – bellowing in call to ancestors long dead; bellowing in defiance of the present; bellowing until rocks and rafters shook, promising their echo to future generations. Snorting and stamping, the mountain paced, chafing against its enclosure.

Soldiers were one field away. Zadie and Nathan lay pressed below the slit apertures, listening intently. Voices came faintly, then firmly, filing past only a rock's width distant. A command rang.

"Wilkins, Smith, cover those openings! Symonds, Trevarnon, check the barn! Guns out!"

A bolt grated on granite. Wood creaked open and stopped. A voice screamed and wood slammed shut. Bone shattered. Blood flowed.　Deep-throated exhalation vibrated the air and a bellow deafened.　Slowly, hearing returned.

"Smith, Trevors, pick up Symonds!　Staunch the flow and get him back down to the farm.　See what you can do for him and hoof it along the road to Tresellyn.　I want you there in thirty minutes. Trevarnon, you're local.　What is this place?　What happened?"

"Bull pen," answered a softer voice.　"Large bull.　Very large bull.　Angry bull.　Butted the door and crushed his arm … Corporal."

The delay before the last word was just sufficient to needle without being overtly insubordinate, and the resultant expletives showed that the barb had done its work.　Coarsely, a command was given, "Move!　Move, you three!　You'll have to do the work of six men now.　Get going – up the slope – there's nothing here!"

Slowly, Nathan and Zadie lifted their heads, squinting through the openings into the hay-loft, staying back from any line of sight.　Pink stains spread the dying sun's blood skyward in the west; southward, an aircraft circled and spluttered to land on the demolished homes of St. Eval; to the east, frightened sheep huddled against walls of stone; to the north, four uniformed figures stood briefly on the brow of the hill.

"That is some bull," whispered Zadie, still not daring to speak out loud.　"I hate it … but I admire it.　In a strange way, I'm rather proud of it and I feel sorry for it … incarcerated in here all its life."

"I know what you mean.　I had forgotten about them.　The old farmers used to keep them – before the days of artificial insemination.　How we get past it now that it is roused is another question.　That door is worrying me, too.　Coming in I could place the weight of my shoulder against it to open and close it.　Going out, I will only be able to use the strength of one arm reaching through to pull it … and there's something else that is worrying me … I can't quite pin it down but – "

"I don't want to add to your worrying, but there are two figures in the field," interrupted Zadie, "heading this way."

He lay beside her, looking out of the northern opening.　The

figures were distinct, though substantially different, and making remarkably quick progress. Grey-haired beneath a flattened cap that might have been any colour between dung and earth, the one was stooped, walking stiffly, a curved pitch-fork resting over its shoulder; the other was sprightly and smaller, running and jumping, carrying a pail. Both were heading directly towards the barn.

"Quick! Push some of that hay nearer the top of the ladder," demanded Nathan. "That's what I've missed! Can't explain! Bury the rucksacks in the far corner. I'll bury you with hay. Whatever you do, don't move; and don't make a noise unless I speak. Hurry!"

Barely had he scraped hay over Zadie's foetal form and flung a sparse covering over himself than the bolt scraped on granite once again, wood creaked, and a sing-song voice began, "You bin a'bellowing today, ol' boy. You bin a'bellowing. Heard 'ee down at The Two Anchors. Did so. What's a you bin doin? Cummen here … let me rub that nose of yourn … there's my boy. Them flier-boys bin a'botherin ye? Young Peter, he cum with me to see 'ee. He be my grandson. He brung 'ee grain … good grain … Ministry men didn't get that. Ye be nice to him and I fetch 'ee some hay …"

Through the gap between two boards, Zadie saw a boy of seven or eight advance, placing a pail in front of the lying form, rubbing the giant head above its eyes as it lifted from rest. A huge pink tongue lowered into the pail, sweeping its contents mouthward. A clink sounded on the iron ladder … and another. A board vibrated under uneven footfall, and rasping sounds carried along its length.

"You a'bin a'bellowing … ye'll be hungry tonight. I'll find 'ee some good hay. Them Germans … they land at Trevennick … I'll let 'ee loose on they. You bellow at 'em … you'll a'send them running. That Mr. Churchill … he be right … fight them on the beaches. Thee and I … we'll fight them here … I still got my Enfield hid away … can't see so well to load. I'd fight now, if I had my leg. Young Goldie, 'e has a gun … 'e be with the captn tonight. Good luck to 'ee, lad."

Once more the pitch-fork scraped across the hay-loft floor. Now, it stood immobile, the old man leaning upon it, reliving some memory, distant in time and space, but real unto the moment. Stirred dust clouded the air. Nathan's nose itched and tickled. It was imperative to sneeze. Tears flowed and eyes boiled, fighting the whole demand of his body. Fraction by fraction he edged a hand towards his face, willing the old man not to see hay twitch. At last, a finger lay beneath his nostrils – inhaling over it, feeling relief flow through him – until his mind said, 'carrots and paper'. He sweated as the old man resumed his scraping of hay towards the ladder. Each scrape and scratch he waited for some cry, some outburst of surprise.

"Grandpa," a voice called up, "Hercules has eaten all his meal. Shall I fetch water?"

"Yes," the old voice answered. "Ye'r a good boy. I were just a'standin, thinking. Now, mind clear while I shovel hay. If ye have bits in yearn hair again, yourn mother 'll scold I."

Clomp by clomp, ladder rungs indicated the old man's descent. Through the crack, Zadie saw him whispering in the bull's ear as the boy emptied water into a narrow drinking trough. Turning, they stood together for a moment by the door, and one wistful farewell later, heavy wood closed out the light. The old bull's head held steady for a minute more before it swivelled and lowered onto folded hooves. Rumbling deeply, a great sigh reverberated from its nostrils, and a giant tongue licked at the thick, brass ring through its nose.

Uncurling, spluttering, cascading hay, Zadie knelt, looking through the northern opening to where two figures climbed, hand grasped in hand, over the distant stile. Three times Nathan sneezed, shedding fragments in imitation of a scarecrow waking to life once its watching masters had passed from view. The western sky burnt red in violence, fanning its fires eastward, igniting the ground below with its lurid shadow. Night soon would extinguish nature's holocaust. In its stead, inflamed man's passions would scar the eastern sky in urban imitation, searing the underside of heaven with their hell.

"He loved that beast," said Zadie simply. "You had the impression they were a part of each other."

For a long while they talked, watching the dying embers of the day, awaiting the fullness of dark, knowing that a moon would follow. She asked, and he told, what he knew of Padstow at war. He thought he had known much; in reality it was insufficient to ensure survival for a single day. Partly, they were stories from those who had survived – memories from which the unmemorable had been discarded; partly, they were facts read or photographs seen – each selective in their own way; partly, they were tangible – objects that remained, bearing their own testament to conflict's legacy.

Figures came and went: an admiral, VC from a former war, charged with the port's defence; Canadian Pioneers blasting rock, sharing sweet cigarettes with children; a boy standing in a garden, watching the glow of Plymouth burning beyond the far horizon; Polish servicemen manning an armoured train; land-girls taking the place of departed men; children evacuated from urban blitz. Objects and events muddled their chronology: sinkings of ships; an unknown Belgian sailor buried in a churchyard; bombs falling on Middle Row, three dead; the diary of a policeman, each mundane call, each imagined alarm, each tragedy; prisoners of war in camp at nearby Wadebridge; bells silent, bells pealing.

Thus dark enfolded them, closing vision, opening imagination. Two hands touched, and a voice said in a different tone, "Time. Time to go."

Chapter 3   Polgodoc

Lifting their packs, they felt towards the opening, reaching to grasp the ladder's topmost rung and descending in silence. Near its base stentorian breathing swirled and sucked, stinking the senses, imposing its proximity. Feet slid across the stone floor, and Nathan's hand touched wood, searching in pattern across the surface of the door until his arm plunged into the night air, and his fingers closed on the cold metal of the outer fastening. Grating more loudly than sensitised fears could bear, the bolt worked across granite. Wood creaked and creaked again, and rusted hinges groaned. Lungs swallowed cool, night air and, fastening the bolt again, each bade farewell to the monster that lay within.

Cloud obscured the stars but not thickly so, and a semblance of light gave shape to the old barn against the sky.

"High pressure is holding," observed Nathan quietly after they had moved a hundred yards. "There must be a weak front out to the west … it is not making much progress though, judging by those clouds. The moon set at dawn today … should rise within the hour … full moon. We need light to climb by … but we don't need it to be seen by. We can talk softly for a mile – three stiles – after that, we must be quiet all the way to the cliff," he added.

Zadie did not feel like speaking and they were over the first stile before she ventured her thoughts, "I suppose these are ideal invasion conditions?"

"I am afraid so … the watch is likely to be sharp tonight."

"Then how do we reach Polgodoc?"

"By the same paths we have used before. The old paths were there long ago; they won't have changed. The rocks are the same rocks I have touched and known: the next stile has two veins of quartz on its left, just where you will put your hand; the one after that is pink granite … not local rock … plundered from some ecclesiastical building recycled from something older. In the darkness there is no time: we could be centuries ago; we could be decades in the future; it is the same place."

"Nathan, there's a strange side to you. Some of that was almost poetic. It makes me feel as if this landscape is a living entity."

They sensed the looming wall before night-vision of a few feet picked out its shape. He let her go ahead, knowing her hand would pause on top of the stile, although he could not see it. He paused too, fingering the rock, suppressing the knowledge that he had not told. His mind was worrying at it. No matter which way he addressed the problem, there was no way round it. Suddenly something cut across them, almost brushing their knees with its closeness, before bounding over the field wall as if it had vanished through the stones.

"Fox," said Nathan, "out hunting."

Not long afterward, they heard the bark of its mate. A solid crumping rolled from the east – cracklings coming with it, each sound growing in intensity. Red dots traced the horizon; pockets of red glow diffused its edge and, as they placed their hands on pink granite, a harvest moon levered its copper-pink sphere over the world's rim.

"Three miles," murmured Nathan. "Walk quietly."

They turned almost immediately, climbing another stile, moon at their backs. By the end of the first field its contents were visibly root not grain. In the second they could make out the far wall before they were halfway across. Irregular rows of turnips stood clear in the third. Sheep moved restlessly in the field beyond, disturbed by the sound from the east or by the foxes. Beyond them a roofline rose, its chimney cutting the ever-whitening cloud; beside it, tops of bell tents glistened in the moon.

Quietly he pulled her down below the wall, mouthing in her ear, "Crugmeer ... farm ... sheep will stir ... no way round ... soldiers ... I was afraid of this." He saw her eyebrows rise before he pointed to the top of the field and continued, "Gate ... into road ... two hundred yards ... very quietly."

She nodded twice. Silently they stepped over rows of turnips, exposed to clear view from the east, hidden from the west. The wooden gate lifted ajar and they squeezed through into a narrow lane. Deep banks closeted the road, funnelling the sound; moonlight illuminated its surface until the banks bent sharply right; faintly, low voices drifted from ahead. Hesitantly, they moved – instinctively preferring to brush the brambled banks than walk in the centre of the lane. Round the bend, the road ran straight for a hundred yards while, upon its left, a solid, stone-built farmhouse lay, a gated farmyard with its range of slate-roofed barns nestling beside. Voices carried more clearly, though still soft and intermittent, and they edged forward until the farmyard gate was only a dozen yards away. Footsteps crunched. Two figures leant on the farm gate, looking west, rifles slung over uniformed shoulders. Zadie and Nathan froze, utterly visible to a turn of the head.

"Captain's been on edge all day …"

"Not surprising … he's been on the go nearly thirty-six hours."

"He suspects something … ever since he came back from Padstow this morning …"

"Still out now … gone on patrol with that local lot …"

"And that's what we had better do. He said, 'Patrol the road'. Get the gate."

Nathan's arm arced. He bent and it arced again. The gate swung inwards at the same time as the stone clattered down the barn roof, clanging onto machinery. The second stone made even more noise. The soldiers turned, stepping quickly, and a dog barked within the house. Zadie and Nathan moved, running silently past the outbuildings, past the open gate, past the blacked out windows. The road bent and a gate opened into a new field. Without pausing they were over it, jogging along its boundary, cutting down the far side to where a stile stood like a broken tooth in the wall of stone. Scrambling over, they slowed to a walk, seeking to control their breathing and pulse.

Diffused moonlight glinted dully on distant water as Zadie whispered, "Where did you learn that trick?"

"Scrumping apples," came the smiling reply; "the old farmers never bought it, but their dogs did." Hardly had the word escaped his lips than a barking broke out behind.

"We've stirred something!" exclaimed Zadie softly.

"Come on," he urged quietly; "ten minutes to the coastal path and ten more to the cliff."

Soon a stream trickled to their left, withered stems of yellow iris standing like soldiers on silent parade amid its muddy borders. Slowly its volume grew, continuing its endless task of carving a valley from rock and stone. Water sploshed into pools, gurgling around boulders that sought to stay its hand, rushing more freely down the steepening slope. Its life brought the realisation of thirst, and briefly they paused, scooping mouthfuls, before pursuing its course again until the coast path cut their way and they turned, stepping into the hidden valley of Polgodoc.

When last they had trodden it, fog had enveloped them, dampening sound, obscuring all from view, protective in its innocence. Now, the cloud was high and the moon nearly due south; the cliffs opposite were deeply shadowed, as were parts of the valley. This was a safe place, known only to a few, overlooked from land from just one point. They slowed their walk, gathering thought, reaching the valley's end, sitting near its final cliffs and looking beyond to where an ocean stretched and Gulland's rocky crown rose as a single different feature. Below them, an adit lay – small, narrow; severed partway by a chasm – following a band of ore; carved with great effort at a time before steel and dynamite, possibly before iron. It was a short, horizontal shaft, ending in a blank wall of rock, and it was upon that wall that the thoughts of both were focused. From his rucksack, Nathan produced a chunk of rock, a third the size of his palm, and held it out. Even in the dull light, it had a lustre.

"Make sure it's tin," said Zadie, holding a similar sized object in her own hand and nodding. "Right. Yours is tin, mine is copper. That's it. Let's climb."

Pocketing the rock, he turned, searching the cliff edge for the exact spot, waves breaking below, unseen in the dark shadow of the cliff beyond. Too far to the right was loose and crumbly; too far to the left, the climb down was impossible. Zadie was staring at him and past him, waiting, moving her head slightly from side to side.

"OK, this is it. There is just enough moonlight to climb by. I'll go first. Keep close to me but try not to tread on my fingers. It's eighteen holds down to the ledge … left hand hold first." He paused, calling, "Are you ready?" before lowering himself over the cliff edge, seeking to prevent the rucksack swinging and unbalancing him. His right foot sought its first hold.

"Yes. Yes, I'm coming," she addressed the disappearing head. "It's just that I kept thinking I saw a light flickering in the corner of my vision."

"What kind of light?" he called back, watching a pair of boots being followed by a bottom and a backpack in silhouette against the lighter sky. "Right foot down and two inches to the right," he added, ducking a few cascading fragments of broken slate that indicated Zadie had let go of the cliff top.

"Like a cigarette glow, only much faster … and there was some kind of sound that I didn't recognise …"

'Fifteen, sixteen, seventeen –' Nathan was counting holds but he could hear a sound himself now '–eighteen; step away with the right foot, find the ledge; two feet flat on the ledge and look up.' Zadie was three holds away. It certainly was a strange sound. It was growing and reverberating from the cliff opposite.

To any who had known it, it was the kind of unmistakable sound that a man might wake to from the deepest sleep and recognise instantly – a deep-throated double roar, epitome of power and speed. But neither Zadie nor Nathan had any knowledge of it. As Zadie landed by his side, it took Nathan's breath away. Majestic, splendid, awesome – aggression, beauty, danger, bound into one spectacle; the great curving phosphorescence of bow waves flung into the moonlight; two plumes of thrashed water spewing skyward in its wake – the Motor Torpedo Boat turned at full throttle. He thrust her in front of him along the ledge, guessing what was coming. Dropping almost instantaneously from crescendo to sulky whimper, the roar ceased and the blinding glare of a naval spotlight seared through the night. To have looked into it would have been impossible; even working away from it along the ledge, the reflection from the cliffs was dazzling and painful.

"Stop! Stop, or I shoot!" a voice rang commandingly from the cliff opposite.

Two paces. Two paces … that was all he needed. The angle for a shot would be difficult. Zadie was in the adit. A shot rang. Nathan felt the bullet embed itself in slate. A splinter of rock cut into his cheek. One more step and he was in. More shots rang. At five feet high by two and a half feet wide, a dark opening recessed in a dark cliff face, the adit entrance would give little target. But Zadie had needed no warning of the danger of a ricochet to propel herself along its uneven floor and over the plank that still spanned the drop to waves swashing on boulders below.

Some illumination from the searchlight bent a little way along the adit, its sides worn smooth by centuries of trickling water and ancient fingers that had worked this rock, but it was dark at its ending – a blank wall, ordinary, impenetrable. Neglecting to duck where the roof lowered, Nathan cried out as he struck his head, feet slipping on the wet floor, hands grasping for the single hold that would steady him. His fingers closed over Zadie's, and he sensed the face turned towards him in the narrow confine. It was saying something to him, but his mind was dominated by the pain from his scalp, eyes watering, tears diluting the blood flowing from his cheek. The voice was insistent, repetitive. Noises and shots from outside were confusing him. Ancient beyond ancient, rock was awakening to a touch that it had known before, the slow throb of eons past stirring an old creation, recalling the inanimate to life until a great band of silvery light spread from top to bottom across Nathan's vision. The living glow was widening, consuming sight, pulsating towards its centre. There was little else to see in the darkness. It dominated. It brought back memories, strange memories.

"Nathan!" the voice yelled, "You have the chunk of tin in your pocket! Put it in the recess before it's too late! Nathan, hear me, please!"

Eyes clicked into focus: the great vein of tin, the mother lode, stretched two feet wide from floor to ceiling in front of him. Emanating silvery light, it was pulsating faster at its heart, light flowing urgently to this single, dark ventricle. He knew now what he must do and, scrabbling in a pocket, his free hand closed on pure, metallic rock. Lifting and reaching, he pressed the object into the dark orifice. Light steadied; its pulse slowed. Grinding apart, the great vein of rock split, opening into deepest blackness.

As he plucked out the lump of tin, Zadie pulled him through the vein's severed heart and into the dark passage beyond. Side by side they stood, hands held, unbending to full height. Behind them rock ground together, thudding its colossal tonnes, sealing them into the cave of Polgodoc, sealing out a world at war. Briefly, the blackness terrified: a blackness without time; a blackness without dimension of space; a blackness in which it was impossible to determine which way was up or down, forward or back; a blackness total, complete.

With an act of will, Nathan opened his clenched hand and rock responded to rock. From the tin that lay in his palm, lustred, silver light dispelled the absolute dark. Thin veins of silvery grey traced up the walls, across the ceiling. From each vein light – neither natural nor artificial, but ancient light captured in the rock's creation – grew as they stepped down the irregular passage floor. In front, it spread; behind, it diminished; above, it penetrated the droplets of water that fell to shatter into a thousand globules of molten silvered-grey, lustering the floor onto which they cascaded so casually. Light called onward, light closed behind, until they stepped the last step of the passage and the full cave opened in front. Duller than once had been the case, the great mother lode of tin – dream of every ancient Cornish miner – illuminated the floor, splitting and circling the raised slab of black slate that lay in the centre of the cavern. Veins lighted into life, tracing their silver outwards and upwards until a thousand dripping droplets plunked and plinked their silvered splendour. Dark archways opened from the cavern – three on the side beyond the monumental plinth; five on the side from which they had entered. In silence, they moved towards the centre, still in awe of the rock's living greeting.

"So, we are here and safe," Zadie said, as they faced each other. "I don't want to linger. Tell me your thoughts quickly. I know mine."

"What are they?" he stalled

"To go out by the passage we used before," she answered, pointing to the dark archway in the middle of three exits; "to wait a few hours; and then to come back through the cave – this time thinking about our own time, not about war."

"And what if the Mortan are waiting?"

"If they are, they are. One war is the same as another war. We'll not be worse off than in 1941."

With a solid clunk, Nathan set his rucksack on the floor, regarding the giant slab of darkest slate longingly. On top of its centre four figurines of crouching lionesses, black as the rock they grew from, faced each other. He fingered a pocket in his shirt.

"No!" commanded Zadie. "Don't even think about it. Don't touch that slate!" His hand fell back and she continued more gently, "Now, put the lump of tin back in your pocket and I will use my piece of copper. It will guide us through the passage out. We need to go out before we can come back in. That was the whole point in coming here. This is our only hope. That is what you thought too."

Obediently, he let the piece of tin slip into his pocket. Slowly, silver light faded, retreating into its rock, to be replaced by a differing light as Zadie held a pure chunk of Cornish copper in her open palm. New veins lived, rivulets of copper-red flowing from ceiling to floor, beckoning to different archways than the tin, turning each drip of water to liquid ruby, pools radiating the rippled redness.

Zadie stepped towards the exit and Nathan turned to follow. A soft click echoed across the chamber and a voice said, "Stay exactly where you are." They both spun round.

Stepping from the black entrance, a figure walked carefully towards them, arm extended, hand held steady, cocked revolver pointing directly at Nathan. Copper light caught the three pips on the uniformed shoulders; a peaked cap hid the eyes but the voice was steady, sure of its intent, "Move away from that rock. Slowly. That's good. Keep your hands in front of you, where I can see them. Good ... I see you understand the King's English. That will help."

It was a young voice – younger than Nathan's, possibly younger than Zadie's – but one that had grown used to command. Two years of war had altered it; only the faintest twang of West Country softness underlay its steel. The eyes were visible now, rimmed red in the light, unblinking; eyes that were pools of history, of events that mouth and mind would not willingly express.

"What do you know about this place? What are you doing here? Who are you?" the voice questioned. "I've lost two good men here: one dead; one insane." The figure took two steps more and prodded Nathan's pack with its boot. "Not talking? We'll see what's in here. You dress strangely, and this material is not known to me."

Carefully, he squatted, keeping the revolver levelled and one eye on them both as he yanked the knot open and felt inside. Lifting out two items, he straightened up, examining each. Very slowly, Zadie started closing her hand. Coppery glow began fading back into the rock. Instantly, the figure thrust the items back.

"No!" it commanded. "Turn the lights back on!" The revolver swivelled at Zadie. Her hand opened a little and light grew. "Zeiss binoculars; a map written in German: you're spies. Move! In front of me ... side by side ... into that lit archway. I'll come back for this later. Keep moving. Hands by your sides."

Stepping through the coppery archway, dull light illuminated the passage – six feet ahead was dark; six feet behind was dark again. For twenty paces they walked without ascending or descending until the floor rose and, at the second step, Zadie caught Nathan's half-breathed, "Wrong passage," as he stumbled deliberately.

"Don't try anything!" came the voice from behind. "A few steps more and there is a rock wall. It will light up when we reach it. Touch the centre and it will open. There is a soldier the other side with a gun trained on the opening," he warned.

The copper glow spread from floor to ceiling in a great vein. Echoes of darkness were flooding through Nathan. Instinctively he twined his fingers between Zadie's, lifting her hand forward with his. She could feel the urgent pressure pushing her arm so that her shoulder was against the wall of the passage and, as their fingers touched the rock, she clenched her other hand.

Rock strained. The copper vein split. Light faded. Before any command could be given, water blasted through the widening crack. Tonnes of pressure tore at hands locked together, hitting the figure behind. Torrents of salt water surged to the full height and width of the passage. Irresistible in force, immense in power, they swept all before them, in them, beneath them. Tumbling, spluttering, clinging tenuously by the hand, Zadie and Nathan were swirled and buffeted back down the passage, bodies banging on rock, temples imploding with pressure, lungs screaming for air. Suddenly, it was there: air under pressure; air squeezed towards the cavern's ceiling; air in the utter darkness. Lungs sucked and gasped; water slowed its swirl. Nathan's feet touched rock. With difficulty he stood, supporting Zadie's head above the water.

Gradually, the movement ceased and water settled to the level of his armpits. Her feet could just touch the floor on tip-toe and, chin upturned, head tilted back, she could breathe above the water-line. It was a rasping breath, painfully fast, striving to slow, seeking control, aware of the disorientation of total darkness; aware too that any move would unbalance her body, plunging her head beneath the water again. His hand caught a submerged shoulder, steadying her. His own eyes were straining to penetrate the blackness, ears deadened by blood throbbing through his temples, but there was reassurance in that touch – a slender contact separating from utter loneliness; the knowledge of a fellow life; a tangible point of feeble hope, keeping absolute fear at bay. A numbed mind began to work.

"Zadie," his voice called into the darkness; "Zadie, can you hear me?"

"Yes," came the slow answer. "You sound a mile away. My ears are full of water. Don't let go of me – I can only just keep my balance."

"Zadie, we need some light. Can you raise your arm above water and open your hand?"

There was no reply but he could feel her body moving cautiously. She knew what he meant and was working her right arm closer to her until she could bend it and raise a clenched hand out of the water. Carefully, she opened her fist, the lump of copper resting precariously on her palm. At first dimly, then with greater strength, a red glow spread eerily beneath the water, tracing its veins across the cavern floor as copper called unto copper and ancient life flowed within it. Absolute darkness became black, stained molten. Red light clawed its way free of dark water to burst in coppery splendour from veins that traced and interlocked, ascending the walls, crossing the ceiling, outlining the tips of exits and entrances.

With the light, it was easier to maintain stability. Instinctively, they edged away from the submerged plinth of slate, lying unlit beneath the water, and towards the wall where the floor sloped slightly upwards. Zadie was able to put a full foot down. Nathan's knee struck an object – soft and yielding in part, solid in others. Fearing the touch, he reached into the water, waiting for his fingers to encounter cold flesh. In the wetness, they met a covering of fabric and, as they moved, a single, sodden strap. It was a strap he recognised and, folding his hand around it, he dragged the rucksack up three steps into the nearby archway. Leaning against its sides they stood, water above Zadie's waist, surveying rippling wavelets of copper-red washing across the cavern into the five dark openings opposite.

"That was not nice," stated Nathan, in unintended litotes, as Zadie asked him to hold the piece of copper. "The cavern is neck-deep in water, and somewhere under the water is a body; the only way out is the way we came in, and that leads to a war zone," he carried on depressingly. "I am afraid this is the end of the line."

She hit him with a walking boot and bent her head beneath the water again, emerging, spluttering, to thrust its mate at him. Backpack and sodden clothing followed.

"We are in the right exit," said a firm voice, as Zadie prised off a wet top and added it to the pile Nathan was holding. "This is no different from a sump in a pothole, and I've done enough pot-holing. The rock will respond whether it is underwater or not. All I have to do is touch it at the end of this passage," she ended, standing facing him, breathing slowly and deeply.

"You mean you are going to dive under that water?" he asked incredulously. "It must be twenty yards to the end of the passage ... and it goes down steeply ... the water will be deep ... it's narrow, you won't be able to turn round ..."

"Listen," commanded Zadie, "I'm not going to argue: this is something I can do and you can't. All you have to do is hold the chunk of copper in your palm so I have a little light, and remember to bring my clothes with you when the water level goes down."

He opened his mouth to argue, but rubied light caught the glint in her eyes, and he closed it again. Before he could say anything else, she had turned away. He thought he caught three small words and his name as she breathed deeply and bent forward. For a moment, a pair of bare feet hung above the water's surface. Arms dug deep, feet kicked, and she was gone.

Silence closed around Nathan. Ripples lapped across the dark water beneath which the feet had disappeared. Time dragged. Bubbles of air broke the surface, disturbing its placid acceptance of a life. It would be dark down there. Light from the veins of copper or tin rarely extended more than a few yards before or behind the hand holding its companion rock. Not only would it be dark, it would be cold; and there had been so little to eat; her body would be sapped of strength. Another bubble rose. How long could she stay down? She must have failed to reach the end of the passage. She must reappear soon. Surely she could not hold her breath this long? Perhaps she had tried to turn in the narrow passage and was stuck – jammed in some dark mausoleum that would never reveal its secret ... separated for ever. His heart burned for her. He had never told her what he felt ... not properly. It was no fault of hers that she was involved in this. She had not asked to be involved ... it had been an accident. It was his fault, it was his doing. Guilt and love spurred him forward until he was four steps down the passage, neck-deep in water, hand held above it. A final burst of bubbles surfaced around eyes staring blankly into an abyss of fading hope – and, as hope faded, so did the copper light. Soon it would be dark – total dark. He would be alone. It would be the end … buried beneath the water … never to see the light … never to feel the air. It would be like the waters below the cliff at Pentire. Perhaps it would have been better to have fallen then; perhaps it would have been a world in which he could have watched and seen from beneath the ocean – felt its currents, had his hopes and fears assuaged by its ceaseless motion. It was calling now. He could feel the water tugging at him. Its weight was pushing, pulling, swirling.

Nathan's foot slipped. Darkness and wetness closed over him. There was no time to take a breath – water was holding him down. His fists clenched. He was being buffeted against rock, tumbling, plunging deeper. His lungs were bursting, but it didn't matter. Nothing mattered any more. It was cold, but his body was feeling strangely warm. It was dark, but there was light in his mind. It was a sarcophagus of rock, but there was space and air.

Chapter 4   Passages of Time

A figure floated into view. Behind it was light – radiant, warming light with the clarity of an unsullied sky. Golden hair fell to its shoulders but, if it were an angel, it had no wings and it was strangely garbed. It should be an angel but it seemed to stand more than fly and it was prising at things in his hands. It was speaking to him. The words were difficult to recognise but there was something familiar to them. One word kept recurring. It must have some particular meaning. Deep within, he felt it was a part of his existence, part of something important.

"Nathan!" the angel demanded. "Nathan," it repeated more softly, "Nathan, wake up! Nathan, it's OK. We are out of the cave. We are still alive. Nathan, it's me!"

His eyes travelled past bare feet and legs, up to the cliffs above which a sun was hanging. They stood dark against its light. To the left, a rock shaped like the chimney of a house rose from boulders and grass; to the right, a scarred and blasted headland led on to the distant form of a lioness at guard over an ancient landscape. He rolled upright, staring out to a clump of hollies on a ridge, and beyond to a hill rising in the west.

"Zadie," he mouthed, before murmuring, "Gulland … we must be back in Soloma's time."

"Yes," replied Zadie, sitting beside him and looking out at the dry land stretching to the furthest west, "a few steps down, and a few thousand years into the past. Somewhere out there is the ice-sheet; somewhere out there is Soloma's home. It's strange to think that now – our time, I mean – all this is buried beneath the sea; a few hours ago, there was a boat with a searchlight almost directly above where we are sitting."

"Any sign of the Mortan?" he asked, staring at the blasted cliff.

"No. No sign of life – only a pair of choughs watching from the bushes by the stream."

They sat a while, absorbing the sun's welcoming warmth from a pale blue sky devoid of vapour trails. Barely a breeze stirred; the weather was different this side of the cave, albeit the season was the same. Finally, touched by its tranquillity, he said, "Zadie, tell me what happened in the cave."

"Some things I will tell, and some I won't. For the moment, let's just say that the dive was longer and darker than I had thought. I hadn't realised what the pressure of the water would be like when the rock exit opened. It spewed me out across the boulders and down the slope all the way to the stream." Livid purple, a bruise was swelling angrily on her left thigh. In one place, her hair was matted with congealed blood and she grimaced as he made to touch it, drawing away. "You kept hold of a few things of mine," she said, placing them to dry alongside the chunk of copper that she had prised from his grasp. "Now help me find the rest."

Thus began a search of the landscape stretching from the cliffs of Polgodoc to the stream, seeking items that had been flushed by water from the cave. Heavier ones, such as Nathan's rucksack, they found rapidly, but it was a while longer before Zadie's legs were re-clothed. Although her right boot was retrieved almost immediately, the left was not discovered until the September sun was well past its zenith. Eventually, they sat beside the stream, drinking ocasionally from it as Nathan searched his pack in vain for anything edible. A small patch of berries were the sum total of food for the day, and hunger gnawed. There was neither house, nor home, nor family from which to seek sustenance in this landscape, nor did they have the skills to survive as Soloma might. To seek her help would be a journey beyond the possible and, in unspoken agreement, the certainty grew that before this day had run its course they must attempt to return to their own time. Through Polgodoc lay the future and the past.

Zadie lifted her head from Nathan's shoulder. Sun, half-down towards its horizon rest, glinted on her hair, reflecting dully from matted patches. He knew what the movement meant and reluctantly he rose, shouldering his pack for a last time. Its contents seemed utterly unimportant now; it was more a question of habit. She caught something of his mood and pulled him forward. Half a mile of grassy slope, followed by a hundred yards of boulders, led up to Polgodoc's cliffs. Bodies were weak, and the pace was slow. There would be enough strength for one last effort, they both knew. Behind them, the sun sank further, beginning to bleed its day's end.

"It matters," said Zadie as the first boulders loomed, and he kept quiet waiting for her to continue; "it matters what we think in the cave of Polgodoc. The thoughts we bring into it, we live out of it." Fingering a thin gold chain around her neck, she went on, "This time, I am going to use my copper token to open the way."

Bending her head, she lifted the object over it and held it in her hand. Light caught its beauty, engravings on its arms and central wheel showing more clearly than either had recalled. Both saw the fine writing – part rune, part cuneiform, blended into some proto-Celtic script – and both wondered at its clarity. His mind remembered his first sight of it – a green-stained, unprepossessing lump of rock, held in a stranger's hand in a cliff top pub. Thoughts of the walk back to Trevennick, thoughts of the old bungalow, thoughts of a figure waiting on a bench – golden hair streaming from beneath a white cap over a blue top, like the sun emerging from behind fair-weather cumulus in a perfect summer sky – flooded through him. Somewhere amongst those images was a dog running on a beach, waves curling in casual perfection; a dark-haired girl moving between rows of tall runner beans, a chicken squawking noisily as it flew to perch on a sagging stone roof; mesembryanthemums cascading colours down an old, stone wall in the sunlight, orange and lemon petals of Californian poppies waving in the breeze.

Skirting a large boulder, Zadie pointed to a cleft in the dark cliff rising above. Rocks had been washed clean by the recent flood of water, pebbles and fragments swept along until deposited in their lee – haphazard piles of history nestled together, awaiting some new fate. Westering sunlight illumined wetted walls as they stepped into the cleft's embrace, feet sploshing in shallow puddles on the floor, their own shadows darkening the way ahead. A single, glancing ray of light fell upon the rock wall that snuffed out the passage and, in its refracted beam, a few flakes of copper ore glinted red, haemorrhaging their reply. Her hand grasped his and, together, they touched the wall. Slowly, the great vein of copper – pure, ancient, flung molten from the magmas of some distant eon – glistened its redness from floor to ceiling, pulsating, throbbing, beckoning towards the one dark recess in its heart.

Zadie reached forward with her free hand, thrusting her copper token into the living vein, murmuring a word – a small word, an old word, a word engraved upon the token by some elder hand with older knowledge. Through each mind the same thought was striving to surface, seeking to command attention, surging to consume consciousness: 'What if the cave was still flooded? What if there were uncounted tonnes of water behind this door of rock?' Each suppressed the thought, pushing it down, pressing it beneath the skein of hope knitting hands and lives together. As if by an act of will, the vein of copper stopped pulsating. Light steadied, emanating from within its two-foot width until, splitting down its centre, rock ground on rock, intolerably huge in the vastness of its weight. Water spurted through the opening fissure, pummelling legs in its cry for freedom, swirling around ankles, tugging at knees; it clawed to take them with it. Then it was gone – a gurgling echo carrying hauntingly from the landscape below.

Plucking the token back into her hand, Zadie urged him through the rock door into the passage beyond. In her open palm, the ancient key called light from each vein to which it was related, each lode, each pocket of ore that had shared its genesis. Whether out of greeting to the master token, or whether for some other reason, light blazed, streaming ahead as they stepped up the uneven passage into the depths of which Zadie had dived so recently. It blazed in the pureness of copper, not some fragment of dissembled white, but an entity in itself. Trickles of water oozed its colour; droplets plinked as liquid rubies, scattering their largesse upon the floor, rippling its existence from shore to shore of miniature pools. Into the cavern light burst, arching up walls and ceiling, circling the floor, stabbing towards the great, black plinth of monumental slate at its centre. Upon its surface, four black lionesses crouched, facing each other. Neither plinth, nor figurines, reflected the light. Of the body of the captain, there was no sign.

"Strange how the table is dry but the rest of the cave is still wet," observed Nathan.

"Don't go near it!" commanded Zadie. The thing had a fascination for him. She had experienced its result before and was quick to continue, "Just find your piece of tin and walk on by."

Reluctantly, he felt in the side pocket of his rucksack, extracting the lump of rock, letting it sit heavily in his palm. Watching carefully, she tucked the copper token over her head and under her top. Coppery light faded, retreating back into its metallic veins; a weaker, more silvery glow, traced through different lines as tin stirred tin to light, etching a single archway thickly. Wisely, she placed herself between him and the plinth, propelling them both across the chamber towards this exit. Light trickled in front and closed behind as they stepped up the passage and, in not much more than two dozen paces, rock showed, blocking their path.

"Ready?" she heard her own voice ask, aware of the turmoil of doubt that was seeking to erupt within.

"Yes," came the flat reply.

"Right exit?" she asked, hesitant to take the final step.

"Yes – this is tin, not copper." The voice was firmer, more alive. "Now we hope ..."

Reticently, rock responded to their touch. A thousand tonnes of solidity groaned and strained. Tearing itself slowly apart, the lode split, widening until two figures could scramble through into the adit's slippery end. In the enclosed space, there was a finality as rock closed upon rock behind. Early evening light showed the adit's entrance clearly – softened light, masked by unseen clouds; light tinged pink on the cliff beyond. Pools on the floor showed dimly. Waves lapped around boulders beneath the dark chasm that split the adit. Across it a wooden plank bridged the gap.

Hope faltered. They sat, staring. A piece of wood – a single, flat, roughly-cut piece of wood, condemned them. It had no right to be there in their time.

"After all this ... after all this ... nothing's changed ..." The voice was close to sobbing. "We're back in 1941 ... back in the middle of a war ... no papers, no food ... no future, no past ... people who don't exist."

He could feel the tears flowing for her. His own nerve was not going to last. It had all been pointless ... foolish ... a false hope. It had cost a life. Now it was going to cost their lives. It had been an endeavour doomed; that wartime plank said it all. Perhaps it would be better not to move. Perhaps it would be better to wait together. Soon, a soldier would come ... or soon lack of food would take its toll. It would not be painful ... just a sleep from which they would not wake.

Yet somewhere deep within something was gnawing at his mind. It was a small thing, a tiny thing, a mere mustard seed. The fraction of his mind that was still working with any clarity was worriting at it like an oyster at a grain of sand. It was something to do with what he could see – but all he could see was an adit cut and carved by the blood and toil of lives that ended centuries ago, and that accursed piece of wood.

Still, it stirred his will, and he said softly, "Come on. This is no place to be. I want to feel the air and see the sun set one last time, whatever happens."

She let him lead her across the plank, out of the adit, and onto the ledge once more. Sea surged and sucked below. An oyster-catcher skimmed its surface, rising briefly against the bank of cirrus cloud cocooning the sun in a sheet of pastel pink as it lowered its orb to rest. Smells of salt and seaweed saturated the senses. It was better here – better to be outside. Air touched the skin lightly and she seemed willing to climb. He watched her launch casually against the cliff, strangely free from anxiety. A fall would not make much difference. Without hope, there was no need for fear. Carelessly, he followed, making the first big step up from the ledge, hanging one-handed half-way up to nod at Gulland's broken frame rising from the water to the west. Stones clattered, chattering past his head to plop into the sea below. A final heave and he was over the cliff's top. Openly, they stood together, facing west, feeling the light breeze, hearing the gulls, watching the sun sink until its lower rim broke clear of the closeting cloud and touched the far horizon, setting it ablaze. Nathan sighed and turned.

"Let's go, before the black-out. It will be better that way." He sighed again. "I shall miss this place."

"Where are we going?"

"I'm not sure – Crugmeer, I suppose. The soldiers are there. We will probably encounter a patrol, but at least there will be food."

In silence, they walked up the hidden valley of Polgodoc … a few last moments of freedom. For each there were words they wanted to say; for neither would they take a form that matched the circumstance. Feet ate up the yards, while emotions lay unvocalised. One more twist and the coastal path would cut across their track. It came, and they stopped – suddenly – together – as surely as if a wall of rock had barred their way.

Four stakes of half-inch, high-tensile steel rose from the ground. Slenderly, between them, blue and white ribbon sagged, bearing the inscription, 'POLICE – DO NOT CROSS'. In effect, it was electrifying. Running their fingers along its simple message, words poured in confusion, thoughts leapt, hope soared.

"Plastic. It's plastic! It's our time!"

"The girls. The two girls who were abducted, that's why it's here!"

"And that's why there was a plank in the adit. It was part of the search. That's what I was missing!" cried Nathan, hugging Zadie and lifting her off her feet. "There were no letters stencilled on the plank."

Elated, they turned along the coastal path, talking rapidly, speeding down into the first narrow valley, climbing quickly over the wall running alongside its stream and up again. Once more the path descended; once more it rose. Beyond the second stile, twinkling lights showed in the distance. Bit by bit, the village of Trevennick came into view – its houses hidden in the half-light; its lights shining unfettered, clear. Surf rolled into the little bay below, washing sand cleansed of barbed wire and invasion fears. Only as they walked above it in the last vestiges of twilight did a fresh wave of thoughts begin to assemble themselves.

"You are right," said Nathan, slowing his pace. "We are prime suspects. At least, I am ..."

"You were on a cliff top with a young girl at precisely the place and time. You were seen. And, as for me," Zadie replied, "I have no alibi – nor do you. We don't know how many days it has been. We don't know what has happened to the girls, although we fear we do. Remember the flip-flop? No one will believe anything we can say."

Darkness was growing as Nathan observed, "If there has been a house to house search, they will have found Soloma's things at the bungalow ... it will look very bad. The place was a mess ... I left in such a hurry. The landrover wasn't there either."

"So, what do we do?" Zadie asked, new fears gnawing.

Wearily, he leant against the metal rail where the coast path wound across Trevennick's stream. Chimneys and rooftops showed solid against sky lightened by a rising moon. Crookedly, the spire of an old church reached toward the blanket of illumined cloud. A badger's head peered out of the thicket of alder and willow that lay upstream, regarding the bowed figure, scenting the air before scurrying ungainly to round her cubs a different way.

At length the bowed figure straightened and said simply, "Lucinda."

Chapter 5   Lucinda

Feet trod the same earth upon which paws had so recently pressed their imprint and, as they pushed through scrubby growth, climbing an old, dry-stone wall into a wide garden, six pairs of eyes regarded them. Unseen, the old raven in her sanctuary of the churchyard yew raised her head from her wing, watching too, remembering.

Uncurtained windows spilt light from the substantial house beyond, fashioned slate and stone lintels reflecting dully. At the further corner, porch light caught the final stem-top blooms of hollyhocks packed in their lower part with their wheels of cylindrical seed, drying brown, shrivelling alongside the leaves that had given life. Nosed on the slate drive against a whitewashed garage, an ancient Austin Cambridge stood with its soft top rolled down, and in the open porch, a chain hung from a pewter bell. Nathan pulled it twice, placing his rucksack on the settle, waiting.

Zadie listened. Deep within, muffled by the heavy door and stone embrasure, something sounded; footsteps clacked nearer across stone-flagged flooring; a bolt scraped, and the ornate brass doorknob turned. Soft light from the hall chandelier fell on a figure still elegant, still tall, still naturally blond. A pendant pair of gold earrings hung crystals that, if they were unsullied carbon, would be worth more than half the village. A satin dress, shaded a gentler hue of faded gold, set off the tanned skin against which a white ornament rested. Patent black leather, studded with silver, circled the waist in a slender belt and gloved the feet that stood by the open door.

"Nathan! Zadie! Oh, you poor darlings!" the figure cried. "Come in. You look exhausted. I thought you might come but I didn't know when."

With a solid clunk, old oak shut out the night and, as Zadie was embraced by the elderly lady, Nathan found himself thinking that he had never seen such genuine emotion in Lucinda, not even at Mabel's funeral. Only once, perhaps, in response to an unexpected question, had she been so unguarded. She embraced him too, ushering them into the dayroom and disappearing to boil a kettle. Tea, sweetened with spoonfuls of sugar – warm, welcoming, restoring strength – flowed through them. Piece by piece, the pile of chocolate slice diminished from its plate until Lucinda broke their concentration on thirst and hunger.

"There is a guest room upstairs. It has some items I tidied from the bungalow," she said, pausing significantly. "You are welcome to use it, and to have a wash, whilst I prepare a meal. There are things you need to hear. Zadie, there is a wardrobe – please use it, if you wish. I will ring when the food is ready."

Lucinda led them up the galleried stairs, past small oils of figures in uniform, switching on the light and pushing open double doors to a room that oozed class. Quietly, her feet retreated as Zadie and Nathan surveyed the scene. Centrally against a wall stood a small, four-poster bed, with an oak table to either side; a cushioned chest resided beneath the mullioned window, whilst another doorway led to a slate-floored en suite, its bath clad with marble. Louvered wood, the colour of clotted cream, stretched the remaining width of wall, contrasting with polished floorboards that were neither beech nor oak. Butterfly patterns in the grain, edging from beneath a Persian rug, suggested solid walnut. Angled by the window, a wingchair sat, and against the nearer wall a chaise-longue nestled below a large, chalk pastel of a seascape. The broken crown of a single island rose through its white-capped waves.

"Some room!" Zadie observed. "Do you have many friends like this?"

"I'm beginning to wonder," replied Nathan, pointing to an object protruding from beneath the bed. "She was expecting us: I don't understand why or when, but that is Soloma's suitcase – the one that Mabel gave her – and those folded clothes beside it are mine. They're clean ... I could have a wash ... and put them on."

"No," stated Zadie firmly, laughing at the same time; "me first. I stink more than you!"

She was both nearer and fractionally quicker to the door to the en suite. The lock clicked. Water gurgled and flowed. Warm, moist smells of scented soap seeped beneath the door, spreading their aroma. Contentedly, he sat in the wingchair, inhaling the fragrance, until a white-wrapped figure clicked open the door, padding bare-foot across the boards. No invitation was needed. Taps poured their warmth and cleanness; pores oozed their dirt; tired mind and muscles eased their tension. Eventually, he wrapped the thick, cream bath-towel around him and stepped into the room. What he saw took his breath away.

"You're beautiful!" he gasped.

Zadie smiled mischievously, savouring the chasm that was opening in front of him, wondering how far she would let him plunge into it, before replying, "Is this some recent revelation, or is it something you have been meaning to say for some time?"

"I mean, that dress is beautiful," he stammered, as she tucked her feet under the folds of pale blue fabric and settled on the chaise-longue. Soloma's leather case lay open on the bed; in one hand Zadie employed a silver hairbrush whilst the other held a mirror; from the gold chain around her neck, the copper token hung, resting half against cleansed skin, half against a sky of powder blue encompassing her form. "I mean, it's beautiful on you," he corrected himself uncertainly. She smiled, waiting. "No, I mean you look beautiful in it ..."

It was enough and she took pity, rescuing him – not for the first time – from a dark hole. "Lucinda has good taste ... and she is almost exactly my fit ... a little tight across the bust, but the length is surprisingly good ..." and she rose, letting the dress fall freely.

"I am going back to the first statement," said Nathan, recognising that he might be close to the surface. "You are beautiful."

"Thank you," Zadie laughed, inclining her head. "Now, if you would dress for dinner," she continued in mock graciousness, gesturing at the small pile of clothes beneath the bed, "I think I will help Lucinda."

He smiled as the blue sky turned and the gold-blond sun led it bare-footed along the landing. Why the set of clothes that he reserved for his more serious evening lectures should be on this floor was a question he would ask Lucinda. In fact, there were a number of questions he wanted to ask Lucinda once he had dressed.

"Nathan, dear," she greeted him brightly; "you look much more human. Come and join us in the dining room and have a glass of wine. It needs to breathe a little but it goes well with the meat ... steak, I am afraid ... it had to be something quick. We are searing them now. How would you like yours?"

'On a plate ... in my mouth,' his body screamed, but the words were more controlled, "I will trust the judgement of the chef."

"A good answer. You have trusted it before and, unless I am much mistaken, you will be wise to trust it again, my dear," replied Lucinda as Zadie bore three bone china plates into the room.

Juices swam across their white expanse. Three matching tureens steamed above protective mats, silver serving spoons reflecting exactly in style the candelabra that shone its five-fold glow along a polished table that would seat twelve at ease. Neither join nor crack appeared in its inch-thick surface. Goblets of crystal rested by a full decanter. Behind it lay the white ornament from Lucinda's neck and a cobwebbed bottle. Nathan's eyes caught the faded label.

"Lucinda, this is exceptionally rare," he marvelled. "This wine is over sixty years old. Didn't you want to keep it for something special?"

"Nathan, dear, and Zadie – you are special ... and I am long past sixty. You cannot keep things for ever. It was a gift. It is the last one ... it seemed appropriate." For a moment she was lost in a memory, looking at the table. Then the voice resumed, "Just a small glass for me. I have been at the Colonel's for drinks; I don't normally dress like this," she laughed. "Now, eat up. Help yourselves; there is fresh bread and butter; the beans are from your garden. Martyn picked them when he brought over your clothes."

"Why did he bring them?" asked Nathan, spooning potatoes onto his plate.

"I had an unexpected visitor three days ago – Goldilocks." Images of long, tapering fingers touching organ stops, and flowing white hair on a tall, slightly-stooped frame standing beside an open grave surged into Nathan's mind as Lucinda continued, "He said he thought you were in trouble … to look out for you … and, if you came, you would be tired and hungry. It was not a long conversation, and he was as enigmatic as ever I remember him. He wanted to leave as soon as he had said his piece. Sometimes he seems to know things …" she explained in response to Nathan's raised eyebrows.

"What happened about the two young girls? questioned Zadie. "Are we suspects in their disappearance? What have the police done?"

Lucinda held up her hand. "I will tell you a little as you eat. These things are linked together. Thereafter, you must tell me about Soloma." She paused just long enough for each to nod, as if some agreement had been entered into, before continuing, "The day you left with Soloma, there was a full scale search: helicopters, dogs, every available person from dawn to dusk. It was the lead item on the national news – two young girls, aged 9 and 11, wandering away from a campsite, feared abducted, sighted with a lone male near Lellizzick. The description of the older one was not dissimilar from Soloma, and it was exactly the area you would be in.

"That night, after dark, Martyn and I went over to your bungalow. It was a real mess. It looked like a bomb had hit it, or someone had left in an extreme hurry. We tidied up and brought Soloma's things over here, just in case. Next day, they began a house to house search, interviewing everybody … not the local force … Metropolitan Police and West Midlands, drafted in. They examined your bungalow. I think someone – probably Kelvin – had said something about a young girl staying with you, but Martyn said she had returned to her relatives in France and you were away on a walking holiday. The young minister was asked about it too and he told them about the funeral. That seemed to put their minds at rest as it had occurred days before the girls went missing.

"Young Trevelyn was less fortunate. He is the same sort of build as you, Nathan, and must have been walking the cliffs that morning. There was something about a helicopter sighting a suspicious figure, and he was hauled in to Bodmin and questioned at length. Fortunately he did not know anything, but they gave him a tough time. Late that afternoon, one of the navy boats – SBS, I think – found the older girl semi-conscious, clinging to the bottom of a cliff near Gunver Head. It took them ages to reach her. The swell was running too high for them to land, and that is an evil place for currents, even on the calmest day; the cliff overhangs and the helicopter was unable to lower a direct line; in the end, they had to abseil down and bring her up in a cradle –"

"Was she alright? What had happened? What about her sister?" interjected Zadie and Nathan at the same time.

"She recovered but it was not until the next day that she was making any sense. Apparently, the girls had been playing at being smugglers and wandered off, looking for a hiding place. All she could remember was the two of them falling into darkness; she found herself in the water being sucked and swept along by the waves; somehow, she managed to pull herself out and up onto the cliff. It was all over the papers – 'Dramatic Rescue', 'Miracle Survival', 'Hope Fades for Sister'. They got their teeth into the unknown stranger who had apparently told them where there were caves; if he had been found, there would have been a lynching. Of course, the search went on for another couple of days before it was down-graded to a body-watch. There was a lot of blame floating around … it was difficult to know whether to be happy about the life that was saved, or sad about the one that was lost, or frustrated at the foolishness."

Those emotions swirled through a pause until Lucinda asked about Soloma. Part by part, the story unwound, prompted occasionally by a new question. Strangely, they found themselves editing by unspoken agreement: of the cave at Polgodoc, they said little; and of the wartime, nothing. By the end of the tale's telling, every potato and bean and carrot had long gone from the tureens; only a solitary slice of farmhouse bread remained, unneeded to mop up juices from plates polished clean by its companion pieces. Lucinda nodded in appreciation as the grandfather clock in the hall chimed its midnight hour.

"I can see why Soloma was pining," she said thoughtfully,

"and it helps me understand much about Mabel. The white coral on the coffin makes sense now. Thank you for telling me so much." As the elegant, old lady rose, Nathan gained the distinct impression that the last few words were not by chance; Lucinda knew there was more, but accepted its withholding. He made to open his mouth but she spoke instead, "It is time to sleep. You deserve some rest." Thanking her, they turned, pausing on the bottom stair as Lucinda added, "I had forgotten, there was one more thing Goldilocks said: 'the girl will need to travel in a hurry.' I assumed it was something about Soloma, but it could have been about Zadie. Does it make any sense to you?"

A whole world came crashing into Zadie's consciousness: dates, times, locations, air-flights, meeting points, job prospects, career, the long period of study as an archaeologist, her flat in London. She told Nathan to go up and was in earnest conversation with Lucinda. As he lay on the bed struggling against sleep, he caught snatches of phone conversation. The clock had struck one before Zadie pulled the covers over herself and stirred him. In his half slumber, he thought he heard a voice saying something about leaving at six-thirty and a Greek island.

*   *   *

Rain was falling – not gentle rain but a steady, heavy downpour. Suddenly, it stopped. He was in a bed. It was a comfortable bed. It wasn't his bed, nor was that his window. There was a light on. He hadn't left a light on. One eye was focusing reluctantly; the other was buried in something soft. It had been a long dream – a nightmare in parts. He felt exhausted from it. Slowly he lifted his head. A figure appeared through the door opposite. For a moment it was wrapped in cloud. Now it was visible. It was a figure wearing old clothes – dirty and worn. It had a small pack on its back. It was reaching towards him, speaking.

"Nathan. Nathan, I must go now. Lucinda is waiting," it said gently, touching his shoulder.

In the doorway it paused, looking back. Silently, it disappeared.

He was awake now, fully awake. Grabbing at trousers, he hopped onto the landing, just getting his foot through the second leg in time to take the stairs in threes. Flinging the front door wide, he caught up with her in the porch. What he said, he couldn't remember. Embracing all too briefly, her reply was smothered. She said she would write. He said he would write, too. Desperate to make some lasting bond, he reached into the rucksack, still lying on the settle, thrusting a much stained map into her hand. "Take it," he insisted against her objection. "It will remind you."

Tooting on the dual-tone horn as Zadie turned, Lucinda called, "Breakfast is on the table – in the dayroom. I'm going to Exeter St. David's … faster train. Pull the door to when you leave … I'll look for you when I come back."

Before the last word had finished or Zadie's door had shut, a gear grated, shattered slate spun, and the immaculate, old car accelerated from the drive with no more caution at the blind turn into the lane than it had shown for the past thirty years. He caught a last glimpse of two blond heads of hair flying in the wind and heard the engine surge into third gear before the Z bend that most modern drivers took in subdued second.

For a long while, he stood staring – a forlorn figure. The bottom had dropped out of his world. Soloma had gone; Zadie had gone. Perhaps she had told him where, but he had been more than half asleep. The old raven, feathers greyed with age, fluttered across his clouded vision, returning to her sanctuary in the churchyard next door. Briefly she regarded him, remembering the figure of an older generation; briefly he regarded her, following the flight. Beyond her, in the west, clouds were thickening. It would rain again before this day was out. It was already pouring in his heart.

Minutes moved with monumental slowness; hours ground glacially. By the clock's strike of eight, a week seemed to have passed. Pulling the door to, Nathan picked up his pack, walking the few yards up the lane to his own drive. Faded blooms of erigeron tumbled in silent greeting down the dry-stone wall. Crunching across fragments of slate, through which occasional poppies struggled to proclaim their hold on life, he looked at the bungalow. Once it had been his grandfather's, but it was older than that. Three worn steps led to a front door devoid of either letterbox or bell. To one side fragmenting, wooden doors of a garage blocked the way. Behind it, the shed roof of sagging stone sheltered a vegetable patch. The last peas, runner beans and carrots would be there, along with his winter supply of potatoes and parsnips, he knew. Among them might still be a few flowers of morning glory, together with dead blooms of valerian and seeded mesembryanthemum, cascading on the wall separating this plot from dairy cattle munching in the field beyond. Feathered movement caught his eye. Striding and squawking, a chicken ran to bear news to its compatriots. They would be perched on the balustrade of the verandah, looking in, before he reached the kitchen, Nathan thought.

The old door opened to his touch. Long-forgotten was the whereabouts of its key, and largely unneeded had it been throughout the generations. The slated hallway, narrow and sporting a single woven rug, opened onto five small rooms. Opening the first door to his left, Nathan deposited his rucksack by the bed. Neatly upon it, a pile of garments lay. Through the door opposite he glimpsed two well-worn chairs and a floor free of debris. The fireplace was laid. Lucinda and Martyn had done a good job. Passing the bakelite telephone on its stand, each circular hole in its metal dial revealing a group of letters beneath, he emerged into the kitchen. Four faces regarded his entry expectantly from beyond the brass taps of the cracked, enamel sink as he pushed the door. In unison each cocked its head to one side, awaiting the sound of latch on wood. Reaching into a tin beside the back door, he grasped a handful of grain and scattered it from the verandah, watching chickens fly from the balustrade and seek each last granule amongst the grass and earth. Water flowed discoloured and brown from the tap. It had always been thus; old piping should have been replaced years ago. Waiting until it was vaguely clear, he filled the copper kettle, turning the gas on and turning it off again. 'No milk,' said a mind distracted by recent events. He walked down to the village shop.

"Morning, Nathan," Kelvin greeted. "Haven't seen you for a week or more. Been away?"

"Yes." He would give as little information as possible. Kelvin's role as shop-keeper was secondary to his well known desire to gather as much gossip as possible.

"Anywhere nice?" probed Kelvin, shuffling containers of milk until he found one with a short expiry date.

"Walking holiday … Wales," replied Nathan, knowing full well what was happening.

"Ah, that's what Martyn said. It's been a bit lively round here. Never known anything like it …"

He was not going to bite. "Granary loaf and six rashers of bacon, please." Why was it that the only things he wanted were behind the counter? Much practice on Kelvin's part, he thought, prodding the loaf in the hope it might be today's.

"That niece of yours gone back then?"

"Yes." His eye caught a paper – some bank in trouble, various platitudes from politicians. At least it would give him the day and date; mundane details like that were rather confused in his mind. "That's it. On account, please." A disappointed Kelvin wrote the purchases on a small card and Nathan allowed himself a momentary smile at his successful escape. Chickens greeted his return and, tea made, they played their usual erratic game amongst the vegetables, seeking to distract him from where they had laid their eggs.

Lunch dragged; the day dragged. He settled to prepare some lecture notes, but his mind kept running in different directions. Finally, he flung them in disarray at the other worn armchair and went for a walk. Stratus cloud was thickening in the west, its gloomy grey laden with moisture being driven on a freshening breeze. 'Front coming through,' his mind said automatically, and his feet turned inland, wending their way towards the moor. Cloud lowered its base to smother the stone-toothed tops, wreathing their substance in insecurity. Almost by accident, he was in the lane leading to Little Vennick, plodding through rivulets beginning to flow down its muddying surface. 'Mabel has gone too,' his thought spoke as the old farmhouse emerged from the spectral embrace of molecules. Idly, he stood, contemplating how life could become so empty so quickly. He kicked at a landrover and was jarred into the realisation that it was his as a key fell from its usual resting place in the wheel arch. Mechanically, he turned the ignition. A gear grated. The old vehicle grumbled down the track, rain driving into its open top.

Even the chickens were absent, as wheels scuffed broken slate, skidding to a stop. By the steps, a larger slate had been turned over so that the word 'Post' read uppermost and, reaching beneath it, he retrieved a brief note from Lucinda. Two numbers were written at the bottom with the annotation, 'flat – answerphone while I'm away' and 'mobile – unlikely to work'. Vainly, he tried each. Later, Lucinda called him, saying that Zadie had made the train. Check-in was at four. She would be away six months on the dig and wanted him to write. Her last words had been, 'Give Nathan my love. I told him where to contact me last night'. Gloom and despair settled further as he replaced the receiver. Dredge deeply as he might, no location surfaced, and he cursed that his body should have craved sleep. She would be remote, inaccessible, lost to him.

Martyn popped by in the morning. Wisely, the old postman's years of experience of delivering bad news led him to sit largely in silence. Nathan tried to talk about Soloma, but his heart was heavy. Lucinda called several times, and the old farmer from next door shambled across on the pretext of having seen a fox near Nathan's chickens. He was aware of their concern, but it did not help his emptiness. A week dragged by. Finally, Martyn appeared again.

"Look, Nathan," he said, "you're moping. Your term starts next week. Why don't you go back early … change of scene … students will cheer you up … give you a focus. I'll look after the chickens."

To some extent it was true, and he thanked him for the thought. It was difficult to be entirely pessimistic in their presence. Life, hope, expectation, laughter, flowed around the campus with their groups. It stirred him to think about his lectures, about the geology and landscape that were his passion. The next day he left.

Chapter 6   A Legacy

December drew in – a cold north-westerly clawing at each unprotected inch of flesh – before Martyn saw him again. He had to admit to himself that he had been half-watching for over a week, and that the geologist's name had been the subject of several conversations over the past months. Smoke, flattened from the squat chimney by a gusting wind, dispersed its faint fragrance of aromatic wood, and light flowed from an uncurtained window onto wetted slate, reflecting off the streaked and dirty landrover, as Martyn stepped up to the door, pausing to hammer with his fist in lieu of absent bell or knocker.

It was a gaunter face that opened the old, oak door, but the eyes had life in them, and the voice had recovered something of its timbre, as he was ushered into the cramped sitting room. Discarding the day-glo jacket of his postal years, Martyn stretched his feet towards the fire, accepting the proffered glass of something that looked likely to have by-passed taxation. There would be trouble at supper; his wife would not approve of drinking at this hour, thought Martyn, deciding that a second glass would make little difference to a sin already committed.

Turning conversation from parsnips and weather, he announced, "I have a letter for you," and passed the odd-shaped envelope across the largely empty bottle. Thick, cream paper felt like linen to the touch; in place of the Queen's head, only an initialled signature adorned the package. Flowing script, written in black ink by fountain pen, proclaimed the message, 'Nathan Petrox'.

"Do you know what is in it?" asked Nathan, certain that the question was superfluous.

"Partly," Martyn admitted. "Delivered a few over the years. Not recently, mind … leastways, not from there …"

"My surname is Peters. Once only, has one person called me Petrox," Nathan said slowly, turning the envelope between his fingers. Martyn dropped his gaze as Nathan reached for an ebony paperknife, breaking the seal on the envelope's obverse. Partly unfolding itself, a single page, written in the same graceful hand on the same heavy paper, consumed Nathan's attention. "Who are Petherick and Kerry?" he asked at length.

"Solicitors ... local firm," Martyn responded, knocking over the almost empty bottle. "Old Wadebridge firm ... off Molesworth Street ... down an opening by Barclay's Bank ... second doorway on the left ... up a flight of wooden stairs. Don't be put off by the entrance ..."

Martyn stood, embarrassed perhaps at his knowledge of the letter or anxious to make his way before the contents of Nathan's bottle took full effect, aware of the inquisition that loomed over supper.

*   *   *

Two days later Nathan found himself in Wadebridge. Collar and tie felt uncomfortable, as he stepped away from the free parking spaces by the supermarket, walking past cycle hire shops closed for the winter, following the line of the old railway that once bisected the town. Wharves and warehouses, renewed as waterfront apartments, showed little sign of life; a solitary Christmas tree winked mournfully in one window; Tourist Information was shuttered and closed on Eddystone Road. He was early for his appointment. Near the place of the old level crossing, he contemplated a pub with the words 'Pons War Gwlan' stencilled high upon its wall. Beyond it the slate cupola of the Town Hall – idiosyncratic, distinct – broke the roofline. Purchasing a paper from the newsagent nearby, he pottered up Molesworth Street. These were the old shops, the traditional shops, the ones that served the local community after the tourists had gone and before they came. Lights, tinsel, streamers – they were trying to make it Christmas but footfall was low, the ghost of Christmas past in economic present. Guiltily, he consumed a free mince pie in a bookshop, having no intention to buy, browsing the poetry instead, moving from Betjeman to Blake to Byron.

'I had a dream, which was not all a dream.

> The bright sun was extinguish'd, and the stars
> Did wander darkling in the eternal space,
> Rayless, and pathless, and the icy earth
> Swung blind and blackening in the moonless air;
> Morn came and went – and came, and brought no day,
> And men forgot their passions …'

More than most, he knew something of the circumstance leading to the verse, and he shut the book before his thoughts pursued that line. It was time.

Shabby and unprepossessing was how he might have described the entry, had it not been for Martyn's comment. The legend 'Petherick and Kerry', in slightly peeling letters, pronounced itself from behind the small glass portion of the outside door. Wooden stairs creaked to a landing where the same names were stencilled on opaque glass, beneath which, a hand-written card read 'Please Enter'. Closing the door, a bell tinkled. A head of brown hair bobbed up from beside a filing cabinet, the label on its blouse bearing the name 'Julia Plaisant'. Behind the labelled figure a couple of desks, laden with files, competed with cabinets, chairs and coffee machine for space. It was not an unpleasant office; it reminded Nathan of a comfortable armchair that had given service to several generations.

The figure smiled, straightening her skirt. "I'm sorry. I wasn't expecting anyone," she apologised.

"I have an appointment," Nathan began, somewhat awkwardly, "with Mr. Petherick."

A giggle escaped the heavily-painted lips, and eyes laughed before she replied more solemnly, "I am sorry, Sir; I don't think that is possible."

"I have a letter – " he persisted, only to be interrupted by her gentle comment, "Mr. Petherick died a hundred years ago."

Confused, Nathan held the letter in mid-air while the voice continued, "May I see your letter, Sir?" Hesitantly, wishing he was somewhere else, he passed it to her. "This is old Mr. Kerry's writing," she pronounced; "he only comes in once or twice a year, a social call to keep in touch. I am afraid there has been a mistake.

This letter seems to concern a will … of one Mabel Vennick. Perhaps I can help," she offered.

Pocketing the letter, he nodded uncertainly, and she knelt beside the last of six locked cabinets, sorting through old manilla files tied with faded ribbon and commenting, "Vennick … Vennick – there's something familiar about that name; I recall looking for it a few months ago. Ah, here it is," she ended, rising and straightening herself again. Unlike the other folders, it was relatively free of dust. Pulling the pink bow open, she glanced briefly at the contents before asking politely, "What did you say your name was, Sir?"

"Peters … Nathan Peters," he replied.

For ten minutes he sat on a small, upright chair until the brown hair reappeared, smiling encouragingly and saying that the partner who dealt with wills and probate was free now and would see him if he wished. She held the varnished beech door half open for him and closed it quietly behind as a younger man rose to greet him.

"Jerome Grabbitt, Wills & Probate," announced a cultured voice bearing no trace of West Country accent. "You are Mr. Peters, I believe – Mr. Nathan Peters," it continued, gesturing towards a single chair with arms drawn towards the partners' desk. Polished oak, inlaid with green leather on the desktop, matched the chair. Three more chairs rested against a wall on which framed certificates proclaimed authority to practice law. Beside a further door a long coat of charcoal grey, exactly in keeping with the man's suit, hung on a stand. Winter light fell weakly through one small window onto a deep green carpet.

"I should ask for some form of identity, as we have not met before, but Miss Plaisant assures me that all is in order." The mouth smiled but the eyes did not and, after further brief exchange, he read the will. Nathan was paying scant attention. His mind would not shift from a picture of Mabel sitting in her wingchair at Little Vennick, looking out through the windows of the old farmhouse down to the little bay below with its Lion Rock guarding the mouth and out beyond Gulland to the distant west. Waves rolled in stately procession; dappled cloud broke the summer light, scattering shafts of gold across the silvered sea; gulls wheeled, dusts of bright white moving in the air – "

"So," said the solicitor, shattering the memory, "it appears that the house and land, the whole estate, are left in Trust. You and Miss Lucinda Venn are the sole trustees. Hmm, you ought to add another – it should be a solicitor, perhaps." His eyes flickered briefly before the voice continued, "The terms of the Trust are somewhat peculiar: 'to benefit those not from these parts'. That may need clarification – "

The door opened unannounced and the solicitor looked up, annoyed. An old man entered. Short in stature, the head was crowned with silver hair, groomed immaculately. A patterned bow-tie clad the starched collar above a waistcoat of lightest grey; neatly folded, a silk handkerchief protruded from the jacket of morning dress; one hand held a silver-topped cane; on the other, a signet ring weighed heavily.

"Sir, how nice to see you." The solicitor was rising rapidly, albeit slightly more slowly than Nathan had.

"Thank you, Grabbitt," a slightly gravelly voice replied. "Do you have young Petrox with you?"

"I have a Mr. Peters, Sir."

"Yes, yes. That's what I mean. Would you mind?"

"Sir?"

"I would like to speak with him. Alone."

"Sir, I was just going through Mrs. Vennick's will with him. There are some oddities – "

"I think I have enough experience to handle a will, thank you, Grabbitt."

"Of course, Sir. I will be in the office if you need me."

The eyes were cold, as he gave a slight inclination of the head, drawing the door to. The old man shut it completely and wandered over to the desk, seating himself, surveying its surface.

"Too big," he announced. "This desk is too big. It's a barrier. I don't like barriers." Their eyes met. Silver the hair might be, but the eyes were lively.

"My name is Kerry. And you are Petrox," he stated more than questioned, nodding slowly to himself. "Yes, yes, I see the likeness."

"Sir?" enquired Nathan. Any other form of address would have been inconceivable. 'Headmaster's study' prompted Nathan's mind, bringing back memories that were not entirely without pain until the old man smiled with a warmth that matched the eyes.

"Sit down, young man. There is something I wish to show you." Reaching into his waistcoat, he produced a gold Hunter, laying it on the desk. "Take it," he said.

Lifting the pocket watch by its chain, Nathan was struck by the weight. "My grandfather had a watch like this," he observed in surprise.

"That watch was lost at the nursing home. This watch belonged to your great-grandfather – Nathaniel. It was one of a pair; the other is long gone. Now it belongs to you. Strange things, old watches," the old man mused; "sometimes they tell more than the time."

Years weighed heavily in Nathan's palm. Sensing their presence, he asked, "My great-grandfather ... did you know him?"

"Yes. I met him from time to time." Silence of memory enfolded the moments until the old man rose, tone changed, "Now I must go before they've gossiped too much in the office."

"What about the will?" Nathan blurted.

"Oh, we'll take that as read, shall we? I'll deal with it."

"There was a Trust – "

"Talk to Lucinda."

"Mr. Grabbitt said we ought to have a third trustee. He suggested a solicitor like himself."

"No! Not Grabbitt." Eyes flashed, the tone was sharp before softening again. "He is right, though ... you ought to have a third. Lucinda is not as young as she was," he added wistfully. "Is there someone you had in mind?"

"Yes."

"Someone known to both of you?"

"Yes."

"What is the name?"

"Zadie … at least, that's an abbreviation … I'm not sure of the surname …" the old man's eyes crinkled in humour "… but the middle name is Barwith."

Suddenly, the eyes sharpened. "Barwith, you say. That is an old family name, a very old family name. Talk to Lucinda … and when you have decided, write to me personally."

By the door, the old man gripped his hand firmly, saying, "It has been a pleasure to meet you, Mr. Petrox. It may be that we will need to meet again."

Through the opening crack, two other voices filtered.

"… I tell you, the old boy is going senile … time we cleared it all out …"

"Well, I wouldn't let him hear you say that."

Quietly Kerry shut the door. He was staring down. Concern struck Nathan that the old man had heard the comment and taken it to heart, but the head came up and the voice showed no sign of strain as it said, "Perhaps, Mr. Petrox, there is something else. Would you accompany me a moment?" Briskly the short figure walked past the desk, thumbing a small key-ring from his waistcoat and opening the further door. "This is the partners' room," he said, closing the door carefully. Nathan's eyes swept round it in surprise. Light fell evenly from four windows on either side, paintings between each; twice the width of Lucinda's table, a vast expanse of polished wood ran nearly full length to a marble fireplace. Another picture hung above it. "Georgian," the voice gravelled, following his gaze; "matching chairs – set of twelve; the fireplace is older, origin suspected but not proven; the oils are Victorian largely – Pethericks on that side, others on this. I see you have recognised the painting above the mantle – opening of Padstow station, 1899 – Nathaniel is third from the right, second row."

Kerry knelt beside a small safe embossed with the name of its Sheffield makers. Below the date a lion rampant stood, one rear paw grasping a world in its claws. 'Dominion of Canada' read black on red while, seated in raised brasswork, Imperial Britannia held her trident defiantly on the safe's other visible side. Shortly the old man rose, placing a package on the table, and standing beside Nathan in the light.

"You have inherited something of Nathaniel's interest in rocks, I believe," Kerry ventured, breaking into Nathan's study of the picture. "Perhaps you would give me an opinion on this?" he asked, slipping the signet ring from his finger.

Surprised, Nathan took it towards the window, turning the object in his fingers. Professional interest was aroused. "Gold," he began, "solid … unusual though … slightly redder than I would have expected … no markings that I can see without a glass … it is either foreign or old; engravings on the signet look like a copy of some Celtic design … one bright blue stone, not sapphire, maybe aquamarine … another one, red, slightly duller, not ruby, could be garnet. There is a silvery-grey stone in the opposite corner, not showing clearly … no idea on that one …" he scanned the gaps, pausing several minutes, angling the ring this way and that "… and just a hint of two other stones: the one looks something like milky quartz; the other could be a small piece of serpentine. For such a valuable ring, it is strange they would use semi-precious stones," he ended, passing it back to its owner.

Kerry's eyes were shining, almost with a touch of tears, as he too held the ring in the light. "Mabel chose well," he murmured, gesturing to a chair, assembling his thoughts. "Before I tell you more, I will ask you three questions." Kerry's gaze locked onto Nathan. "What do you know of Polgodoc?"

"A little," Nathan replied cautiously, startled by the use of the name so few knew.

"Have you been through its cave?"

It was a direct question, a lawyer's question, allowing no fudging in reply. "Yes," Nathan answered slowly.

"And the landscape beyond?"

"Yes."

For a few moments longer Kerry held Nathan's gaze, before beginning, "This is indeed an old ring – a very old ring. The gold it was made from was brought as tribute. It is Cornish gold. There is none left now. Only three things were made from that gold and in each were embedded stones of Cornwall. The crown was lost;

the hilt of the sword was buried with its legend; only this ring remains. It is old Kernow. It tells me much. Each stone responds to a key, or the presence of one who has used the key, or has close knowledge of it. Seldom in my long life, Mr. Petrox, have those stones showed – and then only two – until today when we shook hands upon farewell. Of four stones, I knew; of the fifth, I have no knowledge. Legend and history run strangely mixed. There is much that I must consider. However, it is clear that this package should be yours," said the old man, rising. "No. Don't open it now. Offices have ears and eyes."

Only the bushy brown hair was in the outer office and, descending the first creaking stair, Nathan caught a gravelly voice saying, "Miss Plaisant, bring me the file on Grabbitt, if you please. I wish to take it home."

Turning along Eddystone Road, Nathan's heart thrilled. There was a fourth thing made from that gold, he knew by instinct, knew with a certainty greater than any power of logic. It was a very small thing … a small thing lying in a small box of heavy tin … lying in a bungalow, in Trevennick.

*　　　*　　　*

The conversation with Lucinda was lengthy and pleasant, aided and abetted by a bottle of sherry-wine and a large plate of mince pies, cooked to her usual standards of perfection. Three times the grandfather struck, hidden behind a Christmas tree laden with baubles of thinnest glass – heirlooms, bearing their own story, like most things in Lucinda's home. They were united in their view of what Mabel intended, and that Zadie should be the third trustee. Somehow, it was a turning point, the beginning of a counting-down, a shared certainty. She had laughed that he did not know Zadie's surname, and expressed the opinion that Samuel would track it down from the Barwith clue. He had wondered at her calling Kerry 'Samuel'. Insisting he take the remaining mince pies, Lucinda had invited him for Christmas lunch.

Flames licked slowly round the logs, sharing their warmth

and company that evening in the bungalow, as he stretched in his usual armchair, cup of tea forgotten. The package had been a disappointment – some kind of pictorial map of local history drawn on linen cloth with writing that was hard to decipher and markings that might once have been in colour. Without more information it made no sense and, putting it to one side, he picked up the pocket watch. With this there was a better chance. The protective front hinged open easily, as was common with a Hunter, revealing the face and hands. Clipping it shut, he turned to the back. With greater difficulty it opened, revealing the maker's name on an inner case as shiny as the day it was bought. Beneath the hallmark of assayed gold, his eye caught a small engraving. Reaching to the cabinet of rock specimens, he pulled out a set of lenses. "IGLOS," he murmured to himself, searching the casing's edge. Four times he followed its circumference, each time more slowly, until he found the slightest indentation. Not risking metal or wood, he prised gently with his fingernail. Infinitesimally, something moved. He ran his nail both ways around the edge. Suddenly, the case clicked. Cogs and levers opened to view. A folded piece of rice paper drifted onto his lap. Carefully, he closed the double casing and unfolded the paper. Ink, faded sepia, met his gaze. Five lines only were written on the scrap.

'To the next Petrox
    Beware the Blue;
    Use the Coral Key:
    Time is but a moment,
    Escaped eternity.'

Embers glowed and faded, crinkling their slow demise, while Nathan slept – a single, folded fragment lying loosely in his hand. Beneath another sky, a hand touched copper on gold, remembering.

*   *   *

Lucinda's invitation for Christmas lunch prompted Nathan to tackle the vegetable patch. Over the next few days as she returned from her usual round of social engagements she found potatoes and parsnips neatly bagged on the doorstep. Brussel sprouts and late-flowering broccoli arrived on Christmas Eve, together with a large root of celeriac. She smiled, grinding a gear on turning to the Trevelyns. They had been invited but had declined. It was just as well, really: she did not know how much the son knew, and they would want to bring the two grandchildren. She liked the girls but they were a lively pair, and her home seldom escaped one of their rare visits without some minor catastrophe. Momentarily, a stone wall threatened to jump in front of the vehicle, and Lucinda wrestled with the wheel. The bird had been chosen several weeks ago … it was a long while since she had cooked goose.

The next day bells pealed vigorously from the crooked steeple of the little church, signalling the village's turn to host the Christmas Morning service. Grasping a single red rose, Nathan passed beneath the lych gate and into the sloping graveyard. Shaken from her sanctuary, the old raven watched as he placed it beside another and stood awhile. An organ played, and he slipped in at the back. Decorated in fair measure from the offerings of local trees and hedgerows, the church was both fuller and with people from further afield than he had expected. Crib and Christmas tree competed for the little transept; advent candles glinted on bronze in the lectern's eagle wings; a scattering of stained-glass shadow shimmered over pews and aisle. A few children grasped newly-treasured toys, and a few adults wore mismatching colours of newly-given gifts. The hymn ended, and the pew creaked heavily beside him.

"Wilf!" he exclaimed in half-muted surprise, as the massive form of the old tin-miner and acquaintance turned to face him.

"Come for the meal. Thought I'd keep you company …" came the smiling reply in what could best be judged as a stage whisper. Heads turned and they fell silent.

After the service, the unlikely pair cut across the graveyard to the private gate leading to Lucinda's garden. Wilf's battered landrover, marginally younger than Nathan's, stood on the slate drive alongside a dirty, red van.

"Martyn the Post and Mrs. Martyn are here," nodded Wilf approvingly.

"We can't call her that. What is her name?"

"I don't know – Verona, I think. He always calls her 'The Missus', or 'Mrs. Martyn'.

Nathan pulled on the pewter bell. Elegant as ever, Lucinda appeared, welcoming them. It was a meal worth remembering; Lucinda was generous in her provision of both food and wine. After his third glass, Martyn asked how she knew so much about wine.

"The Bridge Club," Lucinda laughed: "the Colonel is always talking about what he has had delivered; he complains about it almost as much as about his bridge hands; whenever he complains, I know it is something that I would like, and I buy a case."

Conversation flowed freely about Mabel and her Trust, about Zadie, about Soloma, about Cornwall past and present. For a while Lucinda was diverted onto heirlooms and local family history. Stories half-remembered from her grandmother filtered in; she mentioned Nathaniel and a brother, their love of exploring, disappearing for weeks at a time until the brother became deaf and insane. Briefly a darkness clutched at Nathan, but Wilf dispelled his thoughts, sharing tales of a still older Cornwall – of families and mines long-forgotten, legends of Arthur and Tintagel, of saints, of myths and history. Too soon, it seemed, evening had come. Wisely, Veronica drove Martyn home, and Nathan offered Wilf a bed.

One night turned to three as Wilf helped with notes on the geology of Carn Menellis. The second evening they examined Nathaniel's package. Wilf made little more of it than Nathan, except to say with a grunt, "Seen something like it on an old mining diagram. I'll have a think." The battered landrover bade farewell to its older sister and Nathan fell into the habit of walking each day. Increasingly, he found his feet leading him to the Pulpit Rock and he sat looking along the cliff-line to Polgodoc, out to Gulland and the unseen west beyond, inland to the moors where Little Vennick lay, and on towards the distant east. Late after one such walk, the phone rang. An operator's voice surprised him, both in that such voices still existed and in its request for him to accept a long distance call. His heart leapt at the thought of Zadie. Instead, a mildly trans-Atlantic voice echoed in his ear.

"James ... James Heal ... phoning to wish you a Happy New Year. I got the job ... I'll be over in the summer ..."

Nathan hoped the disappointment had not sounded in his voice. With him it lingered. Only when term restarted did the dull ache diminish, as day followed counted day.

Elsewhere, time moved differently.

Chapter 7   Fragments of Many-coloured Glass

Soloma was unhappy. She was concerned about the home that she knew and, above all, she was concerned about Elana. She was sitting talking with Tarma just beyond the eastern guardian, speaking in the language Elana had taught them that winter. Exciting as it was having a secret language in which to communicate, experience had taught them that it was viewed with suspicion by others and they had adopted the habit of coming to this place when they wanted to talk. Indeed, it was just as well that they had done so: the men had come early this year – a few weeks ago in March – and the two girls had been sitting on the same rock, looking across the ice-free bowl of land they knew as home, when they had seen them arrive at the southern guardian. Despite her young age, Soloma had nearly been 'chosen' on a previous visit of the men and she did not want to be taken away from Elana. Tarma had no desire to be chosen, either; going with the men would mean leaving her twin brother and, worse, almost certainly encountering the Mortan again. As a result, they had climbed quickly up the path, through the warm mist, and onto the ice. Two days they had stayed away on the great ice-sheet, losing themselves in the white wilderness. It had been very cold and they had been faint with hunger when they had finally returned, avoiding the men's departure by a matter of hours. Neither Meroa nor Elana commented on their absence or expressed displeasure, although others did – particularly Simona's mother.

The choosing had not gone well, apparently. Five men had come – more than usual – but only two girls had been deemed to be of age and had been chosen to go with them. There had been division amongst the men, and harsh words had been spoken. What made it worse was the lack of boys to replace the men lost in the mining. Ruan had refused to go – again – and there had been further disagreement. In the end, it had been settled by the giving of gifts. This had pleased the men, and they were intrigued by them, talking eagerly amongst themselves.

Two weeks later, one of the Mortan had arrived at the same guardian – on his own – and had spoken with the women there before leaving again. It was unheard of both for the Mortan to arrive so early in the year and for one to come alone. Elana had needed help to climb the steep path up to the guardian to speak with him. She was looking very old now and wearied, and she seldom left her hut. It had been a trouble to her. The bond between them had strengthened since Soloma had lost her own mother to the creature at the Little Lake, and the girl felt a great sadness for the old lady. There had been much for her to bear this winter and, after the visit of the Mortan, the atmosphere had turned tense. There were mutterings in some of the huts.

Soloma looked across the land that lay below her. Smoke from the slowly burning wood was rising in irregular strands of blue-grey opacity, spoiling the purity of the veil of mist in the afternoon sunlight. Myriad droplets of ascending water no longer shimmered the rainbow hues that she was used to as their prisms split the light. She knew that Elana was concerned about the amount of fuel they had used that winter – there would be barely enough for cooking over the summer months until the new growth of wood could be coppiced and dried. They were reaching the low point in their food supplies, as well: the first of the berries would take another month, and the crops another three months to yield; meanwhile, the fish-ponds had been depleted, and the remaining fish were wary and difficult to catch. Perhaps Elana would ask more of them to forage in the land beyond the ice for the next couple of months. Maybe that was why Elana had called a meeting of the eldest from each family that night. Tarma thought the reason was more sinister but would volunteer to leave with Soloma if it were a question of fewer mouths to feed. Neither of them could remember a meeting being called before and, try as they might, they had found out nothing firm about its content. Soloma looked past the lithe figure of the black lioness crouching, alert, a few yards away and beyond it to her home. It was the only home that she had known, and she was not sure whether she loved it so much for its own sake or for the sake of the elderly, white figure that she could just make out in the distance, sitting by her doorway in the sun. Of course, briefly there had been another home, but that had been too brief to call home, really; and it had been strange – dreamlike, unreal. She touched the chain hanging against her skin at the memory of it and turned as Tarma intruded upon her thoughts.

"It is most unlike the old ones not to talk. And it is only the eldest from each family going to the meeting tonight. Meroa has not said anything either, but she banned Ruan and me from going anywhere near Elana's hut – and threatened us."

Soloma thought that Tarma's mother knew her two children very well and answered, "I can't imagine Ruan sitting quietly, waiting to find out what's happening. And you know you would follow him."

"Well, how are we going to find out? No-one is saying anything. I've never known anything like it."

"I think," said Soloma, "that Elana might let me stay. If I make her meal slowly and I'm still clearing things when they come, she may not tell me to go. And someone needs to tend the fire to give them light …"

"And, if you can't stay, you will come to us?"

"Yes. But if Elana tells me not to be there, I'm not taking part in one of Ruan's plans."

"I don't think he's got one."

"I very much doubt that," ended Soloma emphatically.

Tarma nodded and skipped up lightly onto the lioness, placing her hand in the cleft behind the head of the carved piece of basalt and hurrying down the path. Soloma followed more slowly, her thoughts confused as she splashed across the stream and followed the track up past the coral pool to Elana's hut.

*   *   *

It had been a pleasant walk back from the village, made more pleasant by the glass of red wine consumed while sitting outside the café in the little square. It was rough stuff but she had grown accustomed to the local red wine over the winter; there was nothing pretentious about it and it reflected the landscape and people that had become a part of this temporary way of life: earthy, rugged, direct, weather-beaten – yet surprisingly soft, and generous at times. Spring had come early this year and the old men had been sitting outside in the sunshine, exchanging stories that had become exaggerated and embellished with each successive telling. Their grey and black clothes had weathered with their faces, and gold fillings in their teeth contrasted with white beards and hair, although there were gaps in both beards and hair. Eyes had followed her as she had walked across to the gaily-coloured post-box set in the pastel-washed wall and dropped the postcard to Nathan into it. She had meant to write more often. Three cards in six months wasn't much, and she knew that he would be disappointed – not that he would mention it. Anyway, it was two more than she had received from him – which was one more than she had expected to receive. She wondered again whether he had remembered her giving the island's name, or how he had tracked her down – probably from her description of the landscape and rocks around the dig in her first postcard. Maybe there had been more. Certainly, the one she had received had been well-thumbed and well-read by the old men and others by the time it had been handed over to her on a rare foray into the village.

If they had exchanged e-mail addresses she could have kept in touch during the hour when the satellite equipment was available for personal use, but he hadn't offered it and she hadn't asked. Not that her news would have been particularly interesting. And there was an indefinable pleasure about receiving the old-fashioned postcard: it had taken time to choose and to write; it required being taken somewhere to post, and the right stamps found; it had been physically carried to her, and delivered by a real person; it was a tangible link to another world. A few more days and she would be back in that world again; she would have reception on her mobile phone; the tiny island and all their painstaking research would begin to dim into memory.

The time had been busy. It was difficult to explain how six months on an archaeological dig could be so busy and, perhaps falsely, she could imagine him saying, 'So, apart from scraping away with that scalpel-like thing and brushing away the dust with something that looks like a glorified toothbrush, what did you actually do for six months?' She chuckled to herself as she thought of several possible replies that would wind him up nicely.

Tomorrow, Zadie would finish cataloguing and photographing the large array of mostly small items that had been unearthed from beneath the layer of solidified volcanic ash. They would remain within the country, of course – only her photographs and notes would travel with her – evidence of a once thriving civilisation. Idly, she turned a few of the items over: barbs of bones, some with holes drilled through; cutting tools made of some hard rock, like flint but not flint; other pieces of smooth obsidian; shards of pottery, slightly curved and shaped. Each had its story to tell and she sat, imagining its creator crafting it for some specific purpose vital to that community's existence and thinking of the labour that had gone into its making and of its loss and burial beneath the layerings of time and nature. She shut the lid of the packing case, looking at the unfamiliar script on the label and wondering how long her treasures would lay buried anew in the storage area of the museum before some researcher unearthed them again – what had been tools of survival now become passing fragments of intellectual curiosity.

Already, two of the team had left to arrange transport to the museum on the mainland. Two more had gone to give a preliminary report to their sponsor. In two days' time the chartered boat would arrive to take the cases. The few of them remaining would have a party, probably at the café in the village square; then they would depart on the fortnightly supply ship when it called at the island, leaving the old men to exaggerate their tales of what had been taken, until they too were interred to become the objects of some future generation's scientific interest.

*   *   *

"So, are the guardians our only defence? And what are they

a defence against?" demanded Tarma in the darkness of Meroa's hut.

"I don't know, I tell you," Soloma answered. "It is something to do with the Mortan. Elana was not saying much and she was very careful about what she did say. But she did want as many families as possible to go foraging beyond the ice, and to go soon."

"It's too early in the year. There will be little food apart from fish, if you can catch them. Why did she want people to go?"

"I've already told you that I don't know. I was spotted and thrown out before they made that clear."

"This is no good," said Ruan. "We are going over the same ground. Start again and tell us slowly, point by point, who said what and whether any decisions were made."

Soloma drew a deep breath, and the conversation in their own language continued. She had done as she had said and delayed the old lady's supper as long as possible. She had been tidying up in the shadows when the old ones arrived, more or less together. Meroa was the youngest and had arrived last, sitting in the doorway, presumably having kept an eye on Ruan and Tarma until the last possible moment to make sure they were not going to disobey her. Several people had spoken about their meeting with the single Mortan, and Elana had explained that more Mortan would be returning soon – she did not know when. Apparently, they wanted something or somebody – or more than one person. What it was, the old ones did not say clearly, and there was a lot of debate about whether the Mortan should be let in past the guardian. Some spoke against defying them again after last year's visit when the girls had been seized for a sacrifice, and some did not believe the Mortan would come – they had never arrived this early in the year. Elana was nervous and tired, and she wanted families to go foraging – not just mothers and daughters, but boys with them. She knew or suspected something she was not telling, and only a few were willing to consider the idea. There were many objections and they had decided to wait and see if the Mortan came. Elana insisted that no-one was to let them in, if they did come.

"That was when I was spotted," ended Soloma. "The only

other thing I remember was that there were some fairly nasty comments about me being a 'bringer of trouble' as I left. They were still talking as I came down the hill to you." In part she said this because she had determined not to tell Tarma what had been said about Simona and her.

"What were the objections to foraging?" asked Tarma.

"Just what you said: there would be no berries, and little food this early. Also, that the route over the ice was still dangerous; that we had never done it this early; that we could go in a few weeks time; and that we were more exposed in the open land than behind the protection of the guardians."

"What did Meroa say?" Ruan intervened.

"Nothing. She just sat there and looked around."

"We'll have to corner her when she comes back. Maybe she'll talk if you are here," he suggested more in hope than in conviction.

"Well, it won't be long. There are voices on the track now," observed Tarma.

Shortly, Meroa appeared at the doorway, lifting the skins against the starlight. She was neither slim nor stocky in silhouette and her arms made light of heavy skins as she moved into the hut with the purposeful gait that her children had grown both to admire and to treat with caution. There was no doubting she was their mother and they were her children, even if Ruan was now nearly as strong as her. They couldn't see her eyes or expression but the tone of her voice was unmistakable and indicated no surprise at finding the three figures together.

"Soloma, go back to Elana – she needs you. You go too, Tarma. And stay the night. There's no-one on the path, now," she added more softly. "Ruan, I want to speak with you. Go and find your cousin and bring him here. His grandmother is expecting you."

There was just time for Tarma to whisper, "Beyond the eastern guardian – tomorrow," as the three smaller figures ducked under the skins, neither daring nor wishing to question Meroa's commands.

*   *   *

Once the vehicle had been new, equipped with air-conditioning and a fully functional suspension system. Now it was older, and the former had long stopped working, whilst the latter gave no relief from lurchings and swayings on the rutted and pot-holed road to the airport. Matters were made worse by the local driver taking it as a personal challenge to be pressing either the accelerator or brake as far as it would go to the floor. Zadie had been sitting in the full sun most of the journey, and the rough, red wine from the night before was wreaking a particularly vicious revenge on the inside of her head.

The situation had been compounded at the airport, where the half-dozen rock samples that she had thoughtfully gathered for Nathan and put in her carry-on baggage had raised suspicions in the rudimentary X-ray machine. And she had forgotten about the copper ornament hanging on a gold chain around her neck. It was the only thing of any real value that she had ever owned, and she had become very possessive of it, wearing it every day, to the extent that it had become very much a part of her and not a thing detached. It had triggered the alarm on the personal scanner as she had stepped through it, and she had been subjected to a body-search by an obnoxious little man who reminded her of an over-officious traffic-warden on a mission to spread misery amongst the unsuspecting. At least he had the courtesy to summon a female security guard to complete the search – not that there had been any great sense of femininity in either her appearance or her touch.

By the time they had finished, customs had taken an interest in the copper token with its peculiar engraving and cuneiform writing, and had accused her of trying to smuggle an ancient artefact from the archaeological dig out of the country. It had taken a great deal of time and two telephone calls to persuade them otherwise. Possibly as a consequence, the flight was delayed on the runway. It had certainly looked like her bags were being loaded separately, and last, onto the aircraft. The sponsorship only ran to bargain fares so there were none of the usual comforts and, when they encountered turbulence soon after take-off, the revenge of the red wine was complete.

It was not entirely to Zadie's surprise, therefore, to find herself still prowling around the carousel in the baggage reclaim hall at Heathrow long after most people from the flight had departed. Various pieces of language that were not part of her usual vernacular were seething beneath her lips, and she had the feeling that, if one of them escaped, the resultant torrent would be sufficient to bring some arm of officialdom into rapid orbit around her.

Finally, half the baggage appeared. Or, to be more accurate, all the baggage appeared in several halves, sticky elephant-tape holding imitation cloth cases closed and covering the torn destination label. Zadie grabbed at it and loaded it onto her trolley with a kind of half-laugh, tinged with that near-hysteria which could follow those strange emotions of sudden release from indeterminate waiting into an unexpected and mildly unpleasant outcome. At least she wouldn't have to worry about customs, she thought blackly: if anyone asked her whether she had anything to declare, much of her personal clothing was protruding clearly through the cases. Doubtless that would also elicit comment as she struggled with them on the Underground, and she contemplated the alternative of an expensive taxi. Thoughts of shutting her own front door, having a bath, and catching up with messages became increasingly attractive, overwhelming the expense. She would be able to shut out the world around her and rest in her own cocoon.

*   *   *

Nathan was looking at a piece of rock. Not that it was unusual for Nathan to be looking at a rock. However, he was looking at it very intently. It was a very ordinary piece of rock. It was a greenish piece of slate that normally resided in his back garden, but now it was under an equally ordinary piece of grey slate by his front door. The grey slate had been turned over so that the word 'Post' appeared on its upper side, and he could see a foreign stamp sticking out from below it.

It had been a while since Nathan had been home and he thought, perhaps unfairly, that the old bungalow had the faintest air of being unloved and neglected about it – rather like the way the old dog had looked at him sometimes when he had been busy with his thoughts elsewhere and had ignored her for slightly too long. No words or sounds were expressed: it was just an unremarked look, an appearance, mirroring in distorted fashion the tendrils of guilt latching somewhere within his mind. Not that there had been much choice in his absence. Term had dragged by, more slowly than usual, and Nathan had found himself losing enthusiasm for some of his work, becoming less immersed in it. He loved his subject. It was a consuming passion that he awoke to in the morning, breathed in the day, and dreamt at night. He loved his lectures as an opportunity to convey his interest and knowledge to others, but several times he had found himself in mid-flow, pausing and re-gathering his thoughts as unintended ones had penetrated from outside. Increasingly, he had begun counting down the days to the Easter break, thinking of cliff walks, of sitting on the verandah of the old bungalow at Trevennick – and of Zadie. Zadie had promised she would write to him. Zadie had said she would come down and stay when she returned from her dig. They would have time to talk – time together.

He had thought she had meant it. He still thought that she might have meant it. But she hadn't given him an address – at least, not one that he remembered. Once he had tried writing to her, piecing together her whereabouts from her description of the landscape in the one postcard that he had received. Actually, he had tried writing several times, and once he had gone as far as posting the card. He felt foolish about it now. Somewhere, floating around some café in some unknown Mediterranean island, was a postcard addressed to someone they wouldn't even know, with his name on it and some comments that could only elicit a condescending smile or, worse still, a degree of pity for the writer. He felt sullied over the matter, like a foolish child who had pursued an improbable line of action under the misapprehensions of its own ego, and he wished now that he hadn't written.

His mind turned back to his work. Some were saying that the latest review had placed the department under threat. Certainly, the professor had seemed less than his usual, confident self when he had insisted on them staying for three days after the end of term and re-working their applications for funding for the next academic year. His own funding for work on hydrothermal veining and secondary emplacement of metallic ores in the metamorphic aureole of the granite batholiths of the South-west ended on August 1st. It was a nice topic with a wide range of personal interests that had allowed him a good element of latitude in where he went and who he saw. Although he had stressed potential economic aspects of the work in his initial application, that had not been reflected in his interest or in what he had written, and he supposed that was why the funding had been discontinued. His proposal to investigate apparent anomalies in near-shore geologies off the North Cornwall coast had been rejected out of hand by the powers on the purse strings. The professor had described it as an unusual and original topic that had considerable merit as an area of academic debate, before letting slip that it had scored 0/10 on 'practical aspects of data-gathering' and 0/10 on 'possible income-generating strands'. He thought he had detected some animosity, over and above the usual personal academic competitiveness, amongst his peers, who seemed to suggest that it had somehow weakened the overall application of the department. It was all becoming so much like a business: dangle a carrot of possible financial return to the university and there was a good chance of approval; attempt to engage in pure academic research, and it was likely to be frowned upon. It riled him. He could hardly have stood up and said, 'I've been there … I know there are oddities … and they're very interesting.'

The rock was still there, staring up at him. It hadn't moved, and he hadn't moved. Both rocks were still there, and the stamp was still protruding from beneath the grey slate. Nathan opened the door and put two heavy bags down in the dusty hallway. The rest could wait in the landrover awhile, and he went through to the kitchen to make a cup of tea, letting the cold tap run until it had cleared from its habitual rusty colour following a period of inactivity. He could hear air gurgling round the plumbing system. Judging by deposits on the verandah, the chickens were still alive, and a beady eye appeared opposite him in the window, cocking its head to one side, looking enquiringly. He unlocked the back door, supposing casually that it had not been the most sensible thing to leave the key in it, and stepped outside to scatter a handful of grain as the kettle warmed. Five feathery figures squabbled over his generosity and he wondered if Martyn, or the old farmer, had kept an eye on them as he poured boiling water into an almost clean mug and fetched the remains of a pint of milk from one of his bags.

Armed with a cup of tea, Nathan retraced his footsteps along the hall and out of the front door. With considerable hesitancy, and some sense of misgiving, he bent down and plucked the card from between the two rocks, settling himself on the front step before focusing on it.

Reading the first words, his heart leapt: 'Dear Nathan, Thanks for the card. That was a lovely surprise. Got it a few weeks ago. Don't know how you found me. We've only had emails'. Suddenly, there was sunshine in his day. It blazed in his face like the mother lode on that first day in the adit. It warmed him from inside like the wine at Polgodoc. It had been worthwhile. It hadn't been foolish. It didn't matter how many other people had read it: Zadie had read it; it had reached her, and she had welcomed it. He didn't care if his funding was going to be cut off or his research application ridiculed. The world was the right way up again, and he read on: 'Another week and I'll be finished here. I don't know if you'll get this before I'm back but I'll phone and let you know when I'm coming down'. Nathan's emotions jumped again. She might be back in the country already. Was there a date on the postmark? No, only a smudged impression. 'Look forward to seeing you. Love Z'. The last phrase was very small and squeezed into the corner, but it was definitely there; it wasn't a figment of his imagination. But it didn't necessarily mean what it said: it was a common way of ending a card; it could be just a courtesy. Nevertheless, something purred deep inside Nathan as he sat on the step and read the little rectangle of pulverised wood pulp and China clay through slowly three times, mouthing the words to himself.

Eventually, he tucked the postcard in his top pocket and looked down again at the grey slate. The word 'Post' seemed an entirely inadequate expression for the card that had lain below it. Abruptly, his sun disappeared behind a cloud and the day felt chill. The greenish slate had no business being there. It belonged in the back garden on top of a neat stack of similar rocks, alongside the dog's grave. He thought of a second cup of tea, but his body, which had been so full of energy a few moments ago, seemed unwilling to respond to the suggestion. He pushed the grey slate away with his boot and was relieved to see nothing further revealed by the movement. Somewhere in his consciousness he was aware of a demand to turn over the green slate. He was equally aware that he did not wish to do so. Indeed, the sunshine had well and truly gone, and a deep, unpleasant sense of foreboding took its place. The ordinary, green rock was focusing his thoughts upon it, becoming impossible to ignore. He felt himself being drawn to the rock, and with great reluctance he touched the surface; with further reluctance he turned it over.

The writing was simple, distinctive, and unmistakable. It was partially in cuneiform, and consisted of a single word and a single letter beneath. Both had been done in haste and placed where only he would realise the significance. It was both a plea and a command, a call to repay a debt of gratitude and a request tinged with hopelessness. It was absolutely, utterly and completely certain that his ordinary little life – his orderly little life – was about to be turned as upside down as the insignificant slab of rock that bore the message:

HELP

ʃ.

Chapter 8   Only a few Words

"Hello, Nathan," a voice said, breaking into his thoughts. "Expected you back a few days ago."

It was a familiar voice from beneath a flat, peaked cap stained with the passage of years of Cornish rain and grimed with the dust of earthen banks on sunny days. The cap resided at a slight angle on the occupant's head and contrasted violently with the orange day-glo jacket around the shoulders. The figure was stationary, surveying him, resting one hand against the early growth of erigeron that clung to the dry-stone wall where his drive became the lane.

"Oh, Martyn, what are you doing? I thought you had retired from the post."

"I have. New chap's on holiday. I'm just filling in for a few days. You've got your messages then, I see." Martyn hesitated at the entrance to the drive and walked slowly over. "Are you alright? You look as white as a newly-arrived Emmett."

"It's the messages ..." replied Nathan.

"Well I thought you'd like them. Zadie says she's coming to visit. I left the corner sticking out so that you'd see the card as soon as you arrived." Martyn had clearly read the card before depositing it and he added, "It came two days ago. She's probably back in this country by now."

Seeing it was Martyn who had delivered the card, Nathan was unsurprised at his knowledge of its contents and, indeed, his heart had leapt at it, but he answered, "It's the other message. I've just read it," indicating it with his foot.

"Ah, that'll be the little girl, I think."

Nathan nodded. "Yes – it's Soloma's writing."

"Don't know when that came," observed Martyn, contemplating Nathan carefully and sitting down alongside him on the step. "Old farmer Trevelyn thought he saw a young figure up by Mabel's place. The rock wasn't there when I fed your chickens the other Monday, but it was when I put the postcard there." After a prolonged and mutual silence, he added, "There's another rock down at Lucinda's."

Mention of Lucinda's name was a ray of hope amidst the uncertainties swirling through Nathan's mind. He could talk openly with her and, if she had seen Soloma, she would have a good idea of what was happening. He could phone Zadie, as well. Maybe Martyn was right and she was already back.

He asked cautiously, "What did the other message say? Did Lucinda say anything about it to you?"

"I haven't seen Lucinda ... away on her Easter cruise ... think she's in the Aegean this year. Always goes at this time of year ... before the garden consumes all her attention. Won't be back for another week ... "

One set of hopes was dashed. Nathan ought to have remembered that she would not be around at Easter, and he let the frustration show in his voice as he demanded, "Well, did it say the same thing?"

"Not exactly," answered Martyn, becoming concerned at Nathan's reaction, "and whoever wrote it had worked out that Lucinda was away – leant the slate against her garage doors so the writing wasn't visible."

"So, what did it say?"

It was entirely in keeping that Martyn should have bothered to check out as small an oddity as a slate in the wrong place, and Nathan asked again, "What did it say?"

Only when he repeated the question for the third time did Martyn answer. "It wasn't spelt right ... and it was quite short. It just said, PLEAS NATHAN COME."

The poignancy of the message – and of the error – struck him deeply. His mind began to form an image of a small figure, unable to speak with those she sought, desperately seeking a means of communication – searching for words. He could sense Martyn's quiet patience beside him, and it was fully five minutes before he asked, "Have you been watching out for me, Martyn, to tell me this?"

"Sort of ..." he admitted.

"Why?"

"Well ... we liked the little girl ... and we thought you would want to help ..." He held Nathan's gaze carefully before continuing, "Look, I don't know what it cost that little one to leave those messages, but it won't have been easy for her ... and they were done in a hurry. Something was very urgent to her."

Suddenly, Nathan knew Martyn very much better. Martyn had been a known figure throughout his life – Martyn the Post – good, old, reliable Martyn – but now Nathan understood why he had remained as village postman all these years. He was beginning to understand the links between a number of names. Martyn was the one who had sent the condolence card addressed to him and 'the little girl' he felt certain now; he had been the one who had found the old organist for the funeral; he had been the one who had taken Mabel to see Lucinda every Saturday; he had been the person keeping the links together. He had kept his counsel with the utmost carefulness, too. Never had he spoken about 'we' before, nor had he ever sat down beside Nathan in this way. But he couldn't possibly understand what might be involved in helping Soloma, thought Nathan. Apart from the cave at Polgodoc and the ice-sheet and the Mortan, there were a host of other hazards; and he doubted what he could do as one person, anyway. Besides which, he had been lucky before. The memories were complete: they were over, finished, a task done. He hadn't sought it out before, and he didn't want to seek it out again. Yes, he would love to see Soloma and Tarma and Elana and the landscape again – but the reality would be altogether different from the memory that had been smoothed and glossed in his mind over the intervening months.

Uncertainty wracked him, and he probed, "Martyn, helping Soloma is not as easy as you might think ..."

"I never said it would be easy."

That led nowhere and he tried again, "Look, have you ever heard of a place called Polgodoc?"

Martyn seemed unphased by the question and answered evenly, "Mabel mentioned it a few times and so did Lucinda." He paused, like a boxer waiting for his moment, before adding, "And so did your grandfather."

Nathan could feel his options narrowing rapidly. This time he asked, "Do you know what lies beyond Polgodoc?"

"Something of it," came the response.

So Martyn knew what was being asked of Nathan. Carefully, he enquired, "And have you been there?"

"No. It is not open to me."

That was strange wording. Nathan would pursue that response later. For the moment he desperately wanted advice or, rather, counsel from someone who knew at least a little of what he might face. He reached down, tracing his fingers over the simple marks in the green slate, and lifted his eyes to the Lion Rock at the mouth of the bay below Trevennick. He could just make out Gulland with flecks of white waves breaking against it: Gulland, where he had woken with Zadie to the splendour of the ice-wall in the dawn; Gulland, where the girls had led him in his blindness; Gulland, whose shadow had rescued them in their moment of need; Gulland, to which Soloma's gaze had been drawn time after time.

"What are you thinking?" prompted Martyn gently.

"That I wanted advice – advice from someone that knew." He could try Zadie but he knew precisely what her reaction would be. He would have to phone her soon – he wanted to phone her – but he wished to make up his own mind first. Mabel would have known. Lucinda would have a good idea.

"You've already had advice," stated Martyn, surprising him.

"I'm sorry. I don't understand. You said you hadn't been beyond – "

"I'm not talking about me," interrupted Martyn. "You had the advice at Mabel's funeral. It was by the side of her grave. Don't you remember?"

Nathan thought hard, caught unprepared by the comment, and said, "No. No-one told me anything about this. How could they have done? The funeral was back in August, and now it's April."

Martyn regarded him with compassion and slowly began, "I was waiting to say goodbye to you at the lych gate when someone spoke to you by the grave. He was old and he gave you three pieces of advice. I happened to overhear them. Now do you remember? You were on your own with him."

"Well, there was the priest ... he asked about the organist ..."

"No, not the priest."

"There was the organist ..."

"And what did he say?"

"Who? Old Goldilocks?"

"Yes." Martyn smiled at the name. "What did Goldilocks say?"

"He said that Mabel thought a lot of me ... and something about missing her, I think."

"Then you didn't listen very carefully, although that's understandable. Unless I'm much mistaken, what he actually said was, 'She thought a lot of you, Nathan. Don't let her down when she needs you. I'm glad I missed you'. You know now how much Mabel thought of you, and I think you may understand what he meant by being glad he missed you. It's the other part that's relevant," ended Martyn

Nathan thought of the old organist with his flowing white hair and long, slendered fingers and of his singing reverberating through the graveyard as they had stood. What Martyn said rang true. He had not seen Martyn at the lych gate but, after the priest, there had been a young Canadian who had stopped him, and they had talked for some while.

Eventually, Nathan said, "So, what did he mean? I thought he was saying not to let Mabel down."

"Maybe. Maybe not," answered Martyn. "Goldilocks has always been very careful with his words – and he's said some strange things from time to time. I think he was referring to the little girl."

"To Soloma?"

"Yes."

"You are saying that he meant not to let Soloma down when she needed me?"

"Yes. And if you don't believe me, I'll tell you one more thing, since your grandfather trusted me and you've not betrayed the trust put in you down the years: Goldilocks was escaping from the Mortan when he came here."

Nathan felt as if several hammer blows were striking him at once. Never had he expected to hear that word from anyone other than Zadie, and she would not willingly mention it. It was only a little word – just two syllables – but it felt like something evil had entered his ears, and he was struggling to cleanse his body of it. It was grabbing at his emotions. He could feel his mind being dragged back to the Stones of Sacrifice; he could hear the sound pressing on him; he could smell the breath of the vile animals in his nostrils.

Weakly, he asked, "Does Goldilocks know you were going to say this to me?"

"Yes. I went to see him when I saw the message on the first slate. He told me, 'If Nathan will not believe you, mention the grave; and mention the Mortan'. I've only heard the word once before, and I didn't like the little that Goldilocks was prepared to tell me about it, but he was convinced that you would understand. I'm sorry, Nathan – judging by the lack of blood in your face, you understand only too well."

There was a cold, clammy chill in the warm, April sunlight as Martyn stood slowly to his feet and grasped Nathan's hand in both of his, and it was a kindly voice that said, "I can't do much but if you need a message getting to Zadie or Lucinda I'll check under the post-stone each day this week and make sure it reaches them. And I'll look after the chickens … they're laying well now … I owe you about four dozen eggs. There are some in the tray at the back of the shed if you don't want to be interrogated by Kelvin … and I'll drop a loaf by at the end of my round. You have enough to do."

It was a peculiar mixture of the mundane on which to end a conversation, but Nathan thanked him and watched the unpretentious figure turn the corner of the drive, starting down the lane with his post-bag. Somehow it was good to know there were people like Martyn around – and, somewhere, he had made a decision without really noticing it. Martyn was right: he had enough to do.

*   *   *

Late that night Nathan was struggling over the last letter. He was troubled over the ending, and had already re-written it several times. He slurped at the cold mug of tea and bit into a boiled-egg sandwich. The loaf had been waiting for him after his hurried and largely abortive trip into Padstow. The contents of term-time had been emptied unceremoniously from the landrover into the hallway, and the shed, garage, and bungalow had been scoured for useful items. The floor around him resembled an overturned bring-and-buy stall, with the rucksack standing as a solid island amidst a sea of discards. Instead of the geological hammer in the velcro fastenings on its back, an ice-axe was fixed securely in place. Finding it had proved time-consuming and it had eventually emerged from a box beneath the broken plant-pots in the shed. The climbing rope, coiled neatly under the top flap of the rucksack, had been easier to find, albeit oil from the landrover had leaked onto it at some point in the past, and there had been the bonus of a couple of chocks still fixed to a carabiner attached to the rope. However, some of his other old, cold-weather gear had eluded him, and he had to content himself with the view that, if an ill-equipped small girl could manage the ice-sheet, then he could. But she had known the way and he didn't. At least, he doubted that he could attempt the way that he had taken before – not without Zadie – and there had been no reply from her. His first message to her on the answerphone had been garbled and confused – little more than saying he wanted to talk with her urgently about Soloma. His second had been better considered and had asked her to seek out Martyn if she came to Trevennick. Obviously she was not back in the country yet.

Three letters lay in front of him and he sighed wearily as he looked them over again and folded them into envelopes. The one to Lucinda was fine: it simply told her that he had gone; that she should talk to Martyn; and asked her to look after Zadie, if she arrived. The second one was formal. Nathan had found an almost clean piece of heavier paper for it from the end of his PhD work and had headed it up 'Last Will and Testament'. Without any living relatives, he had never made a proper will, but he didn't like the thought of his grandfather's bungalow being taken by the state. He used the language that a layman thought a legal person would, and had decreed it to be his last desire that his estate and possessions should pass to the girl known as Zadie Barwith. He had post-dated his signature and the envelope was addressed to Martyn, with a covering note asking him to act as witness, along with Lucinda, and take the whole thing to Kerry in Wadebridge. He didn't doubt that it was not the proper way of doing things, but Kerry would make it work if anyone could.

Nathan licked the envelope, sealing it without much thought, and turned to the last letter. He scanned it through again: '... sorry not to be here ... message from Soloma ... Martyn the Post knows a bit ... had been looking forward to seeing you ... thanks for the card ... taken it with me ... also, taken the memories ... I don't know what it all means but if I don't come back, please know this – somewhere, I'll be thinking of you. Stay as long as you want, and good luck in the future. You have so much talent; one day I'm sure you will be a famous archaeologist! With my love, N'. It was pretty pathetic really, but it would have to do.

One of the chickens was anticipating the dawn, and the beginning of a grey light was seeping into the room as he sealed the envelope and put it by the heavy, tin box that Mabel had left to him. He looked for a last time at the four empty recesses in the polished wood before he fitted the lid carefully back onto it and went through to the bedroom. He would grab a few hours' sleep now and leave the letters under the Post-rock when he set off later in the day. All being well, he could reach Gulland in half a day. He could spend the night there and choose his route with the sun behind him. If the northern route looked viable he would try it, but that would mean starting a day from near the ice-sheet if he was to reach Elana's land in two days. The heavy rucksack would slow him down considerably. If it didn't look viable or he couldn't find it, he would have to risk the lake and the ice-cave. Although it was shorter, he didn't trust himself to find the route through the cave system, and he reckoned that, the closer he came to the ice, the more likely there would still be snow piled up, and ice-floes on the lake. Perhaps he would come across some footprints of Soloma: it could not have been more than two weeks since she had made the journey, and whatever route she had taken would be the most secure – unless she had been fleeing from something. His subconscious mind moved from practicalities to possibilities in an uneasy sleep, and he was troubled by the image of a small figure with dark hair striving unsuccessfully to complete a return journey against the embrace of cold, not having found the help she sought, running out of food and without warmth or shelter, her hope finally dashed. Nathan shifted uneasily, calling out into the empty world of his imaginings.

Chapter 9   A Heavy Blow

When it came, dawn broke suddenly – not the dawn of the chickens' noisy greeting, but the dawn of Gulland: isolated amidst the vastness of another world's tranquillity; silent; unsullied by sound or movement; complete in its own existence. The rock against which Nathan had slept was eating into his back uncomfortably and his muscles were stiff with the previous day's exertion of carrying the rucksack across uneven ground and up to this eyrie spot. It was a very heavy rucksack, and it had taken him much longer than he had anticipated to make the journey. Partly it was his own fault. On impulse, he had decided to take the long route from the bungalow to Polgodoc. He was not aware of having made a conscious decision about the matter and had found his feet leading him towards the cliff-top path. Thrift was already welcoming the warmer sun of early April, and waves had been curling in slow perfection as they broke into the sandy bay below Trevennick. A line of froth hugged the rocks on the north side of the bay and dragged out past the Lion Rock guarding its entrance. In a week or so a few of the regulars who had displaced the continuity of village generations would be scattered in the more secluded nooks, their woollies and wind-proof garments protecting them from the pretence that it was summer and their children running across the empty sands. The path would be busier as walkers revisited their favourite views, expecting them to be the same as when they bade farewell last September, but greeting them with a freshness tinged with relief. Now there was neither a person, nor dog, nor sheep in sight and Nathan had made his way past the lonesome cry of distant gulls to the Pulpit Rock. This had been where Soloma had loved to sit, looking down at the Lion Rock, along the coastline towards Polgodoc, out to the island of Gulland, and into the unrelenting expanse of ocean beyond where, at some indistinct point, sea met sky. He had sat there a long while, repeating her circumnavigation of the vista. Crests and troughs of restless energy approached the coast in ragged trains – beckoning like a lullaby, fearsome as a nightmare. Increasingly, it had grown upon him that he would soon plunge beneath their temporary interface with atmosphere and land, seeking an older landscape, searching a route leading to that island standing proud against their onslaught. Thence over the ice to a small community, struggling to maintain its marginal existence, and to a small girl whose single word had summoned him from his comfortable familiarity of life. Only the love in her heart, and the determination in her will could have cut so cleanly through the logical objections to such a course of action. A little later, reaching a high point where he could glimpse a corner of his bungalow, he had paused, nodding at it in a half-deferential way, as one might to an old acquaintance whilst thinking, 'I don't know if we will meet again but I have appreciated you'. Faintly, he had imagined a dog's soft bark and his grandmother's voice raised in some old hymn. Thereafter, the path had been littered with memories: crumbling cliffs at the furthest end of Porthmissen Bridge where the village boys had kept him penned for two hours, its precipitous drop to the water below obscured to his eyes by the darkness of that night but not to his ears or imagination; the entry to a cleft in the last recess of which he had discovered a rock dove sitting on her nest, soft and demure, nursing her eggs – last survivor of a species once plentiful but driven from her habitat by the aggression of invaders; the oldest of the ravens on her inaccessible pinnacle of rock, greyed and weakened to a point where fluttering flight seemed almost beyond her strength, grandmother to the nth generation of offspring who watched over this landscape.

Too soon, it seemed, he had reached the point at which the path into the hidden valley of Polgodoc diverged. No plastic tape barred the way. He had sat and eaten briefly alongside the same flat rock where Zadie and he had shared their meal last summer. A few paces more, and he used the climbing rope to lower his rucksack onto the ledge below, following it down. Entry to the adit was a moment of finality. Squeezing uneasily along it and over the chasm, its plank removed, he had reached the pinched-out ending. With Wilf's lump of pure Cornish tin held in his hand, he had concentrated on Soloma. At first the rock had seemed reticent to yield its secret but, as he cried out her name, the great mother lode had blazed in front of him. Switching the tin for Soloma's gift of copper, he had stepped past the lure of the great black slab in the cavern's centre with only a single glance at its mute lionesses. Soon he was following a coppery light into a passage until a vein stretched from descending ceiling to rising floor in front of him. Touching it, he had stepped cautiously through, reaching the first semblance of slanting sunlight before the solid clunk of closing rock had shut behind.

Nathan had found himself leaning against the rock wall just inside the exit from the cleft, shaking uncontrollably. There had been a subconscious debate consuming his mind. Suppressed, it had threatened frequently to puncture its way into his consciousness, and now it overflowed. The mental and emotional effort of excluding all other thoughts than Soloma's need when he had entered and exited the cave of Polgodoc had drained him, and he had been suddenly overwhelmed by the mire of doubt and uncertainty that sucked and gurgled below the surface. Polgodoc was not a place to toy with. Polgodoc was not a place to attempt to use to his own ends. Whilst there might be some likelihood as to where he would emerge, there was no certainty as to when. Doubts had crescendoed into his overt thought screaming, 'Am I in Soloma's time? Are the Mortan waiting?'

Slowly, he gained control of his body, fighting with his mind. The landscape in front of him was that which he remembered, albeit different in parts. Boulders gave way to grass, but snow hid in hollows. Months did not change through Polgodoc's passage, but this near the ice-sheet spring had not fully come. Neither sight nor sound of movement was present, except for a stream some way distant, talking to the rocks it caressed. He had looked to the nearby headland for evidence of fresh rockfall from those few months ago, and he had laboured down to the water and up the slope to the first group of hollies, entering to find a scattering of snow nestling in their shadow. In the centre of the holly ring stood a plinth of solid rock – as he had known it would – six feet or so in length by three in width and height. Its nearer half was slate – dark, matching the cliffs behind; its further part lighter granite, rock of the geology beyond. In each flat surface was a recess of the opposing rock. Only through using the plinth might he pass from one geology to another – thus much had Zadie discovered at this same spot as he had tried to walk past the plinth. Invisible, impenetrable, the barrier had thrust him back. Rock yielded passage to rock only with a token. This was an older place – an ancient place – a place where rock still felt the pulse of its creation, a living landscape.

He had looked for signs of footprints in the snow but it had melted and refrozen. It was unlikely that Soloma's weight would have broken the crust. On the ground a few granite tokens lay where snow had thawed. Inspecting them carefully, he had picked up one and put it in the granite recess in the dark slate beside him. Plucking it out again, he had stepped through onto the granite. It seemed strange that these crudely carved tokens from the next geology were the only way forward and that he could lob the token back through a barrier that was not permeable to him. He watched it scuttle over the snow, wondering what hand would touch it next.

Peering through the exit from the holly ring, Nathan had seen the landscape falling and rising before him. Patches of snow softened its outline but there was still an unpleasantness, a pervading malevolence, lurking beneath its surface. The feeling had intensified as he had neared the patch of badly damaged yew trees halfway across the granite. Light glinted off the Stones of Sacrifice. At least the damaged trees and missing pillars of serpentine pointed to him being in the right time period, even if there was still no evidence of Soloma having journeyed this way. Taking the whole stretch without a break, he had been sweating vigorously when he reached the clump of hollies on its further side some two hours later. He had been half-expecting not to find any tokens by the plinth within the hollies. In his mind he had been fingering the blue stone lying in a soft bag in his pocket, considering whether he would dare to use the master-token.

As it turned out, three of the dark-veined tokens that would let him pass onto the geology of Gulland were discarded at the base of the plinth and, using one, he had sat beyond the holly clump, looking out to the west. Veils of cirrus cloud were thick enough to partially obscure the sun's orb as it made its final descent beyond the low ridge in front of him, and he had turned his gaze to Gulland's broken crown, rising to his right. Whether it was the memory of that first night spent on it with Zadie, he couldn't say, but there was a comfort in its outline against the colouring sky. It spurred him to climb to the summit. By the time he had reached it, the light had nearly gone, and he settled against the rocks below its peak.

It had been a long time awaiting this dawn. During the night the sky had cleared and the panoply of stars, free from urban pollution or vapour trails, had sparkled into the occasional opening of his eyes. Later the waxing Easter moon had shone softly on him until a broad swathe of alto-cumulus had spread its dappled patches from the east. Now his eyes were open, and the fulness of nature's transient splendour assaulted his senses. He reclined like Zeus on Olympus, whilst the sun's strengthening colour radiated its majesty over a landscape swathed in cloud, white opacity gilded and rubied in the fractured clarity of solar light. Below, the shattered slope of Gulland fell into a sea of undulating softness, its surface reflecting light in soundless expression of such casual munificence. Ten miles away the wall of the ice-sheet towered a thousand metres, closing the horizon from furthest north to faintest south; over it spilled molecules of water, chilled by still night air's contact with ice into a layer of cloud that flowed and cascaded, obscuring its serrations, plunging in its greater density to spread across the land below, cosseting it in a cold embrace. It flowed as inexorably as runny icing-sugar from the surface of some great cake to settle in pools of varying intensity and hue as the interplay of sun and cloud and Earth's onward rolling into light gloried momentarily upon each passing part. And, as he watched, it seemed as if some great, diurnal battle between forces – immense and unrelenting in their ancientness – was taking place, until at last intensifying light stilled the chill hand of night and the cascading blanket of obscurity was torn and ripped, revealing spires and pinnacles of halted ice: gemstones, gleaming in distant adoration of the new day's insolation. Layer by shallow layer, nature's cocoon was evaporating like a tide that had turned, an army that had reached its Gettysburg, a melancholy dispersed by the blaze of life. Slowly a ridge of higher ground emerged, cleft by a notch through which Nathan knew a passage from the dark-veined geology of Gulland led to the pinkish rock beyond.

Nathan reached for his binoculars and examined the landscape carefully. There was much snow this near the ice-sheet; low cloud and fog still obscured many places. It looked less dense towards the Little Lake and up the slope beyond. What he really needed was some guidance, something to indicate which way Soloma had come or gone. Doubt gnawed at him: he had never taken the northern route, and there was no indication of its start; moreover, it would mean at least two days on the ice. On the other hand, the western route had substantial obstacles of its own, and he doubted his ability to overcome them.

Looking away to the south, two slow spirals of smoke circled lazily upwards into the still air, puncturing its purity and giving an urgency to his decision. He did not want to be caught here if there were men around. Reminding him of his need for food, his stomach spurred him into action. The heavy rucksack was no easier going downhill than up and it pushed him past the foggy hazel thicket part-way down Gulland's western slope until he stopped by a stream, contemplating breakfast. It was much colder in the dissipating cloud, and he thought of using the Calor gas stove, before deciding to save it for emergencies, settling on cold, sugared porridge and the last of Martyn's bread. If he used it wisely, there was enough food for a week – which was twice as much as he had brought before – and he broke off a couple of freezer bags from a roll to double-wrap the packages against the wet. Nathan's mind was beginning to work on practicalities, and he struck westward. Visibility was good enough to see by but not so clear as to be seen, and he skirted the shore of the Little Lake, pausing briefly to remember a single red rose cast by a slender hand to sink beneath its surface, before trudging up the slope beyond.

It was a matter of a few minutes between being encompassed in the clammy greyness of reluctantly retreating fog and bursting into the brilliance of warm April sunshine reflecting back at him from patches of snow – their surfaces crusted and edges glazed translucent, each tasselled with miniature icicles dripping their winter legacy drop by drop onto the darkened ground. He hurried towards the gulley above, grateful for the warmth, aware of his own visibility, squinting against reflected glare from the increased snow cover. A few weeks more and it would all be gone but now the light was angling up awkwardly at him; he could feel his three-quarters closed eyelids warming. A few hours of this and they would burn most painfully, and he regretted not finding the snow-goggles that he had sought before departing.

The cold shadow of the gulley brought both relief and its own problems. The gulley ran almost exactly east-west, ascending steeply for some seventy metres before breaching the sky-line in a narrow cleft, perhaps ten metres deep and with precipitous sides. Nathan's memory of landscape was good – nearly photographic, in fact. He knew what lay beyond and he did not like what he saw of the way up to it. Moreover, as he rested and surveyed the surface of the snow, he could see no evidence of footprints or disturbance. This was the most obvious way for Soloma to cross from Gulland to the pink rock. It was the only way that Nathan had actually used. It could not have been more than three weeks since she had made the journey and it was more likely to have been within the last seven days. Yet there was not the slightest indication of anything to show human passage. Albeit, Soloma was light on her feet and the far side of the gulley was glazed and crusted where south-facing snow had melted and re-frozen frequently. It would not show an imprint but he doubted whether even she would gain a grip on a surface that shrieked 'slip and fall' at him. The near side, where he stood in the shadow, was also crusted but thinly so and might have borne her weight if she moved rapidly. It was not going to bear his, with or without a rucksack, and he suspected he knew what it would be like beneath its veneer of apparent solidity. Nevertheless, he knew of no alternative.

Edging forward from one half-buried boulder to another, like stepping-stones in a child's game, Nathan gained some ten metres before he reached a point where he had to trust the snow slope. Cutting steps gently with the ice-axe took him further. The gulley had filled deeply with snow over the winter and its slope stretched smoothly and steeply above and below him. Suddenly the crust gave way, plunging him spluttering into the snow below until, weighed down by the heavy rucksack, it closed over his head. It was not the usual wet snow of English winters that would compact and bear weight, but fine-grained powder-snow – each flake no bigger than a grain of milled salt – formed in the intense cold of a glacial blast of Arctic air, shrivelled and huddled into itself, unable to spread its molecules into the infinitely varied patterns of a gently drifting flake that could waft caressingly to settle on eyelashes. No: this was snow like fine grit that would blast and scour, stinging every portion of exposed flesh if driven by the wind; snow that had no bearing weight at all. Nathan sank through it, flailing with his arms to try to gain some balance, keeping his mouth closed rather than sucking the super-chilled, tiny particles into his lungs as snow closed over him and darkness prevailed. This was like a swimmer thrown overboard with a huge weight on his back and no time to breathe deeply or prepare. Feet and knees grounded on solid boulders, themselves slippery and ice-encrusted from the first of the winter weather that had frozen as a sheen on their surface and never melted, entombed within a powdery grave. Feet of snow lay above, hiding the light, blanketing him in darkness. Nathan twisted, banging his knee on rock, letting gravity point his body down the steep slope, fighting the rising panic in a mind that was demanding he take a breath. He could feel his temples beginning to throb and hammer from the lack of air as he spread his arms in breast-stroke fashion, attempting to swim downslope within the snow. He felt his body slithering and snagging on the rocks below as he kicked and pushed himself onwards. His mind screamed, 'Breathe now!' and another part of it cried, 'No, don't breathe!' His head was scraping against something ridged and sharp. It would be bleeding. It was faintly lighter near the taste of blood. Twisting in one last effort, he brought the ice-axe up, puncturing the shallow layer of crusted ice that separated him from the world above and spilling head-first, gasping and retching, like an out-of-control toboggan down its surface, bouncing from rock to rock until he skidded onto the rocky ground below the snow slope.

He rolled onto his side, looking back up at the mangled state of the slope as his body prioritised which of its injuries should claim pole position in an increasing hierarchy of pain. The slope looked like a small whale had belly-flopped onto it, gouging a trench beneath its surface before spilling out onto it again – an injured, harpooned whale, in fact, as he saw the pink-stained surface and felt the warmth pulsing from his head. Blood dripped off his hand onto the ground beside him and he lay back, probing a twisted knee.

Half an hour later Nathan had determined that his injuries were not serious – blood had stopped flowing from his scalp and the congealed hair was now concealed beneath a cap, whilst the knee throbbed but took his weight – and secondly, he was going to have another attempt at the slope. Whether it was out of love for the little girl, or admiration for her bravery, or through a sense of injured pride, he was not certain. This time, however, he would stay off the snow and tackle the rock. Moving a short distance to the south, he sweated as he climbed in the late morning sun. Early cloud had all but evaporated, and the Little Lake lay largely still below him, occasional breaths of wind ruffling its surface. Rippled bands of alto-cumulus had broken into a mackerel sky, while a slight bluish haze hugged the abandoned coastline to the south and he was conscious of his visibility as he reached the crest of the ridge.

Looking to the west, the wall of the great ice-sheet was beginning to tower. Ice floes from the winter freeze stood immobile in those parts of the marginal lake that he could glimpse in front of it. From somewhere beyond there, the simple cry for help had come. Beneath his feet the landscape fell away and rose again in gentle folds, patches of pink rock showing through the widespread remnants of snow cover. To his right and thirty metres below him was the hidden clump of hollies to which the cleft at the head of the gulley would have given access. Immediately below him lay the problem: a steep cliff twenty metres or so in height, composed in its upper part of the dark-veined rock of Gulland, and in its lower of the pink rock of the land beyond. As an ordinary descent, it was possible; it was the change of geologies that rendered it improbable.

Only through the clump of hollies was the route ahead. He looked at them again, lying with his head and shoulders over the edge of the cliff. Although they inhabited such a marginal environment, there was the suggestion of new growth on each bough as small leaves, tinged reddish at their sharpened points, longed to embrace the strengthening year's sunshine. In shadowed patches between their trunks he could see the snow, resting in shelter from the winter winds that had blown it thence and lying, awaiting its proximate demise as the angle of the sun's rays ascended with each rotation of the orb upon which they played. A plinth of rock glistened partially in the centre of the holly ring, its further side embalmed in a clutching cloth of snow, its nearer part clear in its angularity. Black-veined rock of Gulland rose from the ground, laying its rectangular shape against the pink formation from the next geology.

Less than a year ago Nathan had stood at that plinth fingering a pink token and pondering its genesis. A vague memory of having looked up at the cliff where he was now perched flitted through his mind, suggesting that somewhere it contained a fissure and a ledge. He elbowed his way slowly to his right, hanging over the edge and peering downwards, seeking some indication of a route. West-facing, the rock was blazed clean of ice or snow and dry enough, although water was seeping out of the pink material towards its base. Minutes later he paused. The solid surface on which he wriggled sideways was slightly riven by the shattering of frost and sun – at least, it was split enough for a climbing chock to grip if the weight pulled out and down against the crack. If he could use a chock, he could use the climbing rope; if he could use a rope, he could belay himself down the rock-face.

Both the old, soiled rope and the two chocks that he had rescued with it were at the top of his rucksack, and Nathan placed them on the ground beside him, sitting with his feet dangling over the edge, looking contemplatively at both them and what lay below. It was a simple question but it involved a gamble. Nathan didn't like gambling: on the few occasions that he had been inveigled into doing so, he had lost badly; he preferred to think in measured probabilities and percentages. The trouble was there was insufficient data to come to a valid choice. He was 90% convinced that the chock would hold and that he could lower himself down the rock-face safely; it would be almost as easy as abseiling. There was a 60% chance that, once down, he could flick the chock clear with the rope and regain it. On the other hand, this was not a normal rock-face: the dark rock of Gulland gave way to the pink rock of the landscape beyond two thirds of the way down it, and past experience was that the geologies would not allow passage between them except by placing a token in the plinth within one of the holly rings. If he could not lower himself all the way down, maybe he could work laterally along the cliff to the top of the cleft and gain the route he had attempted two hours ago. If that was not possible, he would have to climb back up again. With a fixed rope and juma clips that would be easy, but he wasn't going to have a fixed rope and he hadn't found the juma clips. Moreover, there was the question of the rucksack. If he could succeed, he would want to lower the rucksack first, before descending himself. If he couldn't, he didn't want the rucksack down there. Free-climbing back up with it would be much more difficult. The multiplication of probabilities was beginning to produce figures that Nathan did not like. His stomach suggested a delay for lunch, and he found his mind diverting onto considering the probabilities of whether this would be a good move or not.

Sun was warming the dark rock and, as he sat contemplating further, beginning to wonder whether he had banged his head more than he thought, his peripheral vision caught the slightest movement. He turned abruptly. Equally abruptly, a small and ugly face turned and plunged over the vertical edge of the cliff, whisking a short, sinewy tail behind it, leaving a foot lingering for a moment. It was the first living thing that he had seen. 'Lizard, not snake,' he said to himself, 'could have been a gecko, if this was a warmer climate.' His mind rushed into gear after idling on probabilities and improbabilities. Here was fact: a lizard meant cracks and niches in the rock; what was more, they would be dry ones; dry crevices meant good holds and a good chance of climbing back up; being able to climb back up meant he could leave the rucksack and come back for it if necessary.

Indecision evaporated and he found himself making a bowline with one end of the rope '– form a loop … twist it over … pull it through … rabbit down the hole –' he mouthed in the familiar mantra, shortening the loop, slipping the carabiner onto his belt, and clipping the knot in place. Testing for slippage, he saw the knot was sound, despite the oiling on the rope, and he fed the free end through the metal loop on the chock, wrapping it over one shoulder before casting the remaining length over the cliff edge and snaking it free from obstruction. Carefully, he placed the chock into the shallow split in the rock, its trapezoid shape grinding against white veining on either side and pulverising the quartz crystals as he pulled on it, at first gently and then with his whole weight. This was always the trickiest moment: the vectors of force needed to be downwards and outwards – feet flat on the vertical rock-face; weight pulling the chock deeper into the crevice; hand controlling the speed of the rope around his wrist and shoulder – an unexpected jerk as he went over the edge would be liable to pull the chock upwards and out, with disastrous consequences.

The moment of faith came and went: arm releasing its last, tenuous grip; knees pushing out; soles anchored on the vertical face; shoulders leaning back; face up towards the sky, its skeletal remains of mackerel cloud fading into an open, azure ceiling; hand and wrist controlling the downwards progress. Walking backwards down the cliff, horizontal in the air, Nathan bent his head forward slightly, seeing dark rock turn to pink. Two other faces retreated into their dry nook in surprise, and he laughed at the little creatures. Exhilaration coursed through him: this was something he could do; even with an ungloved hand and an oily rope, he was in control, and he revelled in the freedom of lying in the air. Indeed, for a moment it seemed as if he was cosseted upon the most comfortable of mattresses, moulding itself to every stress and strain of his muscles, taking all the weight and burden from him. He felt like he could release his grip on the rope … fling it away … lie back and rest, unsupported, staring for ever at the firmament above. Softly another blanket settled over him, grain by grain in its gentleness; beneath, the mattress was moulding and firming, adopting his shape; above, more blankets were settling.

A grating thought intruded into his bliss. It was a buzzing fly at the moment of contented sleep and he wanted to swat it out of existence. The mattress was almost a part of him; the blankets above were piling more and more. Moments, years, decades, millennia, were flying through his sight. Unasked, the thought came again, more urgently, like a persistent salesman calling. Blankets were pressing down around his body; there was no need to move; they would hold him, snuggle him, envelop him. With the last flickerings of commonsense, his mind screamed, 'Get out of here! Move! The rocks are making you a part of themselves – fossilised, lithified, absorbed into their being!' He struggled to raise himself, pulling on the free end of the rope. Pain bit into him as it slid, burning his fingers. Pain coursed through him – awakening pain; pain bringing clarity – and his feet scrabbled for a purchase on the rock. His head was clearing now. Veins of quartz with their tiny pockets of grip were coming into focus. His right toe found one. His left hand thrust its fingertips into another. He pulled on the rope with his right hand, pushing with his right foot, searching for a purchase with his left. He had it now. He scraped his right knee up the rock, seeking another hold. His left hand was too low for another move – he would have to let the rope go, abandon it, and reach up with his right. Sweat trickled coldly down his neck and dripped uncomfortably off his eyebrows as he sought to prevent a fall. He could sense the shaking beginning. He knew the feeling. If he started to shake, he would fall. He must not fall; he must stay calm; he must force his limbs to behave. He must ignore the rope entirely and concentrate on climbing this rock-face with two hands and two feet anchored on it. He needed to do it himself – without help. This was like the old days. He was losing focus – working by feel now: tears were flowing, obscuring his vision, stinging in their saltiness; longing to elbow them away, he could feel the rasping, uneven breath unbalancing him. "Focus! Focus now!" he cried out aloud and, as he looked through the blurring cataract of vision, it seemed as if there was a small face scurrying up the rock from one miniscule hold to another, until it whisked over the top of the cliff. His right hand grasped the cold angularity of the metal chock, fingers wedged and crushed just like they had been at Pentire. With the last of his strength, he pulled and fell.

*   *   *

Low-angled sunlight was bouncing off a patch of quartz-rich rock into Nathan's eyes when he awoke. The trailing end of the rope, still fastened to the carabiner around his belt, fell away over the cliff edge; of the chock, there was no sign. He groaned in unwilling processing of memories and rolled onto his side, encountering the rucksack, still upright against the boulder where he had left it hours ago. Mechanically, he began to haul and coil the rope, unclipping the bowline without bothering to undo the knot. Whatever else, the rocks were not going to let him pass by way of this cliff.

Touching the rucksack stirred thoughts of food and, with difficulty, he retraced his climb back to the foot of the gulley. A chipped, enamel cup gathered drips from miniature icicles edging the snow-pack, and occasionally Nathan emptied the contents into a tin brewing hot, sweet tea on the camping stove. He let its warmth wash down the last fragments of a whole bar of chocolate and chewed on dried apricots before repackaging tea-bags and sugar. Cooling the tin in the snow, he packed all the items back into his rucksack, emptying more water from the cup into a meal that was set to rehydrate and checking its lid was secure. He slipped his arms through the straps of the rucksack and lurched unsteadily to his feet. In the west the sun was sinking behind the ice-sheet, casting its last virulent rays in farewell.

It had not been a good day. He had achieved nothing. In fact, he had achieved less than nothing: he had wasted a whole day; he had drained his physical and emotional strength; he had consumed part of his emergency food and gas supplies; and, whatever the reason for Soloma's urgent cry for help, he was now a further day behind her, with no indication as to how to proceed. All he knew was that the route he did know through the gulley and over the great lake was closed firmly against him.

As he walked, the Little Lake extended to his right, its surface gloomily reflecting his mood. He stopped in the faded light, looking towards the faint definition of the flat rock on which he had first glimpsed Soloma and thinking of her own brief remembrance of her mother's death as her will had driven them on through all impossibilities. He missed her. He missed Mabel, too. And, he missed Zadie.

An Easter moon was riding lazily, low in the south-eastern sky, as the light diminished further and his footsteps brought him to the foot of Gulland. Speckles of light from the distant cliffs towards the south impinged upon his consciousness, and the slightest haze drifting across the reflective orb spoke of fires, and men, and mining. If there were men, there would be Mortan. He did not want to meet the Mortan again. Even the name brought an aura of evil and he felt that the bale-fires were sweeping the horizon with their red gaze, seeking his presence like a lighthouse sucking information into itself with each sweep of its beam.

A stream trickled by, oblivious to his melancholy. Moss softened his footfall, and hazels rose in unassuming greeting as Nathan ascended the slope. This thicket had been a good spot: it had been a kind place – a safe haven in uncertainty and danger – and he leant against the boulders on its upper edge, loosening his pack, scraping together moss for bedding with the blunt end of his ice-axe. Moonlight filtered through the undistinguished leaves – each stilled in the expiry of the day, each awaiting the chill of a cloudless night, each offering its minor modicum of warmth to one who lay below.

A grumbling of stone shifting on stone carried in the air.

Nathan sat alert, sensing the direction. It came again – not once but several times; not one stone but a whole cascade, moving and scattering beneath the summit of the slope – perhaps slightly to the south where the flickering searchlights of fires still swept. Silently, he reached for the axe. If they were animals, only bears could be so clumsy, and he struggled to recall if bears were nocturnal or if they moved in groups. More stones slithered. The thought of animals reminded him of the evil half-creatures encountered once before, and he rose, crouching and tensing, raising the ice-axe behind him as the source of clattering stones drew nearer. It – they – were coming directly towards him. Another stone rolled past his foot. Now there was breathing: fast, panting, rapid. There was no time for fire or matches, no other defence. The scalloped end of the axe would cleave bone; the serrated pick would penetrate and rip flesh, if that flesh was real. More stones clattered and slid, until the first shadowy form of limbs and body accelerated into half-view around the boulder.

He swung the axe.

Chapter 10   The Past Calls

A door kicked to, shutting out the noise of London traffic and the ribald comments from the group spilling out of The Hope and Anchor. Normally she hated kicking doors, and it was a measure of her frustration that she had resorted to closing this one in such a fashion. She turned the key, double-locking the door and putting the chain across before stumbling into the little sitting room cum dining room cum everything. Three neat piles of post were stacked on the drop-leaf table, accompanied by equally neat labels: 'Dealt With' – that looked like bills and official stuff; 'SPAM' – the largest pile by far; and 'Personal Not Urgent' – mostly, this one seemed to be Christmas cards. A small bunch of freesias stood in a vase or, at least, a narrow glass pretending to be a vase, and a note below it read: 'Welcome Back! Cleared the rest of the phone messages yesterday – nothing urgent. Milk in fridge. Will pop round tomorrow to sample the duty-free and hear the gossip. Love, Fee'.

Zadie smiled at her friend's efficiency. For a moment she was tempted by the piles of post and the little red number 2 on the answerphone but a more urgent debate took over: cup of tea … or bath … or gin (Gordon's, LHR duty-free on exit, export strength) and tonic (can still in fridge, unless Fee had drunk it) … or all three … and in what order? The bath won, after a glance across at the boiler on the wall of the little kitchen told her that Fee had put on the hot water, and soon the vacant carpet was submerged beneath untidy piles as the two damaged cases disgorged their contents in search of the few items of clean underwear and personal effects that were needed. Zadie peeled off shoes and clothes, leaving a trail of discarded items as she moved through to the bedroom, turning on the light and finding it strange to have to draw curtains after all the time on a small island that had only the emptiness of nature to wrap its eyes around her. The bath in the ensuite was not large, but the water ran warm and steam soothed each pore, cleansing the sweat and grime in superlatives of soporific soapiness. Its restorative qualities, as the last Greek grit gurgled down the plug-hole, spurred her to use the shower attachment above, freeing the gold-blond hair from its matted mess. Consequently, it was a much refreshed Zadie who emerged, clad in a bath towel, back into the debris-strewn sitting room to locate a large, yellow carrier-bag, generous-sized glass and (small) tin of tonic water. Idly, she flicked through the 'Personal Not Urgent' pile, looking at the handwriting on the envelopes and scanning Fee's brief summaries of telephone messages she had deleted, before refilling her glass.

Two-thirds of the way down the glass, she thought vaguely of phoning Nathan, but it was an hour from midnight. Instead, she gathered together the rocks that she had brought him – rocks that had started so much trouble for her in the airport – and placed them on the table, wondering what he would make of them. There was one that was of particular interest to her and, as she rolled it irregularly across the imitation wood of the surface, it was almost out of habit that she pressed the play button on the phone.

"You have two new messages ..." it began in synthesised modernity, intruding upon Zadie's much-improved mood, and it was only because she was slightly too slow reaching for the skip button that she heard Nathan's voice cut in. This wasn't the voice she remembered. At least, it wasn't as she imagined she remembered it – steadily paced, articulate, careful with words: it was garbled and muddled, with an intensity and emotion amplified by the machine. Three times she replayed it, skipping back to the message, seeking to make sense of the phrases, but all she could gather was something about the need to talk urgently and something about Soloma. It was only on the third occasion that she let the second message play: Nathan again, more measured and calm this time ... factual ... detailed ... giving options – until the parting valediction. She could sense the emotion in that and his attempt to push it down, to suppress it beneath logic.

So something had happened. There had been some message from Soloma that had been urgent enough to make Nathan drop everything and go, almost immediately. How immediate was immediately? He had said he was leaving in the morning but he hadn't said which morning. There was a chance that it might be tomorrow – or today, as it nearly was according to the wretched red digits ticking by with remorseless insensitivity to her feelings or the imperative need to slow time down. She might catch him on the phone. What was the number? Where was the number? She had written it somewhere and she yanked at the little cabinet by the table, pulling at the top drawer with such urgency that it came out of its fittings, turning it upside-down on the table, scrabbling through pieces of paper with phone numbers on them. The bath-towel fell off and she ducked for a moment, glancing at the unclosed blinds of the kitchen window and the London world beyond, before ignoring it and throwing herself at Fee's carefully-stacked pile of 'Dealt With' papers. She had phoned Nathan in September. The phone bill was itemised. Somewhere in here would be the number. Rapidly she cast envelopes on the floor, guessing that Fee would have stacked them in chronological order. There, she had it: September statement, 01841 ... that was it! And she grabbed at the phone, punching the little, discoloured keys, willing him still to be there. Five rings and no reply. "Answer! Please answer!" she commanded as she surveyed the disaster area around her and flicked an outstretched toe to recover the towel from amongst the mess of suitcases, clothes, letters and belongings. A late-night bus passed the window. Ten rings ... this was no good. And she sat, as the little numbers ticked on, downing the rest of the glass in a gulp and knocking over the freesias in the process. She put down the phone.

Right. He had gone. But not long ago. Twenty-four hours at the most. She knew where he was going. He had said to contact Martyn or Lucinda. She could think about that on the way down. Now she needed to get there. Suddenly a cold logic cut in; straightening up, she reached for the phone again and dialled.

"Yes ... fifteen minutes ... lone female," she heard her voice say; "... Victoria coach station ... must make it there by twelve forty-five."

It had sounded as if the taxi firm had understood her urgency, and she fell on the rummage of clothes on the floor with clinical efficiency, stuffing some into a small pack and pulling others on herself. It didn't matter if they were worn or smelly – not where she was going. Three minutes more. She walked calmly through to the bedroom, reaching for the newly-framed picture above the bed and casually smashing its glass against the pine bed-end before ripping out the picture and picking up a chunk of silvery-grey rock that lay on the bedside table. A vehicle hooted outside. That was it then; and she opened the front door, scribbling a note as she waved to the waiting taxi: 'Fee. Had to leave in a hurry. May be away a while. Sorry about the mess. Love Z'. Zadie placed the note on one of the few clear pieces of carpet and locked the door, wondering at Fee's reaction when she let herself in with the spare set of keys. Life had suddenly accelerated again to an almost impossible speed. Why did it always do this with Nathan? Why couldn't it be normal?

The taxi driver was as good as his word, waving aside the proffered extra note as he pulled in front of the coach, blocking its departure from the bay, and escorting Zadie on board before casting a final glance at the driver as though his fare had been a parting daughter. A few heads turned but most were ensconced in an i-pod world, or their inquisitiveness was dulled by the lateness of the hour. A dapper, old man moved his silver-headed cane and nodded politely to her as she passed. The furthest seats were taken by a straggle of students, still in animated good humour, the remnant of some post-term hockey tour, judging by the strange-shaped bags not trusted to the coach's luggage bin. Zadie settled at a window, watching the sodium glow of crowded humanity fade and inadvertently starting to count the oncoming BMWs with their little lights illuminated in the shape of glasses once favoured by her grandmother's generation.

"Gimmick," a voice said from within, "can't imagine granny's glasses on the front of a fast car ..." and the Barwith memories poured back: stories of Tintagel and wolves, and bears, and wild boar; portrayals of woods where there were none now, and of waves breaking on a further shore; tales of names and events that lurked in the nether-land of Cornish history – that ancient cyber-space where myth and legend intertwined, reaching out occasionally to penetrate the shallow surface of present being. Fleet passed after a brief pause to pick up a disparate group of the un-automobiled society; the counter-flow of BMWs declined in density as the A303 and A30 led to Salisbury, Golding's illumined spire standing centuries proud above a sleeping city while an elderly couple disembarked to the waiting welcome of more mobile relatives. Dawn's earliest light echoed the arrival of the Exe and a somnolent group shed the stuporous comfort of the coach, awakening to the freshness of misted air at the foot of the university campus as the first milk-floats plied their anachronistic trade, prior to the opening of the ever-open shops that had eaten their livelihood.

They retraced their route in part, and a sudden voice, its West Country accent amplified, said, "Exeter Services – one hour stop," as the driver pulled into the lorry park behind the low complex to take his legal break. A few curtained truck-cabs were stirring to begin their distant distribution, reckoning to pass Bristol before the day's commute began. Occasionally, another twelve-wheeled monster settled with a shush of brakes from its overnight run. Zadie followed the handful of travellers stretching limbs in relief from cramped seats and purchased a few envelopes and stamps before sampling the all-night breakfast. She had not realised how hungry she was and surprised the lone cashier by settling down to the same again as she wrote a longer note of explanation to Fee and posted it to her own address. Not that the note was particularly long, nor did it explain particularly much, but at least she could apologise for the mess and tell her to dispose of the remains of the duty-free in her much-accustomed way. Soon it was time to step out of this strangely still-awake place, feeding off its throb of adventitious trade like a sea creature filtering krill.

Zadie dozed as dual carriageway consumed the signs to villages that had once been a thoroughfare of delay. Each mile ate up the time to decide but each sign soothed with the thought that another was yet to come. Okehampton stirred in its clefted valley and the coach ground up the old road into the first full light, regaining the twin tracks of uninterrupted flow that led on down to the sudden, smooth passage of the Tamar, Launceston's castled crown standing in passive western view. Soon factories arose upon the left, attracting early workers for the dispersal of their goods: pasties to Scotland and products nationwide. An early-season caravan, proudly displaying its motif of St. Andrew, laboured onto the A395 to pass the wind-farms of renewable society, perching as invaders upon a coastline that once sought its own defended solitude. Moors closed in, timeless beyond the tarmacadam, obscured in part by the settled mistiness of night, its shallow roof of white gilded by the morning's rays and yielding suddenly to Bodmin's monument. Newsagents had opened doors to retrieve bundles of papers left at some unearthly hour, and road-workers were assembling warning cones and temporary traffic-lights by the old hospital to provide an obstacle to flow as ungainly machines began to advance upon their advertised task of resurfacing the road.

An old, uneven railway crossing on the steep hill down from Bodmin to Dunmere jolted Zadie out of her reverie. That had been unpleasant for those towards the back of the coach and it seemed to have jolted the driver as well: he was taking the narrow stone bridge and bends much more carefully as they crawled uphill again. She looked around, surprised to see that she was almost in isolation in the rear part: gone were the elderly couple opposite; gone were the large group of students; only the strange, old man with the walking stick remained, dressed as if he belonged to some Edwardian film-set. He smiled at her, and she looked toward the front, counting a dozen lolling heads resisting the recent attempts to awaken them. Soon they would pass the garden centre and traverse the speed bumps into Wadebridge, before turning left over the old bridge, widened now, but its predecessor allegedly built on bales of wool to prevent it sinking into the mud of the estuary and being only the width of a pack-horse train with angular passing places for pedestrians or single horses. The rumour was untrue, she knew, although the wealth of the wool trade was the foundation for its building, and the pub on the corner where they were about to turn left still bore the words 'Pons War Gwlan' high on its wall, words which in Celtic – or Cornish, at least – meant 'Bridge on the

Wool'.

The coach came to a stop at the end of The Platt, near a small cinema, and only the old man disembarked. The driver pulled away through narrow roads, presumably attempting a short-cut to avoid back-tracking around the by-pass, but Zadie found herself looking rather too closely into the window of a bookshop as Sat-Nav and Street-Nav came into open conflict. 'Molesworth Street' the sign read opposite; 'Cross Street' said the nearer one. She wondered why the driver should have attempted such a way – it was a deliveries-only route, semi-pedestrianised, with steeply banked-up curbs to keep traffic and people very separate. The curbs were just high enough for the middle of the coach to ground upon as the driver attempted the tight, left-hand turn and, even as she thought it, a nasty grating sound jarred through the vehicle, waking the remaining passengers.

"Hmmm, holed below the waterline, dear ... port side ... life-jackets under the seat ..." floated back to her in elderly good humour from the couple a few seats in front. Further grating and revving followed and another voice joined in, its tones more clipped, "Know what I always say? If in doubt, advance – fast! Man should give it more revs." They were enjoying this; there would be a few dinner table stories in the making here. So were the little group of early morning workers who had stopped to watch the predicament unfold, some making helpful signs and comments to the driver. He certainly wasn't enjoying being the centre of attention, and Zadie shuffled seats across the aisle to gain a better view. She could see straight into the bookshop. She liked bookshops and this one had a nice look about it: brightly coloured cards dangling in the window, posters carefully displayed, and an inviting space inside to read or browse – not like some of the cramped and shabby ones she knew, where there was hardly space to breathe. One poster caught her eye – 'A Guide to walks in Ancient Cornwall' it read – and suddenly it thrust back at her the reality of why she was there and her potential loneliness in the task ahead.

A day-glo orange jacket with emblazoned crown moved, obscuring the poster, and Zadie reached for her little pad of paper, scribbling furiously before rapping hard on the window, pressing the paper to it. The weather-beaten features of the postman nodded in surprise, and he pointed to the front of the coach where the driver had abandoned his seat to peer through the open passenger door at the uncharted reef that had beached his vessel. Zadie scribbled again, sealing the envelope as she pushed down the aisle and round the door.

"Is it urgent, Miss?" the unknown figure asked.

"Sort of …"

"He lives near the end of my round. I can drop it by myself. That do you?"

Her thanks were cut short by the driver stepping back on board and curtly telling her to be seated again. Perhaps prompted by her indiscretion, he used the microphone to remind all passengers to remain seated and to make sure their seat belts were fastened. He had decided to use gravity in his favour and risk the result. The postman was keeping the opposite pavement clear as the coach revved in reverse and the driver slipped the clutch. A short grating and a rolling bounce culminated in a more solid crunch as a parking restriction sign, its cylindrical, grey column and little, yellow sign now angled artistically away from the vertical, performed a useful function in preventing the rear of the coach from progressing any further. This time, the driver was on a different angle and could swing wide of the corner, pulling clear and up the street to the spontaneous applause of those who had been engaged in watching the whole exercise. It was strange how that had happened: it had been a foolish way to come and yet, now, people were expressing appreciation; there was even a, "Jolly good show. Told you that was how to do it," carrying from the front. Indeed, 'clipped tones' and 'holed beneath the waterline' seemed to have struck up a friendship that continued all the way through the brief stop to check for damage and on to Padstow. As Zadie finally disembarked, she could see them exchanging neat, little address cards.

'Nine-thirty' a clock read. Nathan would be a day ahead of her at least. She could complete essential purchases in an hour and would go via Trevennick to Polgodoc. That would cost another hour but it would be worth the delay if she could find out what was happening from Lucinda, or find Martyn. Nathan's message had mentioned Martyn. Maybe there was a note for her at the bungalow.

Even though it was early on an April morning, there was a smattering of visitors pursuing their way from the old station car park to the pretty harbour. The tide was in and the last vestiges of mist were curling over the estuary; Rock was partly visible, a few masts showing through the shifting, white softness as the sun began to warm the dunes beyond. Most of the shops were open, or opening, although some still had signs advertising restricted hours for the off-season, and she plotted her progress with care: camping store first; food and perishables next; Spar on Middle Street last for dry provisions. True to her word, it was just over the hour when she tumbled out of its door and turned up Duke Street. The new rucksack that had replaced her smaller back-pack was well filled and a comfortable fit after she had adjusted the straps. It had been a good price too, and she forced a chuckle as she caught a reflected glimpse of it in a window, its orange fabric clashing dramatically with her hair as she fingered it loose from beneath the pristine white cap and veered past an old, red post-box set in a wall by Fentonluna Lane.

Soon tarmac gave way to earth, lightly trampled and squelchy at this time of year. Leathery ferns sprawled their long leaves from the mossy moisture of an old, dry-stone wall beneath the lichen-encrusted branches of an ancient wood, its life straining yet again to burst into leaf above the carpet of competing bluebells and aconites. In sunnier spots, primroses blazed in glorious proliferation; milkweed and campion thrust stems upwards in anticipation, tiny closed buds of colour awaiting their full awakening. A pair of long-tailed tits gathered long strands of hair, snagged on last year's bramble from some passing retriever that had unwittingly given a part of its coat to cosset the birth-place of their tiny young. A few months hence, a whole family of the attractive little birds – ten or twelve in number – might bounce their chattering flight along the same path, pausing momentarily in gratitude to such a gift before moving on in restless energy.

On one stile Zadie stood awhile, pursuing her own remembrance of two figures looking up at her: one small and slim, its dark eyes wondering; the other taller, slightly stooped with the emotion of the parting. "I'll find you," she whispered, "I will find you; I will find both of you."

The sweeping vista of Trevose rose distantly into view, extending like a right arm flung out into the great expanse of an Atlantic now lapping gently at the fingers clenched in defiance against the ocean's moody storminess.   Between its nearest knuckles the lifeboat station glinted white, its steep ramp plunging into Mother Ivey's Bay, and behind its lowered elbow sheltered Constantine.   Clouds spread slowly across the horizon beyond, their flattening expanses at varying altitudes reflecting differently the light in shades of grey – not a bland, uninteresting greyness but subtle passages from near warship grey to almost white – encroaching slowly landward from the south. A brimstone fluttered by, strong in its early season flight, rejoicing in the light airs of warmth rising from the dry-stone wall, its brightness dulling the first few heads of rape that were testing the month with their yellow blooms.   Soon the whole field would burst into pungent colour, patching the landscape with its explosion.

"Nathan would have liked this view today," Zadie spoke as she walked, "He would have told me what the clouds were, and how the weather would change ..." and she looked across the fielded slopes to glimpse the corner of a bungalow and the upper storeys of a more substantial house.   Strange emotions ran – anticipation equally of hope and disappointment – as she rounded the tumbling growth of erigeron and crunched over the broken slate drive. A chicken squawked in half-remembered greeting before scuttling round the corner of the bungalow to bear news to its fellows. Her eyes fell on the post slate, its wording facing down, and she turned it over, hoping for a note, heart sinking in unfulfilled response, logic telling her she had not expected anything else. The old door opened to her touch and Zadie stepped inside, lowering her pack halfway down the hall and staring at the sitting room. Whatever mess she had left, this was worse. Nathan had certainly left, and left in a hurry. Only a small space near one armchair was free from jumbled, tumbled piles of discarded clothes and items. That must have been where he had packed his rucksack, she thought, casting around for some note and trying to work out his intention from what had not been taken. She went through to the kitchen, feeling the kettle for the slightest warmth but knowing its cold touch would greet her fingers. She turned the tap and it gurgled its usual colour of rusty brown from inactivity. A chicken looked in hopefully at the window and she took pity on it, scattering a handful of grain from the container before settling on the verandah to pull out all her stuff and pack the bright new rucksack in some more sensible order. Idly, she picked up a green slate lying there and turned it over. Her entire attention was arrested by its simple message.

Chapter 11   Stones of Sacrifice

HELP
S.

That was Soloma's writing!

Waves of comprehension hit like Atlantic rollers pummelling a surfer who had misjudged their coming, breaking upon her, plunging her to the sea-bed, stirring up the sediment of emotion, until she came up spluttering for air, only to be thrust down by the next great wave.

So that was why Nathan had dropped everything and gone; that was why he couldn't wait; that was why there was no note; that was the cause of his garbled message. The next wave hit, and she cried out Soloma's name. What had been so urgent, so desperate, that she had come through ice, and rock, and cave, seeking help but unable to wait, unable to write more than the briefest message? She would have travelled alone through dangers they had struggled to overcome together – and Zadie found the tears streaming uncontrollably, wetting the slate into living colour, as if it too could add its message, "Come."

Still the waves broke upon her. What of the Mortan's dogs? Had they hounded and surrounded the little figure as she attempted to return, driving her to the place of sacrifice? What had she done for food? Was even her will strong enough to drive and guide across the ice, or would her slender strength have failed, leaving a crumpled, frozen heap in the white enormity of its cold embrace?

Shaking hands discarded their tablet of news and Zadie half-stumbled, half-ran to Lucinda's house, attacking the pewter bell until the chain fell off, rasping her knuckles against the door until they were red. Slowly her emotion drained, and she sat on the settle in the porch, leaning against its tall, curved back. There was no Lucinda; there was no Martyn to give news; there was no choice. And the realisation came that there had never been a choice; never, since the first suppressed emotion of the answerphone had cut through her post-bath gin and tonic, had there been any real choice.

Steadily she walked back to the verandah, packing carefully and writing a brief note – 'Martyn. Have gone after Nathan and Soloma. Please tell those who need to know' – placing it under the post stone and shutting the door behind her. The first high layers of advancing cloud were sucking colour from the sun as she passed the stubby steeple of the church and crossed the stream beyond. One lone, white butterfly fluttered weakly on tattered wings during the upward climb to where a sheep-pen marked the joining of four fields. Ducking beneath its lintels, the long stretch of cliff-top path opened to view. Only the eldest of the ravens, standing in her inaccessibility and greyed with knowledge of the years, saw her pass and turned her head to watch the figure disappear into the first of the narrow, deep-cut valleys through which the path wound its way to Polgodoc.

Zadie stepped off the well-worn path, picking her way to where a flat rock rose from springy grass. Button-headed mounds of young thrift abounded before their summer desiccation, and clumps of primroses were already fading from their fulness on the south-facing slope; past its zenith, the sun was obscured behind the gathering cloud. Less than a year ago she had shared a meal at this same spot and she paused, slipping off her pack and prising a pasty from the family of four squashed into a container. Four days of food should be enough for one way, she reasoned, but she was reticent to break into the other supplies and contented herself with refilling a flask from the stream nearby. Waves were beginning to break on Gulland's distant outline, and low cumulus was invading the horizon, displacing its altostratus cousin, as Zadie packed up and moved the few yards along the cliff-top.

It was eighteen holds down to the ledge, she knew; also, that the rucksack would make it more difficult. Too far towards the sea, the rock was crumbly and would come out in her hand. This much Nathan had taught her. She had not anticipated this difficulty: he had simply walked to the cliff edge, looked a little, and lowered himself carefully over it. But the cliff was thirty metres long, and just as high. Where had he begun? She took the mid-point, lying on her stomach, peering over. No holds were visible. Even leaning dangerously far out, there was nothing to show a starting point. The first reach for a foot-hold had been a long one – and the last step down had been worse. Always, she had been guided to them. She shuffled to her right and felt herself slipping forward as loose rock clattered down, pushing herself back and sitting, breathing rapidly. This was no good. She moved ten metres to the left. Here rock was more solid. She had to try. There was no alternative. Those looked like handholds on the cliff top. Nathan had said you had to trust for the first foot-hold.

Pushing the rucksack back from the cliff edge, Zadie lowered herself carefully over it, clinging to the handholds on top, swinging her feet across the vertical face in a series of slow sweeps, searching for a toe-hold. Sweep after sweep produced nothing. A smattering of raindrops heralded the arrival of the first low cumulus, and a gull soared by in the gusting updraught. With elbows bent and forearms flattened, at the extremity of her reach, she could feel a hold with her left foot. Struggling and sweating, nose pushed against the cliff face, trying to work back up for the rucksack, she felt her wrist grasped and her hand being loosened from its hold. She panicked, losing her footing, looking at the waves crashing below. The grip was tightening and pulling – both wrists now – her cheek scraped over the edge and she slithered and rolled after it, lying against the rucksack as a voice said, "That's not the place."

"Martyn!"

"Are you alright?" the kindly tone continued. "You look about all in. Glad to find you … you'd never make it down that way."

Zadie hugged the old postman in her delight and sat leaning against the pack as he continued, "Got your message. Winston delivered it at the end of his round. You were lucky to meet him … not many as would have done that … not now, anyways. Just missed you at the bungalow. Came straight here."

"Thanks, Martyn," she mumbled, straightening her thoughts. "Can you help me?"

"Depends what you want. I'll do my best. Can't climb any more … but I can show you where."

"Tell me about Nathan and Soloma; tell me what you know."

"Not much more than you," he replied, slightly economically. "Nathan read the message from Soloma ... same message as you've seen by the look of it ... set off yesterday. You're about thirty hours behind him ... probably be on the ice by now."

"You know about the ice?"

"Yes. Always knew a bit ... not much, mind you. After he left, I picked up his letters ... went and saw Goldilocks. He told me much more. And he has a message for you. He said that when you see Nathan – mark that, he said when, not if – when you see Nathan, tell him to be careful ... the Mortan are moving ... things are not as they were. Don't ask me what he meant by it," continued Martyn, forestalling Zadie's question, "With Goldilocks he'll only tell you what he wants to and seldom says at all."

Zadie thought for a while and asked instead, "Martyn, have you climbed here before? How do you know the way?"

"Yes, I've climbed," and he stopped, as if unwilling to continue. "Several times ... a long time ago. I was looking for someone."

"Who?" she blurted out, realising her mistake too late as the kindly gaze averted hers and looked out towards Gulland, its outline blurred by falling rain while angled shafts of light played between scattered showers.

"My father," came the soft reply.

Now it was her turn to avert her gaze and murmur an inadequate, "I'm sorry."

For a moment their gaze latched onto the same beam of light striking the shattered island crown, and then he said abruptly, "You must go, if you are going. You will struggle to make it there by tonight." Almost as an afterthought he added, "Gulland is safe; leastwise, it always was so."

Reaching for her pack, she stood. "Show me where to start, then."

Martyn turned away from the cliff, lining up two unseen rocks before pointing to a spot much nearer the crumbling end of the cliff than Zadie had ventured to try.

"Start here," he stated simply. "Left foot first, or you'll find it too large a step at the bottom. It's eighteen holds. Leave the rucksack ... I'll lower it down to you. I've brought some string ... not much good for climbing, but it'll do for this."

Zadie slithered over the edge, lowering herself carefully until her searching foot found a solid hold, and looked up at him for a last time.

"Call clearly when you're down," he said, "and tug twice on the string to say you have the pack." As she released her last cliff-top grip, he continued, "Don't be afraid of the cave: be yourself; it matters what's in your heart."

Her weight reached the point of no return and she reached down with her right foot, sight of the old postman lost. It was too late to ask him more. Perhaps he had intended that? Perhaps he had said more than he intended? The last comment had been meant to reassure, she contemplated as she moved on smoothly. Perhaps that was his intention too, to take her mind off the climb? And suddenly she found the holds had ceased. One large step out and she was balanced on the ledge, calling clearly up. Almost immediately an orange pack appeared, sliding steadily downwards until she grasped it and undid the string. It was an unknown knot, securely tied, but such that a simple pull unravelled the whole thing. She tugged twice, and the loose end slithered rapidly upwards, waving its farewell in the wind. For a moment she paused, waiting to see if a face would appear over the edge, but she knew it wouldn't. Shortly she turned, shuffling along the ledge until the adit's narrow mouth gaped blackly at her. Had she but been able to see it, the face remained for a long while – stationary, seated, staring out to sea, its vision blurred until the fading shafts of day stirred old limbs to retrace their path.

*   *   *

Zadie pushed the rucksack in front of her, sullying its orange fabric on the muddy floor, waiting for her eyes to adjust to the loss of light. Gurgling and swashing came from a little way ahead and refracted light at lowest tide showed the chasm's edges.

Straightening her cap, muddying its whiteness too, she lobbed the pack across the gap far enough to prevent it sliding back and jumped across, remembering to duck before grasping the dry hand-hold in the rock and pushing the pack further with her feet. Briefly she adjusted her grip of hands and feet as she felt the rock begin to throb its greeting to the echo of her heart. Slowly the blank wall gleamed – its dull, silvery streak from floor to ceiling of the old adit's end growing in intensity, emanating its own light, thrilling and pulsing towards the single blank recess in its centre. It would have been easier if she had thought of this before; she didn't know what would happen if she let go her grip of the dry socket, and she was scrabbling with a free right hand to undo the pocket of the rucksack. The rock was growing urgent, quickening pulsations of its light raising her own heartbeat, and her fingers were swelling in their hold, or else the hold was contracting upon them. That was a silly thought. With sudden fear thought became reality. The hold was contracting. It was impossible to move her fingers now. Her left hand could not move; her wrist was held; fingers and bones were being crushed. A watch face shattered. Its casing was pressing unbearably upon her veins and nerves. Pain was increasing – pain adding to fear – and still the pace of light increased. It seemed to be dragging her heartbeat with it. Sweat was pouring off her. She shut her eyes, concentrating on ripping at the new sack's pocket with her one free hand. Finally it tore, and the chunk of tin fell, just out of reach. The bones in her fingers would break soon. A foot hooked at the rock. It slid, and Zadie grabbed. The heavy chunk of unsmelted tin touched her palm, and she thrust it into the dark centre of imploding light, pushing it further, holding her hand against it.

Pain eased. The finger-tips of her left hand could wiggle in the socket of rock. Pulsating light was ceasing; her heartbeat was coming down from attack levels to merely that of fear. The great, silvery-grey gleam in front of her was widening. Her hand came free. Rock split, growling apart to reveal its uncanny illumination beckoning down the curving steps ahead. Swiftly she scooped the rucksack's straps and thrust it through the gap, holding the piece of tin in her open palm and sitting on the top step, calming her breathing, forcing back the fear. She slid forward a step as the rock ground to behind her, crushing the objects that had straggled from the rucksack's pocket. What else had been in the pocket? Answers filtered into a mind that was beginning to work again: new toothbrush, toothpaste, soap and flannel from Spar – that didn't matter; matches – that could matter; torch from camping store – that was a blow. It was no good thinking about the things that were lost: she was better prepared than last time; and she was in the cave now.

Veins of silvery-grey stretched silently in front, threading their unthreatening light up passage walls, arching over its ceiling, casting their gentle illumination in tiny mirrors of still puddles on uneven steps curving down and left. For a while longer she sat, remembering a kindly face and its parting words, "Don't be afraid," until, following the light, the cavern opened in front, light spreading across its floor and around the great, black slab; light curving its path up the walls; light splitting and rejoining, silvering the plinking droplets of water into their pools. The slab had never possessed the same attraction for her as it had for Nathan, and she gave it a wide berth, resting the dragging rucksack against her foot as she faced the further wall. Silvery light dulled and retracted when she closed her hand and bowed her head, drawing a thin, gold chain over her golden hair and resting the copper token at its end in her other palm. Great veins of coppery-red surged into life, obliterating the fading tin as she slipped it in her pocket, springing and spreading in responsive welcome to the master token, scintillating in liquid rubies from every dripping surface, rippling their glow across each pool. Zadie gasped at the splendour of the moment. It seemed as if the rock's response was never the same. This time every beam of coppery radiance was pointing her towards the middle exit, arched over and over in incandescent glory.

The rucksack bumped against her back as she stepped down the passage, veins flooding forward until they met in one last weal of red from roof to floor, barring her path. Reaching forward, she touched it. Rock moved on rock. Silently, she passed into the light filtering beyond. There was barely a clunk as the passage sealed behind, and she picked her way down the opening cleft into the boulders and onto the grassy slope. A few dozen paces more and Zadie sat, absorbing the scene.

Dappled cloud patched the landscape with shifting shafts of afternoon light as the sun hid and emerged from behind their drifting form. Fog clung to the deepest valley floor; snow lingered in the shaded aspects. To the south, a blackened cliff still bore testament to Nathan's pyroclastics and, not far away, a veil of bluish smoke spread in a thin, horizontal layer.

So, there were men around. And, if men, Mortan too. She had feared that. She had never doubted that she would emerge in Soloma's world and in Soloma's time but this was not the world as she remembered – it was a world still partially in winter's grip, poised on the brink of its more rapid transit through the seasons. That would make life much more difficult. So would the fog. On the other hand, it provided concealment, although it seemed to be thinning and draining away as she looked towards the clump of hollies standing on top of the further slope, measuring in her mind whether they were nearer or farther from the source of smoke. Whichever it was, they were the only way. They had found that before. What was clear was that she could not stay here, exposed in the light, and she let her feet carry her down the slope, regretting the bright orange of her pack.

Clammy fog embraced her, and she moved more slowly, letting gravity be her guide until the stream cut across her course. Visibility was not as bad as it had been on the ice – perhaps a hundred yards – and at least there were objects to see. Pausing to drink, she smeared the pack with wetted earth, seeking to obscure its colour, working on times and distances, regretting that her watch had been another casualty of the entry to the cave. The upward slope was uneven, and she reckoned she was veering from a direct route. The apparent lack of progress was frustrating, contributing to a growing sense of urgency. At last, the fog was thinning and she burst out into the warmth of direct light, blinking and basking in it. Apprehension was well founded – the holly ring lay a fair distance to her left – and the north-east facing slope had patches of snow, masking some of the boulders. On the other hand, it was out of sight from the source of smoke, and Zadie quickened her pace, looking ahead gratefully as the dark trees grew closer. Two dozen paces more and she was through the entrance to them, resting safely in their concealment.

A plinth of stone stood before her, just as she had known it would. Unlike Nathan, she had no misapprehensions as to what was needed: the rocks in this place still lived; it was a landscape whose heart still beat, albeit to a different pace; there would be no deceiving them, no way through, except the one that they allowed. Resting a hand on the black rock of Polgodoc, she regarded the socket of granite set into its side of the plinth – granite that she disliked, granite that brought back memories, granite that was waiting to be crossed. Fingering the master token of copper lying against her skin, she wondered over its use; once before it had caused trouble and led to a trap. It would be safer to use the poor imitations of it that should be scattered somewhere near – provided she was sure they were the right rock – and she searched for one, kneeling on the ground, brushing at the snow. In part it had frozen, melted, and re-frozen – too firm to move and anchored at its base, deep shadows of hollies protecting it from each day's increased elevation of the noon-tide sun. Now, with the sun lowering fast, the shadow was dense. An angled shape caught her eye and, suddenly, her heart leapt. To its right was the indent of a boot, its patterned sole still visible upon the crisp surface. It was a large foot; it was a booted foot; and the surging certainty that Nathan had passed this way – and recently – thrilled through her. Lifting the granite token from the snow, she placed it in the recess, plucking it out again and moving lightly past the slab, casting it behind her, causing it to skid across the snow and settle in a drift of withered holly leaves, their brown and sharpened points covering its existence.

At its further side the dense ring of holly trees opened onto a new landscape, lighter in texture but darker in meaning, and Zadie stood, arms outstretched so that her fingers rested on their boughs, their last withering berries reddening in a sun two-thirds

towards its rest. Her eyes scanned what lay beyond. Twice, maybe
three times, they had met near disaster here. It was two hours'
fast walking without deviation from where she stood to the small
crown of hollies that glinted on the half-horizon; beyond that, and
to its right, another forty-five minutes at least to the shattered shape
of Gulland. It was not a simple landscape that lay between: there
were downward slopes and climbs; two rivers of fog still obscured
the deeper parts, and snow grew more common in the distance.
The sun would give her two hours of good light, by the look of
its elevation, and maybe an hour more of deteriorating sight. She
would not willingly be caught on this expanse of granite. It was
almost as if the great forces that had forged and formed it eons ago
had left some lurking imprint of their consuming power resting
uneasily beneath its skin, waiting to break out afresh and consume.
Zadie shivered at the molten cry echoing faintly from depth and
time unknown. Her stomach rumbled hungrily. That simple sound
broke the siren song of stone, and she lurched forward. Food could
wait. Nathan had gone this way. Soloma had gone this way. She
would go this way – and now. Unquenched cords of love reached
out to her and drew her on.

*   *   *

Without a watch the journey to the first fog seemed both short
and long. High cloud had nearly evaporated, and the sun shone
strongly in her face, illuminating the upper layers of clamminess
with a strange quality of light as she stepped into them, part-bathed
in a diffusing glow, part-chilled by her immersion. Boulders that
had been dry glints of mica, quartz and feldspar became wetted
obstacles to her path. Snow was no relief: sometimes it gave soft
steps of passage; at others, her feet skidded on its refrozen surface,
and she grabbed at rocks for support, finding their bluntness
sharpened against her skin. A stream trickled beneath her wrists
as she fell and, pushing herself out of its chill, she worked up the
slope, rock by rock, until a gloriously increasing golden haze hung
just above and, puncturing its radiance, she emerged into the clarity

of light.

So soon, though, the slope turned down again, its shadowed side already severed from the direct sun, a few dark branches showing like stationary seaweed through the blanket at her feet. For a moment Zadie had the insane impression that she could walk across its still, flat surface and up the hill to where a small patch of hollies broke the skyline, flickering dark green and gold. Instead she found cold dimness embracing her as she slipped and struggled. Fine-toothed leaves of scarred branches forced her aside and she followed the slope downwards, seeking its lowest point to cross in the darkening definition of form and substance. It was taking a long while. Ten yards now was all she could see. A stream gurgled, and she stepped through it, striking upwards again, picking her way between rocks cloven by the forces of an age of weathering: heat and cold; wet and dry; living root and death's acid venom. Tall and angular, a pillar rose upon her right, another to her left. The light was better here; soon she would be through this fog. Five paces on, a circular mass of rock, flat as a table, blocked her way. Dark it was; darker than the ground around; and darker far again. So nearly did she touch it. Only something in its darkness – a hint of green and speckled red – and some unspoken thing – held her back. Cold breath swirled, rending the fog. Pillars rose in a toothed ring around her. And suddenly she screamed, plunging unseeingly between two fangs, tumbling and falling down the slope, scrabbling and splashing up again, running, crawling, gasping until, at last, light lessened the cold fog and she flung herself into the dying embrace of the day.

*   *   *

The moon rose over Zadie's still form, silvering her shadow on the hard rocks where she lay. She shivered and moaned. Away to the south a red fire flickered its sweeping gaze across the landscape. Something moved. A large bird circled low, eyeing the softness of unprotected flesh in anticipation. The breath of its landing wings stirred a groan, and it flapped unwillingly from its feast, stirring the air again with its beat. Zadie moved. Her fingers touched her face and a realisation of pain trickled through their chance meeting. Pain brought consciousness; and consciousness spurred thought. Slowly, she rolled over. Comprehension of the silver orb dawned upon her, and she struggled to her knees, lifting her eyes up the slope. Against the faintest light of the distant sky branches rose, their pointed leaves ascending.

She staggered to her feet, surprised at the weight on her back. Above all things, she wanted not to stay on this geology a moment more. Kneeling and crawling in the darkness, she entered through the silent arch, seeking with her fingers for the feel of a token on the ground – a token that would let her off this granite, onto the dark-veined rock of Gulland – before remembering the chain that lay so close to her heart and thrusting the master-token on its end into the plinth, plucking it out again and walking through the hollies' only exit. Gulland: the thought of it stirred something within her, and she sat beyond the holly clump, draining her flask, looking at its moonlit silhouette. That was a safe place – a good place – a place she had been before. The moon was clear in the stillness of the night. It was sufficient to move by. A little while more, and she could rest there – rest without fear – let Gulland watch over her. And for the last time, she stirred herself.

Wearied feet led down, and up. Rocks shifted under her. She would not attempt the summit … she would skirt round the southern flank. Again she fell; again she rose. Here was the hollow where Soloma had pinned her down as the procession passed below. Thought of Soloma's name gave strength for another brief ascent, and then she was sliding, slithering, slipping downwards towards the hazel grove – its soft, mossy floor awaiting, welcoming. Dislodged stones tumbled ahead of her and, finally, she rounded the last boulder, almost like an animal scenting its safe lair.

Too late she saw it.

The axe fell, cleaving the night, penetrating with its curved end, forcing her weakened body to the ground.

Chapter 12   The Taming of a Camel

Nathan knelt, his knee in the small of Zadie's back, tugging urgently at the handle of the axe. It ripped out again, tearing as it came. He rolled her on her side, the face bleeding from where her final slide had arrested on the rocks, hair wrapping across it, cap fallen. Eyes opened in pain and lips murmured his name weakly. She made to move and Nathan lifted her gently in his arms, muttering her name over and over again as he carried her to the comfort of the moss, moonlight falling on tears that washed blood with stinging saltiness. Propping her against his own pack, he raised a flask of water and held it to Zadie's lips.

"Thanks," they said. A while later, they moved again, "Take my pack off, will you. It's hurting me."

The orange pack slipped free, its new fabric muddied, a torn pocket hanging loose, a great, blade-shaped rip in its back.

"You certainly made a mess of that," a weak voice observed; "glad it wasn't my head."

A black fright shuddered through Nathan at the thought that a head or neck was what he had intended to strike.

"I'm sorry. I am so sorry," he stammered. "I thought you were a creature ... a large creature; I had no idea ... I thought I was on my own. I am just so glad to see you ..." and words fell away as he embraced the seated figure.

"Could I have some more water, please; and something to eat?" Zadie asked eventually. "There is some food in my pack."

The pasties had taken the brunt of Nathan's attack, and they sat beside each other picking at the crumbled mess in the skewered, plastic container, each silent in relief until, finally, words began to pour into the night. The old hazels bent their leaves in the slight breeze, listening, and the Great Bear moved silently above, watching as it pointed ever north. High cloud began to filter from the east, its thin lace curtaining the heavens' scintillations.

"I'm glad to have found you. I thought you'd be on the ice by now," Zadie was saying as she tipped the last few crumbs into her cupped palm.

"I would have been," replied Nathan, finding a bar of chocolate, "but the fog delayed me, and the cleft was impassable. There was no way through."

She listened as he told his story. Eventually, she asked, "What do you think happened on the cliff when you were abseiling down?"

"I don't know. Maybe the rocks knew that I was trying to breach their barrier … maybe I was becoming tired and had lost more blood than I had thought … maybe many things – there's so much that I don't understand …"

In the silence they both considered, until he asked, "How did you get down the cliff at Polgodoc? It's not an easy route to find."

Now it was her turn to speak and, in the sharing of the tale, it brought a healing to her mind – until she reached the serpentine. "I so nearly touched it, Nathan; I so nearly touched it … a huge, flat circle of it, with those pillars standing round. There was a depth of evil about the place … a very great depth of evil … something you could sink into and never emerge from … I panicked, and ran – "

"The Stones of Sacrifice, Elana called them."

"Yes. Yes, that was it. That was where the Mortan were taking Tarma and Simona. Oh, Nathan, I can see it all now …"

And they both thought of Soloma, as if by instinct looking upward and seeing a great, illuminated circle in the sky – two circles – one larger, one smaller, each perfect in its form, their edges touched with the faintest colouration of yellow and red.

"That's beautiful. What is it?"

"Lunar halo … two lunar haloes," Nathan replied as they lay back; "a layer of very thin, high cloud – two layers, in fact, at different altitudes – so high that their crystals will be ice and so thin that the moonlight can shine through them, refracting like sunlight in a raindrop. It's a kind of lunar rainbow, if you like."

"I like it very much," she observed, settling against him. "Is it a good sign?"

"Yes, the clouds will thicken and lower from the east; it

promises no fog in the morning."

Its beauty caressed their gaze and, as it slowly faded, sleep shuttered the short remnant of the night.

*   *   *

Dawn stole over the sleeping figures in its regiment of greys, one pink banner leading briefly. The crown of ice ten miles distant – immutable, immense – cleared of its descending airs by the vanguard of a breeze – stood lordly proud, immobilised in time, awaiting the transient passage of another day.

Unusually, Nathan woke first and hobbled off for water, gradually restoring movement to a bruised knee that had lain uncomfortably. There was a flat, green stone on the mossy floor of the glade and he unpacked half his rucksack, setting the camping stove upon it and screwing the cylinder tight. By the time Zadie awoke, porridge and dried fruit were swelling in a tin and water was bubbling on the stove. He put the porridge to heat and added sugar liberally to the two mugs of tea that he was stirring.

"Hot food. Wonderful!" Zadie exclaimed, feeling her face and back. "You've brought a stove – that's great!"

"It is just for emergencies – on the ice, or if smoke from a fire would be too dangerous. However, I think what you have been through qualifies as an emergency. Welcome back," he said, smiling as he handed her the cup of tea. "It's hot and very sweet. Help yourself to porridge …"

Zadie needed no second invitation and she sat eating and drinking gratefully, while he spread out the entire contents of both rucksacks on the mossy floor, re-wrapping packages and putting food in freezer bags.

"Time for a little sorting out," he explained in response to her look. "There is some duplication of items … no point in carrying more than we have to … and both packs can have their weight distributed better. I'll leave a little food here, too; we have enough with what you brought. I'm almost inclined to leave the rope as well, now that we can't use the route we took before: it's the bulkiest item by far. However, I think I'll take it a bit further before deciding."

"When you say, 'take it a bit further', do you have any particular direction in mind?"

"Well, not the one I tried yesterday. Elana's northern route, if we can find it," he added, pausing in his repacking.

"And do you know where it starts?"

"No." He had stopped now. There was a confidence in Zadie's questioning, and he stared at her.

"Ha! Thought as much." She smirked, wondering whether to toy with him a little longer but relenting with a twinge of guilt. "That piece of paper … the one that you've just shoved in the side pocket of my pack … bring it over here." She cleared the stove and tins from the flat rock before commanding triumphantly, "Now spread it out."

Nathan knew better than to question Zadie in this mood – a remarkably recovered Zadie, he thought with pleasure, as he followed her instructions. The thick paper unfolded several times until it reached A3 proportions. He gasped, staring at his own writing; at pencil lines and figures; at words written in German; at question marks, bearings, distances.

She leant against him, peering round his shoulder. "You remember drawing it then … not far from here … sitting on top of Gulland, looking out at the ice?" He nodded, already wrapped in the map in excitement. "Fee had it framed for me as a Christmas present … it was on my bedroom wall." As if to emphasise the point, a shard of glass brushed out of one of the folds as Nathan traced his fingers across the figures.

"This helps tremendously. At least it gives us a direction."

He was lost in it … on his knees … compass out … sighting through the hazel boughs before bowing his head to the map again. Zadie washed out the porridge tin and filled the flasks, finishing the repacking with occasional glances across at his studious exuberance in the simple piece of paper. Eventually, she came and stood facing him. He looked up, folding the map.

"Good. We should have put in more detail, but good. We need

to head north north-west towards the river – "

"What river?"

"A kind of ancient River Camel ... probably much larger ... there will be meltwater from the winter snows. We'll sort out how we cross it when we get there. I wish we had marked more holly clumps, though ... there are two geologies between here and the ice. That will be our problem ... or one of them."

Nathan rose, ready to make a start, but Zadie continued to stare. "That rock," she said, "did you mark it?"

"No. Why?"

"It looks like it has been scratched ... bit like a zigzag ..."

"It was probably scratched when it was moved here. It's not the same as the rocks around here."

"Moved by whom?"

Almost at the same instant, the scratch resolved itself in their eyes as a hurried letter N, and they both dived for the rock, flipping it over. The underlying surface was wetted from contact with the ground but it was clearly scratched – and in considerable detail. Zadie began to make sense of it first.

"This is Soloma's doing," she cried excitedly. "Look: there's her S in the bottom corner. There's a hill ... that must be Gulland; and two lakes ... a big one and a little one; and that must be the ice-wall ..."

"That wiggly line is the river," added Nathan, "and that could be meant to be a tree ..."

"... Probably a holly clump. What's that round thing and the two straight lines?"

"There are three straight lines ... that one has an angle in it, near the tree. I think," Nathan continued, after a substantial pause, "that they are bearings and the round object is the setting sun ..."

"Soloma knew that you hadn't travelled the northern route and she's left you a map ... left it in the one place she thought you would be sure to visit ..."

"And if it hadn't been for yesterday, I would have missed it. If it hadn't been for you now, I would still have missed it." It seemed so obvious that the atypical rock was something that would be expected to attract his attention, something that had been placed there deliberately for him to find, that he could not believe his own blindness.

"Why does the map stop at the end of that second line?"

"Possibly because that is how far we can reach in a day's travel from here," Nathan responded. "Anyway, Soloma's message at Trevennick was on a green slate; this one is on a green slate – we had better keep a look out for flat, green rocks! Meanwhile, I am going to check these angles against your map."

Some time later Nathan had annotated Zadie's map further and confiscated it to a pocket, announcing himself content to move. It was an interesting landscape – not one they had travelled before – but not one in which it was easy to keep to a bearing. The slope fell away in little pockets and rises – to have called them valleys and ridges would have been too grand a title – the veining in the rock producing its own micro-variations, sometimes standing proud and sharp, at others etched deeply as the elements had weathered each small part differentially, according to its resistance. Whatever its past history, the outcome was a slope needing a considerable amount of care in plodding and picking the way over it. Each pocket tended to have a short patch of icy snow at the top of its shaded lee, followed by firm snow that was walkable to its base, where another icy stretch gave way to bare rock on the more southerly ascending aspect. Occasional scrubby bits of plant suggested that berries might be found here later in the year; there were drips of water but nothing by way of clear pools to drink from or a stream to follow on its course. However, it was a secluded landscape, distant from smoke and eyes: to be seen would require a presence only a few yards away.

Eventually, Nathan called a halt and asked, "What's the time?"

"I don't know. I lost my watch entering the cave at Polgodoc. It was brand new, too ... bought it in Padstow ... it had a couple of dials and a luminous compass on one of them," answered Zadie.

"A pity," said Nathan, chuckling softly; "I think mine is at the bottom of a snowdrift in that cleft. I am finding it difficult counting paces in this uneven ground and I'm not convinced I am keeping to the bearing," he continued, more seriously.

"What do you want to do?"

"Stop and have a think – and something to drink, and a bite to eat. I don't want to use the gas – we may need it later – so it will have to be cold water from the flasks ... and there is a pack of muesli bars somewhere ... they would be good."

"How would Soloma have found the way?"

"There would probably be very clear markers, if we knew what to look for ... odd shaped rocks, a different plant, a hollow that looks like a face – just like we might navigate a route by buildings and features – you know ... turn left at the pink house ... large pub on the corner, turn right after it ... sharp right bend, speed camera fifty yards, etcetera. And I think she is good enough to sense where the sun is, even on a day like today when you can't see it. I have been trying to feel its direction by its heat but I can't."

"So what do we do?" enquired Zadie, spluttering bits of muesli in the process.

"Carry on, and if we find a stream flowing anything like north or north-west, follow it."

"Isn't that dangerous? It might lead anywhere."

"It has got to go downhill. So have we. I agree with you, but this does not look like a landscape that will have sudden waterfalls or precipitous drops, and my stomach-watch says half the day is gone."

Perhaps an hour later – more by accident than design – they found a stream. Zadie had disappeared for a moment and had stumbled across the tinkling rivulet, her cry alerting Nathan, who arrived at pace, thinking she was in danger. Disappearing beneath a patch of snow, the stream emerged again to tumble between smoothed rocks, part-iced with its splashing. Progress was slow rock-hopping down its course, and sometimes they had to search for its re-emergence from beneath a larger expanse of crusted snow, wondering how much weight the surface would bear and what lay below. Once, Nathan turned too suddenly at a comment from Zadie and slid ungracefully down a steeper incline, cannoning into rocks at its base. Thereafter, the ice-axe was brought into use on the snowy sections, making progress more secure but slowing it with the difficult downward cuts. Other rivulets joined until it was no longer necessary to seek the water's course, and it plunged into a cascade of ankle-snapping boulders that bruised shins and knees on every slip. It bottled and gurgled between two final boulders of long-tumbled landscape, and disappeared.

Zadie and Nathan rounded the boulders from opposite sides and stood, looking at the scene in front. Vast braids of sand and gravel undulated irregularly before them; somewhere water flowed, rushing and eddying in hidden urgency across the beds of channels hidden by sloping banks and bars; and to their left a few low islands of pink rock rose – isolated points of solidity.

"Well, this is the River Camel – as it was," announced Nathan; "and we need to cross it, according to Soloma's map."

"It's huge!" exclaimed Zadie.

"Yes," he acknowledged softly, almost in a professional voice, "all the rivers this near the ice-sheet would have been much larger than we know them: frozen in winter; swollen with melting snow in spring; grumbling and growling with a bedload of rocks shattered by freezing and thawing of the land; carrying vast volumes of quartz and mica that had been loosened by the decomposition of the rock inland. What we are about to tread on may be the same grains of sand that we saw at Enodoc, or Rock, or at Tregirls, and the larger stones the pebbles trapped at Greenaway, driven onshore by rising sea-levels. In summer the rivers would dry to a trickle and wind would whip up the sand into fields of dunes – unstabilised, mobile – like in some of our deserts."

She sensed a maudlin air about him but could not repress an admiration for the picture of past and present, present and future, that he saw as they stood, and she found herself asking what she knew to be true: "So, we have to cross it?"

"Yes."

"Where? And how?"

"How, I know. Where, I don't. And time is not with us."

Nathan lowered his pack and began to unwind the rope, passing an end to Zadie.

"Tie it on, please. Try a bowline, but don't make it too tight," he half-asked, half-instructed, impressed that he did not need to explain the knot, watching her slip the loop around her waist. "The water will be very fast-flowing in some of the channels," he continued. "The rocks will be slippery beneath your feet and liable to shift suddenly. If there were three of us, this would be easier – we could brace in a triangle and work our way across – but there aren't, so I will have to be on the end of the rope and you will have to lead. We are heading for that low island of solid rock, over there. Take the streams at 45° so the current pushes you towards the far bank. If the water comes higher than your knees, stop: if it reaches your thighs, it will be fast enough to sweep you away. If you do fall," he ended, "fall on your back. That way I can haul you in and your head will be above water against the current. If you fall forward, the water and your pack will push you under when I pull."

As a briefing, Zadie had to admit it was succinct. As a source of encouragement, she did not feel quite the same. Cobbles and gravel crunched under their feet as they crossed the first abandoned bar on the edge of the channel. Feet sank into gritty sand, and Nathan braced himself against what was to come, paying out the rope slowly and trying to hold it against the current without unbalancing Zadie by a sudden pull as she waded tentatively across. Twice she slipped as the fist and head-sized rocks shifted beneath her, and once she plunged forward, pushing back out of the water with her arms and knees, soaking herself to thighs and armpits in the process. She sat on the first island of loose material and began gathering in the rope, as he prepared to follow. What Nathan had not told her was that he had the more difficult part: the rope would hang into the water in front of him and tug in the current; there would be no tension to hold him against it; and his heavier pack would almost certainly plunge him beneath the water if he fell. He could work downstream along the bank and come back towards her: that would give him tension for balance but it would mean working against the current. Besides which, he had not explained that possibility. In the end he opted to follow Zadie's line of crossing, falling at almost exactly the same point and emerging spluttering and wet.

"Well done; bad pothole," he mumbled, as they made their way to the next channel and looked across towards the island.

This channel was considerably wider. Indeed, the rope would probably only just stretch across it – which would be a huge weight dragging in the water. Beyond it, the recently abandoned bed of the channel, showing up as the next bar, was much sandier. It must have been a raging torrent for the water to have been that high, and it looked as if it had been submerged quite recently. Glacial streams had a diurnal regime, reaching their maximum flow in the warmth of early afternoon and their minimum just before dawn, and he hoped that this river was not experiencing any such changes, at least not in an upward direction. Questions of lag-times – how long it would take snows melting further upstream to reach this point – permeated his mind.

Zadie was off before he had reached any conclusion. She was taking this quite fast, and he was having to pay out rope rapidly. Now it was beginning to drag in the current, and she was up to her knees in the water. He could see it tugging at her as she leant against it with each step. This wasn't looking good: the current was pushing strongly from right to left, turbulent and thrusting – and she was already deep in it. The rope was dragging from right to left, heavily and in bursts, as it surfaced from beneath the water, only to be caught and dragged down again. He was pulling back, and she was struggling to lean both to the right and to move forward; meanwhile, rocks were slipping and moving under her feet. She was paused now, halfway across, and he could sense the uncertainty. Concentrating hard on the far bank, she was making little progress. Only one item was under Nathan's control. He would have to shorten the rope to try to stop its vicious tugging on her. That meant two of them in the water at once: if she slipped, he would struggle to hold her; if he slipped, she wouldn't even know until the rope pulled her over as well. If he didn't do something, she was going to fall.

Nathan slipped the rope off his shoulders and stepped into the water, coiling it in front of him, holding it clear of the water. It was wet and heavy. His arms were already aching and water was trickling down them, inside his clothing. It was cold water; his feet and legs were becoming numbed with it and with the effort of steadying himself against its relentless pressure. No wonder she had found it hard going. He risked a quick glance up, regretting it almost immediately as he struggled for balance. Zadie was making progress again. The rope seemed to be dragging less on her. The rocks were exceedingly slippery and mobile in the middle of the channel: this was taking him an age; each step was draining his body and mind. Soon he would have to put the coil back over his shoulders; his arms were struggling with its cold weight. Suddenly he could feel the erratic, tugging tension of the rope slacken; it tightened again; once more it lessened, and he saw her on the bank, holding it above her head, trying to keep it clear of the water, trying to give him a steady tension. Two thirds of the way across relief was palpable – and instantly false. That moment's inattention to his footing produced a slip, and he was plunged into the water, submerged by the weight of his pack, swallowing water. In desperation, he wrapped his wrist around the rope, kicking and rolling his body, spluttering in the icy water, bumping along with the current until the rope bit and cut into his wrist. He rolled and rolled again, scrabbling for a purchase with his knees and feet, pushing with his one free hand and pulling with the other, coughing water and sucking air. Water was eddying around a large boulder. He grabbed at it, willing his fingers to find something to grip. Uncontrolled movement abated; no longer was he being swept downstream. Crevice by crevice his fingers were hauling him in until he hugged the rock, kicking and splashing, pulling himself like a deadweight onto the sand, the rope snaking from his wrist towards the figure running over the soft surface.

Half-deadened brain cells reacted slowly – too slowly. He saw it coming, as if in slow motion. Her feet were sinking further with each step. This was sand that had been hurriedly abandoned by the water – loosely consolidated – like sand on the beach between Rock and Brea Hill where the tide had retreated rapidly – only there a footstep would sink a few inches; here, Zadie was shin deep in the material, brought to a standstill, sinking further as she struggled. There was nothing for her to grip on; nothing to pull against; one leg was already knee deep.

"Throw yourself forward!" yelled Nathan. "Flatten your body so it doesn't sink!"

A face looked towards him in incomprehension. He tried calling again, urgently, as he shifted into a sitting position, bracing his feet against the rock. At the third time of calling, she understood, throwing herself forward onto the sinking sand. The bowline tightened under Zadie's armpits and Nathan leant forward, using his leg strength like a rower in an eight, feet braced against the rock, bottom sliding forward and back, both wrists locked around the rope, pulling with his arms and upper body as well.

"Spread-eagle your arms! Don't let the rope slip off." Zadie's head rose briefly. "Now, try wiggling your feet so they point backwards and crawl – very gently. Don't put any more pressure on the sand than you have to."

He hauled again. The rope gave a little. Another haul ... he was looking directly at her ... one knee was free and on the surface ... the other was flexing. If he hauled much more strongly, he would be liable to break a rib, or her other leg if it was stuck fast. If the knot slipped, it would suffocate her. The last haul had made six inches ... the next made another six ... both legs were free ... she was flat on the surface, face raised expectantly.

Nathan let the tension relax and called again, "Roll! Roll down the bank and into the water!"

He could see her struggling to roll with the obstruction of the rucksack on her back. She was rocking to and fro like a stranded, upturned turtle. With agonising slowness she toppled over. One slow roll followed another, as Zadie maintained the momentum. He concentrated on keeping the rope clear of her rotating body – stopping it winding around her neck – as one last roll tumbled her into the water and the current gripped. Fast, as fast as he could, Nathan was reeling her in. Zadie was helping, swivelling her body, kicking towards the rock like a giant fish that wanted to be caught.

The current eddied her into the rock's lee, pushing her head under in its turbulence. He grabbed at the straps on her pack, pulling the struggling, spluttering body with it, until Zadie collapsed on the bank beside him.

*   *   *

Recovery had taken some time. They had lain together exchanging few words, each grappling with the images, graphic and immediate, of what had happened, each drained of emotion. For the second time that day the emergency stove came into action, brewing hot, sweet tea. From the east the gentle wind was surprisingly mild, but sodden clothes were unpleasant and still dripping, as they stood again, contemplating the way ahead.

Edging along the great sand bar, not trusting the inviting surface that rose in gentle convexity to block the view to their right, they worked from rock to rock along the water's shallow margin, its rippled surface slipping by much faster than their progress. Occasionally half a branch, discarded from its origin, swept past, coursing and tumbling on its final journey, buried for a moment before resurfacing yards downstream. The sand bar narrowed and lowered to a point, curving like a talon into the clawing water; another channel – yet wider, yet deeper – emerged into sight, washing on its farther side against the pink rock of a low island.

"That is a big channel," stated Zadie's voice. It was a long while since she had spoken, concentrating as they had been on the foot by foot task. In essence, her tone was neutral, but to Nathan's sensitised ears there was a hint of fear. He tried to suppress similar emotions as he replied, "We must go on."

"We have come the wrong way, haven't we?"

"Yes, I am afraid so," Nathan acknowledged sadly. "I'm sorry."

Somehow the admission of his fallibility cheered Zadie and she dragged him onward. At the finest, sharpest point of the sand bar's curving talon they saw it and its pair – black, flat, and just beneath the water. It was like turning over the card that said,

'Advance to Go', when faced with an impossible roll of the die. Simultaneously, they realised their fortune.

"Stepping stones!" cried Zadie.

"Stepping stones," Nathan echoed. "This must be Soloma's route!"

Almost in deference, water split around the stones, spilling shallowly across their surface – menhirs of passage laid laterally across its path – its violence reserved for the steps of faith between. They took it without roping up, confident that they had stumbled upon Soloma's way, knowing that no rope would rescue a mistaken move, passing from solid place to solid place, until they made their landing and walked over the pink surface of the island to its whale-back summit.

If it was a whale, it was swimming upstream. What was more, there were a whole school of them, separated only by shallow shoals of wetted stones. Rapidly, they moved from one whale island to the next, until the wetness began to diminish and gentle fold of land gave way to gentle fold. The pinkness was beginning to diminish, too; the first banks of snow appeared, clothing each animal upon its northern flanks. They sat on a higher point, guessing the remaining light.

"How long?" voiced Zadie.

"An hour, maybe a little more. It will fade quickly, and there will be no moon tonight."

"That whale, two whales away ..." she began

"Which whale?" Nathan had succumbed to the analogy some time ago and felt disinclined to fight it.

"The one over there," Zadie answered, pointing. "It looks like it's spouting water, coming up for breath."

It was almost as casual as sitting on a beach, idly watching the shape of clouds – 'Look: dragon – see the tail and mouth?' ... 'It's breathing smoke' ... 'Chicken with one chick' ... 'Platypus'. Nathan was about to give a pained answer but there was something about the hill that appealed to his curiosity, and he unearthed the binoculars instead. One lens dribbled water but the other was clear and its monocular vision was sufficient to bring the feature into closer detail.

"Trees!" he exclaimed. "Not big … dark … small clump of them." His cry of, "Well spotted! Let's go!" was entirely unnecessary as Zadie was already off before he had lowered the binoculars or picked up his pack. It was only on the snowbank at the splayed tail of the first 'whale' that he caught up with her.

"Do you notice anything, Nathan?" Zadie asked, as he walked alongside her in the dimming light.

"Other than the fact that it is growing dark and hills have become whales, you mean?"

"It's about the hills … about the rock they are made of …"

"This rock?" he asked.

"Yes."

"It's a lightly metamorphosed limestone … pink in colour … probably formed in the shallow waters of submarine rises within the tropical Tethys Sea during the Devonian orogeny – "

"Whoa! Stop! You've lost me already, and that's not what I was asking …"

With regret, he reined in what had promised to be a good fifteen minutes of enthusiastic explanation and asked, "What are you getting at?"

"This isn't the same rock as Gulland, is it?"

"No, of course not, Gulland is heavily metamorphic with veins of – " and he stopped in mid first-sentence, suddenly realising what she was meaning. "How interesting. How very, very interesting."

"Got it?"

"Yes. I think so: we've moved from the dark rock of Gulland to the pink rock here without passing a plinth, or using a token, or encountering any barrier …"

"That's what I was thinking, although I'm not too sure about the 'no barrier' bit. We have by-passed a holly clump … perhaps not by a route to be recommended, though."

The land was rising to a shallow ridge as they looked ahead. It was less than half-light but they were definitely the tops of trees standing in shadowy silhouette against the dull shape blocking the horizon beyond. Slowly, they gained in definition until, cresting the rise and descending a few steps further, stunted forms of holly rose in huddled welcome, arching a passage for the two figures to walk within. A plinth stood in their centre – a block of pink rising rectangularly near them and ending abruptly in its counterpart of clear, glassy quartz. Snow wrapped around its side, sloping smoothly up to its flat surface and extending into the holly roots. Halfway astride the unsullied drift a single dint – small but distinct – broke the perfection of a winter's work; and in its crisp imprint, a solitary, glassy token lay.

"Soloma!" cried Zadie.

Chapter 13   A Matter of Some Bearing

Stunted boughs threw their ancient protection around them for the night. Darkness had come fast, and long had they talked about the import of their find, impatient for the dawn. It came with no great splendour and found them awaking stiffened limbs in stiffened clothes, beginning again a conversation thrice pored over.

"She marked that spot and put it there as a clear sign," Zadie was saying as Nathan stirred the porridge. He had relented into using the stove again but was making sure he did not keep it lit a moment more than necessary as he handed her hot tea and food.

"I agree, but there is no sign of any green rock within the holly ring – and this is as far as her last map took us ... even though I didn't follow it well," he added as a self-depreciating afterthought.

"Perhaps it's not green."

"We have turned over every flat rock of whatever colour ... and a whole lot that weren't flat."

"So what do we do?"

"Well, I am going to finish my mug of tea and find some dry socks."

"You and your socks! We're wasting time!" exclaimed Zadie in frustration.

Something chimed in Nathan's mind as he extracted a nice orange pair from a freezer bag and tied the wet ones on the back of his rucksack to flap dry as they walked. That was it! That was the reason! His comment brought Zadie abruptly upright from her latest unproductive search within the holly ring.

"What do you mean?" she demanded.

"You said something about wasting time ... I don't think Soloma had time to do anything here ..."

"Go on." She was interested now.

"The mark she made was about the quickest thing she could do. It must have been light for her to find the token. There is no other evidence of her having been here. If she'd had the time, she could have done something much more detailed. I think she was being followed."

"By the Mortan?"

"Possibly. Certainly, by someone to whom she did not want to give any information."

"So, what is she saying to us?"

Nathan paused and caught Zadie's gaze before replying, "First, to go throught the barrier; secondly, to look for a distinctive mark in open snow – probably some way from here; and, thirdly, to be careful not to be seen."

Zadie nodded, slowly accepting the reasoning, and asked, "Have you ever thought of taking up detective work?"

"I used to do it with the students," he replied, laughing with her, "tracking down the bits that didn't sound like them, or like my lecture notes – nowadays there's a computer programme that will do it all, mind you … I don't need to think or know much any more." He still chuckled though as he fiddled with his compass.

"What are you doing now?"

"Just a little thought. I don't think it's relevant – but if it is, Soloma deserves a starred 1st."

"Would you mind explaining?"

Instead, Zadie received another question in reply, "Which way round was the token – longways to the imprint or crossways? Do you remember?"

"Longways, I think." She was intrigued by the conversation.

"It was pretty dark when we arrived, but that's what I thought too," he said as he turned the compass housing a bit further.

"So, are you going to tell me?"

"I'm just wondering," he replied, mustering a dramatic pause, "whether there is any significance in the angle of the footprint? If she gave us that as a bearing, Soloma goes straight to the top of any class I ever taught: in haste; pursued; not wanting to leave any tell-tale evidence but wanting to give a sign … simple, elegant, superb!" He was humming a tune to himself – an old tune with half-mumbled words – exuding a confidence that wrapped warmly around her, lifting her uncertainties by his manner.

Together, they leant on the plinth of pink rock and placed the quartz token into the recess in it, lifting it out again and stepping through the invisible barrier. Casually, he pocketed the token, humming to himself again, more loudly this time, and running the fingers of his right hand along the smooth surface of the monstrous piece of quartz that formed the glass-clear compatriot to the pink landscape that they had left. His other hand held hers. They halted momentarily beneath the gnarled remnants of over-arching holly, looking to the west.

The landscape below was largely white, part-crusted, part-soft in its covering of unmelted snow, falling away in jumbled heaps of semi-smoothness interrupted by angular rocks of all shapes and sizes. Southwards, a lake grew in width, its margins narrowed by winter ice that had grown flat into it, its centre littered with fallen chunks that floated in random confusion. Towards the north a vast river ran, splitting and rejoining its endless bars and braids – some proto-Severn draining the winter's legacy from land beyond their view. Above all, towered the ice: a great wall of ice, eight hundred metres high; ice, pinnacled and creviced; ice, ridged and vertical; ice, pristine white; ice, decaying black with the dead-toothed debris of a hundred millennia of moraine scoured from the Irish Sea, plucked from Snowdonia, carried from Skye, Arran, Antrim; awesome in its immensity, the last great bastion of an ice sheet sweeping south, locking time within its cold embrace. Onto that ice sheet she had gone. Onto that ice sheet they must go. And he nodded twice towards it, breathing in, as if acknowledging the strength of some old foe.

"It's awful," murmured Zadie.

"I'm not sure how you are spelling that," came the unexpected response as he swung her clasped hand forward and marched down the slope, humming still. "Awe is a funny thing. It is certainly a thing of awe. But there are bigger things than its cold vastness … and one of them is Soloma."

This was a different Nathan. There was a determination, a confidence about him, a steadied warmth that flowed from grip to grip; and, in his strength, she found her own, allowing her strength to flow back to him, until he smiled amongst his tears, turning his face and saying, "Thanks. We're going to do this."

"You seem much more confident," she ventured.

"I am," he replied; "a worm has turned. The way is marked – all we have to do is follow."

"We tried to follow yesterday …"

"Yes, but I started in the wrong place. We should have started at the top of Gulland – that was where the bearing was meant to be taken from. Today we have started in the right place, on the right line."

"Shouldn't we be looking for footprints or something?"

"Not yet … too near the hollies. She will have kept off the snow here … avoided giving her tracks away. We are heading down to that big jumble of black rocks … ideal place to not be seen."

The jumble was more than that – it was a demolition yard of discarded fragments ranging in size from a two-storey house to a fist and mostly angular enough, at least in some of their dimensions, to puncture a car tyre – or flesh. Soon Nathan was sitting on top of a bungalow-sized piece with his compass, directing a slightly suspicious Zadie across a rubble-strewn lawn of black and white.

"Stop!" came the command. "Wait until I join you. We'll do a box search." The seated figure waited as Nathan slid alongside and continued, "We are sitting at the most likely point that Soloma had in mind; we start ten yards out from here, pacing a ten by ten box, then another ten yards – twenty by twenty – etcetera, until we find what we are looking for; we use the compass to give right angles at the corners."

Nathan was sounding enthusiastic, and she was careful in the tone of her response. "You're still convinced about the bearing?"

He nodded.

"I think it will be difficult in these rocks," she continued cautiously; "and I don't think Soloma would have expected it."

For the first time Nathan could see a flaw in his logic and he asked, "Have you an alternative in mind?"

"Yes." She hesitated, watching him, before judging it wise to

continue. "Climb the highest rock and look down. After all," she
added very gently, "you said that yesterday we should have started
from the highest point."

As with any choice, there were competing possibilities.
Certainly, there were no certainties. Zadie's suggestion had an
elegance about it, and he found his thoughts veering towards
accepting it as a working hypothesis. It would be a lot quicker to
climb one rock than to conduct an entire box-search. Moreover,
if he took the binoculars with him – assuming they were not still
being monoculars – he might be able to look down on the river and
find a potential crossing point. It was at the end of this process that
he nodded to Zadie and said, "OK. That's fair. Which rock?"

"The one behind the one you climbed."

He was inclined to agree with her, and they slid round the base
of the bungalow rock, clambering through the curling edifice of a
frozen drift of snow before arresting their slide down its smooth
lee-slope at the same place. In the middle of the snow, three clear
footprints had been stamped and, below them, a flat rock lay.

"There: told you so!" was met with, "We would have found it
on a box-search!" but neither seemed inclined to argue the point as
they turned the rock over and held it between them.

Much less well engraved than the one on Gulland, it was a
common piece of black rock. Nevertheless, it marked a high point
– presumably the rock in front – and four lines. Again, there was
a setting sun. Confusingly, there was another circle and something
that looked like a striding figure, with marks alongside. Some
scratches crossed and re-crossed, and little dots looked like eyes
between them. In one corner an S was clear and Nathan oriented
the rock so that this was at the bottom, extracting Zadie's map and
laying each alongside the other. It was a game that appealed to
both of them – part intellect, part survival.

"That scratchy triangle is this rock, where we are," said Nathan.
"S is at the bottom and north is at the top."

"In that case, the circle with the line two-thirds of the way
down it is the sun rising in the east," continued Zadie; "and there
are two more suns. Look how that last one has the line two-thirds

up it."

"Setting sun, not rising sun," replied Nathan. "So that's North, East, South and West. Why is there another circle in the middle?"

"Could be the moon … not the most obvious way of drawing it, though … and what are those little triangles?"

"The circle in the middle has two lines through it …"

"I wonder," questioned Zadie, "how long did Elana say the northern route over the ice took?"

"Two days."

"Then I think the circle with the two lines represents a rising and a setting sun – a full day's journey."

"Maybe those little triangles are markers of some sort – five of them," contributed Nathan.

"What about the start? It looks like a figure …"

"There's a line – that could be a bearing – and some other scratches alongside it."

"How did Soloma write numbers?" Zadie asked.

"Above nine, I don't know. Four was single strokes. Five was a stylised hand. It doesn't look like any of those. What about the scratches and dots beyond the first line?"

"I've no idea …"

Conversation continued in vigorous fashion until they found themselves double and triple-tracking back over unknown ground. Eventually, the rock was placed amongst other, similar coloured fragments and Zadie stood, watching Nathan turn the dial on his compass and move his open palm until the floating red needle matched north. He sighted on another large rock in the distance.

Snow lay over much of the landscape but it was not a nice smooth sheet. In parts, it was hard-crusted and slippery, not yielding any imprint to their feet; in other parts, it was soft and powdery, driven by the eddying winds of months to accumulate in varying depth; and through it all tips of the jumbled mass that lay concealed beneath broke the whitened cloth. It was difficult terrain to cross. Zadie could see Nathan checking his compass frequently and slowly beginning to shake his head as the river drew nearer.

"What's wrong?" she asked.

"Nothing. Well, nothing much ... it's just that rock is troubling me ..."

"Which one? And why?"

"That one two hundred yards away," he pointed. "I thought the bearing from Soloma's slate would take us to it – but it's not, and I can hear water ahead."

Flat ice, dusted with powdery snow, extended into the river in front, creaking and groaning at its unexpected burden of two rucksacked figures as they edged over it. Finally, they stood looking across an enormity of channels and bars stretching a mile or more to a point where the ice-wall began to rise, its fractured face frowning in enmity. Water – cold and black – raced and tumbled over the unseen burden on its bed; an island bar – smooth-sided, ice-rimmed, dusted with snow – rose on the farther side; and, beyond that, other raised banks hinted at wider and deeper channels yet.

"There is a safe way across this," said Nathan absently, fingering the rope.

"And a lot of unsafe ones! I'm not going in there," Zadie responded.

"This is where the bearing ends," argued Nathan, turning and sighting back. "I checked it very carefully."

"Then it's wrong. We won't even get a third of the way across that channel before we're swept downstream. Are you sure about the bearing? Maybe your compass isn't working properly."

"The bearing is right ... and there is nothing wrong with my compass!" came the sharpened retort.

"I'm still not going in there."

He could understand her reticence, or rather, the point-blank refusal. There was no obvious way across. Nor would the rope stretch more than half the distance. Even if he offered to lead, the water would drag viciously. Eventually he tapped the compass and put it away, saying, "OK, what do you want to do?"

"Go back off this ice and along to that rock. It's the highest thing around. Maybe we can see from there."

"See what?"

"I don't know ... a crossing point ... something, anything."

There was a tension as they retraced their steps, walking apart, and diverted to the rock. It was not particularly high – perhaps eight metres – but it was larger than anything else around and its steep, black surface had absorbed the insolation, cleansing it from winter's grip. Zadie was climbing before Nathan had lowered his pack, and he could tell from her demeanour, standing on top of the slightly flattened summit, that something had caught her eye. The phrase 'I told you so' emanated from her body-language.

"There: I told you so," proclaimed Zadie as he joined her.

The wide channel with its great volume of water stretched below. But with their elevation something else was visible: flat, darker patches beneath a smoothing of the flow, each separated by the seething of constricted water. Beyond the first water's ending, black rock showed on the island bar, and on the next one too. In summer the rocks would provide dry passage, standing proud above the water's withered arms; now, shallowly within its clutch, they promised passage still; and she smiled at him as he acknowledged their potential. Descending together, they paused to adjust and balance packs before pursuing the steps unroped, confident that this was Soloma's way. The last channel gurgled behind, a mis-fit stream already abandoning its attempt to bar the way. A final rock rose – dark, its flat surface anchored into the ice that soared above, spilling its untold years in steep advance towards them – and they sat, looking back over the expanse of sand, stone, snow and water, and up to the distant point of dark leaves showing against the grey blanket of cloud.

"We still can't see the sun," observed Zadie, "but it feels like time for food. I need a reward for that crossing!"

"Yes, this is a good place to eat ... and there's a long haul to come. It is the last of the water, too ... there will be nothing on the ice-sheet, except what we melt with the stove or body-heat. I think I will cook a meal and fill some of the dried packages to rehydrate as we go," answered Nathan, and he spread some of the contents of his pack on the rock between them.

The compass lay beside the stove as Nathan stirred rice to

expand and emptied a sachet of curry powder into it, adding a handful of dried fruit. Occasionally, he prodded the compass too and fiddled with its housing, turning the dial in miniscule amounts. Putting it aside, he handed her the food, heating water in a different tin and stirring sugar into black tea.

He was sipping at his mug and clearing up, when Zadie observed between mouthfuls, "Something's eating you."

"Oh, it was your comment about the compass not working properly. I don't see how I could have been that far out on my bearing with that rock today ... and yesterday it was the same," he answered, accepting the food tin from her and tucking in to the remainder whilst she made a face at the sweetness of her own mug of tea. "On the other hand, there is a possible explanation ..." A lump of relatively unstirred curry powder brought a temporary halt to Nathan's words.

"Is it important?"

"It could be," he continued. "What time period do you think we are in?"

"You mean, how many years ago?"

"Yes."

"About five thousand, judging by Soloma's society – no iron tools, no settled agriculture – and what you've said about sea-levels and this ice-sheet. Why?"

"It's the magnetic declination."

"What?" she asked, as he ran his fingers around the inside of the tin and licked the last remnant of sauce off them.

"How the north pole changes ..."

"I thought the north pole was the North Pole: it's a place."

"I'm talking about the magnetic north pole: it is not the same as the true north pole, and it wanders – slowly – and sometimes it flips."

"You've lost me. Start again and tell me as we go up the ice," said Zadie.

They cleared up the remaining things and started up the great cascade of ice, sloping sharply towards its summit eight hundred metres above. There was not any real choice of route: to either side ice cliffs rose from the frozen edge of the great river's course, their bevelled shoulders falling from high above onto the sloping tongue of ice that formed their path; and on that silent tongue the almost year-long freeze had closed the crevasses of forward motion and buried the litter of moraine that two brief summer months might show. It was a simple task of kicking forward and stepping up, like an endless stairway into an endless white above.

"Compasses point to magnetic north," began Nathan again – it was a good conversation for the long trudge upwards as it could be a lengthy discourse and would occupy the mind – "and magnetic north shifts."

"Explain," commanded Zadie.

"Magnetic north is the result of the movement of vast bodies of iron-rich rock deep beneath the earth, in its outer core. They set up a magnetic field as the Earth rotates but it fluxes – becomes weaker and stronger – and moves as the molten iron itself moves. It's not the same as Polar North or True North." He was aware of a great deal of over-simplification at this point and paused, considering how best to continue.

"So, there are three norths?" asked Zadie, easing him into the task.

"Yes. Polar North is where the North Pole lies: it's fixed, unchanging." He nearly diverted onto the Earth wobbling on its axis but decided against that complication. "True North is the Pole Star: that's celestial, immovable." That was truer, but not entirely so. "Magnetic North is where a compass points to. It changes quite rapidly – a degree every two years or so, first one way and then the other – and that is what is called the magnetic declination. Sometimes it flips," he ended.

"What do you mean, flips?"

"North becomes South, and South becomes North."

"Sorry. Try that again. I was just getting used to the idea of three Norths, and I appear to have lost one of them."

"The polarity reverses – "

"That's saying the same thing in words dressed up to obscure it," retorted Zadie.

She was sharp with her thought, and Nathan cast a glance at her in acknowledgement as he continued, "Some movement of the masses of molten iron, coupled with the Earth's own movement, causes North to become South and vice versa. In simple terms, a compass would point in the opposite direction. We don't know precisely what the causes are, as we have not lived through them. It only occurs every hundred thousand years or so."

"So how do we know anything about it?"

"Well, that's a very interesting question," he answered, and she chuckled at an image of a student who had successfully diverted him onto a pet topic. "It is all to do with the Mid-Atlantic Ridge and the rocks that have formed there over the recent past. The ridge splits the Atlantic down the middle – hence its name – and it's an active volcanic area. There are great fissures and fractures that allow molten rock to well up from the Earth's Mantle – the bit below the solid crust – and spill out onto the sea-bed, forming new rock. The rock is basalt, rich in iron, and as it cools tiny fragments within it orient themsleves like trillions of compasses pointing to the magnetic pole. In the rocks that cooled and formed when the magnetic pole is as it is today they point north; in the rocks that cooled and formed when the magnetic pole had flipped they point south."

"And you can measure the way these tiny compasses point?"

"Sort of … they create anomalies which can be measured and plotted … and if you plot them on a map of the Atlantic, you get a remarkable pattern."

"What sort of pattern?"

"Imagine a piece of paper with blotches of ink or paint on it – you probably did this as a child – fold it over, press it down, and open it up again, and you have a perfectly symmetrical pattern – butterflies' wings, or whatever. That is what it looks like either side of the Mid-Atlantic Ridge: the youngest rocks, nearest it, have cooled pointing north; the slightly older ones, further away, point south; the next group point north; and so it goes on, again and again."

It was a measure of his enthusiasm that she could almost see the image being projected onto a board and she asked, "So when did the last flip occur; can you date it?"

"Possibly as little as ten thousand years ago – although we don't know if it was a sudden flip … or a slow one."

"And we are probably five thousand years ago?" she mused, thinking that the ice beneath her feet was becoming slightly less steep.

"Exactly."

"Which, coming back to the point, means that you are not certain that your compass is working properly. You don't know where north is … and we are about to go on an ice-sheet with no other means of navigation."

It was a slightly abrupt twist to a conversation that Nathan had been enjoying. It was not an entirely valid conclusion and he rebutted it in part, "It's not that I don't know where North is; it's just that it may not be the same North as on your map. That is why my bearings were out."

Perhaps it was as well that the slope was definitely levelling out and their attention was drawn to what lay ahead. Eight hundred metres of solid ice they had climbed, and now a great plateau of white eternity opened in front. This was a world of whiteness, locked in its monochrome as it had been for a hundred thousand years. Up above, some great battle in the air was taking place. This whole day, and that before, grey cloud had blanketed the sky, obscuring sight of sun or stars, driven from the east by a wind – not strong but persistent in its advance – forcing the chilled atmosphere that flowed from the ice to yield. Somewhere, summer was amassing its regiments of warmth, but here eons of winter dwelt in permanent abode.

"What are we looking for?" asked Zadie, taking the binoculars Nathan had offered.

"Anything not white," came the reply as he broke a chocolate bar and put the other half beside her. "It will be small but fairly obvious, probably a cairn of black rocks, and probably not more than a mile. This is the only spot we could have come to, and there is no sign of anything here."

"There!" cried Zadie, almost immediately, pointing into the distance and giving him the glasses while she ate.

As a feature, it was entirely unremarkable, either when viewed from afar or from nearby – merely a small pile of rocks. However, in a landscape consisting of unrelieved white, it was remarkable enough. They found Soloma's marker stone immediately – a distinctive S and a short arrow pointing between two fainter lines – not much detail to go by. Zadie was circling the cairn carefully, looking for other signs, whilst Nathan was sitting on it scribbling numbers on the back of her map with a blunt pencil – probably the same pencil, with the same bluntness, that he had once used on its front.

"What are you doing?" she called across to him.

"Trying some calculations … I can't get them right in my head and I don't have enough information."

He looked up as she wandered over and leant a hand on his shoulder, peering at the figures. "What are you trying to do?" she asked sympathetically.

"Work out the right bearing to the next cairn. I was wrong earlier today, and I was wrong yesterday … and it nearly cost you your life in the sinking sand."

"Can I help?"

"Not unless you know pi to at least eight decimal places, and your sin, tan, cos tables by heart."

"You're working on geometry – in the middle of an ice-sheet!" she exclaimed in disbelief.

"Yes," he answered, and put the pencil down before explaining. "Soloma's map was drawn to true north: the sun rose on it in the true east and set in the true west; your map was drawn by some unknown German in 1938 for some unknown purpose, probably connected to the use of submarines, and it used the magnetic north of that time. They don't match up. That is why I was out with my bearings."

"What are you trying to do?" she persisted.

"Work out my error. We were two hundred yards out when we missed Soloma's rock – the one that you climbed. What I don't know is the distance from the high rock where we found her map to the other one. If I did, I could use triangles, or radians and pi to correct my error. I can't even use time instead of distance because neither of us has a watch. Put it this way, if we miss a target by two hundred yards over a distance of one mile, say, how far will we miss the next cairn by if it is a third of a day's travel from here – let's say four hours if we count a day as being the hours of light?"

She could begin to see his drift and offered a response: "Four hours at slow walking with packs might be twelve miles; twelve miles with an error of two hundred yards per mile would put us something like a mile and a half out."

"Exactly – and with no hope of finding any cairn in this wilderness … and no time to backtrack here – lost on the ice … very cold ice."

"So what are you going to do?"

"Subtract 5° from 287°."

"Why?"

"Gut feel."

Zadie could not imagine anyone more unlikely to go by some gut instinct than Nathan and objected, "What about your calculations? What do they tell you?"

"I can't complete them. I don't have the data. Look: if you don't like 'gut feel', call it an estimate, or a guesstimate, or extrapolation, if that makes you happier. All I can say is that we have consistently missed to the right of Soloma's intended target and that I think an error of two hundred yards over one mile equates to about 5° off course. Therefore, I've corrected it to the left. Anyway, we can't stay here," he ended; "we have two times a third of a day's travel left, according to Soloma's map, and my stomach-clock tells me half this day has gone already."

The idea of an estimate was somehow more reassuring – it was strange how a different word for the same thing could change its impact – and Zadie had a clear picture of Soloma's map in her mind. Five cairns had figured on it: this was the first; the last two she knew; the middle one was the one that had an image of the sun alongside with two lines drawn through it. That would be the night stop; Elana had said that the northern route took two days. There had been other marks on the map, too. What was troubling Zadie now was the thought of walking on a bearing. Nathan had sensed it as well. She'd had experience of this before – bad experience.

"I suppose," she said slowly, "that you want me to walk ahead while you keep me on a bearing of 282°?"

Nathan rose and hugged her gently, before saying, "Please – but it won't be as bad as last time: there will be no fog with this cloud and breeze; and there are things I want to talk about – tell you about; the wind will carry my voice to you and you will be able to call back – and you will be able to see, even if it is all white."

Carefully, he lined her up a good distance ahead and set her off, holding the compass in his palm and calling occasionally 'left a bit' or 'right' as they marched over the smooth surface of the great ice-sheet, leaving the vestigial view of land behind its eastern precipice. And he began to tell of many things, things they had not had time to talk about: of Lucinda and the meaning she had given to 'Polgodoc'; of Goldilocks and his strange knowledge; of Kerry and the solicitors; of Mabel's will; of Martyn and Wilf; and of Lucinda again and her memories. Her questions, called against the wind, had prompted further comment, sometimes revealing things of which he himself was only sketchily aware.

"I don't know," he was saying, "of all the strange things we've encountered, that was the strangest ..." when he became aware that her figure was higher than his, and he heard a cry as she stopped.

"Oh, no! Not again! I hate them!"

"What's wrong?" he asked, reaching the stationary form.

"Ice pressure ridges. What did you call them – 'sastrugi'? Up and down, up and down, and, all the time, blown snow in the troughs between them. I hate them!"

An apology in acknowledgement of the difficulty of navigating across these natural obstacles died in Nathan's throat, as he looked at his compass and checked it again. Instead he commented, "For once, they might be friend, not foe. I think you might just like them, this time."

"Why?" she demanded.

"Because this trough trends in exactly the right direction for us to follow. In fact, I think we could walk together along it. If I am not mistaken, these are why there were those two lines to either side of Soloma's arrow at the cairn."

Whether they were tears of relief, he didn't know but they walked steadily, walled in from the flat whiteness to either side by two white ridges, thrust up by pressure of the ice upon itself. Hemmed in by grey-white cloud above, only the colour of their attire broke the singularity of vision – and only their conversation, the solitude of sound. The walls went on – undeviating, unyielding – and checking the compass became more a cursory thing, until the ice ramparts lowered their defences and a vast breadth of whiteness spread to each horizon. Even above was whiter, tinged with a suffusion of the slightest colour from an orb that hinted at its presence. Zadie stopped mid-sentence in the story of her run-in with officialdom at the small, Greek airport and tugged at his hand, the small black speck growing in form before them.

"Cairn Two," she announced, quickly locating Soloma's mark. This time the arrow crossed two lines and bent to run between the second and a third. "Back into the ridges and along the second trough," she interpreted.

"Yes," he agreed; "two-seven-zero; that will do nicely. It's just a question of the light."

As he spoke the first weak shadow fell, the last covering of stratus yielding to a thinner veil of cirrus high above. For the first time in two days a golden circle heralded the position of the sun and a single shaft bounced brilliantly off distant ice. The interplay of light and white cheered them as they ate briefly, but its lowish angle spurred departure. Once in the trough and convinced of its direction, Nathan prompted Zadie into resuming the story of her flight from Greece, smiling slightly less than sympathetically at the impact of rough, red wine.

"It sounds like your friend, Fee, will have quite a shock when she opens your door," Nathan observed when she ended.

"Yes, although it's not really as bad as it looks – apart from the glass in the bedroom; and her present of the duty-free will calm her down. She'll probably sit and consume it in between tidying up. Anyway, I brought you a present as well," Zadie announced. "There was actually more than one but I only grabbed one in my hurry to leave."

Nathan was halfway through, "That's kind of you. You shouldn't have bothered ..." when Zadie picked up her rucksack again and thrust the object into his hands. "It's a rock," she added, rather unnecessarily.

For most people, receiving an inauspicious lump of pink, crumbly material of absolutely no value or beauty would have required a considerable act of false gratitude in response. However, for Nathan there was neither falseness nor a lack of gratitude as he turned it over in his palm while they walked. A low ray of sunlight illuminated its true colour for a moment.

"I don't have a specimen of this," he observed, nodding at it slowly. "Do you know what it is?"

"No. But I know where it's from – there was a whole layer of it above the layer that we were excavating."

"How thick was the layer?"

"Ten feet ... more in places."

"And what was the civilisation you were excavating?"

"Pre-Minoan ... how far pre, we don't know yet."

"That would fit."

"I thought you didn't know anything about ancient civilisations?"

"Mostly, no. That name, I know." He paused, turning the rock over again and holding it out to her. "What you are looking at is a chunk of destructiveness, the like of which has never been seen in mainland Europe since. Geology meeting man ... there's only ever been one winner." She looked at him as he stared towards the reddening sun that was beginning to set the western clouds on fire, until he asked, "Ever heard of Santorini?"

"Of course; it's an island in the eastern Mediterranean ... about two days' sail from where we were working," she replied.

"Well, that gives you your scale then. This is ignimbrite, and it is from Santorini."

"I didn't go to Santorini; I picked it up on the island," Zadie objected.

"You didn't have to go to Santorini. Santorini came to where you were. Santorini was a large volcano. It erupted explosively, spewing columns of ash tens of kilometres into the atmosphere, spreading it around the globe, blocking out sunlight, bringing winter whatever the season; it blew away 90% of its mountain in a single moment; it sent shock waves across the entire Mediterranean basin – some even say that it broke open The Straits of Gibraltar and water poured in from the Atlantic, tsunami after tsunami, hugely bigger than the one that hit Indonesia in 2004, engulfing every bit of coast – submerging, destroying, obliterating. If that wasn't enough, the columns of ash – millions and millions of tonnes of rock – kept collapsing, falling on the land around, rushing across it at a hundred miles an hour, burying everything within a hundred and fifty kilometres. It was a big enough eruption to create its own weather system – lightning, torrential rain – and the ash that fell was compacted and cemented together to form a rock – ignimbrite – and that small piece that you are holding in your hand is the tiniest fragment of an apocalyptic force that obliterated any trace of life within its reach.

"Listen: you've probably seen images of Mt. St. Helens erupting in 1981 or heard of Krakatoa in 1889. There's something called the VEI Scale – Volcano Explosivity Index. It's logarithmic, rather like the Richter Scale for earthquakes, and runs from VEI 1 to VEI 8. Mt. St. Helens was a baby – VEI 4; Krakatoa was an adult – VEI 5; Santorini was a collossus – VEI 6: it was bigger than anything in our recorded history – bigger than Pinatubo in 1991, bigger than Katmai in 1912, as big as Tambora in 1815. That was a volcano in Indonesia – it spread so much ash in the stratosphere that they nick-named the following year 'eighteen-hundred-and-froze-to-death' – snow in Calcutta in the summer, frosts hard enough to kill the crops in Europe and the USA. Byron even wrote poetry about it: 'I had a dream that was not a dream'. That wasn't the worst in Europe, though. Laki (1783) wiped out 95% of the

Icelandic population: fissures 27 kilometres long splitting open the earth, throwing curtains of lava five kilometres into the sky; rivers of liquid rock; aerosols of sulphur dioxide turning to sulphuric acid droplets in the air and killing animals and people in the most painful way – we've found it in growths and legions on the bones of skeletons from the few who had a decent burial. Before it was Hekla 3, spreading shards of volcanic glass and sulphuric acid from Iceland to Ireland, tipping ancient communities into extinction. But even it didn't rival Santorini for destructiveness."

The sun's orb lowered itself beneath the thin veil of far-flung cloud, blood-red, its circumference complete, stabbing the rays of dying day straight in their faces. The canopy of cloud above reflected them downwards in further waves of rolling fire and, from each side, the low ridges of ice ignited in their light, until the whole world around them seemed to burn.

"Nathan, what would a VEI 8 mean?" asked Zadie softly.

"The end of everything as we know it," he answered simply. "A computer society could not withstand that shock: no food at Tesco; no petrol at the garage; no satellites and mobile phones; no electricity. Maybe in 1800 there were the skills to survive ... maybe in 1900 some would. Not now, though; society has become too complex, too inter-linked, too unskilled in life."

"What about this society ... the age we are in here?"

"They would have a better chance than us ..."

Still the sun sank lower. Its rim touched the shield of ice and its body enlarged, distorting and squashing itself towards its rest. If it were possible, the redness grew – deepening to magenta, dulling in intensity, like blood congealing, ebbing back towards the disappearing day that had given life. The great circle of life was a third gone. Soon there was but a third remaining. And in its final demise, a single, black speck showed firm.

"How much light have we left to walk by?" asked Zadie.

"Enough for a mile, perhaps a little more."

"If that speck was the next cairn, how far do you think it is?"

"More than a mile, I suspect, but there is nothing to judge distance by, and it depends on how big it is. So long as this trough and these ridges continue straight, we can keep going for the moment," he said, grasping her hand.

"And if we don't reach the cairn?"

"I don't really want to think about the consequences. There's a survival bag in the bottom of my pack," he added, neglecting to mention that it was designed for one body.

"What about your head-torch?"

He shook his head sadly. "Not much use over more than fifteen yards ... no good for finding a cairn. Anyway, I don't want to waste time unpacking until we absolutely have to."

Light from beyond the horizon was lingering longer than expected, and some time later they had a sense that the ridges and trough were flattening out. It was only then that they stopped and Nathan consented to find the torch, giving it to Zadie and using the luminous compass point to guide her from behind. A few stars showed clear in the west and he was navigating as much by these as by the compass. For Zadie it was unpleasant work in front, with no sight of human company and the patch of light seeming to fall on the same unchanging surface. Soon it became a question of will to force the next step forward, and each time the will seemed weakened. For Nathan, he at least had Zadie's light to fasten on. More stars showed and his night-sight was less blinded by the light. Perhaps that was why he saw her first small stumble and called a halt. He turned off the torch, allowing the darkness to deepen, sitting close to her on his pack, feeding her with most of a bar of chocolate. Soon he would unpack the survival bag and stove. The night must bring what it would. Without any shelter, cold would seep from below – seep through clothes, through flesh, seep into bones, chilling to the marrow ... working its insidious way towards the heart. Warmth would evaporate from uncovered faces, minds retreating to numbed sleep from which awakening might not come – dawn's rays cast on two forms for ever silent, two bodies frozen into ice, enmeshed within its oblivion of time.

"I'm sorry," he murmured, "we must have missed the cairn."

"I'm sorry, too," she answered. "I wish I could phone for a taxi."

They laughed gently for a moment, looking up. And he laughed more loudly as a patch of cirrus showed. And she laughed, pointing at its glow.

"Moon! The moon is coming," they said together.

On that night its rising was as beautiful as the sun to them. Beams of reflected day struck ice, bathing its whiteness silver, except for one small patch of dark. Together they headed towards it until, at last, dark rocks separated within the shadowy form. Not so much a cairn, it was more of a shallow ring of stone, six feet in diameter at most, floored with pieces of flatter rock. Snow dusted their surface and a loose drift huddled in the lee of a wall barely two feet in height. At best three, perhaps four, bodies might lay beneath those walls, sheltered from the wind. Dark against one side, a thick fur was rolled.

"No taxi, but here's the hotel," announced Nathan; "shall I call for room service?" and he set about lighting the stove and pouring the last of the water into a tin. The second mug of sweet tea was even better than the first, and Zadie lay wrapped in the large fur, sipping it, head propped against her pack, watching the near-full moon edging clear of the final strands of cloud. Stars sparkled vividly further from its light and night air chilled rapidly as heat radiated back into space. Nathan warmed a tin of rehydrated food.

"What's for supper?" asked a voice.

That was better; that sounded more like an interested voice. He looked up, smiling unseen, and answered, "I don't know … didn't want to waste the torch; I couldn't read the label in the moonlight … felt like rice … with larger bits in it. Limited menu tonight, I'm afraid, but there's another pack from earlier that will do for breakfast; I'll keep it in my rucksack so it doesn't freeze overnight, and the rest of the tea can go in the flask." Whatever it was, it was food, and Nathan said, "Budge up," pulling a portion of the fur across him as they lay consuming the contents of the tin.

"There was a package and a stave rolled inside the fur," Zadie observed. "I've put them over there."

"Good: we'll have a look in the morning. I'm tired and it is going to be very cold tonight. Let's sleep while we can."

A few minutes later a soft voice persisted, "Nathan, that volcano you were talking about – when did it erupt?"

"About 1650 BC."

"Would it have caused tidal waves in the Atlantic?"

"It might have done; why?"

"Oh, I was just thinking."

Soon, she dozed and slept. Nathan slept too, but fitfully. Somewhere in his dreams was a vision of great walls of water striking a strange, bright land, lifting it, carrying it away.

Chapter 14   Elana

Dawn came – not as expected from the east but from the west. Bereft of cloud, crystal skies refracted the moon's light, its sinking disc tinged pink, bathing the western ice a sea of the same discolouration. Slowly it sank, coppery in its dying, until the first true light flooded over its departure.

"Not a cloud to see anywhere," said Nathan, stirring breakfast and handing tea to a stirring Zadie. "You missed a good dawn," he added, describing it to her as she stretched. "Just as well we are going west; this sun would be almost impossible to walk into with the glare off the ice."

"Did you check where it rose?" she asked, dredging some memory of his concern about navigation from a mind that was rapidly awaking with porridge and dried apricot.

"Better than that," came the response as he tended a second tin; "I took a sighting on the Pole Star during the night. The correction is 6°; I know where we are going now, and it is due west from here." He sniffed at the tin, eating some before passing it across and saying, "Here: try this."

"What is it?"

"Bangers and mash. Full English this morning. Well, full rehydrated English, anyway."

"Any chance of toast and marmalade?"

Laughing, he replied, "No, but you can have the last muesli bar."

"I'll settle on that. When are we leaving?"

"Soon … we don't seem to walk as fast as Elana's people."

"That's not surprising: we wasted time at the river yesterday; they are not carrying heavy packs; and they don't stop to cook a meal." Her eye caught the package that had been inside the fur and she continued, "I expect they just take a block of those honey-cakes, which is probably what this is – an emergency food dump for when they take this route."

Nathan was several sentences into a discourse on how water could be just as much of a problem as food, when he realised that he had lost Zadie's attention entirely and he looked up at her. Sitting on the low wall of stones, she was reading a small piece of blue paper, engrossed in its contents, oblivious to him. Only on the third 'What have you got there?' did he gain any attention. She handed it to him, and it was his turn to become engrossed as he read:

'Dear Nathan,

If you are reading this, I know you are on your way. Come due west. We are trapped. They have sealed the guardians against us. Only a child may pass, but you may be able to do so. The ice-gates have been opened. Soon they will return. The food and fur are for you. Eat as you walk. Make haste.

Yours in hope,

Elana.'

The writing was in a large hand, ill formed in places, and made with some improvised quill, perhaps cut from a woody plant, but there were touches of shape pointing to a copper-plate taught in infant schools in the 1920s and 1930s. Dull red on the faded, blue paper, it had run in places as it was written, and fragments of letters were missing where the congealed liquid had fallen away. A sobbing sound intruded on Nathan's ears. Tears were flowing uncontrollably down Zadie's face, and a breaking voice said weakly, "There's something on the back." Nathan turned the small sheet over. This was a different hand – stronger, much better formed, faded from black to sepia, its message only a few lines long, starting mid-sentence:

'and so, my darling Eleanor, I long to be with you and in your arms, to put mine around you and to feel yours around me. This war is nearly done. Soon I will be home – home to be with you, home to stay. Our wait is nearly over.

I love you with all of my existence,

B.'

"That dear, dear, old lady," sobbed Zadie, barely able to string the words together. "All these years she's kept that letter … kept it … kept it safe … taken it out to read it over … knowing that she could never return … remembering the person who could never find her … and, now –" she broke down completely at this point, flinging herself at Nathan and sobbing on his shoulder "– and, now … something so awful is happening … that she parts with her last treasure … to write a final, forlorn message …"

Nathan was struggling with his own emotions as he wrapped Zadie to himself, crumpling the paper, seeing through blurred eyes an image of a small, white-haired figure seated at the doorway of an improvised shack, bowed with care in the early morning sun, and recalling her last words: 'Farewell. Remember me to Cornwall'.

Slowly, the sobbing stopped and Nathan's eyes began to see again. They pushed apart, arms extended, hands resting on each other's shoulders, each searching the other's eyes.

"Tell me the message won't be forlorn," Zadie said.

"It won't be forlorn," came the slow response. "It will not be forlorn. We are going. Now."

*   *   *

There was no question of one walking ahead of the other. The mood that Zadie was in, if she had been in front she would have run off into the distance. Besides, they had much to talk about as they dissected each word on the crumpled piece of paper, passing it from one to the other, speculating endlessly. On one thing they agreed: somewhere, the Mortan were at the bottom of Elana's troubles. Fear drove and love pulled them at a much faster pace than the day before, and the sun was not yet at its full height when they were seated on the next black cairn, Nathan resplendent in his white fur, munching at the gift of honey-cakes, washing them down with the last luke-warm tea from the flask.

"Something has happened to those great, black lionesses, guarding the way in," Zadie was saying as their feet sped forward again. "Remember how we couldn't pass them until 'someone who had given birth' stroked their back and let us through?" Nathan grunted agreement. "This time they can't get out. Soloma and

Tarma and Simona went by without any problem. We had to wait until Meroa arrived. That's what it means by 'only a child may pass', I'm sure of it."

"Why did Elana think I might be able to pass? I couldn't do so before. We both had to wait."

"I don't know, but she would have had her reasons."

"And I don't like that bit about the ice-gates," he continued. "That sounds very nasty."

"I think she's more concerned about someone returning. Returning means they've come once already – "

"At least once," added Nathan.

"I agree. Maybe the Mortan came."

"Why? Why would they? It's too early in the year."

"They have power over the rocks. We've seen that before," countered Zadie.

"Yes: evil power – very evil power. We were lucky before. We have nothing to fight them with this time. You were lucky as well, at the Stones of Sacrifice."

Zadie shuddered at the memory and was about to continue the dissection when she cried, "Animal!"

"Where?"

"Coming straight towards us – fast … quite large!"

"Right. I can see it now! I'll use the ice-axe; you use the stave. Put the packs down. If you stand behind them, I'm less likely to hit you this time!"

The creature was bounding forward at a great pace, fairly upright in gait and gobbling up the distance fast. Suddenly, Zadie threw the stave aside and rushed in front of Nathan, crying out. It was a wild moment of embrace, the two forms locked in contact, rolling on the ground as Nathan ran forward to them trailing the axe from his wrist.

"Miss Zadie! Miss Zadie! Mister Nathan!" the creature cried, detaching itself from Zadie's grasp and flinging itself at Nathan. Black hair flew; dark eyes glistened with pleasure; and Soloma's face broke into a huge smile. "I waited so long for you. Every day I come. Tarma comes too. But today, Meroa sent her away with

Ruan …" and they both caught the anxious glimpse to the south before Zadie buried the little girl in her embrace again.

"Your English is very good," Nathan observed in genuine admiration as they broke apart.

"Mister Nathan, all winter Elana teach me and Tarma. No, that is not right … she teached Tarma and I," and they all laughed together, eventually settling on 'taught Tarma and me'. It took a while longer to persuade Soloma not to keep calling them Miss and Mister. Both the joy of meeting and the innocuous conversation carried them to the last cairn without noticing the passage of time. Sitting on its loosely piled rocks, the mood changed.

"We must go," announced Soloma.

This was Soloma moving back in charge, the momentary childhood evaporating, and Nathan asked quietly, "What has happened, Soloma? Tell us as we walk."

With much prompting and many false questions they gathered some of the sorry tale, while the cylindrical pall of mist grew in the west, blocking the sun's direct glare, curtains of rainbow droplets spiralling within its upward motion. Somehow it seemed different to Nathan though, both more transparent and more opaque. Ice sloped gently down. Soon it steepened and patches of rock appeared, until pink rock took over from ice. Descending through the veils of mist, they began to understand more fully and it was a changed sight that met their eyes.

A bowl of land opened before them, mists rising around its circumference where warm springs, heated deep within the rock, melted snows, maintaining this small pocket of life amidst the vast ice-sheet stretching to every side. In its centre a conical hill rose, contoured around by narrow fields, a straggle of huts on its south-facing slope. A few figures moved, Lowry-like in the distance. Three paths led downward, each with its black lioness guarding the way. Thus much was the same, but the clarity of light within the veil was dimmed by a haze of remnant wood smoke. Hazel trees raised their topmost branches above still water, their twigs unsprung with growth, their lower stems submerged; where the fish-ponds and washing pools had been only the mirror of water was visible.

"What has happened?" cried Zadie.

"Ice-gates have been opened," Soloma replied. "The water is rising. We cannot catch the fish – the pools are gone and they go too deep. Soon waters will cover the path to the hill. Soon they cover the first fields. We have only what is stored."

Long had they been looking forward to seeing Elana's land again. Now it lay marred before them. Grief and anger rose in equal proportion.

"Why? What has happened?" exclaimed Nathan.

"Mortan," was the single-word reply. "We denied the Mortan. They will come … Elana knows it."

"When?" burst out Zadie. "What will they do?"

"Soon," said Soloma calmly, picking her way down the steep track. "What they do, I do not know. It will not be good. Elana fears for us."

Massive and complete, black in its entirety, the figure of the lioness barred their way. Once before they had reached this point and they waited for Soloma to climb its back and place her hand in the cleft upon its neck. Instead, she cast it a passing touch, wistful if that were possible in one so young, and walked on by, turning beyond its swishing tail to watch – not with her normal interest but as if some thing of great moment hung upon their next move. Zadie followed her course, only to find herself arrested, unable to move forward further, firmly thrust back by an invisible barrier. Nathan leant against the great animal's jaws, running his fingers between its teeth, caressing the smoothness of its cheek, sliding his palm along the smooth flank of carved basalt until his hand reached hers. Together, they walked past the tail and stopped in front of Soloma's quietly nodding figure. There was a smile of satisfaction on her face, and she was speaking quietly to herself in her own language. All that Zadie could elicit was an enigmatic, 'Elana said'. After much prompting this was finally amplified into, 'Elana said … guardians would let Nathan pass'. They gave up at that point, looking across to the central hill where figures huddled, watching and pointing, drawing others from within the huts as they descended towards the stream at the bottom of the slope, crossing its shallow stepping stones and beginning their ascent. Soloma walked in front, weaving her way up past the huts, engaging in little conversation, aware of some figures retreating back inside and of others greeting her. Zadie and Nathan walked behind, feeling like exhibits in a small world that was closing in – a world that was uncertain, disturbed, questioning.

The path levelled out before rising a final step. A circular pool, fringed with rock growths in pastel shades, lay on their left. In its centre a mound of living coral grew – sharp, white – descending and spreading beneath the water, but no offering of petals lodged in its embayments. Soloma hastened their steps, leading them to the hut beyond, skins hanging across its doorway and a legacy of smoke clouding the dim atmosphere within. Wrapped in its wreaths of slow circulation, some stabbed blue by chinks of late-afternoon light from between layered walls of hewn wood, a figure sat. White hair fell beyond the drooped shoulders, a chain of copper ornaments hung loosely, and a hand rested to one side on a small, pink, rock-slab table. Slowly the figure rose and spoke.

"I bid you such welcome as it remains to give. Soloma has watched often for you. She was determined that you would come. Now you have; and there is little time."

Nathan's half-prepared words in the language of this place died in their assembling as Zadie burst out, "Elana, what has happened? What has happened to your land and people?"

"To my land, you have seen. The ice-gates are open; the water is rising. The wash-pools and fishponds are lost to us. The coppiced wood and hazel grove are gone. Soon the first fields will flood. We have only a little of last year's grain and wood. It is insufficient for the mouths."

"Has this happened before? Why has it happened?" demanded Zadie

"There are no simple answers," responded a voice, resigned and saddened in its reflective ancientness. "Waters have risen and fallen before, but not by this much. Only legend speaks of such a rise. Maybe it is myth. I do not know. But these people have a strong oral history … memories passed from grandmother to grandchild … stories recited in the sheltering from the long winter darkness. One such story there is. It tells of other lands like mine – further to the west. We have not found them, although we have wandered as far as the world now ends. Perhaps they lie beyond. Perhaps the story is true. Most usually there is a seed of truth in what the stories tell."

"What did this story tell?" asked Nathan gently.

"That there were other lands like mine – oases of warmth and habitation within the vast expanse of ice – but that they perished … drowned by rising waters. Some few persons escaped, moving ever onwards, seeking a safer place. It was not a story oft-told, for it spoke of vengeance reaching out … cold darkness obliterating life."

The figure lowered itself wearily, waving to them to be seated as Soloma ran to her side and she continued, "What has happened to my people is more difficult. I will tell you some, while we are waiting. In part I tell you because you must know, in part, because it concerns you, Nathan. It is a long story and there are many parts to it; but I will make it brief.

"When you bade farewell to Soloma at the turning of last year, you gave her a gift. It was a small thing, generously given I deem. She brought it here and laid it on this table where my hand now rests. There, it drew the attention of others. It was a thing of beauty. Its shape was known to us, although its metal was not. I should have realised and hidden it – as you had kept it hidden. To that extent the fault is mine, if there be fault in all of this.

"Winter's grasp came early. Even here, snow fell. There was little to do and some were drawn to this thing, discussing it. One experimented with ornaments of tin and copper. Soon, others were using their winter fuel, and the clear air burnt blue, until they fused the two, producing a metal like yours. It was harder, more shiny than anything they knew; it could be shaped and polished well. As winter dragged its course, they worked, creating ornaments to give to the men they had once loved. The men came for a choosing of wives earlier than ever I recall. Maybe the paths to the south were freer of snow than those of which Soloma tells. Maybe something else drove them. Their losses had been bad and they sought boys too, for mining or for war. No boys would go; nor were there sufficient girls of age. There was argument. It was placated only by the giving of gifts. Amongst those gifts were ornaments, smelted of tin and copper, gleaming and hard.

"But a few weeks passed and one Mortan came, demanding the secret of this metal to make weapons and seeking two girls for sacrifice. We shut the guardians against him, barring entry; and none were willing to yield a daughter. Thus he was denied. But we found that he too had power. The rocks were sealed against us – only a child might pass. We were trapped in this little land of ours. We thought the Mortan might have set the rocks so that a man might pass but we have no men with us, as you know. The village was muttering – anxious about what had been done and fearful of the Mortans' wrath. We called a meeting of the oldest of each family."

Elana paused, sighing deeply, as if recalling some profound pain buried from immediate consciousness. As she made to continue, voices broke out on the path below. An arrow of gold from the sinking sun caught Soloma's hair as she flitted from Elana's side towards the door. The voices continued, abating in the end as Soloma reappeared, followed by a figure whose face spilled its delight in greeting. Warmth was genuine as Tarma clasped Zadie, and Nathan, and for once Elana's face seemed less lined with care. All too soon the moments were gone and Tarma knelt beside the old lady, engaged in urgent and rapid conversation, the speed and quietness of which were beyond Nathan's comprehension of the tongue.

"So it must be tonight," said Elana, reverting to her English of decades past. "Nathan, I have something to ask of you – and Zadie, too. It is not a thing of ease. Nor is it lightly that I ask. Consider well before you reply: in this place, as perhaps it was once in the world that you and I have known, a word given is an action to be performed." Holding him with that rare clarity of gaze of eyes that have seen much, maybe too much, she continued, "Do you wish me to ask?"

Eyes were fixed upon him; he could feel Zadie's boring into his back. If she were the sort of person to carry a handbag, he sensed it would now be extended to its greatest extreme, waiting to accelerate toward his face. Soloma's eyes were dark, unblinking, hopelessness reflecting her aged and un-aged life. Tarma's were wider – more uncertain, more remembering, more fearful.

"You may ask, Elana, if these two girls wish you to do so," he heard his own voice saying, as he gestured with open palms towards them, sensing that the handbag was no longer threatening.

"It is what they have asked me so to do. It is what I wish. It is our hope," and Elana paused again, regarding him. "I ask you to help my people – those who wish to go. They do not wish to go east to enter your time, nor do I think so many would be allowed; they will not go south to where men and Mortan are; the west is closed. Will you take them? Will you both take them?"

He could see the vicar in front of him – a thousand images in celluloid, a dozen in reality, rings on a cushion, a packed audience of unseen witnesses: 'Do you take this people ... in sickness and in health; for richer, for poorer; to love and to cherish; 'til death you do part?'

In unison their voices rang, "We will."

Eternity paused its rolling spheres. Elana lifted herself, wrapped on her right by Tarma and on her left by Soloma, hobbling towards the standing pair, reaching to kiss the outstretched hands.

"Thank you," she said, and bowed her whitened head. "Now go with Tarma. She will explain. You will stay there, this last night. Soloma must be with me. Soon others will come. I need her. This is my last task."

In silence they withdrew, turning for a moment to see a small, frail figure supported in the doorway by Soloma's young frame. A single, crumpled petal floated on the water of the coral pool as they followed Tarma down the path, stepping aside from the oncoming voices into a smaller hut.

"Meroa is gathering the elders to Elana," announced Tarma, confident in her use of English. "Ruan is with her but he will return soon. This is my home. Come in. We will light a fire. We cannot take the wood with us. We will cook. We have a little food."

"Where are we going?" asked Nathan, as the blaze grew and Zadie looked inquisitively around, prompting him to add two handfuls of rice to the small amount of coarse grain in the heating copper utensil. He laid his fur on the bamboo-like leaves in one corner and began a comprehensive unpacking of his rucksack as he awaited a reply. Ruan's stocky figure blocked the doorway, delaying his response to the question. He must be taller than his mother now, and his body and muscles were beginning to fill out, thought Zadie, watching the face hardening slightly, protective of an environment in which he had been the only male, and relaxing only after his twin's lengthy greeting.

Dried fruit had been shared, and the meal was bubbling fully before Tarma began her explanation. North was their heading. Long ago, Meroa's mother and Elana had been far distant on the ice, lost in unexpected cloud, when they encountered a man in the last stages of exhaustion. His lips and face were puffed and blackened by wind and glare, swollen to the extent that he could not swallow the little water they had to offer. His garb had been strange, and that night, on some unmarked flatness of ice, he had surrendered his life to the cold. His language had been only partially understood, but he had told of a land to the north before he had died. Three days it had been before they themselves returned, hardly alive. Some had doubted their tale. Others spoke with pity of the elements. A few believed their words and into the long winter nights entered an odyssey to a land unfettered, unsettled, free.

"And we are going there on the basis on that story?" asked Zadie, more searching for denial than for confirmation.

"Before she died, my grandmother told my mother. My mother told me. Elana was there," said Tarma simply. "We will go."

Zadie felt strangely diminished by Tarma's certainty. She wanted to cry, 'Wait! What if?' All the university training of argument and counter-argument, of cerebral consideration, cried out for inactivity, for delay and weighing words, weighting and waiting until their meaning was apparent. Another language cut across the upheavals of her thoughts as Nathan uttered words she did not understand. The unasked questions died on her lips as he grasped her hand and answered softly, "I said we would go with them."

Chapter 15   North

Early next morning a reasonably sharp elbow dug into Nathan's ribs. At least, he assumed it was morning. It was still dark and he had been enjoying planting peas and runner beans between the lines of broad beans that were already reaching skyward in the garden at Trevennick. Somewhere in the dream had been a golden tail of a retriever and a fluttering of chicken wings. A tap had gurgled rusty water, and cows were munching beyond the dry-stone wall upon which the first carrot-like leaves of Californian poppies were exploring the Cornish air. Suddenly he was awake and focusing on two heads – four eyes – looking down on him. Slowly, they separated and both said, "Come," one in a familiar language, the other dragging and dredging him into a different existence.

"Come where?" he replied.

"To Elana," they both answered, confusing him in their different languages.

He recognised Meroa, the eyes smiling slightly in the flickering firelight at the use of her elbow to wake him. Tarma stood out of direct sight. Both guided his steps up the path to where Ruan lifted the skin curtain and a fur-clad Zadie greeted his entry to Elana's hut.

"I am glad you are awake," said the unseen voice. "My people have met. Seventeen there are who will be ready at first light. Others are too old or burdened in expectancy: they will slow you too much. Some prefer to wait and trust. Tarma says the Mortan will be here before this day is ended. You must hurry. Head north by the Pole Star. Meroa will go in my place, and Soloma also. And, Nathan, one more thing ..." she added it so quietly that he barely heard "... take care of the boys: they are our future."

*   *   *

A seldom used path climbed to the northern guardian – last

of the three. Stones slid and feet slipped on rock clothed with its own thread-bare blanket of lichen and moss, three figures ascending in the first of dawn's pre-glow, its light not yet enough to tell one colour from another. Others were there before them: huddled shapes of human form detaching themselves from the guardian against which they leant, furs lighter against its darkness, faces unseen, backs bowed by baskets, staves in hand. A murmur ran in greeting, pathetic as an infant's cry suppressed, hopeful as a bird calling after the fledglings that had left. A shadow stepped forward becoming Soloma, greeting and guiding his hand towards the great, lithe figure of the carved, black lioness. His fingers touched its haunches, caressing their smoothed blackness, and it seemed almost as if there was some inner life pulsing and vibrating in response beneath the veneer of rock-skin. Murmur grew behind as those who had been held by the invisible barrier slipped through its grasp, following and leading on as Nathan stood with his hand in the animal's jaw, fingering its feel until Soloma beckoned and Zadie's arm propelled.

"It was almost as if it was alive," said Nathan sadly, "almost like the old dog saying farewell on that last morning ... knowing her time had come ... giving one last look before her closing eyes had sunk."

Zadie sensed the tears of his remembering flowing quietly as they clambered upwards through warm curtains of mist. Keeping his arm firmly locked in hers, she followed the straggle of humanity until the last veil was torn and dawn's true light blasted its vision upon them. The glassy sea of ice stretched infinite in front, pink wave-crests and golden coronets crowning its immensity in greeting to the day. Night's last stars faded in the firmament above as the sky sprang into celestial blue, cloudless in its entirety, opening to the great orb's passage across its field. Without talking they walked on, absorbing the day's splendour until the sun was halfway in its morning climb, and Meroa called a halt, gathering around a few frost-shattered stones. Ruan was sitting on them, his cousin by his side, and Soloma came across as others rested on their furs, baskets laid aside.

"This is as far as we know," she said. "There are no more cairns. Now you must lead."

Meroa joined their conversation as Tarma translated. North by the Pole Star was all that Elana had given. How far was unknown. How long would it take a man to be exhausted – so swollen and blackened of face that he could not drink? Water was going to be a problem. There would be no streams on the surface of the ice-sheet, not this far into it. Vaguely Nathan thought he heard an infant's cry and it distracted him. Zadie repeated her question. Soloma was giving an opinion too. Eventually he nodded, leaving her to explain.

The group was moving again now, more bunched than before, and Nathan was speaking to Zadie, "We'll bring up the rear … Soloma will tell Meroa to halt if we stop, and we can use hand signals. Ruan and his cousin will act as runners if necessary."

"Where's Tarma?"

"In the middle, keeping people together," he answered.

"What are you steering?" asked Zadie, looking at the compass held level in Nathan's hand as he gave signals to Tarma and Soloma, lining them up ahead.

"Five degrees east of the Pole Star, according to my sighting of the other night. We've done this before," he continued, dropping his hand and watching the whole group begin to move in response; "only this time it is a lot easier – good visibility, no fog, at least four people who know what they are doing, and enough distance between us and the front to maintain an accurate bearing."

"What if there is fog? That was horrid last time. Or those ice-pressure ridges …?"

"Yes, they would slow us up … but not impossibly … with this length of line we can keep going," he replied as they walked across the featureless expanse of ice. The few black rocks of the cairn had long since been absorbed into its white oblivion. "Fog would be the killer … we would have to stay put … and we haven't enough food or water to do that. However, it is not going to be foggy today."

"I'm glad to hear that. How can you be so sure?"

"Look at the sky – there's not a cloud in sight; feel the air – it's dry, crisp, but not bitter-cold. These people have their furs loosely open, not wrapped tight against it. Ice sheets create their own weather systems and this one has high pressure sitting over it – descending air, spreading downwards and outwards across it, taking cold to the surrounding areas. That's why it was dry and there was still powder snow around Gulland. It's not like the Cornwall we know with Atlantic depressions hurling their winds and wetness in from a relatively warm ocean. All that is blocked by the ice. There will be no Gulf Stream out to the west – no warm conveyor belt of the North Atlantic Drift to raise the temperature. After all, this latitude is the same as Labrador in Canada, and look at its climate – minus 20°C in winter, snow-covered half the year, patches of permafrost. To the east of us is the dry landmass of Europe, stretching into Asia … no moisture from that direction. Only if the winds go round to the south will there be warmth and moisture … that was what happened before. Mind you," he ended, "the morning is a different question. If the night is still, the air will be chilled by contact with the ice …"

Foregoing the morning's meterology of cloud, organised or otherwise, Zadie pursued another question. Nathan was in the process of answering, "They have nothing to cook with … and precious little food to eat. The stars are a better guide than my compass … if there is enough moon to see by, we will walk as long as we can. Anyway, you can ask the others soon. The sun is nearly at its zenith and I expect Meroa will call a halt … she seems to be dividing the day into quarters. It's a good job we are going north, though … any other direction and we would have a very difficult glare off the ice."

The zenith halt was brief when it came but not without intrigue. Zadie nudged Nathan as he drank sparingly from a mug, and they both watched with interest as each woman laid out a small square of some black skin and set to work with a flint, scraping thin, curled flakes of white ice onto it, rather like one might decorate an expensive dessert with fragments of fine chocolate, except that the colours were reversed. She nodded in admiration at the initiative, watching the dark surface absorb the sun's rays, melting the curls until each was able to gather a mouthful of water and repeat the process.

"Not much, but enough to tide them over," she said, eyeing the last fragment of honey-baked bar with regret as Nathan measured half the remaining water into a meal to rehydrate and snapped the lid securely in place.

"Yes," he agreed, "better than sucking ice. That does really nasty things to your insides even if it doesn't freeze the skin off your tongue." Vaguely she remembered as a child putting her whole tongue on a lolly straight from the freezer and the pain of trying to pull it away again.

Reassembling the human line took time, and without Tarma's bossing, it would have proved difficult. Eventually, they were under way and Zadie decided to test Nathan's powers of observation. Sometimes he could miss the most obvious of things.

"Nathan, have you noticed anything?"

"Other than the fact there are no taxis or hotels, you mean?"

She gave him a gentle punch and continued, "Have you noticed anything about the people?"

"This sounds like the beginning of 'I Spy' or 'Twenty Questions'. I spy something white; it's all around and there is rather a lot of it. Are you going to give me any clues?"

"It's about what Elana said and the number of her people ..."

"Go on."

"She said seventeen would go. Have you counted them?"

"No," and he began to do so. After a while, he responded, "Well, I've made it nineteen twice and eighteen once, but it is difficult with everyone moving."

"Yes, I counted at lunch," (the word brought incipient pangs of hunger), "and I made it nineteen. It is actually twenty-one."

"You mean including us?"

"No. Twenty-three with us. You see those two women nearest us?" He nodded. "They are barely older than Soloma and yet they are moving more slowly than the rest. Tarma is keeping an eye on them and drops back from time to time. And they keep their furs closed. Even at lunch, they did."

"Are you going to tell me?"

She debated whether to prolong the conversation before stating, "They are each nursing a child. I heard an infant cry gently once." Nathan stopped, amazed. "No. Don't stop!" Zadie commanded, "Soloma will take it as a sign to halt the line." Slowly he fell into step again, struggling for speech.

"You mean we are in the middle of an ice-sheet, heading towards an unknown location, with no certainty of reaching it, and we have two babes in arms with us?" he asked incredulously.

"Yes," came the quiet reply. "And Nathan, I want you to do something for me ..."

"What?" he managed, wondering which impossibility out of many was about to descend.

"When we stop tonight, make them each a hot, sweet drink." He spluttered at the inanity of life's turn. "They need more liquid than the rest of us and they are weakened. Will you do that? Not tea – that will trouble the babies. Will you? You can use the stove and have the rest of my water ration," she ended. He shook his head in disbelief and Zadie took his lack of words as affirmation, reaching across and mouthing, "Thank you."

"Oh, and Nathan –" he lifted an eyebrow "– I don't believe you have no idea where we are going. Why else would you be steering five degrees off Elana's course; and why else would you want to walk at night?"

"It is true I have an idea," he granted, "but I can't remember the maps. We will know by noon tomorrow. And anyway, there is another reason for going five degrees to the East."

"Nathan saying he can't remember a map is like The Plough saying it doesn't know where the Pole Star is," and they both laughed. "What's the other reason?"

"Just caution. Something has scared these people," he said slowly, "scared them enough to leave the only home they know, scared them enough to gamble everything. Elana was reciting an old story; Tarma recited it to you; others will know it amongst those left behind. By moon-down tonight we will have covered the best part of thirty miles. Five degrees over thirty miles is enough to put any pursuer out of sight – so long as I don't use the stove or torch in the dark," he finished ominously.

The stop at the sun's mid-descent had come and gone. Meroa had agreed to walk by night if the ice was flat. For some reason it had been Tarma who had been most forceful in support. Soloma had held her counsel. Now the sun was close to touching the far west, and they stopped again. This would be a longer halt as food was consumed and eyes waited for the inflamed orb to flood the ice surface with its parting gift of blood before adjusting to the lesser light of the moon, already riding high above. Zadie manipulated their stopping skilfully so that they were nearer the young mothers, who themselves were slightly apart from the others, and she beckoned to Tarma, falling into earnest conversation. Nathan set up the stove behind the rucksacks but went to find Soloma before lighting it. They were too small a group for there to be secrets, and it troubled him.

"Elana said that none were to come who might slow us down," she ended.

"They have not slowed us down today," countered Nathan.

"If you give them your food, you will be slower," she argued. "You do not have our skills."

"Elana trusted me. You will need children. We will not leave them. They cannot go back," he said firmly, looking at the eyes glittering in the reddening rays. "Let us ask Meroa," he continued as Tarma and her mother came across.

An animated, three-way conversation ensued – far too fast for Nathan to follow the words – until Meroa held up her hand and the two girls fell silent. Speaking slowly, Meroa waited until each girl alternately translated her words, each checking the other:

"They are with us now …

… to go back would be danger …

… to them and to us …"

"Elana told us …

… to let you guide."

"You must do …

… what you see …
      … is best."
"We must be one."

"Each of us needs the other," answered Nathan slowly, pausing for the two translations before turning to light the stove.

Whatever had happened, the line formed more easily in the moonlight and kept more closely together as they walked. After a while Soloma dropped back and Tarma guided by the star he had pointed out until they swapped again. An infant cried briefly, shushed in a gentle lullaby as the moon descended towards its rest. Long after it had gone, they lay huddled – fur insulating from the ice beneath, fur protecting from the chilled airs above. In his dreams, Nathan saw sheet-lightning flickering upon a cloud-bank in the furthest west and heard sea-birds against the Cornish cliffs. A post-van bumped down a track, two friendly faces turning to smile at him, and an organ played. A single red flower floated to its music.

Chapter 16   Of Nunataks and Nests

Super-cooled molecules of water vapour drifted in the cold grip of night, seeking a surface to condense upon. Dense air hugged the ice and they changed their form, adding a thin layer of frozen water, covering furs so they crinkled stiffly as sleeping forms awoke to dawn's diffusion of pink and gold. Some found microscopic particles of dust, lifted from a distant place, to implant themselves around and a misty fog hung thinly dispelling the day's warmth but not its light.

There was a reticence to move: limbs stiffened by the previous day's exertion objected to a new demand; only close by were two forms active, each hunched over, protecting their child as it fed. Elsewhere, eyes were awake, but warmth was being conserved beneath the furs, waiting for the sun's strength to grow. Nathan forced his legs to respond. It had been a long while since he had walked so far in one day with such a heavy pack; there would be pain this day, but less the next as muscles adapted to the old demands. It was cold – pervasive, not bitingly so as there was no wind – and he tucked the fur back over Zadie before the warmth could dissipate. She stirred slightly and eyes flickered as he shuffled to his rucksack, loosening the ice-axe and scraping at the surface. Flame from gas sounded loud in the stillness and more were awake, ears alerted to the chink of tin on stove, eyes watching as he poured and stirred, pouring again and repeating the process until two flasks were full. He reached for two large slabs, snapping pieces within the foil, and stepped to where the infant sounds escaped from their embrace. It took a while to persuade the two girls to eat and drink in full view of the others, and it wasn't much: warmed water with sugar dissolved and a chunk of chocolate – but they took a little and he made his way to Tarma and Soloma, giving the rest to them and pointing.

An improbable start to the day became more surreal as the girls circulated like two young ordinands offering communion to their flock, encouraging each to eat the strange food and instinctively measuring the mouthfuls of precious liquid that each could be allowed. Nathan watched as he stirred again, shutting off the flame and passing a lukewarm mug to Zadie.

"Sorry it's not tea," he said, smiling. "I couldn't waste gas bringing water to the boil."

"It's fine ... I'm grateful ... and so are they," she answered. "You'll have them eating out of your hand today."

"Not your best choice of idiom," Nathan laughed sadly; "I have barely enough food for us for three days, and the gas cylinder won't last long if I do that again. However, the real problem is water ... that and the cold. They know it as well," he added seriously.

"You are cold, too. Here: have your fur back; it's still warm from my lying on it, and I want to get up anyway."

Others were moving, and the movement seemed to stir the air so that a few glimpses of true sunlight penetrated. Here and there a figure was standing, absorbing its warmth. Elsewhere, small portions of food were being consumed and baskets made ready for travel. Meroa was creating some kind of order and sent a message that they would be ready soon. Visibility was not great but it was good enough to attempt a bearing.

The line began to move, walking from nothingness towards nothingness it seemed, a vast expanse of silent whiteness stretching in every direction, absorbing the sound of feet or voice in its infinity. Far above, the sun moved: no cloud; no wind; nothing but a lingering, cold mist fuzzying the boundary between ice-sheet and sky to the east. Morning was near half-run when Tarma's form appeared, walking alongside to bear a message that the ice was changing and they would stop soon. There was nothing obvious to Zadie or Nathan until some time later when they realised Soloma's figure appeared shorter at intermittent intervals.

"It's undulating," said Zadie, eventually – "very gently, but the ice is no longer flat."

Now that she had voiced the thought, they could see it more clearly. The wavelength of the change was too long to be perceptible to walking feet – at least, not to theirs – and the rises too low to be obvious, but it looked as if Soloma, furthest in front, was losing a little of her legs into a distant trough before they climbed out again, becoming fully visible. Neither Nathan nor Tarma possessed the subtlety of adjective in the other's language to pursue an accurate discussion of what it meant, although that did not prevent the attempt, aided by Zadie's imaginative use of sign language, and the conversation was still flowing strongly when Meroa called her half-zenith halt. Black skin squares and scraping flints appeared immediately, sucking at warmth to provide a mouthful of water. A few ate a morsel but most were concentrating on the surface or the sky, talking more than was their custom. Even Nathan had noticed the change in their behaviour.

"Do you think they are discussing the ice?" he asked Zadie as he sucked on a boiled sweet and offered her a choice of colours.

"Probably," she answered, thinking that the plethora of E-numbers on the packet seemed rather less important in the middle of an ice-sheet, "the ice is so much a part of their environment that even the slightest change must be like us coming across a sign saying 'Dual carriageway ahead' – "

"Or, 'expect delays'," he added gloomily.

"No. They seem quite positive. And there is something else they are talking about … Ruan was pointing a moment ago … and now he is lying on his back, talking to his cousin, Mawgan … Tarma is there, too; so is Meroa."

"Where's Soloma?"

"Coming towards us."

"That's good. She's not spoken much to us recently."

"You are getting in a sullen mood," observed Zadie. "She can hardly speak with us when you put her in front with Meroa to respond to your hand signals, can she? Anyway, she's nearly here, so you can ask her yourself."

As it happened, there was no need to phrase a question since an excited Soloma announced, "Ruan sees something."

"What?" replied Nathan and, "Where?" asked Zadie simultaneously, confusing the sounds of their words in the process and immediately reversing their questions, with the same effect.

"OK, you first," said Nathan to Zadie.

"Where?" she asked.

Soloma pointed to the sky. There was nothing – not a cloud, not a stirring of air – nothing either could see, and Nathan asked, "What?"

"Bird. High bird."

"Where?" they both burst out, looking very interested.

Again, she pointed. Zadie was quicker to Nathan's rucksack than he was and claimed possession of the binoculars as he waited impatiently. She was adopting a logical search pattern from low to high and left to right along the line of Soloma's raised arm. It was amazing how long it could take with binoculars to find an object that Soloma could obviously see with her naked eye.

"Got it!" cried Zadie eventually, as Nathan looked carefully at the angle she was making with the binoculars and the slow movement of them as she followed the bird's flight. It was clearly high above the horizon and must be circling, but he still could not see it.

"What does it look like?" he asked. "Any idea of size or height?"

"No. It's not much more than a speck in the binoculars and there's nothing to measure it against. These people must have incredibly good eyesight to see it."

"If they have seen the bird, the bird will have seen us – it will have a hundred times better sight. What is it doing? How is it flying? How do the wings compare to the body?"

"Have a look for yourself."

"No. You keep the binoculars on it. You have found it and it might take me a long while to do the same. Just tell me what you can."

"OK. Answer (a) is that it's flying in slow circles – very slow circles; answer (b) is that it's not flapping its wings, if that's what you are asking; and answer (c) is that each wing is longer than the body."

"Do the wings come to a point at the end?"

"Difficult to tell … no, they look more squared-off, or fairly much the same width throughout."

"They are straight, not kinked?"

"Yes."

"Any tail feathers visible?"

"Can't tell … possibly fan-shaped." Nathan fell quiet for a while until Zadie remarked, "Is that the end of your questions? Do you have your answer?"

"I have an answer – and a very interesting one."

"Good. Can I give the binoculars to Soloma now? My neck is beginning to ache."

"Of course," he answered, laughing for a moment and offering a second sweet as she rubbed the nape of her neck with the palm of her hand.

"So, are you going to tell me? After all, I've done the hard work. Your mood certainly seems to have changed for the better, anyway."

"It is not a question of mood … it is about processing the facts."

"If you want facts, why didn't you ask Soloma?"

"Because I don't think she will know. You can try her if you want. Think about it: there are no birds or animals in Elana's land; either there never were, or they killed them for food long ago. Soloma was unfamiliar with them when she was at the bungalow in Trevennick – look at what she did to my chicken and Mabel's geese … probably old Trevelyn's sheep as well." He paused, watching her nod in agreement and waiting to see if Soloma would offer any comment. "No," he continued; "it runs this way: they associate birds with something beyond the ice and they are thinking that we may be within reach of the edge of it."

"Birds live beyond ice," stated Soloma, having understood more of Nathan's conversation than he had imagined, as usual.

"There: see!" exclaimed Zadie.

"Hmm."

"What do you mean 'Hmm', and why did you question me so closely about the bird?"

"Let's try a chat with Meroa, and I'll tell you my thoughts – or some of them – as we wander over," he answered, taking back the binoculars from Soloma. "What you described to me sounds like a predator – and a big one. It could have been a buzzard – they are carrion eaters – but I don't think so ... there were others in the past throughout Wales and the West Country until medieval peasants and Victorian shooting parties killed them off ... big birds like bustards on Salisbury Plain ... and predators like red kites ... and eagles – golden eagles, even this far south. We've seen choughs, don't forget ..."

"Why are you so interested in predators?"

"Because they are at the top of a food chain ... and, if there is a large predator, there is food further down the chain ... and near enough for it to feed off ... and it needs fresh water."

"How near is near? How far would an eagle fly?"

"I don't know. The range is usually proportional to the height they fly at and the amount of food available. That one was high by the sound of it." And he greeted Meroa, trying a question in her own language, and several more in English via Tarma and Soloma.

Meroa summoned the eldest of the women and engaged in detailed conversation, whilst several others gathered to suggest or listen. Some twenty minutes later a certain amount had been established: the bird was not known to them; the bird meant there was an end to the ice within a day's march; and there were stories of birds as big as a small child that once inhabited the area beyond the ice that they knew until the men had killed them. There were also stories of the Mortan keeping birds chained and feeding them – on what she did not say. On balance though, the omen was good and the people were eager to begin walking. It was less easy going as the ice undulated more – not with any regular pattern and with the rises much shorter than the troughs. Occasionally, an arm was raised, pointing to the eagle circling almost invisibly above. A breeze filtered across their line of march and not long before the zenith halt, Ruan and Morgan stopped abreast a slightly higher rise, pointing east and north, others gathering around them as they arrived, waiting for the last. Nathan had barely joined them and nodded in interest when Meroa mistook the sign and the group was off – not following a bearing, nor in line, but little pockets of figures moving hurriedly in the direction in which the boys had pointed and where they were now leading, well in front. Tarma was with the young mothers. Only Soloma hung back a ridge away.

"Call them back!" cried Zadie. "We are scattering."

"Too late," he answered; "they won't hear – the breeze is against us – and they've got the bit between their teeth." Nevertheless, Zadie cupped her hands and called and waved as Nathan continued, "It would be too difficult to explain and, anyway, they are probably right ... we will have to go there. It is our turn to follow this time. Come on, Soloma is waiting for us."

The young face was upset and angry. "I am sorry, Mister Nathan," she said rather formally; "the people have run off. Elana would not like it. She told them to let you guide. I am sorry, Miss Zadie."

"It's alright," said Nathan consolingly as Zadie hugged her and he bent to kiss the dark hair. "They think it is land; they think it is the end of their journey; and they are very thirsty and very hungry. Still, at least I know where we are now," he went on reflectively – "not bad ... four miles out on a day and a half's march – maybe less ... it is difficult to tell the distance. It means the ice is quite thin too, perhaps only two or three hundred metres thick."

"Since you seem to know where we are, are you going to tell me – us – anything useful? It certainly looks like land to me," Zadie responded.

"The Inuit have a word for it – nunatak," he observed playfully as they walked freely, side by side, not needing to concentrate on compass or feet.

"Once we come across something archaeological, I'm going to throw so many obscure terms at you that you'll regret this," Zadie proclaimed, wondering if she could hit him without clobbering Soloma's head as she walked between them. "Now tell us what it's all about. It certainly looks like a dark mountain – well half dark and half lighter, glistening in the sun."

"You are not far wrong," he answered. "It is a mountain

of kinds. A nunatak is a mountain that is high enough to stick up through an ice-sheet – but it is also an island; it is isolated, surrounded by ice on all sides, not joined to other land."

"How do you know it's not joined to land? You can't see the far side."

"True. I may be wrong … but the timing and location are about right. You have seen this mountain before … on a very clear day from some of the high cliffs near where your grandmother lived …"

"I don't remember seeing anything like that …"

"It doesn't look like this in our time … it is only a dark splodge on the distant horizon … out to sea. It is a proper island …"

"I can't think of any islands west of Cornwall, apart from the Scilly Isles."

"Wrong direction … too far south … there is one further north … there is a bay named after it, near Port Quin – the village that lost nearly all its men when the fishing boats went out one night and never came back …"

Suddenly, she had it. "Lundy!" she cried. "You mean we have walked to the island of Lundy?"

"That's right. Half an hour and we'll be there. I've never been there but I've looked at it on maps. The geology is part granite, part metamorphic from memory – that will account for the two colours we can see – and its highest point is just under 150 metres above our sea-level. Assume a sea-bed depth of 80 metres and we can start telling quite a bit about the thickness of ice and therefore how close we are to the edge of it. I wasn't sure if it would be clear of ice. I am quite glad to see it actually: it's our halfway mark and the course is almost due north from here – Pole Star north," he ended.

Zadie was struggling with the idea of having walked to Lundy, even though her mind accepted that sea-levels were lower and the great Irish Sea ice-sheet had ground round the western coast of Wales and pushed within grasp of Cornwall. For a moment she missed his remark and it was something in her heart that shuddered and jarred her mind onto it.

"Wait a minute. You said 'halfway'. What do you mean?"

"Well, perhaps we are a bit over halfway. It depends."

"Why? Where are we going?" she demanded, forgetting to carry on walking until he turned and waited.

"South Wales ... Swansea Bay ... ideally, the Gower Peninsula, if I can hit it."

This time, she remained rooted firmly to the spot, looking at him in incredulity. "You mean we are walking from Cornwall to South Wales?"

"Yes," declared Nathan simply – "in as straight a line as I can manage. In fact, we have already walked at least half of it," he smiled.

They were nearing the 'nunatak' of Lundy before Zadie had come fully to terms with the concept. Even then she found question after question welling up. The discussion was lively as Nathan explained his reasoning. Prime amongst this was Elana's encounter with the dying man and the directions he had given, but also the people's desire not to encounter the society of men and Mortan. To the east the great meltwater channels of the Severn, Wye, Usk, and Avon would bar their passage; to the west was deep ice and deep water; but to the north the Brecon Beacons would shield an enclave of southern facing land that might be free and welcoming. Moreover, at the back of his mind he had an idea of the affinity between the peoples of Wales and Cornwall that had stretched back before history was properly written. He felt almost as if he stood at a beginning.

"Ice is changing," said Soloma, interrupting the exchange of thoughts. "You follow," she commanded, picking a winding route over the last few hundred yards to where a dark, rocky slope rose in moderate steepness. Her skill was good, and looking back from the first few feet of rock they could see the shallow bridges of winter snow that she had avoided – broken in places, opening into deep crevasses where moving ice had pulled away from solid rock. Water trickled and gurgled into them from snow patches further up the slope, warmed by the afternoon sun and offering their precious burden to groups scattered on the rock below. Ruan and Morgan were returning from the highest point, bearing twigs and dry pieces of last year's stunted growth, surprisingly many for a landscape so barren. There were no trees and little moss but they had found enough for several small fires to be nursed to life – grain mixing with water and stirring in utensils carefully removed from baskets.

Soloma settled by Zadie, caressing a flame and feeding it with consummate economy as Nathan stirred porridge and dried fruit in a tin above and set aside another packaged meal to rehydrate. She had already filled and refilled their flasks. Around them others had drunk deeply too and now divided themselves according to the number of fires. Tarma and the boys were with the young mothers, further down the slope; Meroa was higher up with an older group; two other groups had formed in favoured hollows; and each was basking in the sun's warmth, sheltered from an easterly wind, intent upon their cooking. Perhaps Ruan had told them this was only an island, only a stopping point, but they seemed content to take the provision of the moment.

They shared the porridge with Soloma, and Nathan broke half a bar of chocolate while they had water to wash it down. He was counting out packages of food and repacking emptied items when the idea came. Soon socks and spare clothing had been unpacked and he was counting again, carefully laying aside a pile of items.

"Don't tell me," commented Zadie, remembering a previous occasion, "you're looking for a dry pair of socks."

"No. Well, yes and no. I'm counting freezer bags – the ones I wrapped the socks and some of the food packages in."

"Isn't it frozen enough with this sea of ice all around?"

"That's just it," he replied, rather more excitedly than was his wont. "Water was our problem on the ice. If we hadn't found it here, it would have been a real problem. Now we have found it, suppose we could take enough for a day's journey for all of us?"

"How? We have two flasks and a couple of plastic food containers."

"Freezer bags," he answered triumphantly. "Fill them with water, knot them tight, keep them under the furs tonight – "

Three screams silenced words. One was young and female; the second was pitifully young; the third was a boy's voice. It had happened in an instant. The child had been put down by his mother's side only for a moment to bathe him as best she could. She had turned away just an arm's reach. Whether Mawgan had reacted in some last instinct to a sound, throwing himself forward, was unknown but one claw caught him across the back, the other scattering rock, missing the child it aimed to kill and lift in one smooth assault. For a fragment of time the image of enormous eagle wings beating to lift what one claw gripped hovered in front of them. A few feet it made. Body tore from claw – just too heavy for the bird to lift – and slid, tumbling, clattering with the rocks, holding itself in one last agonising look on the edge of the crevasse, until the final, crying fall.

Tarma was the first to react, diving, grabbing the infant as it slid with the moving rocks, thrusting him back into his mother's arms. Ruan was standing, throwing stones at the retreating eagle. Others were moving. Zadie was off down the slope – far too fast; she would have trouble stopping at the edge of the crevasse. Nathan was two steps after her and halted, turning back to the rucksack and the pile beside it. The coil of rope was over his shoulder, and the bowline was completed on the run as he joined the others peering over the edge. Barely six feet wide at the top, the crevasse rapidly became narrow, dark and nasty. Somewhere below, water emptied through it to the base of the ice-sheet.

"I'll go," Zadie stated, grabbing the bowline and slipping it under her arms. "Don't argue! You are too heavy. We'll never pull you up again. Besides, this is more like a pot-hole. This is my scene, not yours. Just get the rope organised and lower me the first few feet until I can brace across that gap."

The sky closed over Zadie, narrowing to a gash of blue. It was narrowing further with each downward move. There were faces looking down at her – not Nathan's – he would be back from the edge paying out the rope, keeping the tension. She dared not look at them … all she must do was concentrate on these irregular walls of ice. Her heartbeat was rising far too high, and she fought to control it, telling herself that this was a simple chimney … that she had done similar things a hundred times before. 'Keep the feet flat against the far wall … push the back against the other wall … keep the lower body horizontal and work down step by step.' That was fine for coarse, dry sandstone that gave grip … it was even alright for wet rock in a pothole … but this was ice – slippery, cold, vertical ice – and she felt her heart hammering again. 'Concentrate!' her mind screamed as the further wall bulged forward slightly. She could feel the whole of her spine pressed against the nearer wall … any narrower and the technique would not work. The bulge cut off more of the sky … there was only a little left to see now, like a bright blade, badly notched, hanging above. Noises came from the dimness below: rushing water and another noise. That was human … half cry, half moan … coming from beneath and to the right. She could glimpse a figure, crumpled across the narrowest part of the ice chasm, clinging with both hands to some stone that had long been embedded in the ice. She would have to work right and down. Carefully she tried, increasingly aware of a limit to the length of time Mawgan could maintain his grip and of the widening drop below him. If he slid any further, there was nothing to stop him falling all the way to the bottom to become a fragment of memory, a human boulder frozen into the ice-sheet base. The rope was snagging, pulling her back towards the line of her descent. Again, she tried. The rope twitched and jerked. Looking up with difficulty since her head was pressed against the ice, a small part of a figure was silhouetted in the sky's dagger … it was holding an arm out sideways … the rope was rubbing and jerking along the edge of the crevasse high above. Her heart jumped. Nathan had posted someone to give him hand signals … it must be Soloma … and she imagined her lying prone, body extended out over the crevasse as far as she could dare … peering down … someone holding her legs … probably Tarma who could relay instructions quickly in a language that Nathan could understand. They had worked out what she wanted, and the rope moved irregularly across the line of sky as she worked right. She stopped and saw the arm above tuck in and point down … they must be able to see the body … there was too much noise for a call to be heard. The rope slackened a fraction, and Zadie's feet were working down again. Suddenly Mawgan's arms and face were alongside. His eyes were wide, his breathing shallow, his hands still clinging to the one rock that protruded from the solid ice.

There were three ways of getting him back up. Of the three, climbing was now out of the question: the ice provided too little friction to work back up in the same way she had come down … and, anyway, she would be too exhausted … it was always much more tiring wriggling up a chimney inch by inch, even when it was good rock. Clasping him to her and having him hold around her neck whilst the rope was hauled up was what her mind had been assuming, but it was clear now that the combined weight would be too great and the rope would crush her ribs. There was another knot that was possible – one that created a kind of cradle to sit in. She had learnt it as part of her pot-holing qualification; but it was complex and would take time. Time was a commodity they did not have. It was only a few instants as the thoughts flitted through her mind, and the decision was made before a full realisation of the consequences could be addressed. It would depend on whether Nathan had told Soloma the rope signals, or whether he could feel them. At least she could brace herself more comfortably across the narrow gap where Mawgan lay, and use his stone to take some weight.

Zadie levered her body upwards to gain a little give in the rope, and tugged sharply, twice. The distant head above had turned. Something had registered. Should she repeat the signal? Repeated signals were dangerous … they led to confusion. 'Two tugs for slack; one for tighten', she ran over in her mind. Delay stretched, and she was reaching for the rope again as it slowly lost tension … it was folding down towards her … no longer supporting her … only her feet and back were bracing her against the drop into the abyss below. That was good … Nathan was paying the rope out very slowly … waiting for another signal to tell him how much slack she wanted. She let it come six feet or more and gave a single tug, watching Soloma's arm move distantly above and the rope cease its descent.

Mawgan was watching intently too, not trying to talk, waiting for instruction, breathing more regularly as she moved alongside him. There were many people who would have grabbed at the rope as soon as it came near enough, and she admired him for his discipline. Blood streaked the ice from his back ... the eagle's claws must have penetrated through fur. That would have to wait. Very carefully she slid the rope under her, lifting one leg through and placing her foot firmly back against the further wall before repeating the process with the other leg. Nothing held her now. The coil lay loose upon her, and it was only seconds to make a second, higher loop. Gently she touched his foot with hers and pointed to the lower loop. Eyes seemed to understand. Her hand touched his, and she passed him the higher loop, tugging strongly once. Soloma's arm was up. The rope was moving, tensing and dropping for a moment as Mawgan let go of the rock and his weight bit, hands clasped in the upper loop, one foot – now two feet – standing in the lower loop. Now he was rising ... the rope was moving upward, carrying him away from Zadie ... smoothly and rapidly ... far too fast for one man to be hauling it in. Nathan must have a line of people walking away with it, she thought, hooking an elbow around the stone ... it would be a bumpy ride. And, as the rope disappeared, the full realisation of what she had done hammered into her.

Twenty metres down a crevasse ... no safety rope ... no way of climbing out ... an unknown depth down into the darkness ... water rushing ... only this narrowed place between each wall of ice and a single long stone – barely two inches thick – holding against a plunging fall that would be out of sight or reach. The stone shifted, its slight movement intensified by her nerves. It had held Mawgan's weight all that time ... but hers was greater. It shifted again and she looked up. Arms reached to pull Mawgan's body over the edge. Soloma's face had disappeared. The serrated sliver of sky mocked in its unobtainability. There was nothing ... no-one to cling to ... an oblivion of cold ice eating into hope – enfolding, embracing, entombing. The stone shifted again. In a few seconds, it would give way.

A rope hurtled out of the light, falling unchecked. It must be sliding freely across Nathan's palms, burning with its speed. A face reappeared. The stone split with a crack and, for a sickening moment Zadie's body paused against gravity, splintered stone held in one hand, the other scrabbling for a grip – any grip. The knot struck her face, dislodging her. Falling, she lunged. A despairing grasp found a loop and she hung on, arm nearly jerked from its socket as the rope snapped taut, foot flailing desperately for the loop below. In the darkness, she found it. Both feet were in place … one arm was through the upper loop, rope twisted around her wrist … the other arm using the stone to stop the spin and push clear of the ice-tomb walls. She was rising … rising through the narrow gap … past the blood staining … sky expanding … light hurting her eyes … and she closed them, letting fear fall, as arms grasped and pulled, rolling her onto warm rock.

*   *   *

Rivers of blood flowed into Zadie's eyes.   Blotches of congealing scarlet streamed into view. Shafts of dying red stabbed at her. A strong arm gripped, raising her shoulders gently, head cushioned, and a distant voice intoned, "Drink this." Hot, sweet tea trickled down her throat, and she leant back, allowing herself to be fed like a child in sips, drawing comfort from the soothing words, easing her body back into being.

"That was a very brave thing you did," the voice was saying, "very brave. Meroa wants to thank you; they all want to thank you. They have nothing to give, except their gratitude, but I want to say this," and as she drained the last of the tea, she felt his lips on hers. Then they were embracing fully – sobbing, crying in relief, smiling, leaning together while the sun withdrew the bloodied day's farewell from ice and cloud.

"How long was I out of things?" Zadie asked softly.

"A couple of hours, maybe," Nathan answered. "The sun was below halfway to the horizon when we pulled you over the edge and now it's set."

"What about Mawgan? How is he?"

"Not too bad … he's over there, asleep," and he pointed to a figure with two women sitting by him. One had a child. "His fur took most of the impact from the claw … he was bleeding but I raided your first aid kit. They bathed him and I found some TCP … it stung and he didn't like it … Soloma didn't half give him an earful about complaining … even Meroa looked a bit taken aback," he ended, chuckling.

"Why am I thinking about freezer bags?" asked Zadie, suddenly.

"Possibly because that's the last thing we were talking about before the eagle attacked … or possibly because you're hungry."

"Of course; it's all coming back now. I wonder why it attacked?"

"Probably it was hungry … no fear of humans … nice little meal –" Zadie shuddered as an infant murmured – "or, maybe because we burnt its nest."

"Burnt its nest!"

"Yes – I can't see what else would have provided Ruan with dry twigs and pieces of wood the thickness of my finger in this environment; it's certainly not growing here."

"Will it attack again?"

"I don't think eagles are nocturnal … but we are sleeping together tonight – all of us – and Meroa has organised a watch. Now that's enough questions. How about some food? The last curry is rehydrated and waiting to heat, and I'll do you a flask of tea as well. Most of the others have eaten."

Zadie nodded and lay back, watching clouds spilling from the east – thin fingers of cirrus, curling at their ends, and broken patches of alto-cumulus playing hide and seek with a moon that was fully formed. Post-sunset light still radiated from beyond the north-west horizon and the twilight lingered – long enough for her to catch sight of an object sticking out from behind Nathan's rucksack.

"What's that?" she cried, pointing.

"It was in your hand when we pulled you over the top. You

wouldn't let go of it ... I thought it might be important and put it there for the morning," he added slightly hesitantly.

"Pass it here," commanded Zadie, taking the object from him, leaving him to stir and sniff at the curry before she announced, "It's a bone ... a human bone. Look: here is where it joined the knee." All through the meal the bone was a matter of contention as she speculated and informed: "Curry's good ... male, I think ... chicken bits aren't too chewy this time ... mature male ... date of bone uncertain ... dried apricots go well with it ... no evidence of disease or violence ... I'll lick the tin out if you haven't ... pity we haven't got the rest of the skeleton ... with my fingers, I mean. Anything for dessert?" she finished as Soloma settled beside them for the night. Nathan pushed the soaking oats out of range of moving limbs and offered them part of a chocolate bar. Slowly, conversation ceased and silence enveloped all, immense in its own eternity, complete in its perfection, original in its existence.

White clouds shone like fabric stretched in front of a photographer's lamp, and between their diffusion of reflected light stars roamed the dark pools, half a Plough hiding its pointers to the north. One fur-wrapped figure sat upright on a rock until it slipped quietly to disturb another and lay to its rest. Three figures slept side by side, a discarded bone marking their place. Far away, on a distant height, a feathered form buried her head against her mate. Further still, a tall figure stood writing at a desk, moonlight falling on long, white hair.

Chapter 17   Clouds of Portend

Cloud and the gentle persistence of an easterly wind had kept
the night warmer so that water was still trickling from snow-banks
when they awoke. Dawn had come subdued, spreading its silvery-
gold awhile and withdrawing into the ordinariness of a day unlit by
clear rays, shadows indistinct. Figures moved, drinking deeply and
eating briefly. Some turned to watch as Nathan warmed porridge
and brewed tea; others gathered around Meroa, packing their few
belongings, talking quietly, awaiting instruction. In turn, she was
waiting for three figures to finish talking amongst themselves.

Nathan had taken time to explain his intentions carefully as the
porridge tin had been thoroughly cleaned by finger. Now he was
reliant on Soloma to convey them accurately. She passed a freezer
bag to the nearest woman and watched as it was passed from hand
to hand, held up to the light, prodded and pulled, discussed and
murmured over – whether in awe of evil or anticipation of good,
Nathan could not tell. Soloma was taking her time and seemed
to be repeating the same sentence over and over, the only phrases
of which he could understand were 'high sun' and 'water'. There
was nodding amongst her audience. This seemed to have become
more accepted as a sign of agreement as they had travelled. That
looked encouraging. Zadie nudged him and whispered, "Now's
the real test," as Soloma took back the reverently passed bag – such
a common thing, yet entirely mystical – and stepped a few paces
to one side. Bending beside the noise that trickled, she turned,
lifting the bag. Immediately, voices broke the peace – some angry,
some confused, some amazed; some had pressed themselves to the
ground, refusing to look up; others were muttering 'Mortana'; a few
still stood or sat. Meroa's voice was harsher as she commanded,
and faces lifted.

Soloma walked towards one of those still standing and poured
the liquid into an upturned mouth, dribbling a few splashes by
accident onto the infant boy who stirred and gurgled. Mawgan

rose, taking the bag, tipping its contents into his mouth and spilling more down his front. A clamour arose. Soloma passed other bags to Tarma, and a crowd gathered by the rivulet – taking, holding, drinking, examining. A bag punctured and Meroa called in command again before fear or concern could take root. Novelty was mixed with awe – water held, unseeingly contained, yet visible. Zadie, at least, had some appreciation of the care with which the group agreed a division of the bags and lowered the knotted contents of precious water onto the top of laden baskets.

Amidst the activity a smiling Soloma was buried in hugs by Zadie. For a moment she broke off and stood looking at Nathan, who stepped forward and hugged her more solemnly, speaking quietly. Young eyes sparkled. Meroa and Tarma talked, while Ruan listened silently, and soon the whole party was moving down the rock, bidding goodbye to this strange island in the ice, picking its way across crevasses, turning with the sun's hidden warmth on its right faces.

"You know," said Nathan to Zadie, bringing up the rear, "these people see more in the surface of the snow or ice than the most experienced mountaineer. We've just crossed some very deep crevasses by a route I would never have picked and now, without the sun visible behind that blanket of alto-cumulus, they are heading as accurately north as any compass. They are amazing. If they had been with Scott, he would have been there and back to the South Pole before Amunsden had eaten the first dog! We think we know everything but they read signs we can't even see."

"I think you're growing a bit fond of them," observed Zadie, watching him closely.

"Maybe you are right," he responded eventually, stepping off the last ridge and seeing the vast expanse of flat whiteness stretching in front. "They don't reject you for what you appear to be like; they bide their time to make up their minds; they are very generous with the little they have; and they are very skilful."

"Would you stay with them?"

He made to reply and shut his mouth, realising slowly the enormities of the question, considering its ramifications. She respected his thought, wondering at the state of her own heart, until he replied, "It would depend on you." Now it was her turn to consider, walking quietly through a silent world, mind and emotion in turmoil. A figure dropped back beside them, and they both looked across, surprised to see Ruan.

After a few more paces, the figure turned and spoke slowly, searching for each word, "I ... speak ... some. Tarma ... teach me. Thank you. You lead ... to new ... land."

There was little emotion in the voice but there was plenty in Zadie's as she burst out, "Ruan, you will lead, too; you will look after the people; you will help them," and she made to embrace him as he stood stiffly. They faced each other and Nathan laid a hand on his shoulder, speaking words that Zadie did not understand – words searched for and as imprecise as Ruan's had been, clasping briefly before they walked on.

All through that early morning they talked, part in one language, part in another, until the half-zenith halt. Some drank sparingly, marvelling at water so contained, and some ate a mouthful; but most rested, content to nurse their strength, conscious of their lessening food, intent upon leaving the last honey-baked bars for the mid-day meal, mindful of the balance between food consumed and energy demanded. It was only at the zenith halt that all ate something and they rested longer. Nathan poured the tepid remnants of the morning tea into two mugs, handing one to Zadie and pointing at the rucksack.

"Try the side pocket – there's a small package," he said, watching her surprise as she unwrapped it, and two oval objects, glinting multi-coloured, fell into her hands. Picking up one and peeling the foil away, he mumbled, "Happy Easter."

Zadie had been no slower peeling and biting and her reply was delayed by a full mouth of chewy, chocolate, cream-filled, mini Easter egg. Eventually she managed something that sounded like a combination of, "Is it Easter today?" and, "Where did you get these from? I can't believe it."

He laughed, licking his fingers and washing the sticky sweetness away with the last mouthful of tea. "We had a few in the department and those two were still in my pocket when I packed at the bungalow. It seemed a shame to leave them. I didn't know I would be able to share them with you when I put them in ..."

"What about this?" asked Zadie, recovering her powers of diction and fingering an envelope that had been in the same package.

"I grabbed those from the shed ... it's usually my Easter task. I was going to give them to Elana but it was all so rushed ... and the water may have soaked through in the river."

"The envelope feels dry enough to me. What's in it?"

"Three packets of seeds: carrots, runner beans and peas ... I thought it might help her food supply," he ended lamely, sensing the incredulity of the moment.

"Should last a while," Zadie observed, looking at the picture of well-formed carrots and reading the back; "it says, sow before 2009 – that gives about 5,000 years! It does say something about avoiding hard frosts, though ... could be difficult just here."

He was still chuckling about Zadie's reply when Soloma came to stir them into walking again. Flat, white cloud was still spilling from the east, obscuring the sun – bright white above, white below, white extending in every direction, except in the furthest west where darker shades emerged. Bulbous, changing slowly, pushing upwards and outwards, shifting in colour and shape as the afternoon wore on, they caught Nathan's eye, and his mind worried at them, entranced by the attraction of something that was not entirely white and nagged by some thought that kept escaping.

"Apart from me," asked Zadie, walking on his left, "what do you keep looking at?"

"Clouds," came the reply.

"We've had clouds all day: boring, flat, white clouds – just thick enough to block the sun."

"They were a delicate gold at dawn," he argued defensively, "and, besides, they mean there won't be fog. Anyway," he continued after a half-offended pause, "it's not those I was looking at. Away in the far west they are different." For the first time she followed his gaze and acknowledged the point. Clouds peered in a line over the horizon like a giant pile of cauliflowers, squashed flat on top, with bad bits that were black and mouldy; light flickered on them. Suddenly, the thought was captured. "Cumulonimbus," he muttered; "we are seeing the top fraction of a whole range of clouds that start beyond the horizon ... and that is not the sun you can see glinting ... it is lightning ... the flashes are too distant for us to hear thunder."

"You mean they are storm clouds? Are they coming this way?" On the second time of asking she gained only a quiet, "How interesting," in response and it was not until the third attempt that she elicited a fuller reply.

"It's like this," he began: "those are vertical clouds – clouds formed from strong updraughts of air. There are down-draughts too ... that's what helps give the shape and create the lightning ... but essentially it's rapidly rising air ... what's more, it's moist air. Clouds are only the visible part of invisible processes ... which is just as well, really. This is very interesting: there are three things that could be going on and they all involve relatively warm, moist air ..." and he became lost in consideration of them.

Zadie coughed. "Excuse me, are you going to continue?"

"Oh, sorry ... yes ... I was thinking." She smiled whimsically. "Yes ... warm, moist air ... rising ... three possible reasons." And slowly he settled into an explanation as they walked over the unchanging ice. It could be a vigorous front with warm air being undercut by colder, denser air and forced aloft – that was unlikely, though, given the easterly wind and the flat clouds above. It could be a range of hills beyond the horizon forcing the air to rise as it flowed over them – that would be a possibility if the clouds were further north but not with them stretching right across the western horizon. He would have to be horribly wrong in his interpretation of the old land masses for that to be the case. Only one real possibility remained: that there was a warm, moist surface – air being warmed by it, sucked upwards, cooling, condensing, forming the great line of growing bulbous shapes with their distinctive flattened tops drawn almost like a ruler across their summits.

"Why are you so wrapped up in those clouds?" Zadie asked,

breaking into another period of contemplation.

"Because they are telling us something we can't see ... something I hadn't considered ... something very big ..."

"They may be telling you, but since you are not telling me, they aren't telling us," observed Zadie with impeccable logic, surprised at her own patience in trying to extract any meaningful information. On the other hand, with nothing to do but plod over the endless ice-sheet, she was warming to any continued subject of conversation. It was better than thinking about food – which her mind promptly did at the suggestion not to.

"I think," began Nathan slowly, that things are much further on in time than I imagined ... much closer to an end ..."

"What are you talking about?"

"I'm talking about warm water ... an ocean of relatively warm water; about the North Atlantic Drift; about this ice-sheet only extending thirty of forty miles west; about it being a last beached remnant of something that was once vast. I am talking about it being near its doom."

"All because of those clouds?"

"Yes. The more I think about it, the more it is the only logical explanation."

What constituted the doom of a chunk of ice perhaps a hundred miles long by sixty miles wide and maybe eight hundred metres thick provided a rich vein of conversation that continued after only the briefest of afternoon halts. Clear sky was opening between Zadie's 'boring flat clouds' and the 'cauliflower piles', and as the sun began to edge behind them, they became more impressive in stature and appearance. Lightning played more obviously within the clouds, whilst darkened bruises turned purple and flattened crests radiated gold from the light beyond. There was a majesty and splendour and power about the spectacle as the sun set and the moon emerged from its invisibility in the cloud-free sector of the sky above.

"About three hours' combination of twilight and moonlight that we can travel by," stated Nathan, spotting Soloma's figure hurrying back towards them.

"Ice is changing," she announced upon arrival. "Meroa wants you," and she took up the rear position as Zadie and Nathan hurried forward along the shortening line. Meroa was going more slowly, allowing them to catch up.

Zadie understood Meroa's hand signs as rapidly as Tarma translated for Nathan. A short while later it was clear even to the pair of them that the ice was becoming less level and sloping slightly. Soon it was definitely uneven. Suddenly the world changed. It was the most unprepossessing of objects: barely a foot across; grey both in the diminished light and in its own nature; slightly jagged on one edge; firmly embedded in the ice so that neither foot nor hand could move it. Yet each hand touched and tried and touched again, pointing excitedly, voices commenting, agreeing, disagreeing. The stored sum of experience exhausted, Tarma translated, "It is not known to us."

Nathan knelt, running his fingernails across the object – such a small, insignificant object, lacking in any beauty or intrinsic value, yet such an incomparable treasure; an object beyond worth. Faces looked on as he pronounced, "Limestone … grey limestone … Carboniferous, Z-series, Welsh." Tarma and Soloma looked at each other, seeking a word to translate. Zadie leant on his shoulder, asking quietly, "Is it a good sign?" His smile and nod brought immediate reaction from those around. Drifting sound raised all their eyes. Black against the moonlit cloud, blackening the moonlight itself, the V-shaped flock pursued their noisy skein, circling and lowering in the last vestiges of light, approaching some twilit runway to their roost.

"Geese!" cried Zadie.

"Geese and rock!" echoed Nathan. "We are near. A few miles more, that's all we need."

The whole party plunged down the steepening slope. It fell and rose, but fell more than rose; rocks strewed their way – most grey, some a darker, blotchy red, and some moved as they trod. One rock tumbled, keeping pace, dislodging others until a whole pack accelerated downwards, slowing as they rolled up the moonlit rise a few yards in front and disappeared from sound or view. Laughter floated after them as willing feet broached the rise, abruptly coming to a halt. One pair slipped, and only an alert arm prevented a body following the unseen cascade of boulders that splashed into the moon-shadowed surface of water below.

The ice-cliff was not high – perhaps fifty metres – but it was precipitous enough to spell disaster for any who slid over its edge. Ripples spread in the moonlight from the boulders that had sunk their existence beneath this lake. Carefully, faces peered down to where water abutted the ice and northwards over its now-placid surface, dimly aware of a further shore, illumined but in part.

"That was a bit too close for comfort," whispered Zadie. "This is impassable. These people are nearly exhausted. They weren't expecting another barrier. They have enough hope and strength left for one more try. Another night on the ice will finish us. We must do something," she implored.

Almost as she finished speaking, Meroa appeared at his side. This was the final choice: a choice without any certainty of fact – only a surety that the route forward was blocked; a choice with very limited time or moonlight available; a choice in the knowledge of bodies weakened and wearied, hopes so recently dashed. Left or right? West or East? It was a very simple choice. Somewhere the lake must narrow; somewhere the ice-cliff might yield a descent; and he became aware of every eye fixed upon him. Moonlight broke clear, bathing the scene, casting soft shadows from its low arc across the southern sky. Soon it would grasp the outstretched summits of cumulus, burying its lamp; only darkness and a scattering of cold stars, watching the cold ice with their long-dead rays, would remain. And still he hesitated. East was the more obvious choice: the ice should thin, its cliff lessening in height until some scrabbling descent to the lake was possible; but they had no means of crossing an unknown width of water. Grey chunks of rock stared back at him, inscrutable in their knowledge; grey chunks of rock scoured and carried by the ice, scoured and carried by slow centuries of flow; and, for just one moment, it seemed they spoke to him.

"West," he said, flinging out an arm.

They rose, unquestioning, pursuing as nearly as they could the edge of the ice cliff, its shadow stretching indistinctly to the north, embracing the cold waters waiting expectantly beneath. Even in the failing light, their skill over snow and ice was remarkable. Occasionally they deviated from the edge for no apparent reason, only to look back and see the dark gash of a drop avoided; several times they retreated part-way across a snow bridge deemed not able to bear their weight; and once they ended on a promontory of ice, a headland of frozen time plunging vertically on three sides. But slowly they made progress to the west, rocks increasing in frequency, their greyness scarcely distinguishable from irregularities in the ice as the wall broke into a series of tumbled, fractured falls vanishing into shadow as dark cloud gripped the moon.

Meroa looked at Nathan. He nodded, calling quietly to Soloma and lowering his pack. "You are the best climber," he whispered. "You lead with me. I am giving Zadie the head-torch. Ask Ruan to come last with her, and ask the others to use the rope." She spoke quietly, waiting for Meroa to repeat, while Zadie took the torch and fastened the rope around her waist.

Silent stars studded the darkness as they descended by feel and intuition, each following their neighbour's breathing, each threaded in hope by a hand upon an unseen line, each moving in quiet intensity, straining with sight, straining with ears, stepping with utmost care. A rock slid, scuttling and sploshing to their right, and an arm tugged heavily on the rope as a foot punctured the surface of the snow. Voices cried briefly. Nathan slipped, his weight dragging Soloma with him, his outstretched arm slamming into a solid surface at the same time as the rope bit around his waist. He could feel the others struggling to retain their footing behind. The rope went slack, anxious breath telling of the arrival of one after another until Zadie's head-torch loomed, dazzling in the darkness. Rock showed in its light – solid, creviced, grey. Without any word Soloma took the rope from Zadie, tying it lightly around her own waist, hands and feet speeding upward as if they had suction on the rock, disappearing into darkness. Rope slithered through the torch beam. For moments it stopped moving. A stone bounced down the cliff, quickly followed by another. The rope began to move again – not upwards but outwards – and almost as rapidly as she had disappeared, Soloma slid to a standstill. After the briefest of conversations, Soloma was climbing again. Singly they followed, each awaiting some unseen signal before beginning; each using the rope for balance and a guide – all except two who laboured in their climb. Tarma accompanied one and Mawgan the other, guiding tired limbs as infants clung beneath the furs. Zadie climbed with the torch, following Ruan's lead. Lastly, Nathan and Meroa remained. Lightly, she touched his arm and pushed him forward, working by starlight, following the rope, feeling for each hold, ascending from darkness toward faint light, from silence toward quiet voices. Soloma's figure greeted them, loosening the rope from where she had tied it around a rock and pointing to where others were gathered in the pool of Zadie's torch. Together they stood, edging across a flat surface, stepping a few hundred yards, working their way across a narrow isthmus, darkness dropping to either side, following the sweeping play of the torch, gaining gradually in height, walking until a single, higher rock, sheltering a hollow to its east, offered a stopping point.

Water trickled and Zadie leant forward, torch on head, as cupped hands were raised to mouths, each drinking briefly before yielding to another. Tarma and Ruan appeared, filling freezer bags, and soon others imitated. Finally, Meroa came, Soloma by her side. It was a short speech, but one of genuine gratitude and, as they turned away, flame burst into the night.

Shortly, a voice said, "Tea?" and two flasks circulated – hot, sweet contents pouring warmth and strength. "Here's yours," said the voice again, settling by his side and casting her fur across them both. Soon he was snoring, while in the distant west a dull thunder rolled. Above, a few stars looked on, wondering, and sounds of roosting birds floated on the air.

Chapter 18   Rhossili

By the time Nathan was awake most of the furs had disappeared.

"Welcome to the world – to a new world," said a familiar voice, proffering him a cup of tea. "Don't worry," it went on, spotting his anxiety; "we haven't used your gas. They've found wood. Soloma brewed you this. Most of them are away hunting. It's very funny. Come and see. I have your binoculars. It's only a short walk. We were to follow once you were awake."

"Who is we?" questioned Nathan, accepting the over-sweetened tea gratefully.

"You and I, the two girls with children, and Tarma," answered Zadie, pointing across to the trio (or fivesome) basking in the early light. "But we don't all need to move yet." And she dragged him to where grey rock fell away in a ragged cliff.

Lying there, a whole landscape opened before them, shafts of low-angled sunlight breaking through dappled cloud to play upon the vista. Curving south and east, ice gleamed, its last wall etched clear against the sky above and lake below. A low island of ice, populated with black specks, floated on the wedge of water that widenened to the east. Occasionally a few specks launched into ungainly flight and plunged vertically into the water, emerging against all probability of gravity, shaking their necks, swallowing, shedding wetness, resuming their station. A little north, waterfowl hugged the shore, bending to seek for food. Further north, grey cliffs rose, indented into hidden bays, and above them valleys and moors. Vegetation clung in tinges of spring growth: moss, heather, stunted trees and scattered clumps of hazel, willow, alder and oak. Amongst them a herd of deer grazed, and above two pairs of birds wheeled high. Further still, hills rose, meeting the sky in a glistening whiteness of snow and stubby glaciers.

A few hundred yards below a chain of figures was working through the shallow water, six in one direction, seven in the other, three along the shore. Ducks and geese paddled reluctantly in front of them until there was a sudden explosion of wings and flapping feet stepping on water, rising aloft like some Barnes-Wallis bomb returning to its cradle. A figure dived forward, emerging clutching a foot, wings flapping around the dark head, other figures converging, smothering the wings, avoiding the darting beak.

"I think we know exactly who that was," said Nathan, watching Zadie lower the glasses, "and what's going to happen next. There are another two fishing on that rock," he added. "This is a good land for them: fish, birds, deer, wood and water; they will do well here. There's shelter too – and it faces south."

They joined the hunting party for a two-goose brunch with fish (six), duck (two), and eggs (unspecified) in a valley of scrubby trees leading up from the wide lakeshore. Soloma had nearly dried in the weak sunshine, and Meroa was organising three groups to explore the surrounding area; she and Mawgan would stay with the young mothers while the others were away. Tarma relinquished her care, sitting beside Zadie as Nathan watched Soloma burying the evidence of fire in her usual efficient way.

"Come on," he said, "I want to climb Rhossili."

"What? Where?" exclaimed Zadie.

"Rhossili Down … that red hill behind us," Nathan stated.

"You mean you know where we are?"

"Yes. OS Map 159, Grid Ref 420888 (approx), Gower Peninsula, South Wales; latitude approx 51° 34' W, longitude approx 4° 17' W."

"You remember grid references and map numbers!"

"Yes, sometimes. In this case I had a cream tea at a hotel about a mile from here on a day when the wind was howling in from the west, driving sand and spray and everything else before it; and I had a holiday a few miles east in Oxwich Bay. There were marshes there with curlews and bitterns and a wonderful collection of shells on the beach walking to Three Cliffs Bay; inland there were castles dating from the Norman conquest, kilns from early smelting, and evidence of Iron Age settlements. Come on. Let's go up that hill. For once, I can tell you what the landscape will be like, rather than what it was like."

The foursome ascended gradually whilst he pointed out the landscape below, grey limestone contrasting markedly with old red sandstone and millstone grits. Each differed in resistance and permeability, and therefore in their resulting landforms and the amount of surface water. Each had, and would have, its own story to tell.

"One day," he said, pointing to the southern foot of the hill where grey joined red, " there will be a village with a church there, and all this land to the west will be sea. A great storm will blow so much sand up onto it that it will be abandoned and only the stone foundations will remain. Away to the north will be dunes and marshes – the Llandrhidian marshes – with a ruined castle overlooking them. Down there," he turned, looking east, "will be burial mounds and barrows at Cefn Bryn, perhaps not too long in the future, and kilns for smelting ore. Further away is a coalfield that will bring wealth and links to tin and copper ore from Cornwall. There will be mills for grain and manors and farms and fields; there will be a port that gives to and sucks from an empire covering half this globe; there will be people – large numbers of people; there will be conflicts and strikes; there will be wars and bombings; there will be cars and roads and second homes; there will be poverty and greed and unemployment and – "

"Nathan, that's the future, that's a future," interrupted Zadie; "we're here and we're now." And she stared at him.

He stopped and stared back, abashed at his loquaciousness.

"What you see is a future. It doesn't have to be the future. It doesn't have to be these people's future. It's our problem if ever we get back to our time ..."

Still staring, he murmured, "I'm sorry ... I was a bit carried away ..."

"Nathan, do you want to go back?" she asked slowly.

"I don't know," he answered uncertainly. "There is something about these people ... there is a value on each life ... there is a care ... there is a willingness to help ... I'm not sure I see that in our society."

"Your vision is jaundiced," she commented carefully. "If it hadn't been for your intervention," she continued generously, "there would have been two young mothers with infants dead on the ice somewhere between Lundy and Elana's land. There are bad things in this world as well as good, just as there are good things in our world as well as bad. We can only take the next step, the best step, the better step."

His eyes misted, clearing slowly as Tarma and Soloma stood by, sensing his uncertainty of mood, not comprehending the words. He reached forward, finding Zadie's hand had moved more rapidly towards his than his towards hers, and they stepped on up the slope. The girls swung behind, exchanging low comments in their own language. Far below, two parties were trekking back across the land. One carried wood, the other had fanned out, seeking unsuccessfully to corner a deer. Unseen above, an eagle soared.

Upon the summit a different rock stood, neither grey nor red, rectangular if it was any shape. Nathan and Zadie leant against it, looking south and east. Soloma climbed, standing on top at the level of their shoulders and rotating, delighting in the view. Tarma was forced to circumnavigate its base but it was her cry that brought them all to the western face. Had the sun not been well past its zenith, the markings might not have shown since lichen covered them in part. Soloma rubbed with handfuls of weathered ground and Tarma etched carefully with the edge of a stone, following each line. Finally they stood, tracing the engraving with their fingers.

"IGLOS," they spoke as one.

"Free, without barrier, open to all," quoted Nathan, remembering Elana's translation of the word that had so puzzled them.

"Free," said Soloma. "The land is free."

"Open to us," said Tarma, smiling.

Only then did it strike them that they had moved from grey limestone onto the red sandstone of Rhossili Down without any barrier, without any holly clump and plinth, without any token.

"It's an old inscription," Zadie observed, running her fingers across the lichen and lettering, "and it faces west, not the way we came."

Turning west, they looked down three hundred metres or more. Land stretched away – land with clusters of hardy trees; land with patches of grass; land bordered by hills to the north and a lake to the south. Beyond its shore the ice-wall rose, curving west until it became the horizon. Only at one point did a tongue of ice touch the land, tumbling downwards to lick the rock where they had slithered and arrived in the night. Birds flew over it from the western lake and others joined them, winging east from unseen gathering points.

"We were very fortunate finding that in the dark. It's the only place we could have come off the ice safely," observed Zadie thoughtfully.

"Worm's Head," said Nathan.

"What?"

"That's what it will be called – Worm's Head – and even in our time it's a strange place," explained Nathan, turning eastwards; "and those ice-capped hills are the Brecon Beacons. This is a little land enclosed on every side – but it's a good land; there is plenty in it; they will be safe here – and somewhere not too far west is the sea. Some of those birds are sea-birds, and the clouds in the west are cumulus – they will have rain and warmth ... see how the snow is already gone over much of the land, and there are colours like flowers near where that group is stalking the deer. This is a good place for them," he ended, nodding as if some moment had come and gone, some thought been dismissed, something unseen passed irretrievably.

"Come on," called Zadie, seizing the initiative; "I can see smoke. They are cooking again, and I'm hungry."

The girls moved fast, eager to share their discovery, and the word 'Iglos' was recurring in conversation as they drew near the source of smoke. Several fires were lit and, judging by the growing pile of feathers and bone, this was a third meal for some. Nevertheless, a goodly portion had been put on one side. It was fishier in taste than the morning's wild geese but definitely waterfowl of some unrecognisable type.

"Different valley," said Zadie, munching and wondering how best to wipe her fingers; "this isn't the same one as this morning … better choice … more wood, opens south, stream with pools, overhang on the cliff for shelter …"

"And there is a cave in it," offered Nathan, facing a similar problem to Zadie and toying between the discarded fur and his trousers as the solution before deciding that the latter could not become much dirtier and rubbing his hands across them. "Hoi! That's my serviette!" he cried as Zadie followed his example.

"Where's the cave?" she laughed.

"Just to the left of the overhang … watch the woman with two baskets. See?"

Zadie watched. Several more figures disappeared with baskets and objects and reappeared without them. The scene was busy and the cave must have extended more deeply or more widely than its opening suggested. Use of wood had been economical and one smouldering fire remained, chewing at bones that had been heaped upon its embers. A few were using a pool and gritty sand to clean hands and fingers but most had gathered by the overhang. Tarma and Soloma were slightly to one side, talking quietly to each other as they had been throughout the meal.

"They seem particularly busy gathering stuff to that cave," observed Zadie. "There's still a fair amount of light left. Do they know something we don't?"

"The answer to that is almost certainly yes, but in this case it's the clouds." And as they wandered across it began to rain – gently at first, then steadily, driven in from the west. Thickening cloud cut the light early, and they spread their furs under the overhang, more for comfort than heat, as it seemed warm after the ice, and lay talking, listening to voices from the cave and to the few who preferred to share the outside. Tarma and Soloma were still deep in conversation, soft snatches drifting across the intervening yards as limbs relaxed, seeking sleep's respite from the exertion of previous days.

"I wonder if there are bears?" yawned Zadie, wriggling away from a persistent drip.

"Probably not … they don't seem concerned … although maybe that is why they burnt the bones."

"It's strange," she persisted, elbowing him out of the most comfortable hollow. "In my first year I read something about caves in South Wales containing evidence of old civilisation … oyster shells, blackened bones, fragments of antlers … and now I see it happening. I wonder how long it will take Ruan and Mawgan to develop their hunting skills …" But Nathan was already snoring.

Some time in the night the moon broke through the wrack of disintegrating cloud, beaming its soft floodlight from the south. A fox stood on a nearby headland, looking at the sleeping forms, sniffing a new smell. It turned and trotted towards its mate, puzzled.

*   *   *

After days of cloud, dawn rose glorious but hardly silent. Waders and waterfowl had been greeting it impatiently long before its first pink flush drove the eastern stars to hide and caressed the distant hills, colouring their snowy crowns. In molten gold the orb's rim cut the horizon, floating upward, flooding its warmth, bouncing its dazzle across the lake's surface, embracing all that lived. A great clattering arose, wings crossing its flight, some hugging the water, scooting to a fresh standstill, others climbing, circling, beginning a long glide down.

"Sounds like the breakfast party is already in action," Zadie observed, pointing to the wide expanse of grass and sand between the grey cliffs and the water's edge and watching two lines of figures working towards each other. "If I could chose my own house, this is what I would have for the bedroom," she continued – "facing east, with a view like this."

"It's good," he acknowledged, stretching feet and legs to see which muscles responded; "however, I was wondering where the bathroom was!"

"It should have a view too," Zadie announced, "and sunlight for warmth." And she was tugging him to his feet to follow her towards the stream.

"Wait a minute," he called, grabbing two packages from the pack and scooping the fur over his shoulder.

"What's that for?"

"I didn't pack a towel, and the hotel don't seem to have provided one."

"What about those packages?" she laughed.

"Clean socks, clean underwear and," he added triumphantly, "a bar of soap."

"I'll take the soap – you can keep the rest – they won't fit!"

"Catch!"

"Ugh!" she sniffed. "Male soap! Never mind, can't be fussy. That sun is warm already," Zadie continued as they followed the stream's twists and turns down the little valley until it tumbled over a ledge of flat, grey rock, splashing into a pool below, gurgling on into another and spreading out to give its life to the grass beyond.

"That will do nicely," Zadie informed; "shower and bidet … solarium nearby. No shower curtain though, so I'll go first. Leave me the fur to dry off with. You can use the other pool." A little while later a cry of, "Soap coming down!" preceded the arrival of an object sliding over the rock in the water. Nathan grabbed it, succeeding at the third attempt, and completed his wash, sitting on a rock to finish drying. The grass felt good on his feet as he wriggled them into fresh socks and contemplated washing the 'serviette trousers' before deciding they would take too long to dry. He slipped them back on and walked the few paces up the slope to where Zadie was lying, mostly wrapped in the fur, as her clothes dried on the nearby rocks and she turned them occasionally in the sun. Putting his old socks to join them, he watched the conclusion of the breakfast hunt.

Soon figures were coming their way. It looked like three medium-sized birds this time, and a freezer bag of eggs with Mawgan. He and Ruan must have been climbing the cliffs. Nathan greeted them politely in their own language and was greeted in reply. Several pointed to the low waterfall and Tarma explained that they were talking about the lost wash-pools of Elana's land.

Eventually she left, saying that a meal would be ready at half-zenith. Soloma lingered, sitting by Zadie and sniffing. She was searching for something in her mind.

Shortly, her voice said, "Soap. Nathan-Soap!"

Bursting into laughter, Nathan held out the bar to her to smell and she took it, shedding clothes and splashing into the waterfall. It was a very small bar by the time she returned, hair curling in long wet strands. A newly-clad Zadie wrapped her in Nathan's fur while another set of clothes was laid to dry on warm rocks. A smell of wood smoke filtered down the valley.

"Do you have the brush?" asked Soloma hopefully, pointing at her hair. Suppressed laughter crinkled in their eyes as they both gave a sad, "No," in response.

For a while they sat together, drinking in the warmth – invigorated, clean – watching the birds searching for food and mates. Slowly Soloma grew quiet until she said, rather formally, "Mister Nathan, Miss Zadie, I am going tomorrow. I go back to Elana. She needs me. Tarma stays here. Tarma cooks me food to take. I thank – "

"Oh, Soloma! You're not going back alone, not over all that ice!" cried Zadie, hugging her. "We need to go back, too. We will go together."

The sun had stopped shining. A cold claw grasped at Nathan's heart and he heard his own voice saying, "No, Soloma. You are not going alone. We will come with you."

It took Tarma's appearance to say that food was ready to break the ensuing conversation. She took one look at the trio and said simply, "You know?" Nods were sufficient response, and they walked past the laughter of falling water in silence, wending their footsteps towards the smell of food. Tarma's parting words had been, "I will tell Meroa while you eat."

The rest of that day both dragged and accelerated. Sometimes it seemed there was nothing that could be done and at other times the moments flew. Nathan spread the entire contents of both rucksacks on the ground, discarding every item that was not essential, seeking to reduce the weight. Mawgan, whose feet were larger, found himself the possessor of a newly washed pair of red walking socks; to Ruan he gave the penknife, explaining its attachments; two handkerchiefs went to the nursing mothers to help with bathing their infants. For a long while he considered the rope. It was the single heaviest item by far. Every time he had thought of leaving it, a need had arisen. Eventually, it was decided that it would be Soloma's charge to carry, coiled and slung over her shoulder.

The sun was well past its half-zenith descent when Nathan and Zadie knelt together going through objects one last time. "That's it then," he said reluctantly: "Your small first aid kit; chunk of tin; your spare sweater; head torch; small flask; space for two containers with the meat Meroa has promised; your cap and scarf; two mugs, one spoon; three tea bags; a quarter of a cup of sugar; two large bars of chocolate – that lot goes in your pack."

"Check," said Zadie.

"Why has it still got a bone fastened on the back?"

"It's the one from Lundy. If I have it analysed, it could be very interesting ..." and her voice died away. He stared at her and she put it to one side, muttering.

"Now my sack: survival bag; chunk of tin; chunk of copper; blue token; compass to my pocket; large flask; last meal to rehydrate – bangers and mash; porridge – enough for two meals; matches; half a bag of boiled sweets; your map; scarf; cap; binoculars; freezer bags; camping stove; gas cylinder; two tins; extra sweater; sundries; ice-axe."

"What are sundries?"

"Freshly washed underwear, very small bar of soap, small piece of ignimbrite that you gave me ..."

"No. No bone, no sundries," stated Zadie.

Nathan put the sundries with the bone.

"It's just what we stand up in, plus furs and staves, then," he observed.

"Where are the seeds?" demanded Zadie.

"In my back pocket. Oh, very well! Where's your wallet?"

"You're not having that!"

"It'll be no use on a corpse in the middle of an ice-sheet. Take the credit card out of it and leave the rest."

"Anything else?" she asked.

"No, only that we need to be moving. We must spend the night as close to the ice as possible. It is a very long day from here to Lundy."

Food arrived again. Soloma arrived with it, forcing them to eat more than they wanted and to drink freely. Meroa arrived with two containers squashed full of goose meat. By the look of it, Ruan had learnt a use for the penknife blade remarkably well. Others gathered, giving their farewell or thanks each in their own way. Lastly, three figures approached. Two drew back their furs and passed a sleeping infant into Nathan's arms.

"They want you to bless them," whispered Zadie intuitively.

Nathan's mind blanked. For a moment all he could think of was his grandmother's old Cornish litany, 'From ghoulies and ghosties and things that go bump in the night, good Lord deliver us', and then it seemed as if an old figure reached across time, dangling a gold watch, wire-rimmed glasses framing short silver hair, and he found himself saying quietly, "The Lord bless you and keep you; the Lord lift up his countenance upon you, and give you peace."

As he passed the children back to their mothers, Zadie's voice whispered, "That was nice, very nice. Where did you learn that?"

"It's old ... goes back a long way," he answered, fighting to hold on to the image of the face and hold back the tears.

Only Tarma remained now. "I am coming with you tonight," she announced. "I am bringing food for breakfast. I will say farewell in the dawn." Slowly the quartet moved up the valley, turning at its ending to look at figures already moving about their tasks, and turning again, into the setting sun.

Chapter 19 Memories

Barely was the lightening east chasing stars to sleep, than Tarma woke them with food. She led them across the rock to its final ending, peering down at the ice below. Briefly she clasped Zadie and Nathan, each face still indistinct, and said, "Thank you. My people thank you. This is a good land. It is IGLOS. We will remember you." Longer she held Soloma – a parting both brief and lasting. Quiet words passed and, in the glimmerings of pre-dawn, Nathan thought he saw Soloma bend her neck, hanging something around Tarma, kissing her forehead once, turning away forever.

Minutes later a rope snaked down the rock, the unseen hand above relinquishing her grasp, breaking the last link. The ice was awkward in ascent, slippery and unclear of route. Several times they slid, averting a further fall only with the axe. They had eschewed the rope for speed, and it took all Soloma's skill to pick a way. Finally, she stopped. A sloping wall, a mere ten feet of ice, with deep drops to either side, barred their passage. Two times she tried, Zadie rescuing her second slide from plunging over the edge by grabbing an ankle as it passed. They looked at each other uncertainly, aware of time passing; aware that this was not the route of their descent. Reluctantly, Nathan took the rope, using the ice-axe to cut steps and climb, ice turning pink in the growing light. He disappeared from view, tugging three times to tell Zadie to climb, hauling her over the top and casting the rope back down. Soloma was carrying his pack and struggling with its long straps, weight swinging out, unbalancing her climb. He hauled more rapidly, tautening and pulling. They could hear her laboured breath. A head of black hair appeared and an arm thrust forward; Zadie grabbed and Nathan pulled, and the figure slid and slithered into them, grinning and rising on its knees. He coiled the rope, swapping it for the pack and all three stood, embraced for a moment by the vast orange disc cutting the horizon, transfixing them with its first true rays. Far below a figure waved both arms, and turned. Far above an eagle soared, its cold eye magnifying the specks standing on cold ice. Farther still, two figures sat in an ancient landrover, talking quietly as the sun rose over a Cornish moor.

"That cost us time," observed Nathan, without malice.

"We're up now, and the ice is flat before us. We seem to have missed the rocks," commented Zadie.

"Right. It is south south-west from here. You go ahead. I will line you up and show Soloma the bearing; she can lead after that. She will be better than a compass and we can all walk together. We'll go straight through to the zenith stop to make up time. That should be eighteen miles, near enough. OK?"

"Fine. Just don't leave me in front on my own."

Soloma grasped what was required without many words and Zadie fell into step as they reached her. Occasionally Nathan checked his compass, each time becoming more confident in Soloma's ability to navigate without any obvious points of reference other than the moving arc of the sun.

"You know," began Zadie after a while, "there's not really any such thing as 'goodbye' in our world … not in a final sense."

"This isn't going to become a discussion of death and life after death, is it?" asked Nathan warily. "I was rather hoping to keep to the life side of things for the next few days …"

"No. I was just thinking that when we say 'goodbye', it isn't really like that. We have the telephone and emails, and you managed to send me a postcard when I was on that Greek island. We can still communicate, even after we have said goodbye. We can still see people – photographs, videos, electronic images – even if we don't see them again physically … whereas for Soloma and Tarma, that was the end. Nothing ever again – only a memory growing old."

Nathan looked at the young girl a pace ahead, wondering how much she had understood, and replied, "It is only the last sixty years when people have been able to communicate so freely. Go back further, and words and meanings and actions were all linked together. Things meant more what they said. Words change too. 'Goodbye' to us means, 'I'll be in touch; I'll write, hear you, see you'. When Lucinda said 'goodbye' to her father in his naval uniform in 1940, it meant something different. When the Pilgrim Fathers said 'goodbye' at the Mayflower steps in Plymouth, it meant something different again. I know what you mean. Today, we have seen the comfortable part of the word stripped away; what is left is raw and elemental."

"I'd like to hope they could meet again, one day," Zadie mused.

"This ice is old – near its own death – and the journey is almost impossible," observed Nathan; "but hope is a good thing."

In the silence of walking, a voice from in front said, "Tarma is gone. I will not see her. I will remember; she will remember," and they both had the impression that, were the young face to turn, it would have tears flowing down its cheeks.

For a long while further they walked in silence, the sun rising in altitude, blasting back at them off the white surface until they screwed their eyes near shut. Eventually Soloma called a halt, pointing to the sun's height.

"One flask of water; half a container of goose; boiled sweet for dessert," said Nathan. "We ate well yesterday. We will have the other flask mid-afternoon."

The container of goose had seemed quite large until it had been divided into half and three, and yesterday's plenty appeared even more distant as Zadie contemplated the boiled sweet, debating how long she could make it last. Nathan had closed the container before the half of goose meat consumed became greater than the half remaining and was licking his fingers in memory of it.

"Good goose," he commented; "nice taste to it … not like the domesticated flocks."

"Very nice taste," said Zadie wistfully, deciding to start the sweet. "Aren't you having one?"

"I'll have mine later," lied Nathan, counting to six and replacing the packet. "Now, let's go. If we don't make Lundy by nightfall, it won't matter how much or how little food we have."

This time they walked abreast, confident in Soloma's instinct for direction. Zadie stirred Nathan into conversation. "Once you said we never had time to talk. I was going to come and stay with you … we were going to have time to talk. Now we have time … all the time in the world. Tell me about yourself."

"What do you want to know?"

"What you want to tell," she answered.

And suddenly he found himself spilling out a life story – memories of grandparents listening on a wireless to broadcasts they called 'The Home Service' and 'The Light Programme'; memories of making soft toffee, dropped into a pan of water to harden, of egg-custard boiled in a chipped cup that had no handle, of crab apples gathered for jelly; of rhubarb, blackberries and apple, in season.   On rolled the memories – of school, of pressures to succeed; of exams, of college and university; of a home far from the sea; of travel and distant stars. Through it all, the thread of an old bungalow ran – older faces and events long gone, waves long-broken on a shore – until the word 'Trevennick' brought speech to a halt, the sun nearing its half-zenith.

"You loved that place," said Zadie softly.

"I still do. It's something special."

"Tell me about Kerry and Wadebridge."

Soon a more recent story was unfolding – one told in part on Gulland but more fully now as Zadie's promptings probed.

"It sounds like Kerry knew vastly more than he told you," observed Zadie reflectively; "and that he told you more than he intended when you first met. I still don't understand about the ring, or Mabel's will."

"Nor do I entirely. The will I think Lucinda, or maybe Martyn, could explain more. The ring, I don't think I understand fully: it was intuitive; it goes back much further, much deeper."

"What about Goldilocks? He seems to know things in a strange kind of way. He gave Martyn the message for you. Come to think of it, Martyn didn't seem surprised to have received a message from me either."

"I hadn't thought of him – although he has been in my dreams. What are you suggesting?"

"Nothing: just that he seems to keep appearing at odd

moments."

"There!" cried Soloma.

"Where? What?" asked Nathan and Zadie, respectively.

"There is the island," announced Soloma, pointing slightly east of south.

"Lundy!" they exclaimed, picking out the darker splodge in the late afternoon light.

Neither a compass nor Soloma's skill were needed as they altered direction slightly and made haste towards the feature, encountering ridged ice for the first time. Rapidly it grew in stature, lengthening from north to south, offering its warmed western slope to the approaching trio. Good light gave ready access over the crevasses, and they were seated, watching the red sun's rim touch the horizon, before any remembered they had not stopped since lunch. A flask was slowly refilling with water from the last of the snow-melt, and the emptied container of goose meat was rehydrating porridge after a partial clean. Nathan swirled and squashed one tea-bag in a tin of heating water on the stove, attempting to extract as much of its darkening essence as possible, dissolving sugar and pouring the contents into the larger flask. They sipped gratefully, sun sinking by the second, stabbing its last ruby rays. Pink and almost round, peculiarly distinct, the moon followed the sun to its setting, leaving an invasion of stars to reclaim their ancient inhabitance. Amongst them two planets stood in confrontation. Cold closed around: old cold, cold long practised at its art, long used to clutching at the heart in night's late hours, long unchallenged, strength undiminished. Together they sheltered as best they could, thanking the animals whose lives had given fur, thanking each other for their warmth, breathing chilled airs cautiously, thinking, half sleeping.

In the absolute clarity, warmth radiated back into space; stars scintillated, winking in their cold eternity, shrinking against its embrace. Cold ascended from beneath and descended from above; it flowed down the slope – merciless, penetrating, numbing mind and body. It clutched, grasped, crushed. It stretched its ancient fingers, seeking to extinguish.

Soloma moaned. Zadie moved. Nathan stirred. Fingers

struggled with a match. Flame burst into being, roaring a tirade against its old enemy – pitiful, small, insecure – yet warming, powerful, altogether different in sort. The last sugar stirred into solution; tea infused – colour unseen – tipping sloppily into a mug. Heat trickled down throats, gurgling life, giving hope. Above, stars rotated on their eternal tracks. A furlong away a head turned from the unexpected glare, talons balanced on cold rock, wings furled. One eye watched until the first pink light cast Lundy's shadow across the ice, and lugubrious limbs laboured an ancient creature into the air's stirring. Slowly it circled north, seeking a quarry with less life.

Porridge glouped firmly in the tin. Zadie sat watching Nathan stir, while Soloma fetched a second flask of water. True dawn had broken, sending its shafts of gold far distant.

"That was the coldest night I have ever known, and the next one we have to spend on the ice," Zadie stated quietly, staring away to the south and west.

"Porridge is ready," replied a steady voice.

"We go soon," said the other, dipping her fingers into the mixture and eating, whilst Zadie used the spoon.

"Boiled sweet?" Nathan enquired, offering them one each. "Have a last drink," he said, leaving the mugs to pack away last. "I've filled two freezer bags but there is no easy water between here and Elana's land. If Soloma leads us across the crevasses, I will set us on a bearing. We were to the west of Lundy when we came and we should be able to cut off a small corner. We need to make as much distance as possible today – no stop until the sun is just past its zenith and we are looking straight into it. One of the nice things about not having a watch," he added, "is that you can't keep looking at it and thinking how long you have been doing something and wanting to stop doing it. We are just going to walk."

There was something about the way he said it that stirred both hearts. In part was the feeling that they were launched on something courageous; something to be achieved against overwhelming odds; something that would pass into folklore, a tale to be told by the embers of a fire on a dark night with the stars gleaming – and in part was the comforting sense that all that was required of them was to walk, to go on walking; to do something so simple, so natural; something they had done all their lives; something so possible that anything was possible.

By the time the last crevasse had been negotiated, the sun broke clear of Lundy's dark form, a rising moon following closely in its wake – visible briefly until the growing enormity of light swallowed its presence. Nathan set Soloma on a bearing, content to let her lead.

"There is warmth in that sun," Zadie observed, peeling off her extra sweater and stuffing it into the rucksack that Nathan held for her as they walked together.

"Yes. Just over two months to the solstice. Things are changing fast."

"The solstice was my grandmother's birthday ... June 21st. She always said she had been born on the longest day and intended to live the longest life," Zadie laughed at the memory. "She didn't quite make that but she lived well into her eighties ... died on the shortest day. The little chapel near Trebarwith was packed for the funeral. I never realised she knew so many people ... and some of them were quite ... strange ... addressed me as 'Barwith'. I've never shared that name with anyone but you ... not even at school. I was always Zadie B Luxillian ... or, if the teachers didn't know me, Zadenia Luxillian ... mostly just Zadie. My parents were at the funeral ... came separately but sat together ... first time I had seen them hold hands in years. They even embraced before they left again for their own lives ..."

"Tell me about your grandmother," said Nathan, partly from genuine interest and partly to divert from maudlin memories. "Did you spend much time with her?"

"I saw a lot of her when I was little ... before boarding school ... and sometimes in the holidays. She used to say, 'Bring all your friends down, dear; I'll take them to see the king.' She was a bit peculiar like that ... I never dared take them. I remember once when I was a little girl we were walking in the woods near Tintagel and she pulled me behind a tree saying, 'Hide now; the wild boar are coming.' Another time we walked to Tintagel – she was a great walker – and we passed the castle ... 'Don't like these modern castles,' she said ... and she took me down the cliffs, ignoring the 'Don't Climb' notices, to the foot of the headland and into a cave full of rounded boulders each the size of a head, with indents in them like blank eyes staring out. 'Don't tell anyone,' she whispered, 'but this is Merlin's cave ... and that is where Gwenhallion worked ... don't let the stones hear you.' She was full of Merlin, although she always called him Merlan, and of Arthur, and The Round Table ... drew me pictures of Arthur ... all clean-shaven and with a nice crown ... nothing like a king would have been in the 6thC. She drew pictures of the Round Table, too ... made me draw some with crayons. The strange thing was, if I drew it round, she would crumple it up and give me a new piece of some cut-up cereal box. She always wanted it drawn like an egg ... and always with two places left blank. If she approved, she would give it a funny tick in the middle with a line across it ... I don't think she ever learnt to read or write very well, to tell the truth. Sometimes I'd find her talking to a bit of stone wall or a worn slate in a stile, as if it were a friend. In the end, she had to be kept out of Tintagel ... she took to standing outside the Old Post Office asking passers-by to bring her a particular piece of slate from its roof. The National Trust didn't like it ... said it was disturbing their customers ... and the Social Services started getting interested. Not very nice really ... she was a funny old thing ... but leaving her home would have killed her. She made the most fantastic toffee. I'll always remember her toffee. I asked her for the recipe once ... but all she said was, 'It's love, and timing ... one day, you'll find out.' I used to call her 'Granny Tree' because of her love for the woods. At least, that was what I thought ... I guess it was supposed to be 'Granny Tre', after Trebarwith.

Somewhere a fact, a name, a passing comment, was resonating in Nathan's mind, but he couldn't place it and asked instead, "Why were you called Zadenia?"

"That was when my parents were still together ... emotionally as well as physically. My mother thought I was the most beautiful baby and wanted to call me after her favourite flower: Gardenia. My father said that I was going to be special and I wasn't going to have an ordinary initial ... so I became Zadenia Barwith Luxillian. I never found out my middle name until I needed a passport."

"I like the names and I like the stories," said Nathan, nodding; "and I think I would have liked your grandmother. At least we could have talked to the same rocks together," he added, laughing. "Let's see what stories Soloma can tell ... her people have a strong oral tradition."

Slowly they pieced it together. Varda had died almost as young as Soloma's mother but Elana had taught her the stories. Lore, legend, and myth mixed as she spoke, sometimes in one language, sometimes in another. Some stories they recognised as touching on Elana's recounting to them: a window in the east; a way of escaping; strangers bearing knowledge both wonderful and dangerous; lands that once were but were no more; flowers on a coral pool instead of sacrifice; a place of great evil; a lake bluer than the summer sky; men coming, men choosing, gifts exchanged; smelting of tin and copper; fields, fish-ponds and washing pools created; warm mist stemming snow and ice. But others were new: the meaning of shadows; names of shapes; subtle differences in the feeling of ice, or light upon it; courses of stars; swirlings of mist; rocks placed in sequence; sources of food; separation of men and women; coming of the Mortan ... and, deeper still, the legend of a Mortana.

Lunch came and went – a meal inadequate in amount, though pleasant in taste: wild goose washed down with water from a freezer bag – and still they talked and walked. Filaments of high cloud fingered their way from the east, gaining upon a slowly declining sun like a pack of marathon runners upon an early leader. By the half-zenith's halt, the pack was touching its quarry. Water sufficed instead of food, the remnant poured into the remaining porridge to swell it for a later meal. Zadie and Soloma sucked a sweet apiece as Nathan told stories of ancient rocks and landscapes in Australia; of young islands in the South Pacific barely higher than a man above sea-level, and an hour's walk round; of volcanoes in New

Zealand and mountains in Nepal. The sun dipped, shielding its
rays in submission to pursuit, colouring the clouds first from above
and then below, changing their white vestments to oranges and
reds, hueing them in shades of deepest dye, distinguishing each
pursuer differently, bidding farewell in one last, defiant burst.

"We'll stop here," Nathan announced. "I'll boil the last two
sweets and tea-bag with one flask of water to give us something
warm. We can have the rest of the goose for supper. It won't be
as cold tonight with this cloud. We've walked well ... we should
see the mists marking Elana's land by noon tomorrow ... and there
will be porridge for breakfast. Elana will have food and water
for us when we arrive." Licking fingers in the intensifying dark,
he spread his fur on the ice as they tucked the other furs over and
around them, drawing close, awaiting the distant dawn.

*   *   *

Elsewhere, a door opened. Dark ebony – blackest of wood
– tapped on a stone-flagged floor, a familiar grip masking its silver
top as the cane was laid against a chair. Curved arms shone with
a patina of age, old beech welcoming the grip it had long known.
A desk lamp, cast in solid brass, shielded its luminance behind a
hood of green smoked-glass. Oak, polished through the years, and
leather, inlaid with gilt, shone back, softly welcoming the light.
Three voices spoke, and spoke at length. Hands leant forward from
the chair, fingers intertwined, resting, feeling the smooth surface.

"If they stop, they are doomed," the old voice spoke in final
summary. "Still, there is hope, albeit, I grant you, little."

"I could go," murmured the largest figure.

"No: there is not time. And, no: I do not think that way lies
open to you any more. Set a watch. That is all that we can do ...
and, friend –" he changed his glance "– in this ending, there may
be an ending of things else, too."

Slendered fingers touched the desk and white hair nodded
twice, answering, "So be it. There is nothing that I would change.
The years have been full. I will not yield now."

Chapter 20   A Final Farewell

In the first glimmerings of dawn thicker cloud blocked its beauty, tinged only the most faintly pink in greeting. For a while the stove's flame shone strongly, until sunlight caught the thinner clouds extending west, and gold diffused from them in rival rays.

"Porridge, anyone?" asked Nathan. "The gas is holding out well," he added, licking the spoon clean and tipping the rest of the boiled-sweet tea to reheat.

Soon they were walking, talking again, exchanging stories of school, of places visited, of past occasions. The hidden sun climbed until its pale frame cast a first, weak shadow. At half-zenith rise its orb was indistinct but clear in its location. Soloma asked for the binoculars, scanning and re-scanning to the south south-west as they paused and took a mouthful of precious water from the flask. Some time later she started veering off course, and Nathan challenged her.

"Do you see something?"

"I think so. Mist rising ... but not as it should."

"Her English is improving from listening to us talk," observed Zadie.

Nathan was inclined to agree, making a mental note to be more careful in his references to 'she' and 'her', as he trained the binoculars on the horizon, only to be disappointed by the glare from the ice. Nevertheless, he let Soloma lead towards whatever she had seen.

"There! There!" cried Soloma, and out of the immense expanse of white a speck of darkened surface emerged. It took less than an hour to reach its low form: a few black rocks in a haphazard pile. "North mark," she said excitedly. "Soon there. Look for mist rising."

Walking and trying to use the binoculars at the same time proved impossible but there was certainly something rising from the near horizon. Soon probably meant noon. The mist was not like he had seen it before, though; it was both thinner and more opaque, although it was difficult to tell its character with no clear shadow and the sun nearing its greatest height. Clearly, something was troubling Soloma. She was moving at great speed and they were struggling to keep up with her. It would not be long now: the spirals were more conspicuous, and the ice was beginning to slope downwards; a rock appeared ... and another.

Soloma was poised, looking over the lip into Elana's land – her land, her home. No warm mists rose, only skeletal plumes of smoke, ascending from charred embers of huts on the uppermost part of a hill surrounded by a deep lake of cold water. Sheet ice, an inch thick, encrusted the path they had trodden only a week ago, and waters edged by ice covered the tail of the guardian. Soloma stepped forward on the steep path to the northern guardian and Nathan grabbed at her, holding and pulling her back. Zadie rolled Soloma into her own arms and held the sobbing head against her shoulder, eyes staring down.

Slowly they worked their way along the circumference of this bowl of once-fertile land, Zadie holding and shielding Soloma, hugging her against herself. A lukewarm stream still trickled near the eastern path, and they picked their way with care, sitting on the forepaws of the carved, black lioness, poised above a flat expanse of water. Zadie lay back against the animal's jaws, wrapping Soloma to her, while Nathan stepped a little way, seeking to fill the flasks. Returning, he stood with his back to them both – immobile, hunched, defeated.

"Nathan, what's happened? What's happened to this place?" a disbelieving Zadie cried. "Nathan, why won't you answer me? Turn round!"

Slowly, he turned, eyes entirely unsighted, ears blocked from hearing.

"Oh! Oh, Nathan ... I've never seen you cry like this before. What's wrong? Can you hear me? Talk to me! Please talk to me."

Struggling, he focused on words, one at a time, and thoughts he didn't want to think.

"We must … go … up the slope. Take her. She knows … she senses it. We must go … away from here. Take her … take her, now." And he stumbled up the path.

"Nathan, what is wrong?" she cried, struggling after him with Soloma. Slowly, so slowly, they plodded upwards, passing the last few shrivelled growths of plant. At the top he stood and turned, choking.

"The huts … are burned. From where I stood … I could see the coral pool. The coral is red, not white … there is a body spread across its centre. She was so small … so defenceless … she loved her people … she gave them so much … she loved her land." And he lifted up his voice, weeping, "Elana; Oh, Elana … we cannot take you back, but we will remember you … we will take your farewell to the Cornwall that you loved. We will remember," and he bowed his head, soft tears falling in silent memoriam.

Turning away, the voice changed. "Soloma, take us to the second cairn."

For a moment their eyes exchanged blurred communication before she nodded and walked on, leading Zadie with her hand. Behind them, Nathan stumbled. Behind him, waters rose – diluting redness, washing it clean, lifting a slender form until it sank, one arm raised in final goodbye … resting at last.

Time passed without meaning. Cloud gathered darkly in the west. A cairn passed, another came. They sat upon it, each lost in emotion and thought. Silently, Nathan unfolded the crumpled map, running over notes that he had made months previously. A precious bar of chocolate lay broken between them. The simple act of touch, the will of eating, brought returning thought and speech.

"We do not have enough food for the northern route," he said in a measured tone; "and we do not have enough time to reach the night cairn. The sun is already halfway down, and the light will fade early with those dark clouds. There will be no moon tonight; it sets with the sun."

"What are you suggesting?" asked Zadie, surprised to hear her own voice sound nearly normal.

"The lake and the cave … Elana's secret route," he answered

with great reticence. "It will cut off a day, and we left food at Gulland."

"You don't like that cave. Last time you found it ... difficult," observed Zadie, choosing her words with care.

"There is no alternative. Besides, this time I have the ice-axe and a rope that will bear my weight. We don't have time to debate this ..."

Worry clutched at Zadie, and doubly so: fear that he would fall apart again in the dark recesses of tunnels, or that the ice itself had shifted, closing the passage; fear of being called to lead on her own over the ridges they must cross, with only a distant voice from behind steering her on a bearing.

"There is no alternative," he said again, as if it were a declaration in defiance of his own anxieties. "This time, Soloma is with us. The ridges will not be so bad," he added, addressing one part of the concerns he sensed. "My notes say, '500 paces and turn on the reciprocal to 280°' ... that will be a bearing of 100° ... 'twenty ridges, followed by twenty minutes flat walking, an hour and a half ascent from the blue lake to the plateau' ... but we will be going downhill so, say an hour. There is a good chance of reaching the cave with some light left. Once we are in it, light is irrelevant: it will depend on your memory of the way through ... and how much battery there is left in the head torch," he ended, doubting the battery more than Zadie's memory.

"And whether you can climb down ..." added Zadie.

"You see to the cave; I will see to the climb; and Soloma can navigate the ridges. She has done it before in the opposite direction."

Both of them looked at Soloma, finding dark eyes staring back, absorbing the conversation, intent in thought. The young head nodded, black hair falling forward, her voice answering the unspoken question. "I know the ridges. I will take us to the lake." More plaintively, she continued, "It was Elana's special place," and a haunting memory touched each heart.

"That is five hundred," announced Nathan shortly.

Soloma struck off, reaching the first low ridge of ice, watching for Nathan to show his agreement by hand signals from the turning point, waiting for them to catch her up. Perhaps forty yards separated this ridge from the next, the intervening trough filled more deeply with powder snow scoured by winter winds and settling in the hollow. It reached to calves and knees, slowing progress, making normal steps awkward. Nathan kicked through the snow, sapping strength, whereas Soloma sank less far, picking her feet up between each step; Zadie struggled, having neither Nathan's weight nor Soloma's lightness, biting back her dislike of it and counting ridges.

"Two to go," she said eventually, half-kicking, half-stepping through the final troughs and standing gratefully on the last ridge, looking at flat ice beyond. Light dimmed rapidly as they stood. Towards the west, cloud had grown enormously, deepening and darkening, billowing and spreading in thick layers of differing height. Its uppermost pall blotted out the sun, casting twilight as the moon, following closely the sun's track, emerged from the obscurity of light. Moon chased sun behind the bank of cloud, or cloud spread rapidly – it was difficult to tell which. Sun broke free and light returned, only for another dense bank to encompass it. For a moment moon and sun both showed on opposite edges of black, billowing cloud, each dulled red, as if the universe had suddenly evolved two suns of equal ray. They stood entranced until Zadie broke the thrall with further speech, "That's the weirdest thing I've ever seen."

"It's the weirdest cloud. Let's go!" snapped Nathan, stepping forward. "I don't like it. We need the light. Let's move."

Twenty minutes later the ice began to slope down, its gradient increasing until it reached a steady, steep descent. Occasional black rocks emerged, but mostly the moraine was hidden beneath winter snow. Constantly they looked for a glimpse of the sky-blue lake to emerge, beginning to doubt Soloma's skill of navigation. Light brightened briefly and all at once the landscape resolved itself before their eyes, minds taking in what they had seen but not understood.

"It's frozen!" cried Zadie. "There is no blue water."

"Snow covered," added Nathan; "that is why we could not see it. What's more, we are already low enough … we need to find the entrance to the cave."

Around them an amphitheatre of ice enclosed the frozen lake, its fourth side formed from the tumbling wall down which they had come. Ahead the highest ice-wall rose six hundred metres or more, sloping not quite vertically – impassable, dangerous – pockmarked with dark spots of varying size, each of which might be the opening of a cave. The dark, flat rocks that Nathan had relied upon as markers from his memory lay buried beneath the winter's fresh deposit. Light fluctuated, fading and growing, but mostly fading.

"This is not the place to be stuck," said Zadie with some urgency. "Last time you started searching too low. Trust your instinct." Nathan's world of logic and maps, of precise bearings and sequences of landforms, was contemplating the idea of what 'trusting his instinct' might mean when he became aware the voice was still speaking. "We will help you. What are we looking for? What size is the entrance?"

That was easier; that was fact. "Approximately four metres wide by three metres high," he found his voice replying – "slight notch in either side, flat floor … rather like a cod-fish with its mouth open … empty aerosol can of fluorescent paint six feet inside it on the right … and two wooden staves we left there."

Splitting and searching, they worked upwards, keeping within sight, occasionally disappearing only to emerge with a shake of the head. Six caves checked … surely they were climbing too high? The great ice-wall towered above, steepening, its upper part darkening improbably before a red light illumined the surface above. Bands of darkness and red light followed each other downwards like blood cascading. Another cave checked. Nothing. Darkness gripped – complete darkness – blocking out sight of each other. Red glow succeeded it. Another band of darkness was hard on its heels, more complete if that were possible. Soloma cried. She cried again and waved, standing like a red semaphore against a bloodied backdrop. Zadie reached her. She was waving. Nathan was further away … another fifty yards. Darkness severed them, burying contact in its suddenness, obliterating all view.

"Use the torch!" he yelled. "Put the head torch on. Give me something to aim towards. Point it at my voice."

A pinpoint of wonderful illumination flickered and settled in his direction, drawing him on, working by feel over the steep ice. The pinpoint became a nail-head. Voices strengthened. He could hear breathing. Arms grasped his and pulled him into the entrance. The torch flickered on the floor, catching the end of a wooden stave in its beam.

"Thanks," he gasped, kneeling, breathing heavily. "Now turn it off."

"What?"

"Turn the torch off."

"Why?"

"We need it. This darkness has come too suddenly. It is something to do with that cloud. It may clear. I tell you what," he added after a moment's thought, "I'll light the stove and cook the last meal. It should have rehydrated by now, and we haven't eaten since breakfast. We need something … and, if it doesn't clear, we may as well spend the night where we are."

Zadie had several thoughts, one of which was that he was putting off the cave, but mention of food brought an immediate longing for something to eat. Soon a warm glow bathed the ice-cave as rehydrated food heated. The heating and the eating were brief enough, as were the few mouthfuls of water allowed to each.

"I'm turning the stove off now," announced Nathan. "It will go dark," he warned. Gas ceased its sound but in the silence it did not go completely dark. Purple-orange light showed the cave's mouth and filtered around its walls, enough for face to see face, growing in its strange anger until walls, floor and ceiling revealed themselves. "Come on!" cried Nathan, hastily stuffing the still-warm stove and uncleaned tin into his rucksack. "We'll try now."

Shortly, they found themselves lying flat on the cold floor, peering over the lip of a waterfall formed in ice, looking at the route down its sheer side – the route that had caused so much trouble before – fifteen metres of friction-free descent – one small obstacle that had nearly unhinged him. Zadie could feel her heartbeat rising as they edged back. She could not help but wonder whether he was forcing himself beyond his competence and would crack again. Soloma waited, unslinging the rope at his command. Behind them orange glared, changing to purple tinged violently with green.

"All you need to do is hold the rope and let it out steadily," he lied in part, slipping a bowline under his shoulders. "I'm going to abseil down and climb back up for you with the ice-axe. The two of you should be able to hold my weight between you. This will take ten minutes, maximum," he stated confidently – more confidently than his mind was telling him. It was the start that was difficult. If he managed that, the rest might work. He balanced his feet on the edge of the ice waterfall, looking them in the face, leaning back, letting the rope take the strain until his body was horizontal, his feet flat against the ice. "Pay it out slowly and steadily on the count of three, hand over hand … keep going unless I call … you'll know if I've fallen."

He saw Zadie's arms moving and let his shoulders drop below the horizontal, bouncing gently off the ice with his feet, bringing them back onto it a little lower. Bounce by bounce he worked his way down, watching the steadily lengthening rope wearing a notch in the ice above, unable to see the hands and arms that were holding his weight. Seeking to judge how far below him the wall ended, he risked a one-footed bounce, trailing the other foot to search for the floor, twisting and slipping as it found only air. Two more bounces and his head brushed the ice floor. The rope went slack and he rolled to one side, standing and seeing the top of the perfectly frozen waterfall in the ghoulish light.

Turning his attention to the face he had just abseiled down, he slipped the loop of the ice-axe over his wrist and chipped at the ice. "Climbing!" he called, tugging sharply, waiting for the rope to come taut. Ice broke free under the axe creating good steps, clear holds. He kept the distance short, aware of the different limb lengths, working rapidly back up the face … over the bulge … nearing the top. A last thrust and he slithered with the rope's pull to Zadie's feet.

Grasping the two rucksacks, he let them slide down the face, hearing them skid to a stop somewhere below before making his own belay and tightening the rope under Soloma's arms. Her descent was as rapid as he had imagined. She was a natural climber, balanced and light, barely needing the rope's support now that the holds were cut. "The holds are good," Nathan encouraged as the rope came up again and he widened the loop for Zadie's shoulders. This time he kept the tension firmer. It took longer as she worked her way, reach by reach. Orange flared briefly. The rope came loose and he peered over, seeing the two forms standing below. He let go of the end, allowing the rope to slither towards them. With no belay above, the rope could be of no use to him, and he lowered himself carefully over the lip. This was free-climbing down: no support; no safety net; no second chance ... climbing on sheer ice – the most difficult of all surfaces – without an opportunity to look down ... that would entail a loss of balance ... feeling for holds ... keeping moving with fingers that were becoming chilled ... aware of a mind nagging about previous failure. The bulge in the ice was forcing his weight outwards. His knee would not bend over it and his foot was flailing for the next hold. He could feel the shaking beginning, and his fingers were becoming more and more numb. Hesitation grew. Into the rising maelstrom of doubt, a single voice called and kept calling, guiding him to the unseen holds below, "Three inches left ... right foot, six inches lower." He was down. He turned and saw that Soloma had already collected the rucksacks and Zadie was standing with the torch strapped round her forehead.

Zadie nodded, in no mood to delay. This was her task now. "Rope up," she said firmly. "Nathan in the middle, Soloma at the end – five yards between you. I'll take the slack coiled over my shoulder." Nathan did not disagree. There were reasons for this arrangement, and he understood well enough, respecting her expertise. It would be a long passage, narrow and nasty in places, without any light, except what the head-torch would give; none at all if it failed. There would be a blackness so complete it would be impossible to see a finger held in front of a face at nose-length;

a blackness that would disorientate; a blackness that would sap at every sense of balance. Nathan slammed his mind shut on the thoughts, watching Soloma's calm expression as she tied on behind him, settling the rope around his waist so that it was clear of the rucksack and did not snag. "Let's go," came Zadie's voice before he could think further. "Steady pace – keep the tension loose, rope off the ground. One sharp tug for stop, two for go on."

Already they were rounding a bend, the ice waterfall shutting from view. This was the old water-course by which the blue lake had once drained through the last, vast fragment of ice-sheet – a monumental block of ice maybe eight hundred metres high and more than a mile across. Floor, passage, walls and ceiling, were all carved in solid ice. Now it was abandoned, water finding a lower outlet. How Soloma's people had ever found this route he shuddered to imagine, although part of the story was known to him. Sometimes there was still a sound of water flowing far beneath as a side of the cave opened onto fissures to an unseen chasm; at other times the roof vanished into distant heights and the cave narrowed to a squeeze. Violent purple light ricocheted along the passage from behind, glimmering off the glass-cold sides. Immediately darkness followed, a darkness total and complete.

Zadie had the head-torch switched on, pointing towards the ceiling, dispensing its hope of life before his nerves could react. Dimly he saw a patch of luminescent paint, no bigger than a hand, and felt some reassurance they were on course, yet knowing that Zadie would trust her own mental map of this ice labyrinth rather than old markers. Another squeeze came, difficult to pass through with the rucksack, light disappearing into the heights. The passage split and split again. On it went, widening and narrowing, sometimes flat, sometimes curved underfoot, sometimes sloping more obviously down. Without the rope and the knowledge of Soloma behind, Nathan's mind would not have held on. Zadie paused, searching her memory, moving on again. Minutes dragged. Time began to have no meaning. Finally she stopped, turning to face them.

As calmly as a tour guide in a coach she announced, "Round the next bend is the ice-bridge. It is narrow and long. When we reach it, stop. I am going to walk straight across. I will pay my own rope out. This rope is long enough to stretch all the way across. Soloma, you grip the rope in front of Nathan. When I give two tugs, start him off and follow him. Nathan, when I reach the far side I will take off the torch and point it at the wall behind me. You will see the light but it won't dazzle you like last time, and you will see my silhouette against it. I want you to walk straight towards me, not looking to either side or up. You will feel Soloma walking behind you. Do you understand?" He nodded as his thoughts began to scream. "Now I'm going through that once more," repeated Zadie. "Stop me if you are not clear." Convinced they understood, she added, "Good. We are halfway. Soon the passage will open out."

The rope jerked forward, and Nathan's feet moved unwillingly with its pull. Rounding the bend, the sound of rushing, grumbling water, ascending from unseen depths, assaulted his ears. He heard Zadie's, "Stop here," and felt Soloma's hands grasp the rope in front of him. Light disappeared as Zadie turned, focusing it downward on the narrow ice-bridge that spanned the chasm cutting across their route. Unplumbed depths on either side reflected no light, nor did the heights reaching above. Water roared. The only light he could see was a small pool, seemingly suspended in the darkness, seemingly shrinking to an impossibly thin thread as Zadie walked steadily across the bridge.

Complete darkness flooded over him like sea closing over a drowning swimmer for the last time. Soloma balanced herself, her breathing a point of human contact. Suddenly light coursed up the wall opposite, as if it were a pale stone battlement rising in faint moonlight. Ghost-like in front of it, a figure moved. He felt Soloma's gentle push and heard her command. One pace, two paces … don't look down to either side; four paces … he could feel the rope take hold behind … Soloma was walking too; ten paces … Zadie was reeling him in … he could see arms moving against the light. Twenty paces … sound welled up in wrath, drowning hearing, attacking balance, tempting him to look and seek its origin. What if the ice-bridge would not bear the weight of two? It seemed more narrow even than the remembrance of it in dark dreams. Had it altered? Had the great block of ice moved … billions of tonnes of ice … an ancient, cold mausoleum? Thirty paces … the shadow figure was growing in size. He could run the last dozen steps … he could fling himself to safety … he could escape this abyss from which every evil thought assailed … he could be free.

"Keep walking steadily," the calm voice of the tour guide called faintly above the roar. "Keep coming." The voice was growing stronger. "Five more paces." She pulled him past her, pushing him away from the edge into the passage beyond, making him sit as Soloma stood beside. Briefly darkness gripped again. Light came, settling upon Zadie's head, cascading from iced ceiling and walls. A voice came, too. "Well done," it said. "You did that very well." Warmth flooded through him; peace pushed panic back; limbs responded to brain; thoughts ordered themselves.

On stretched the passage but it had lost its terror. Minutes passed at normal pace. Walls widened, and they walked three abreast, the rope held lightly. Gravel crunched on the ice floor as the passage turned and turned again. A cleft passed. Gritty sand scuffed beneath their feet, and suddenly – unexpectedly, unanticipated, unannounced – two stars glimmered in floodlit greeting.

Sitting on sand-covered ice, the torch extinguished, their eyes began to adjust, watching a night sky faintly outline the exit from the cave. Placing a fur on the sand, three figures laid on it, drawing the other furs around them as stars moved from floor to ceiling in the east. Exhaustion took its toll, and heads lay together, excluding thought. Ice groaned on ice, torturing its own soul. Periodically the sound intruded, vibrating through their rest. An eye opened, wondering what the ear had heard, and flickered shut again, mind sinking back into dreams of part-consciousness, fearing, hoping.

Chapter 21   Life Seeks Life

Light stung Zadie awake. Soloma's form was edging in front of her. Together they reached the cave mouth and lay, looking along an iced ledge of rock across which a buttress of ice blocked the way. Above, the vast ice-wall stretched vertiginously out of sight, compressed millennia of snow exposed in the ice-sheet's final boundary. Below, water spewed into a seething pool under pressure from its passage beneath the ice. Before them a lake stretched, frozen to where its further shore touched a snow-covered slope through which black rocks protruded in confusion. In the distance a single, shattered hill blocked the sun's rays, casting them in golden aureole around its broken crown.

"Gulland," whispered Zadie as the first true ray of light struck the entrance to the ice-cave and Nathan crawled beside her. Now the sun's orb was part-clear, its lower portion bitten by the hill but its upper part indented. Rapidly light diminished, rays cut from their creation. Soloma cried out. A smooth bite ate and consumed the rising sun until darkness spread at dawn. Stars shone again. Glowing pink-copper, the moon stood low above Gulland, flames extending from its circumference. The landscape hid, plunged into a second night. Time retreated into its formation, and Earth paused her life, while the heavens regarded creation's glory in silent adoration. In second dawning, a red lip mouthed its way beyond the cold sphere, restoring light, bringing golds and whites, flooding its life across the withdrawn world.

"That was very special," murmured Nathan in awe. "We have witnessed something not seen for generations."

"Well, before you feel too privileged, spare a thought for Soloma. And how are we going to get down from here, across the lake, and anywhere near home? And I'm hungry," Zadie observed with some asperity.

Nathan withdrew his gaze as the sun escaped fully from the moon's brief containment. Accepting the reprimand, he answered softly, "Try up the cave in the cleft; take Soloma."

Now it was Zadie's turn to gasp, remembering forgotten items discarded so easily, suddenly significant. She rose, walking over the gritty sand with Soloma, passing the furs, proceeding into the cave until it bent out of sight. Words floated back and sounds … sounds of scraping, and words hopeful in tone. Soon they returned, depositing their trophies as full light bore straight in through the cave's mouth. Nathan was seated, dangling an object in the rays, watching them flash from fine gold, regarding the gently spinning shape that hung, almost transparent yet tinged the faintest blue.

"It's your blue token!" exclaimed Zadie, lifting a hand to touch the chain around her own neck. "It's so beautiful … more beautiful than ever I remember it. It's so long since I've seen it."

"The last time we really looked at it we were sitting exactly where we are now," he replied. Beauty mesmerised as the token passed from hand to hand. "We found a way of escape then; we need a way of escape now … and only Soloma can give the answer. I will ask her when we have eaten," he continued, changing tack. "You found the things by the look of it."

Together they examined the objects that had been carried from the cave's recess … strange objects, secretly hidden for the few who had known this way. Two were half-spherical, stacked originally like a giant Easter egg but now lying side by side, the one slightly larger than the other. Skin – old skin – was stretched across their light frame – looking older and more frail than when they had last been seen, patches showing in the strong light. Protected within the now-halved egg lay two furs. Within one of these lay a further package wrapped in skin and, in the other, two shaped pieces of wood the length of an arm. Zadie stroked one of the furs, remembering packing it away, regarding its whiteness, recalling the circumstance, while Soloma unwrapped the small package and spread its contents carefully.

"Well, that solves breakfast," stated Nathan, looking at four small pieces of dried fish and two honey-baked bars of grain and hazel nut. "You didn't spot if there was any water trickling, did you? Tarma found some last time."

By way of answer, Soloma retreated with the cooking tin, returning with it part full. At least it was enough to give a couple of mouthfuls each to help chew dried food. The two shaped paddles looked sound enough but the coracles were sadly old, skin cracked, stitching frayed in places. Holding each up to the light and slowly rotating it, there were points at which the skin was thinned almost to translucence. Sadly, he put them down.

"I was rather relying on these to cross the lake," he observed. "I was going to go upstream to where the water is flowing if it was frozen here."

Zadie finished munching a honey-bar, savouring the lingering taste, and picked up the nearest coracle, holding it against the light as he had, marvelling at how little it weighed but inclined to share his gloomy prognosis. Soloma said simply, "Too old," and shook her head.

"I feared as much. It has probably been a generation since they were used, nor will they be used again. We are the last who know this route ... Elana's land is gone ... there is no reason for any to come this way again," he added mournfully, sitting near the mouth of the cave looking out and down. "The ledge I can manage," he continued thoughtfully. "It is badly iced but should be passable with care; the ice buttress is more difficult ... I will have to use the axe ... take the rope with me. It depends what lies beyond ... and whether I can find a safe stance to bring you round. You will both have to come together ... there is no way of feeding the rope back ... and you will have to bring the rucksacks, unless we abandon them ... I can't climb round that buttress with mine."

"Is there any alternative?" asked Zadie, knowing the answer before she spoke. One slow shake was sufficient response. "In that case, what are you waiting for? We can't work out the next move until we are out of here and down."

"I know, I know. It's just that I feel I am leaving something for the very last time, losing touch with something I will never see again." And he stood, looking back up the cave and forward over the ledge. "Leave the coracles and the other stuff ... no-one will need them any more ... bring the rucksacks and sort out which you each want to carry. Don't tie on until I am round and I tug twice. Soloma can hold your end of the rope. I'm not tying on, only a loose bow," he explained in a matter of fact kind of way. "If I fall, you won't hold me with this drop, and there's no way back up. If I do fall, use the rope yourselves. Let Soloma lead … she will have more chance."

Before she could respond, he stepped beyond her reach onto the sloping, ice-covered ledge. Soloma watched intently as he edged forward, letting the rope slide through her fingers, holding the end loosely. Slowly, he made progress. Water spewed out under great force from the base of the ice-wall fifty metres below, curling upwards and forwards, swirling in a turbulent plunge pool, roaring its thirst for him to join it. The rock was iced, requiring each step to be an art of balance. Occasionally he chipped with the axe, seeking to make an easier footing for the others, each blow risking imbalance. His fingers stretched and touched the buttress – years of slow flow of ice from above that had built out across the rock, blocking the ledge, bulging out in an overhang, forcing any who sought to pass to take two long, sideways steps around it with nothing but the drop into swirling rocks and water below. He paused, chipping patiently near shoulder-height, creating a series of finger-holds as far as the axe could strike. Suddenly he disappeared from view. The rope slid and stopped. It slid again, moving rapidly through Soloma's hands until it stopped once more. For a long while nothing happened. Finally, two tugs came along its length.

"You go," Soloma said with an assurance that bode no argument. Nathan's pack hung loosely from her slim shoulders and she watched Zadie's first step slide tentatively. Soloma knew well why Nathan had told her to come last. Hers was the most difficult task … to keep her balance, to move at exactly the same speed as Zadie, to use the rope to steady her, to be close enough to keep her moving. It was not a thing of pride, though had she thought in those terms she might have felt such an emotion; Nathan had trusted her with this task; it was simply the next task in survival – her task – a task on which they all depended, just as so many tasks in her young life had been. She had thought to only hold the rope. In the end she tied her own knot, more like a bow. If she slipped and fell, one pull on the loose end would undo the knot; the rope would come free; she would not drag Zadie with her. If Zadie slipped, the knot would tighten; she might stop her fall. These were her people now ... this was her task; there was no Elana ... there was no home in the ice, no Tarma; somewhere there was a land ... a land beyond a cave; a land with strange animals and walls built of stone ... a land with flowers and many things to eat ... a land with a low stone house. It was her task to get them there now.

She stepped after Zadie, anticipating her moves, keeping just enough feel in the rope to correct a slide before it began, keeping close. Above the roar of water, her voice carried faintly, "Walk softly ... foot flat ... move slowly." She sensed Zadie about to lunge for the buttress and was there, guiding fingers into a slender hold, gently urging by her presence, encouraging Zadie to move on. Soloma's fingers hung on tiny grips as Zadie stopped then moved too rapidly, rounding the buttress out of sight. The rope was coming taut. It would pull Soloma off. Dangerously fast she moved, hand following hand, feet not gripping. The last bulge of ice forced the rucksack backwards and, as her foot landed on iced rock, Soloma could feel her weight following, beginning to topple. She reached towards the loose end of the knot to release it, and the rope jerked strongly. Suddenly she found herself face down, pulled forward, sliding over cold rock, being hauled in, being buried in Nathan's arms.

A few sliding steps and all three figures were nestled in an angle between two giant, black rocks, a muddled slope of rock and snow falling away beneath. Blindingly white, ice towered above, reflecting the late morning sun. They kept moving, each preferring to focus on a task ahead rather than to dwell on the ice buttress in their minds. Pockets and pinnacles of black rock had absorbed the diverted energy, themselves warming the snow under which they had long lain and melting its translucent form so that it crinkled and dripped from fragile crystals, yielding reluctantly to this seasonal retreat. In one place they stopped to fill a flask, allowing the liquid to roll around the tongue as if it were the finest wine. In other places snow gave way, causing unsuspecting feet to sink through its surface and slide on unseen angles of rock beneath; whereas in others still it stood undinted by passage of foot, frozen and re-frozen, crisp, shiny. It was treacherous, ankle-breaking territory, requiring the utmost concentration.

At last they sat, looking over the flat expanse of white-iced lake, grateful to be down, growing in awareness of the next uncertainty. Silence stretched, each unwilling to voice their thoughts, each searching for some alternative, each knowing there was none. Nathan sighed and reached into a rucksack pocket.

"Here, have this," he said, breaking the object carefully. "Half now half over the far side; it's the last one." The chocolate was somehow normal ... a day's walking ... a stop by a lake ... everything in order. "Soloma, you will have to go first," he continued, tying her onto the rope. "If the ice starts cracking, fall flat and we will pull you back. Zadie, you go next. I will follow and tie the rucksacks separately behind me. That way the weight will be spread as much as possible." He stood, searching his mind one last time for any other possibility before shaking his head and ending, "Good luck, everybody. Once we are across, life will become a bit easier ... and there is food that we left at Gulland."

One hundred yards – not much more – was all they had to cross at this, the narrowest point, narrow but deep. Soloma stepped, feeling her way, sliding her feet. Zadie followed. Nathan looked up from tying the rucksacks and glimpsed the foremost figure untie the rope, holding it in her hand instead. "She's the bravest little girl I've ever known," he said quietly to himself, realising why she had done it, and his heart went out to her – his heart went out to them both ... they had both done so much, helped so much, carried his fears through the cave ... kept going when it seemed impossible ... and still they were keeping going. They deserved to live. Two rucksacks jerked into sliding motion behind and ice creaked under him. He slid his feet, seeking to prevent any shock of impact or resonance from his steps. Far ahead he could see Soloma tying onto the rope again. So she was past the worst point and now concerned to rescue Zadie rather than to risk dragging her in. Zadie's motion was strange – she was sliding her feet but one foot kept disappearing from view and then the other … almost as if she was skating across a gentle swell. Ice creaked under him. It was clearer here, and there was the suggestion of water beneath as his shadow fell brightly in the sun. His own feet were beginning to slide fractionally up and down. That was it … the ice was rising and falling, buckling like the shallowest of swells.

Zadie shrieked. She was trying to run, propelling herself forward like an ice-skater. She turned her head, yelling, "Nathan, move! Run!" The ice was buckling higher and lower in its imitation wave as Nathan stirred himself, attempting to gain momentum, but the rucksacks were dragging like a sea-anchor. A shadow passed below, and another; ice rose and fell more vigorously, creaking and groaning. Chill cut through him. Abandoning the rope, he was speeding as fast as frightened limbs could move. He had seen before what these creatures could do. Soloma knew too well what they had done. They had all seen five adult men dismembered in less than a minute. Ice shuddered from below in front of him and behind. Cracks were beginning to appear. Again it shuddered – this time directly from below – both creatures attacking at once, knocking him off his feet. He was up again, sliding feet forward again, desperately trying to move. Ten yards to the white ice … maybe the water would be shallower there … maybe the ice would be thicker … maybe his shape would be less visible through it. The others were at the rocks, staring aghast, powerless to intervene.

Simultaneously, three things happened. Ice finally broke under Nathan, lifting him, flinging him forward like a sled across the white ice towards the rocks, and a cavernous-toothed mouth opened, ingesting the orange rucksack as it closed. Soloma was jerked off the rock, rope tightening around her body as it accelerated across the surface towards the thrashing mess of broken ice and water. Zadie screamed. Nathan lunged, grabbing the rope, feeling his body whipped round, cannoning against Soloma as they were both dragged irresistibly towards the broken ice. Another set of teeth rose, breaking more ice, spilling chilled water in a wave over it, surfing an object that struck and thrust them back. Suddenly they were stationary, clear ice washing with water only a few feet in front. A hideous mouth rose, clamping and crushing at orange fabric. Another set of teeth were joining in the dismemberment of a once-new rucksack. Water and fragmented ice were surging across the tortured and groaning surface, washing over Nathan and Soloma. One monstrous mouth disappeared into the depths. In that moment they were moving, moving onto the white ice, moving away from the thrashing water. Zadie was moving towards them – tugging, pulling, hastening them onto the rocks, into the rocks, away from the shore.

*   *   *

Together they sat on the snow, absorbing the sun's rays, backs against a huge rock that obliterated all sight of the lake's shattered surface. Water dripped from hair and clothing. Two feet of severed rope lay in Nathan's hands as he tried to unpick a knot that had come under several tonnes of pressure and which, strangely, still fastened the remnant end to his rucksack. His ice-axe had been ripped from the pack, stitching coming away with the fastenings.

"Sunk, like some ancient Excalibur," he murmured, as he worked with fingers that were beginning to regain some circulation, the pain of warmth chasing spasms of cold through them.

"I hope that animal swallowed it on the way down, or that my rucksack is giving it the most awful indigestion," contributed Zadie, looking up briefly from inspecting Soloma for bruises or cracked ribs where the other end of the rope had tightened around her.

Soloma was protesting there was nothing wrong with her and, as if to demonstrate the point, tugged gently on one end of the knot around her stomach and watched the rope fall free. She stood and passed it to Nathan who could not avoid an involuntary gasp of admiration.

"That is a brilliant knot, Soloma," he said – much to her pleasure – as he took the six feet or so of mangled rope from her hands. "Here, have a go at this, will you? I still have no grip in my fingertips and I can't shift the knot at all," he continued in frustration, passing his rucksack to them.

A combination of Soloma's teeth and fingers finally induced some movement in the tortured rope and Zadie emptied the contents of the sack onto the snow. Two cooking tins had been re-oriented in shape from rectangular to rhomboid but looked as if they would still hold something, as did one dented metal mug. The flask tumbled out in shards of many sizes, whilst the binoculars protruded at an unlikely angle through their case; the cylinder of camping gas wheezed its last few gasps through an incision where cold teeth had bitten into its double skin. A shattered compass, crushed box of matches and sodden map joined the growing heap of damage and destruction. Nathan picked over the pile and rummaged in the pockets of the sack. The amount that was still of use barely warranted him slinging the much-savaged pack across one shoulder.

"I think we'll leave these here," he said in wearied slowness, shoving the pile of broken items to join two fragments of rope beneath the rock and burying them all with snow. "We know the way. We must make Gulland by nightfall. I'm sorry, but the last of the chocolate is at the bottom of the lake. We left food at Gulland … not much, but enough … it may still be there. Soloma, you lead us to the hollies. You have the best eye for this ground."

As she nodded and moved away, picking a path up the jumbled slope of rock, Nathan moved closer to Zadie and slipped an object into her hand. Her eyes flashed in surprise as she caught the metallic gleam and felt its heavy, irregular shape. It was nothing of beauty and she made to refuse it, only to find his hand tightening over hers and his eyes warning in response. Faintly, she caught the words mouthed close to her ear, "Keep it … just in case: yours is at the bottom of the lake." The fingers of her other hand went to the neck of her fur, pressing gently for reassurance, and she caught his nod as he tapped his pocket. Soloma turned and hands parted as they heard her warning of unstable ground. Loosened boulders cascaded, gathering blackness to themselves while scattering a powdering of snow to scintillate briefly in the still air.

Soon they left the main boulder field, angling across snow that had melted and re-frozen, its crisp surface yielding no imprint of foot or passage, eyes three-quarters closed against a sun at its zenith, feeling its power to burn the soft skin where eyelid meets eye-brow. Whichever way they turned or tried to angle their heads, its direct or reflected penetration followed. They shuttered their eyes more closed still, taking to closing one and then the other, keeping only one the slightest squint open, listening to follow Soloma by her breathing rather than looking for any sight of the slight figure ahead, longing for a shadow to give relief.

At last, it came. Stabbing, burning searchlights diminished, dulling in intensity. Far above, the sun rode behind cloud spilling from the west. It was both high and medium cloud, layered in form, neither grey nor white in colour, and the sun reddened behind it – an orb of molten copper in the early afternoon. Stumbling against dead, prickled leaves of stunted holly, a shower of tiny icicles tinkled around as they lowered themselves against the boles of the old trees. Slowly, eyes opened more fully. Soloma had led them well to this first holly clump. Whether she had led by sight or instinct, her feel for this landscape was good. She was breathing heavily – much more so than usual, Nathan thought as he looked across and eased his eyes open, touching the skin around them. The resultant expletive was almost simultaneous with Zadie's cry as she instinctively touched her own eyelids

"Foul language!" rasped Nathan through a dry throat.

"Yours was fouler than mine!" retorted Zadie, attempting a laugh.

The exchange had raised Soloma to a sitting position, and she was looking at the scene inside the ring of hollies. Snow sloped down from each tree, covering the ground thickly until it reached the great plinth of rock in the centre of the ring. There the rock rose a few inches above the snow, a dusting of flakes snaking at random across its exposed surface. A surface of crystal-clear quartz lay nearer to them; pink limestone composed the further half, and each was only the uppermost portion of a great slab inset with an inlay of the other rock in its centre. In that inset piece lay a carved hollow, sculpted to receive a token of passage from one geology to the next. Without the right token, there was no passage. Thus much they all knew. Thus much they had proved before. In easier times coarse tokens would lay scattered on the ground around the plinth. Soloma moved beside the quartz, lowering herself to touch its surface, looking forlornly at the depth of snow around, clawing at it in vain. Moving her arm forward, she felt the invisible barrier resisting, pushing her back, and she turned her face as Nathan knelt beside her. Zadie stood behind, leaning a hand gently on each shoulder. Momentarily, the young face fell. In another it would have been a sign of resignation, of defeat, but it lifted again as Nathan drew a soft pouch from his pocket.

"I thought you had lost it in the lake!" cried Soloma.

"No, and Zadie has her copper token, too." The face lifted. "Here, you take this and put it in the plinth."

With reverence, Soloma lifted the thin chain of gold from its pouch and watched the translucent blue token spin on its end. Pure light broke free from cloud and, for a moment, chain and token glowed and shimmered so that beauty bathed the spot. Beyond all surety of mind, Nathan knew in that instant that this gold was as native and pure as that which he had seen on an old man's hand. Whether it was imagination or not, a breath seemed to stir the ancient hollies and their leaves rustled, leaning towards the spectacle. Gently, Soloma blew powdery snow from the recess in the plinth and placed the token in it. By some trick of light, even the great cube of quartz seemed to respond, emanating hues of faintest blue and gold that grew in greeting and faded in farewell, as if to some companion remembered but not seen for an eon past.

"Hands," whispered Zadie. "Hold hands … we must go through together."

It was softly spoken but broke the spell, and Soloma lifted the token from its rest, stepping through the barrier with them across the snow, around the pink portion of the slab and through the further arch of withered boughs. Behind them a column of ice two hundred metres high and fifty metres thick calved from the great ice-wall across a front four hundred metres long. Billions of tonnes of history relinquished their tenuous grip, falling lazily into the lake below, exploding its surface into pulverised molecules, rolling its death-thunder before it, driving the very air as a gale of final breath, impelling tortured water to fling itself forward, entraining rocks the size of houses as if they were pebbles on a beach, crumbling and crashing to its own oblivion.

In unspoken consent they turned from the cold chaos, stepping into a landscape reddened by the partly obscured sun. Here snow was less, and more of the pink rock showed through in ledges sloping down. Scraggy fragments of vegetation hugged the surface in favoured crannies and, at the bottom of the slope water trickled over a rock. Tips of yellow-budded flowers dotted mossy growth as they knelt to fill a battered mug, taking turns to drink.

"Up to that cleft on the sky-line two miles away ... there is a clump of hollies and another plinth ... down again, then on to Gulland," Nathan mused. "It doesn't seem like more than mid-afternoon, but the light is going early. There is no sun to be seen."

"What is that cloud?" asked Soloma. "I have not seen cloud like it before. With most cloud, I can feel where the sun is, even if I do not see it, but not today."

"I don't know," answered Nathan, pondering. "I don't know, but the sky is clear in the east ... although that will not help us much as the moon rose just before dawn today and will set with the sun. We must make haste. We need food. Guide us well, Soloma."

Despite her skill, the going was difficult in places as ledges needed scrambling up and over. Limbs were weary. Topping one ledge, a patch of snow broke free ahead, careering down the slope away from them, bouncing and bounding across the pink rock, invisible on the white snow. In a matter of seconds it had covered half the slope they had toiled up so laboriously. Another patch moved – larger, discoloured with brown streaking through its white surface. It was moving more slowly at first, gathering momentum, gaining on the bright white patch that was slowing and turning.

Soloma cried out a word in her own language at the same time as Zadie exclaimed, "Hare! Arctic hare … still has its winter camouflage," and Nathan added, "Fox! It's after it, it's gaining."

The hare was turning again, going back upslope, invisible for a moment … slowing … hesitating in the middle of a clear expanse of rock, standing like a white beacon, inviting its adversary. Too late it turned. The end came swiftly in a flurry of tumbling fur rolling over rock, across snow, trailing a stain of red across the pristine surface until a final death-cry floated over the landscape. Predator and prey disappeared from view.

Nearly two hours later they stood at the entrance to the holly ring. Shrivelled, red berries still clung to sprigs of leaves and only the most shaded depths possessed patches of snow. It was considerably darker within the ring and they wasted no time looking for tokens on the ground. This time the blue key evoked no strange response from the slab of pink limestone as they moved onto the dark-veined rock beyond and clambered down the cleft. This was as far as Nathan had reached before, at cost of great effort, and the cliffs seemed to mock him, looking down on their ease of passage now. The gully was deep, already shadowed heavily, snow still present in places. Nevertheless, the great drifts that had thwarted Nathan were gone, and it was passable with care. Part way down Zadie slipped, dislodging a small cascade of stones. They slid over the snow patches, clattering and clunking against each other – all but one pebble, that was. It seemed to 'clink' rather than 'clunk' and something about its shape caught the eye. The others were becoming frustrated with Nathan's diversion after it – already it would be fully dark by the time they reached the Little Lake – when his cry of, "Ha!" brought them rapidly to his side and he held the pebble triumphantly aloft.

It was a peculiar pebble – almost circular, disc-like, with a sheen on it as Nathan rubbed his fingers across its iced surface and flipped it over to rub the other side against his trousers. Finally he announced with great solemnity, "I can now say with confidence that the time is 5.47pm."

"You've found a watch?" asked Zadie incredulously.

"Yes. Well, to be more accurate, I have re-found my watch –
minus its strap," and he told the story of its loss as they picked their
way onto more open country, walking side by side. A confidence
flowed through Nathan from the chance discovery. Here was one
small certainty, one exact measurement, a link with a society that
could make such an intricate object, a link with somewhere where
such a thing was regarded as the common right, a link with order
and predictability, a link with the bedside table on which this thing
had lain so many nights, a link with the bungalow – his bungalow,
his home. Zadie could not help but sense his change and in the
gathering gloom she was moved to begin a long argument.

"It's unlike you, Nathan," she continued, "You've been content
without it all these days; you haven't needed it. Just because we
can measure time accurately, doesn't mean that we can control it:
we can't stop it, or start it; we can't possess it or lock it away to be
brought out when we want; sell it or buy it …"

"I know, I know. It is just reassuring. With an accurate measure
of time and distance you can map, plan, organise …"

"… and what do we plan and organise? Does it make us any
different from these people, from this time, from Elana's land?"

Mention of Elana brought them all to a halt. By coincidence
it was at the shore of the Little Lake. It was too dark to see the
flat rock from which Zadie had rescued Soloma or the expanse of
water beneath which the girl's mother had been taken. Early stars
in the east glittered on the still-frozen edges of the lake but from
the water they did not reflect. To the west, there was neither sunset
nor any light – it was as if the sky was riven, divided in conflict.

Briefly they paused, acknowledging the significance of
the place, but thoughts crowded in. Despite her protestations,
the episode of the watch had set in train a series of longings in
Zadie's mind: for hot food, and a soft bed; for a bath, and a phone
to communicate; for pubs filled with noise and company. Nathan
found his thoughts following a different direction. For him, it was
the mention of people and Elana that had jarred. He had pushed any
thought of the Mortan deep into his sub-consciousness. Now it had
resurfaced. If there were animals moving back into this landscape,

following the receding snow, there would be men hunting them. If there were men, there would be Mortan. Their passage from here to the cave of Polgodoc would be unlikely to pass unnoticed ... and any defence that he had was at the bottom of a lake. Soloma agreed there would be hunting parties but seemed disinclined to talk. Whether she was concentrating on picking a way in the little starlight or whether she was wrapped in thoughts of Elana, Nathan left her to it, resuming his own measuring of possibilities in his mind – until his stomach reminded him with increasing clamour that it had been unattended many hours.

Water trickled between boulders on the steeply rising land. Occasionally, one or other would stoop, guided by the sound to scoop a palmful of the liquid and lap from a cupped hand, endeavouring to quell the demands of unsatisfied hunger. Distantly, a fox barked to its mate, the reply coming more faintly. Something brushed against Zadie. More things brushed and snagged on her fur. One sprang back, catching Nathan across the face. Blood trickled into the corner of his mouth, and he licked at it with his tongue – it tasted good ... thicker than water, and it was warm. He wondered idly about the death of the Arctic hare and whether the fox had taken pleasure in the warm blood. It had stopped seeping into his mouth now and he regretted it somewhat, thinking to scratch at the cut with his nails and feel the comforting flow again. There was no noise ahead. Maybe the others had gone on ... maybe they had found somewhere else to rest ... maybe they had found food. And he thought of the blood again. Somewhere a noise was intruding into his thoughts; he wished it would go away. They were pleasant thoughts, warm thoughts. It was a familiar noise ... there was something about it that he recognised ... something that brought back memories. There were chickens in those memories ... and shafts of sunlight streaming from behind a white cloud floating in a pale blue sky ... there were orange and yellow flowers dancing in the breeze ... and there was a dog running across the sand, barking at gulls that rose into flight before it. Soon he would fly too ... lift off the ground with no effort. There was the noise again. It was closer, louder; too loud. Something flung itself at his legs, and he crashed onto the ground. It was moist and yielding. The damp cold stirred his mind.

"Mister Nathan, stop! Stop!" the voice was crying. Another joined it, out of breath and urgent, "Nathan, we've been looking for you. We are there. We've made it to the hazel thicket. It's Gulland! Nathan, speak to me," it commanded.

Slowly the mists were clearing. "Zadie," he whispered. "Zadie, I was dreaming ... it was a nice dream ..."

"You were hallucinating. You need food. Come with us now. Take my arm. Follow Soloma down the slope. We've found the food we left. Foxes got some of it ... but there are two packages left. Soloma found them. They feel like rice ... and porridge. Give your pack to Soloma ... she needs the tins to fetch water. One more boulder to go round, then it's flatter and mossy. You can sit and share my fur."

Warmth seeped from her body to his as Soloma appeared, placing battered tins on the flat slate she had used as a map and pouring a packet carefully into each, working by feel, stirring with her fingers. Once more she disappeared, returning with the cup and offering him a drink. Some order was beginning to trickle into Nathan's mind and he blew on his fingers, working at their circulation before observing, "Twenty minutes."

"What?" questioned Zadie, alarmed at the illogicality.

"They are quick meals. They only need twenty minutes to re-hydrate. Just as well I have my watch," he stated, attempting a chuckle.

"Except you can't see it," she countered, relieved all the same.

"I can when I push this button. There, see: 9.10pm. It will be ready by half past. In fact, there might be enough glow from the watch to see what it is."

"Don't knock it over!"

"I'll be very careful ... I'll crawl," a wearied voice replied. Prodding with one finger, the verdict came, "Ready mixed curry, probably vegetarian ... can't see any meaty chunks ... which is just as well as they take longer to re-hydrate. The other is definitely porridge – with dried apricots mixed in. We can leave that for the morning."

They knelt around the tin, dipping fingers in turn into the cold, curry mixture, holding a palm beneath to make sure that none of the food escaped between tin and mouth, licking fingers and hands until all was gone. Distant groans alternated with animal noises across the landscape below as they chewed in grateful silence. Irresistibly, sleep overwhelmed, and soon three figures lay, resting on one fur, covered by two others, inert to the world around.

Late after midnight a hare's ears twitched as she lay listening to the sounds, wondering in her loneliness. Later still Nathan dreamt. Thunder rolled through those dreams, and a red marine flare kept descending into them. He turned, moaning quietly.

Chapter 22   The Last Day

Pre-dawn and dawn broke in ultimate splendour, curtained by Gulland's eastern flank. The moon rose, waning from its Easter fullness, bathing the landscape in its lesser candle; the sun followed, bursting in glory. Sun chased moon; moon chased sun. Briefly they kissed in airless embrace, relinquishing their closeness until the centuries should roll on to another appointment made ere time began. Eastward, the sky was clear – no prisms to refract the purity of light, nothing to dissemble its beauty. Westward, clouds banked high in layers, pendulant beneath, each returning the dawning's rays reddened and oranged, yellowed and purpled, as if some bruised anger lived and moved within. Magenta hung in a veil far above as clouds stirred, fingering their way east.

Surreptitiously, Soloma slipped from between the half-woken figures, gathering a battered tin and mug to fill with water from below a hazel thicket green with budded leaves. By the time she returned, Zadie had levered the girl's fur from beneath a sleepy Nathan who was massaging and moving various parts of his body that had locked into discomfort during the night. To encourage his movement further, she reclaimed her own fur and stepped over to the porridge.

"OK, OK," he muttered grumpily. "I get the message – bed's gone, no blankets, if I don't get up now, the food will be gone too."

"I thought that would move you," she replied, smiling and handing Soloma her fur. "Why are you shaking the rucksack like that?"

"Because somewhere in it there may still be a spoon. At least, that's what it felt like my ear was lying on when I woke up … and porridge will be a lot easier with a spoon. Ah! Here it is," he exclaimed unnecessarily as the somewhat bent object settled on the moss. Straightening it to something like its original shape, he handed it to Zadie and said, "You can use it first – I'll trust you to judge a third of a tin. I'm just going to … find a bathroom," he added lamely.

She shot him a glance. "Don't go near any serpentine or yew trees this time!" Relenting, she continued, "It's alright. You go – I will count out the dried apricots."

In the light the route through the hazel thicket was easier to pick. He could see where he must have deviated from following the others and crashed through the thickest part, breaking young branches as he went. Beyond the low ridge in the west, thunder rolled, although no lightning showed and the top of the great ice-wall was obscured by mist. There was something not quite right about the scene below, and he was worrying at it as he made his way back towards the others.

"Good porridge, then?" he greeted them.

"No, actually," responded Zadie, swilling her mouth from the cup. "It's a bit grey and gritty … apricots are the best part … there were eight. You get two and a large chunk," she ended, as if her maths was about to be challenged.

He decided to leave the apricots to last. There was definitely something wrong with the porridge. It was grating between his molars, and he could understand why the others had been washing out their mouths. The apricots were juicy, though. A pity there were so few. The last piece was hovering near his mouth when a huge clap of thunder shook the ground beneath. Hazels bent in the wind accompanying the sound. Quickly he swallowed the piece, regretting the missed opportunity to chew and savour its taste, and pushed through the thicket after the others.

Soloma was pointing and exclaiming. Zadie was standing watching, her fur reflecting light emanating from beneath clouds in the north-west. Suddenly it became blindingly clear to him. The Little Lake was filling, spilling, overflowing the shallow valley below, rising by the minute. Noise was growing and, in full sun, the western clouds still hung in malevolence of colour.

"Move!" yelled Nathan. "Move now! I'll explain as we go! Please move," he pleaded, grabbing Zadie roughly by the arm.

"What about your rucksack and fur?"

"Leave it! Leave everything. Just move!"

Impelled partly by the slope and more by his urgency, feet moved, picking their way over rocks, angling across the southern flank of Gulland towards the shallow valley lying at its foot. The way seemed stubbornly slow: each boulder an obstacle cast across their intended path; each defile an unwanted clamber; each rivulet a hazard into which to slip and slide. He was pushing, pulling, cajoling, leading and snapping at their heels, driving them down. This was important. This was the first hurdle. The next would be worse. Fail here and there would be no next. Water sloshed shin-deep, and they were through. To the south the landscape was changing. He could not afford to look that way. It was uphill now … uphill to the hollies … uphill over more open ground. Soloma drew by his side and Zadie grasped an arm.

"Tell us what is going on. Tell us!" she demanded.

"Keep walking," came the response. "Keep walking – fast as you can. Time has run out. We are nearly too late. There is a deep valley half way across the granite …"

"What are you talking about? I don't understand. You've never been like this before."

"I'm like this because I care … I care for you both … I love you both … and I'm frightened, I'm scared. Keep walking. I'll talk as I can. I didn't see it and I should have done … I've studied it but I didn't know what it would be like."

Deep within she was riven between the desire to pull him to the ground, to demand that he stop, to say that she would not move another pace, and by an equal impulse to throw her arms around him, to hold him to her. But it was Soloma who spoke first.

"I understand, Mister Nathan. This is an ending. This is my ending. We will be together," and she hooked her arm around his elbow.

Another arm reached around his shoulders and, more steadily, they walked on up the slope. He seemed more stable now. Whatever happened, they were together … that mattered … mattered more than he had realised. He was talking about a subject that he knew, even if there was little normality in his voice.

"It is like this," he began slowly, "the light in the ice cave; the clouds in the west; the grit in the porridge; the lake spilling over – they are all connected. I know when we are now: 2310 BC, give or take a dozen years – Hekla IV."

"Who is Hekla?"

"Not who, what. Hekla is a volcano, an Icelandic volcano. It has erupted massively only a few times over the last seven millennia. Each time it has spread deposits across much of western Europe, spewing ash and lava kilometres into the atmosphere, sending out explosions and shockwaves that sped tsunami across the entire Atlantic. Each major eruptive cycle lasted months. The main ones are given numerals, going back in time: Hekla 1, 1104AD; Hekla 3, 950BC; Hekla 4, 2310BC; Hekla 5, 5050BC. The volume of material ejected from Hekla 4 was hundreds of times what was emitted from Mt. St. Helens. Mt. St. Helens erupted once; Hekla went on for week after week, month after month. It sprayed sulphur gases into the atmosphere – they combined with water to rain as sulphuric acid droplets; it sent aerosols into the stratosphere; the volcanic dust from it blocked sunlight for decades to come."

Talons of dark cloud roiled above, reaching to grasp the sun as they entered the hollies. Dramatically its light diminished, a red disc behind a spreading veil of darkness. Thunder rolled from some further massive collapse of ice in the west and the wind from it propelled them through the entrance to the ring, loosening a tinkling of volcanic dust from the leaves. A pittering of fragments fell briefly from the sky, glittering like shards of frozen blood onto the plinth in the distorted light.

"Volcanic glass," said Nathan, "tiny shards of glass formed in the molten froth of the eruption, blasted into the stratosphere, carried in the upper airs to fall two thousand miles away. This must be a huge eruption …" he ended, blowing the granite recess in the dark-veined block clear of fragments. "Ready?" he asked, hesitating for the slightest moment as he held the blue master-token above the recess. Two nods came and he plunged it in. Whether there were still fragments of glass in the recess, or for some other reason, the token resisted his attempt to lift it out.

"Take it out," said Zadie urgently.

"I'm trying. It won't come ..."

"The barrier is still in place. We can't get through. Take it out!" came the demand from a voice laced with quavered warning.

Desperately he pulled at the fine gold chain, sensing for the tension it could bear. It was not going to take much more. It must take more. It must come. It must ...

Suddenly it came free. Zadie had whisked them through the barrier and to the exit of the holly ring before Nathan could think about inspecting the token or chain for damage. Weird light illumined the granite landscape stretching below. The hidden sun, not yet at its zenith, lighted the westward facing slopes dull red whilst the moon, still clear of cloud, cast its ghostly pallor white across the eastward slopes – each orb etching its own claim on every minute change in aspect. Southwards the land was flattened – valleys filled with liquid, hints of pale light moving on their surface. Yew trees stood in a distant clump at the bottom of a long slope where a stream surged by them. To their right a small hill rose, five obelisks penetrating its skin like upright nails. Another shower of fragments tinkled around them from the sky above.

"I don't like it. Something is wrong with this landscape," stated Zadie.

Feet moved. Speech was deadened. In the malevolent unreality of the scene only two white furs seemed clean and real – beacons moving at haste across an environment that begrudged their existence, across rocks that sought to slow their passage, across a distance that diminished so unwillingly. Nathan was troubled by his inability to remove the token at the plinth, troubled, too, by the landscape. Zadie was right. Even given the effects of the light, there was something wrong ... something he felt he should have spotted. Soloma was moving fast, keeping away from the main area of boulders, keeping Zadie and Nathan abreast of her, taking the slope as a slalom, cutting every corner she could identify. She kept glancing to the south. There was something she perceived, something she knew or feared. Perhaps it was the animals: horrid half-creatures; obelisks of serpentine; sentinels of evil; hounds of the Mortan. But the Mortan themselves were not masters; there was a deeper evil; an evil more pervasive, older, ancient, rooted and grounded in this place, absorbed by it, a part of it, eons old, inherent in its creation. There would be no defence this time; there was no means of fire, no distress flare to ignite. Perhaps she perceived the Hill of Sacrifice … a few more turns and it would come into view … so would the yew trees. The sound of water was much louder. They must be near the bottom of the slope. It felt like an hour they had been hurrying down it … no, it felt like time had lost its meaning – it could have been a day, a month, a year.

Soloma stopped abruptly, ending Nathan's thoughts. For fully a minute roll after thundering roll of noise swept over them from the west. Above, the moon had touched the first, veiled tentacles of cloud. In front, dark water stretched for twenty yards, its surface stirred by the vigour of a plunging stream. As they watched, it widened, lapping towards their feet, consuming the slope beyond that led up to the final holly ring, to the last plinth, to the last barrier. Already it had buried the yew trees to half their height and, downstream, the Hill of Sacrifice rose as an island. Sentinels of serpentine watched, awaiting a touch of warm flesh to awaken what lay within.

"There was no lake here before," cried Zadie. "What is happening? It's growing as we watch. It's reached my feet. We've got to do something. Can't we go upstream?"

"No." It was Soloma who spoke. "The rocks change soon. There is a barrier. We must cross here. We must reach the holly ring."

"It's the ice-sheet," broke in Nathan. "It's disintegrating. The whole of the Blue Lake must have poured out. Water is pouring under it – "

"Never mind why – "

They both turned, regarding the girl for a moment. Both made to speak and stopped. Both spoke, confusing each other in their attempt. The decision was made on a mere nod from each to the other and, together, they stepped into the water.

"Keep together, if we can," called Nathan. "Soloma, keep hold of me and loosen your fur; let it float ... I'll carry you when it gets deeper."

The water was cold – bitingly, icily cold. Already it was past Nathan's knees and he was dreading the moment when it reached beyond his thighs. Soloma's fur was beginning to float like a white mantle behind her. Zadie had loosened her fur too. She gasped involuntarily as water reached higher. The ground was slippery, uneven, difficult. Soloma lost grip and kicked, using Nathan's shoulder as a float, trying to swim. Nearly halfway and it was up to his armpits. Current and buoyancy were lifting him ... it was difficult to keep moving. Zadie was having the same problem; she was dropping behind. She was going to have to swim but the fur was weighing her down in the water. It would stop her kicking. He turned and missed a footing, plunging under the water. It was cold, so cold, black, so black. He could feel it grasping at him, killing warmth, squeezing out life. Soloma was hanging on ... he could feel her ... the current was taking them. He kicked, spluttering for air, going under again, coming up, being swirled round, thrashing with one arm. Something touched it and he grabbed. It gave way. There was something else. It broke. No, it was holding. He pulled against it, breaking the surface, spluttering, coughing, wrapping his arm around a yew tree. Soloma was pulling herself onto a bough. It was prickly, awkward, weighed down by the current. She was up, clambering higher, stepping on his arm. Crying out, he swivelled for a better grip. In the corner of his eye a white fur eddied. It went under. Part of it surfaced again. It was out of reach ... ten feet away ... floating ... sinking ... close to a pillar that rose out of the water. Now it was wrapping around it.

"Zadie!" he screamed.

At the moment that he let go and sank with the current, an answering scream came, "No! Come back! I'm here!"

Water closed over him. The current was strong ... it was eddying, tumbling, turbulent. He struck out with both arms. Clothes and boots were weighing down ... it was tiring to kick ... he needed air ... he must have air. Cold fingers touched something solid. A stone? A branch? It was difficult to tell. He held onto it. There was something softer ... it was pulling him ... pulling him to the surface ... pulling him out of the blackness ... pulling him towards air. Gasping, retching, trying to heave up swallowed water, trying to breathe, trying to focus, trying to hear, his head surfaced.

"Keep hold!" a voice came faintly.

His head went under and up again. There came the voice again.

"Keep hold! We're pulling you in!"

There were arms ... fingers that had warmth touching his, gripping him, touching his face. Arms were wrapping around him ... lips breathing on his ... hands pressing on him ... voices in his ears ... arms under his shoulders dragging him ... bodies close beside him. He was having trouble focusing. Two red blobs kept swimming into view. One was larger and circular; the other was mis-shapen. They kept wanting to merge but every time they came together they separated again. There was noise – noise accompanied by great waves of pressure. Intermittently, he could feel himself being dragged across rough ground until he was propped against something solid. A voice was entering insistently into his sub-consciousness. It seemed to be saying, "Nathan! Nathan, you didn't need to do that. Nathan, don't you dare die on me here!"

Again it came: "Nathan, I love you ... Soloma loves you. Nathan, I'm not going to leave you."

And there was another voice: "Mister Nathan, please wake up."

Slowly his eyes cleared. Holly leaves came into focus. In front of them was something pale ... two pale things; one of them floated on a white covering. Behind was darkness ... darkness punctuated by two shapes ... dull red, glowing – two blood-red orbs dripping their rays upon a dying landscape. He moaned. A hand reached out, caressing his cheek. Things were snapping into focus. The hand belonged to an arm; the arm belonged to a shoulder; and beyond the shoulder was a face, Zadie's face. It had a mouth and its lips were moving ... it was saying something. There was another face close by … it was speaking too. Both faces were smiling … their arms were lifting him. He was sitting on something solid. They were rubbing his legs and moving his feet.

*   *   *

Time would not let them rest. Too soon three figures were standing on the far side of the plinth, looking down a shallow slope and up to the cliffs of Polgodoc. This was the last lap. Wearily, they walked. The slope was easier and the stream at its base little more than three steps across. Primroses dotted its grassy bank, and early thrift thrust its close-budded heads through clumped leaves where they knelt to drink. A red-beaked bird followed its mate towards the land beyond the cliffs; two long, brown ears swivelled and bounded after them.

In the growing darkness of a day not long past its noon, they rose, taking the few paces to the slope's lip and two paces more. It was less than half a mile to the cliffs now, a gentle uphill climb. They froze. They stood in disbelief. Figures were strung across the slope … figures in long furs, belted, sheathed, hands gripping curved knives, walking towards them, eyes fixed, unyielding, unblinking.

"Mortan," mouthed Zadie. Turning, she took one step. "Men … men coming down the slope behind. We're trapped!"

Soloma slumped against Nathan, and he put his arm around her. A small voice echoed plaintively, "I am sorry. I am sorry, Miss Zadie; I am sorry, Mister Nathan. I have failed you. Let me go. Maybe they will let you pass. They want a sacrifice. It should have been. It should have been long ago."

Nathan seethed. If any one single thing could have ignited the last reserves of emotion and will that lay within him, this was it. The child would not go. The child may not go. This child must not go. If they were to go, they would go together. It was better to die against overwhelming odds, it was better to fight against unassailable evil than to allow this.

"No!" he cried. "No! You may not have her! You shall

not have her!"

He marched directly up the slope towards the oncoming figures, Zadie and Soloma following on either side. Men were breathing heavily up the slope behind. Dredging his memory for the language Soloma had taught him so long ago, he flung his arm upward a few paces from the advancing Mortan. "Do not touch her!" he commanded. "I call on sun and moon. I call on sky and cloud to see what you do."

For a moment, the Mortan paused. For a further moment, they pointed. In a moment further they broke and ran – ran for the cliffs. The men behind ran. They ran past Zadie, gratuitously hitting her head as they passed; they ran past Nathan, thrusting the end of a stave into his back; they ran past Soloma, kicking her in the stomach.

Slowly, unexpectedly, the three figures rose. Men were flinging themselves at the base of cliffs. To the west, an utterly apocalyptic sight arose: blocks of ice sky-scraper high, mountain wide, were rolling, grinding, surging across the landscape; wave after wave was washing in front of them; Gulland was all but submerged. Rolling, roaring, it tumbled on, breaking the sky-line with its height, trembling the ground with its strength, rearing, crushing, consuming. On it came – massive, unimaginable, a force beyond all reckoning.

"Run!" cried Zadie.

Soloma tugged at Nathan's hand. They were off up the slope. Half a mile ... 800 yards ... one hundred gone ... noise growing from behind ... valley filling with water. That must be two hundred yards ... surely they were half-way? A man had fallen from the cliff ahead ... his friends had stopped to help ... no, they were climbing again ... he was crying out ... he couldn't move. Water rushed by, spilling against the southern cliff, sweeping up it. The man was gone. So were three more, plucked from the face.

"Keep moving!" Zadie called. "Two hundred yards ... I've got the key ... tell me which cleft ..."

Soloma was dragging at Nathan's hand. He was struggling. She was willing him up the slope into the boulders. Ground was vibrating beneath them. Noise was becoming overwhelming from behind. She knew the entrance. She had found it before. Zadie was moving towards the wrong one. She pleaded in her heart for her to stop. Nothing she could say or do would carry in the noise. Water furled and crashed, flinging them forward, propelling them towards the cliff. Mountains of ice were rolling behind them. An ocean of water was pouring and surging. Soloma's hand grasped Zadie and she hung on as water sucked out again. Another wave was rearing, vaster by far, a hill of ice rolling behind it. This was their chance, their only chance, and Soloma shoved Zadie to her right. The wave broke, flinging them around the rock face, forcing their bodies deep into a crevice. Water dragged against them but she urged them forward. It was dark, wet, without any light. The next wave was grumbling and rearing behind – immense, immeasurable – slowed only by the giant block of ice that it was rolling in front of it. They were against a rock wall, and Soloma was yelling, crying, calling.

Deep within, a memory stirred. Zadie was lifting a small object over her head. Now she was thrusting it against the rock. The wave was breaking behind them. The pressure of air propelled before it was becoming unbearable in the enclosed space. In a moment the water would reach, and pound, and suck. It would be the final end. There would be no escape, no alternative.

Suddenly the darkness in front was riven by a glow from floor to ceiling. A vein of copper widened and split. Rock opened. Water surged, pushing and thrusting them through the opening, far up the passage into the cave of Polgodoc. Gurgling and sucking, it fell back until a solid clunk sealed the rock again.

Zadie rolled over, gasping, the copper key in her open palm drawing light from veins in the rock. Nathan crawled to her side. Soloma stood, staring. The rock had illumined rapidly; lines of coppery red were glowing in the passage; a blaze of colour emanated from beyond as the cavern welcomed a master key. He could picture the floor of it: a great wheel of copper, thick as an arm, circling the slab of finest slate, and above would be other veins, tracing, splitting, rejoining. Droplets of water would be dripping, plinking into pools like molten ore, rippling their colour across the surface.

"We've made it! We have made it, Zadie!" he cried, hugging her to her feet. Shambling and stumbling forward, he added, "It's alright, I am not going anywhere near the table ... I don't want to touch it ever again. Just remember, 'middle entrance in, middle entrance out', and keep thinking about Trevennick – keep thinking about our time."

Soloma stopped abruptly as they stepped into the cavern. Nathan and Zadie cannoned into her, knocking her a pace further forward. Mouths fell open, staring, speechless.

"No," sobbed Zadie. "No, not now, not after everything else."

Soloma's head fell. Her shoulders slumped. Her knees were buckling.

Nathan felt his own mind swimming as the great copper vein lit their figures from below. The anger, the malice was palpable. Black eyes were cold, unyielding, colder than cold. Beside the broken, hooked nose – all down one side of the face – a scar, more lurid in the light, burnt into flesh. The beard was malformed, flesh showing like leprosy in patches where it would never grow again. Broken nails, yellowed and dirty, wrapped round a curved copper knife, its fine point pressed against the young neck pinioned between one figure and the next. Furs clothed both men. The young neck belonged to a girl, so far as the dishevelled, unwashed hair gave any clue; of its colour there was no indication. Beneath some torn fabric another vestment lay, the letters TCH still apparent through its grubbiness. But the eyes were not blank – they sparked and watched from beyond the monumental slab of slate, flickering from Nathan to Zadie to Soloma and back again.

'Mortan," breathed Zadie. "Mortan, between us and the exit ... and that girl ... Nathan ... the flip-flop ..."

"Long I have waited. Long have we watched," the cold-eyed voice spoke in a language known to Soloma and, in surprising part, to Nathan. The eyes fixed on Nathan. "That girl belongs with us. Come, Soloma," the voice continued. "See, I know her name."

The eyes were drilling into him. "This girl is your time ... I offer you an exchange. Give me Soloma and I give you this one ... and you may follow the copper light to your own future," he ended, flinging his arm at the passage behind him.

The girl's eyes were fixed on Nathan, willing him to look at her, desperate to convey unspoken thoughts, pleading for him to catch her eye. Well she understood the language she had been forced to learn; well she knew this man; well she knew the evil of his intent. She moved. The knife tightened, pricking her skin. "Choose!" the voice continued angrily. "Choose whether you have this one whole or in parts, living or dismembered."

Suddenly his eyes met hers, and Nathan laughed. It was a coarse, gravelly laugh, lacking entirely in humour. "So," he said, "you offer an exchange ... you ask for trust ... you point to a way out." He tensed himself. "That way is closed. You offer only death ... death now, death soon, death as the only certainty in – "

A huge crash shook the cavern. Copper light trembled. Water spurted from each passage. All stumbled. The girl launched herself forward. A foot caught her. The knife clattered. Her head hit solidly against the base of the great slate slab. Both Mortan grabbed at her, leaning on the slate, reaching, searching for the knife. Nathan lunged into motion, Zadie and Soloma moving around the other end of the slate. The slab itself was responding to the Mortans' touch: vibrating, resonating, demanding its offering. Each Mortan had a hand locked on its surface, pulling, straining, struggling to free it from the force of the lionesses that held it firm. One had put both hands on the slab; the other was kicking and flailing at the girl. Noise was growing and growing. Mobile mountains of frozen millennia impelled by the long-pent sea ground and shuddered against the outside of the cave, echoing and reverberating within. No sound was fading. Each blow was amplified. Unbearably, the roar of lionesses was rising above the crescendo of cacophony: lioness cheated by no token offered; lioness holding its deceptor to it; lioness in anger. Vastly beyond the ability of words to communicate, noise was pulverising ears, paining thought. Soon it would deafen, madden, kill.

Nathan skirted a flailing foot and grabbed at a pair of tattered jeans, hauling the body and head attached to them roughly across the floor. Remarkably, its limbs were still working; its eyes flickered in some dazed moment of understanding. He looked up and, for the last time, a face loathing with hatred stared directly at him. Every sinew and muscle of the Mortan's being was straining to break the force that held him to the great, black slate, straining to delay Nathan's movement until sound could kill, straining to impart a final doom.

Zadie tugged. In her palm was the chunk of tin. Copper light was fading; silvery threads were opening instead. Soloma stood at the archway they illumined most, reaching for the girl, urging them forward. Steps up the passage were uneven and slippery. Noise pounded and pounded. It assaulted in great waves of pressure; it pressed upon the brain; it unravelled the mind. It was pounding off the wall in front, pounding off the end of the passage, pounding from behind.

Suddenly it lessened. Suddenly it stopped. All was stillness. Ears hurt, hearts hammered, minds clawed their way back from oblivion. Bit by bit, breath slowed. Sound came again: gentle sound, the sound of lapping water, the sound of swash and backwash, the sound of distant gulls. Smell came: the smell of salt upon seaweed, the smell of sun upon grass, the smell of recent rain, the smell of spring flowers. Light flowed: clear light, clean light, the gentle light of a late afternoon's sun reflecting off rock and cloud ... the light, the sound, the smell ... of Cornwall.

Chapter 23   An Old Acquaintance

"Just for a moment," said Nathan quietly, "just for a moment, don't say anything. Just breathe. Just believe."

It was a long moment.

Finally Zadie shifted. Warmth flowed from the head cradled against her cheek. Soloma knelt by the chasm in the floor of the old adit, looking on, her figure silhouetted against the rough-hewn entrance and the cliff beyond. Waves splashed and sucked over the boulders below.

"This child is bleeding, Nathan. She needs help," Zadie ventured softly, caressing the forehead. "We must move."

Carefully, they handed the dazed figure across the gap. She was still moving, mumbling words in response to questions, looking with eyes that drifted in and out of focus. Zadie kept her against the cliff face as they emerged onto the ledge, working their way to its extremity. A passing gull squawked at the disturbance, dropping in its ungainly fashion to examine something the waves had smashed against the rocks before wheeling and rising past them in the updraught.

"Easy for a gull," muttered Zadie as they stood contemplating the climb. Only then did the enormity of difficulties strike home. Consequences were breaking upon her by the moment. This was a girl who was dead ... at best, missing for seven months. There would be questions, accusations ... the police would want to interview, the press would grab it. The girl's story would make no sense, Soloma's would be nonsense ... neither she nor Nathan had any alibi. There was nothing ... not a shred of anything substantial ... Soloma would be taken and put in care ... they would end up in prison – or maybe sectioned under some mental health act.

"Right," Nathan's voice cut across Zadie's rising panic. "We haven't time to delay. Do you recall the girl's name from the press coverage? I have a name in mind but I can't quite get it right."

There was nothing wrong with his mind. He must have been

working at this, thinking on it ever since the cave had closed behind them. He was standing patiently, waiting for her answer.

Instead it was Soloma who said, "Look," pointing at the frayed collar of an outworn fleece.

Admiration for the sharpness of her eye and mind bounded through Nathan, and he blessed some unsung hand that had stitched the name tag onto the now tattered remains of a once-prized possession.

Zadie bent, moistening and rubbing with her fingers until, rising again, she announced, "It says Eve ... Eve Elliott."

"Good. Well done. Now let's see if we can stir a response," he continued, facing the girl and watching her eyes drift in and out of focus as he placed her hand in his. "Eve," he called, "Eve, if you can hear me, I want you to squeeze my hand. Eve, can you hear me?" The eyes were struggling ... no pressure on the hand ... the merest suggestion that something was flickering in recognition. Again he tried and again. Zadie tried. She kept on trying until, in despair, she hugged the girl close to her body crying, "O Eve, Evie, please answer us!" A hand twitched against Zadie. For a moment the eyes were fully focused. The hand twitched with the name again. A response was coming most times now.

Some while later they had persuaded Evie to lock her arms around Nathan's neck and tuck her knees against his waist. Soloma was poised, waiting to be unleashed. Zadie was arguing.

"No," came Nathan's final answer. "Soloma goes, you go. If I fall, I fall. The top is where I need most help. I won't be able to wriggle over with Evie on my back. I need you to pull her over."

Before there could be any further reply, he nodded at Soloma who flung herself forward. She was climbing ... up and up ... flying up the cliff – discoloured, white fur billowing like wings in the wind. Zadie turned after her and launched herself ... right foot, left hand ... steady on the hold ... left foot, right hand ... don't try to look down, don't think about Nathan with Evie. She could hear a scrabbling below, a boot scraping and sliding, a muffled thud. Keep going, don't look down. How many holds was it to the top? She wasn't counting ... she had forgotten to count. Left hand ...

left foot, right hand … right foot, left hand. Get to the top, get over the top … then she could turn. A dirty, white arm with a dirtier hand on the end of it reached and pulled. She was over, lying alongside it, peering down. He was labouring two thirds of the way up … the girl's arms were tight around his throat, throttling him. The breathing was wheezy and pained. He was searching for each grip, moving slowly to compensate for the swaying of Evie's body. The girl's eyes were closed. His lips were moving, counting. She willed him on. Two more hand holds and they could reach … another one and there would be something to grab. He had stopped. He was stationary. Why didn't he move?

Muffled sound from a face pushed against the rock carried up to them. "Two more holds … let me come two more holds. Grab the girl, not me. My weight will pull you both down. Grab her under the arms and pull her over my head. Have you heard that? Don't grab me."

The reply seemed to satisfy him. A hand moved; the other hand moved and retreated. Again it reached, searching, feeling for the finger hold. A foot scrabbled, steadying under the weight. The girl was within reach. They had their arms under hers, pulling, lifting, dragging her away from the cliff top. Her eyes were open. She was mumbling something. Soloma was whispering back.

Loose stones scattered, careering over the cliff edge as Nathan hauled himself over. He rolled to their side, lying against the rocky slope, breathing heavily, closing his eyes, opening them again, breathing the sunlight … drinking in the sounds of gulls wheeling, the sound of the slow swash and gurgle of waves … absorbing the view of short cropped grass, of primroses and early thrift, of an island crown standing far from the shore – proud, undefeated, outlined against the westering sun.

"How is she?" he muttered, levering himself to his knees.

"Eyes open … still looking dazed … talking a little with Soloma," came the reply.

"See if she can stand. We need to find someone to look at her. I don't think I can carry her again."

Soloma bent, speaking quietly, slipping her arm under Evie's shoulder. Zadie reached to help, and the girl stumbled to her feet, trying a step forward, trying another, moving slowly in the lopsided embrace. Thus they walked – in half shuffles, half steps – up from the hidden valley of Polgodoc, climbing slowly until a spring burbled across their path. There they paused, lapping water, washing grime, bathing away congealed blood. Resuming their path, the corner of a deep-sunk lane broke their way, its dry-stone walls clothed with moss and leathery fern, rooted in crevices between sprouting valerian.

"Half a mile," stated Nathan – "and there is a farm. We can find help for her."

"I don't think she can walk that far. And what are you going to say about Soloma … about us …?"

As if it had been waiting, the sound of a vehicle's engine throttled along the lane towards them – the sound of an old vehicle with a slightly blowing exhaust being driven by someone who knew the road. No gate was accessible either to hide or for safety. A gear crashed. They stood, strung across the narrow lane. A dull, red bonnet rounded the bend ahead, dipping as the driver braked hard. A wing-mirror crunched on stone, objecting to the unfair contest. The vehicle slewed and stopped. Without moving his feet, Nathan leant forward, resting his hands on the bonnet. The driver's door opened, jamming against a patch of last year's brambles, and an anxious face appeared. Sliding from behind the wheel, a figure stood in the little V of gap that the wall-wedged door and vehicle would allow.

"We need help!" cried Zadie from behind Nathan. "This girl is injured. She needs to be looked at … please help us."

"I don't believe it!" cried Nathan. "I don't believe it! How can you be – "

How Soloma had squeezed round the vehicle and flung herself on the figure from behind, he didn't know. But she was there, hanging on, wrapping her arms around, calling out, embracing.

The old face smiled. "I'm sorry," it said. "I'm sorry; it was my watch … I was delayed by Treverne's cows crossing … I was hurrying."

Finally Zadie forced her way past Nathan's shoulder, past the battered wing of the old red van, and virtually wrenched the old man's head off as she wrapped her arms around his neck, exclaiming, "Martyn! Martyn the Post!"

The conversation became increasingly confused. Each spoke simultaneously – questioning and answering, starting an explanation and seeking an explanation. For a moment they all drew breath at the same time, and a whimper echoed from the road.

"Who is that?" questioned Martyn. "She looks like she needs help."

Briefly, the story unfolded – solemn, rapid, factual – and heads nodded, expressions settling in seriousness, words exchanging anxieties.

Martyn's voice was older, more subdued, "I'll take her ... take her now. Trevelyn's place is up the road. She was a nurse, she can advise – and she knows; she won't ask awkward questions. If necessary, I'll take her to Truro or accompany her in the ambulance. I'll think about what to say on the way. I won't involve you. There are plenty of rocks for a girl to fall against and hurt her head. Now let me get back in this vehicle and turn it round. No, don't argue any more."

The door slammed, and the vehicle edged by the standing figures, grating gears as it turned in the next available gate and accelerated back, squealing to a halt. Evie slumped into the passenger seat, as Martyn cleared packages.

"Here," he said, through a window that had long since refused to budge from halfway up or halfway down, "take this ... the wife made them ... no use to me now. And Nathan," he added, stirring the gear lever in a random search for any forward gear, "you look awful ... a total mess. Try not to be seen. I'll phone Lucinda ... warn her you are coming." With which comment, gear lever and clutch suddenly combined to jerk the vehicle into motion.

Three figures stood, watching at least one brake light work as the van rounded the bend. "I wonder what will become of her. I hope she is alright," Zadie observed, stretching out her hands in front of her and adding, "I guess we all look a complete mess."

Soloma leant against Nathan, sniffing.

"I think she will be OK. It is better than we could have expected … a lot better than we could have expected. But maybe we should take the coastal path. Martyn is right about our appearance. It will be too late for walkers … the sun will be gone within the hour and we can slip through the village in the half-light."

Soloma sniffed again, inquisitively this time, and he found himself opening the brown paper bag.

"Pasties!" he cried.

Barely had the corner of the lane given place to the coastal path than the last crumbs were being licked from fingers. Over the stile they climbed, and on they walked – two figures side by side, deep in urgent talk, the third walking ahead. For two, the conversation was about the third: what would become of her? How could she exist in this world? Could she be hidden? What questions would be asked? What answers could be given? Who would lay claim to her?

Eventually, speech ceased; they were content simply to walk as three. Sheep separated in silent objection, and landmarks passed; a cliff of marbled rock dipped seaward in the evening light; white horses in serried ranks cantered to its base; a fulmar rose, an oyster-catcher angled down; green sward rolled their passage towards a final marker. There, rose a rock, a pulpit rock. Together they stood, leaning against its resonance – looking north to where Polgodoc plunged its cliff … looking down to the worn imitation of a lioness at guard … looking out to where an island stood, to where a sun lowered its orb majestically to rest. Gently, a tune was humming in the air, the music of an old hymn, a familiar hymn, words half mumbled, rising and fading, phrases rolling into the passing light.

The last, lingering lip of light sank beneath the western waves, and Nathan spoke:

"That world has gone.
We saw its ending.
It was so sudden,
So unexpected.

It was as if
It never existed."

Abruptly, they turned.   Lights in the village shone from uncurtained windows – flickerings of civilisation staring into a twilit world.   From a single chimney, smoke rose, spiralling in the still air.   And suddenly he knew the chimney.   There would be chickens nearby that needed feeding ... there would be a bed ... there would be a bath ... Lucinda would have brought food.

Striding across the short-cropped grass with its tightly-curled clumps of thrift, reflected rays from the dying day cast a largesse of rubies on waves washing the shore clean in the little bay below. The eldest of the old ravens glanced at their passing.   Sand stretched up to the shallow head of the cove, wrapping it in a soft embrace. A stream trickled in its eternal task past tamarisk and marram; a badger lollopped from its path.   Beneath the landscape's skin, something stirred, slow in its genesis, infinitesimal in its movement at first – and high above, in antiphonic form, airs moved.   Distantly they seemed to murmur, "Remember me ..."

Far away an eagle settled by her mate, watching the strange flicker of fire below.   Elsewhere slendered fingers lay on the arm of an old wingchair whilst long, white locks rested against its back, and nearby a silver-topped cane slipped onto a stone-flagged floor, echoing its fall.   In another place, media gathered beside a home; and outside a hospital in Truro a postman stood bemused by camera lights.   In London Town, locks snapped shut on a hand-tooled briefcase, and a chauffeur bowed in practiced fashion to bespoke suit and shoes.

Over the wall three figures climbed into Lucinda's garden. A rabbit scuttled from stealing its evening meal and, passing the private gate to the churchyard, another voice seemed to echo, "Remember me ..."   Slate crunched beneath feet.   Briefly they stepped on tarmacked road, street light spilling on Soloma's fur until, turning a last time, young leaves of erigeron brushed Zadie's shoulder.   Light from a part-open door tumbled down three steps, illuminating a slate on which the word 'Post' was roughly engraved. A postcard of a cruise liner on a placid ocean protruded from beneath, the corner of an envelope cutting across its bows. Aromas of bacon and eggs and mushrooms frying floated with Lucinda's voice. Somewhere a chicken squawked. Two pairs of feet paused, hesitating against the confrontation of normality. The third pair ran on, flinging the old door wide, the young figure silhouetted against the streaming light – welcoming, beckoning, smiling.

END OF BOOK TWO

Author's Note

The Camel of Soloma is a book that I did not anticipate writing so soon. It owes its publication in large measure to those readers of *The Three Camels* who wrote asking how the story continued and encouraging me to publish through their comments of approval. To learn that the story has reached across the generations from teenager to great-grandparent, and far beyond the Cornwall for which I imagined I was writing, has been an entirely unexpected pleasure.

The landscape is not passive. Shallowly beneath its present form lies the past; and in that past is an expression of the future. Each step we take treads upon that past; each step affects that future. As unborn generations step upon their past, what echoes will they hear from the present? What stories will they want to tell? And who will hear?

My very grateful thanks are extended to those who made this book possible: to my family, to the poet David Caddy, to Elisabeth Jenkins, to Bill 'the printer', to the five readers of the manuscript, all of whom gave freely of their time; without their enthusiasm, interest and technical advice, *The Camel of Soloma* could not have been published.

And if any reader should ask, "Does the story continue?" the answer is, "Maybe."

This is a limited, numbered first edition, of which this is copy
number: 848.

Further copies of *The Camel of Soloma* may be ordered through
booksellers. They are also available by post from:

The Bookroom, Bryanston Conference Centre, Blandford, Dorset
DT11 0PX (01258 452411).

By the Same Author

'The Three Camels'
(ISBN 978-0-9559577-0-3)